Silks and Stones
Quinn Lawrence

Fondence City Press

Silks and Stones

Quinn Lawrence

Published by Fondence City Press

Copyright © 2026 by Quinn Lawrence

https://www.quinnlawrencebooks.com

All rights reserved.

The characters and events portrayed in this book are fictitious. Any similarity to real persons, living or dead, is coincidental and not intended by the author.

No portion of this book may be reproduced, stored in a retrieval system, or transmitted in any form without written permission from the publisher or author, except as permitted by U.S. copyright law.

Also by Quinn Lawrence

The Cinna and Hokuren Series
Cinnamon Soul
Silks and Stones

1

The target squatted on the roof of the apothecary, looking imperiously down at his would-be captors. Cinna squinted up at him, leaning against a nearby olive tree. Her quarry stretched and yawned, then taunted her further with his next act.

"He's licking himself right in front of us," said Cinna, disgusted yet enthralled.

"Of course he is." Her boss, Hokuren, fingered the lapel of her coat. "He's a cat."

The cat's white fur and royal purple collar matched the description given by Lady Belladonna, their client. This would be Quartz, who had run from Belladonna's home three days ago. Cinna was glad to see him, even if she had to watch him clean his nethers with his tongue.

She'd held up the old lady's amateurish drawing of her pet to scores of the city of Velles's denizens for the better part of the last three days to track him down. She was embarrassed to possess the drawing, let alone to have shoved it in the faces of people trying to get through their day.

"That roof looks precarious," said Hokuren, not taking her eyes off Quartz. She had brown skin and black hair tied into braids that ended in golden rings, and she touched one of those braids nervously. As always, Hokuren dressed up fashionably with her tan coat, sensible pants, and leather boots. Not an outfit for climbing, as if she would ever dare to do such a thing.

Cinna's basic tunic and trousers, gray against the light brown of her skin, were much more suited for the task. She ran her hand through her thick wavy brown hair, barely restrained by the blue headband that she never took off, and gauged the slope of the roof. It would prove a challenge, but she hated when things were too easy. She pictured it in her mind: climb to the highest branches of the olive tree, leap to grab the ledge of the roof, and pull herself up.

"And can you really make that jump?" asked Hokuren. Cinna had learned not to take offense to questions like this. A less secure person might take this as doubt of her abilities, but the boss wanted her to be safe.

Cinna nodded toward the cat. "Of course, boss. A climb and a quick hop over. Tricky part will be getting down."

"Try not to let this one get hurt. Remember Ginger?"

"Ginger shouldn't have jumped. I'll tell Quartz not to," said Cinna. "Hopefully he listens."

"First time for everything, I suppose."

Cinna plotted her route up the olive tree's trunk. The tree was over eight hundred years old, making it the oldest living thing in Velles if you didn't count Senara, the millennia-old goddess residing in Cinna's soul. A sign near the tree asked that passersby refrain from climbing it or eating the olives, out of respect. Cinna planned to do both and so pretended she couldn't read it. Until recently, it would have been true.

The tree sported plenty of branches to grab, and its rough bark provided enough traction for her bare feet, making her climb easy. She paused to pick an olive that looked ripe and pop it into her mouth. She chewed once and almost choked with alarm, taste buds overwhelmed by bitterness.

Horrified, she spat the olive out, sending it several feet to the ground, where it landed with a splat.

"You have to soak olives to make them palatable," said Hokuren, amusement in her voice. "They don't come like that straight from the tree. Didn't you read the sign about not eating them?"

Cinna bit back a retort. Hokuren was the sign-follower in their partnership.

Working her tongue over her teeth didn't get rid of the awful bitterness. It lingered like cigar smoke. Cinna sighed and continued to climb, practiced hands and feet hauling her up with ease. Near the top of the tree, the branches became too thin to support her weight. She stood on the highest branch she trusted, which was only wide enough for her to balance on the balls of her feet. From here, the jump was not exactly easy, but far within her ability.

Quartz continued to ignore her, his leg straight up in the air as he zealously groomed himself from his perch on the slanted roof. A more perfect opportunity to jump, run, and catch him before he could pull his head up to flee didn't exist.

The branch cracked when Cinna slid her foot out another step, so she brought it back. This would be as close as she would get. With a deep breath, she crouched down, swung her arms, and jumped—

SNAP.

Cinna's leap lost most of its momentum as the branch collapsed beneath her. She sprawled out to grab for the building before she fell the two stories down. Her hands found the rain-eroded stone of a windowsill. She dangled for a moment, then brought her feet up. There was just enough room to stand on the sill.

The roof overhang, extending several inches past the walls, was within reach above her. She had used the olive tree because she'd wanted to avoid this pathway to the roof, but the tree had failed her. She would have to adjust.

"Cinna!" yelled Hokuren from below. "Just come down! We'll figure another way."

She ignored Hokuren's plea, spat in her hands, and grabbed the nearest beam supporting the overhang. The edge of the beam cut into her palms as she shimmied out, hanging precariously over the ground. Her right hand slipped as she reached the end, and for a heart-stopping moment only her left held her up. She regained her composure and twisted her body to pull herself up.

Cinna now stood atop the roof, none the worse for wear.

"Meorrr," growled Quartz as welcome. So he had kept tabs on her. It would be nice to see at least one cat run into her arms, purring in gratitude, but the job was not to get the cat to like her. It was to return him to his owner.

"Good kitty," said Cinna, pitching her voice into a high falsetto. This never helped, but it was how everyone else always talked to cats. They must have had a reason.

Quartz got to his feet and slunk down, ears pinned against his head. Cinna recognized this from previous cat encounters as a bad sign. He growled, backing up. Cinna braced her toes with every step upon the sloped rooftop that wanted nothing more than to send her sliding back to the earth.

The cat bolted, racing for the edge of the roof. "No!" cried Cinna, not wanting to see a repeat of Ginger's fall. But Quartz's jump put him on the adjacent roof of the tanner's shop, where he preened, apparently assuming Cinna would not follow.

Foolish cat. Cinna threw caution to the wind and ran along the clay tiles of the roof, smooth from years of wind and rain. Traction was poor under the soles of her bare feet, but she kept her balance with body control developed over years of training and exercise and vaulted to the tanner's roof. She landed in a roll that brought her next to the startled Quartz. She snatched him up before he could react, wrapping her arms around his body.

He struggled in her grip, hissing and scratching at her, inflicting several thin wounds with his razor-sharp claws. Lady Belladonna did not cut her cat's nails often enough. Or, possibly, ever. But Cinna held tight, letting the cat work through his energy.

Finally, Quartz calmed down. He seemed to realize that Cinna had an ironclad hold on him, and in one last act of defiance stuck his claws into her torso through her tunic, clinging to her.

"Ow," Cinna said. She tugged him, but his curved claws dug deep.

Cinna peered over the edge of the tanner's and found a route down. Her limbs were free to make the descent easily with Quartz stuck to her. The cat, perhaps sensing the danger in letting go, pressed against Cinna and, if anything, buried his claws further. Each incremental step down the side of the tanner's rewarded her with a fresh pain, but she fought through it.

Once on firm ground again, Cinna grabbed the cat and pulled, but he refused to let go. She was still puzzling over how to extract him without tearing chunks from herself when Hokuren arrived at her side, holding their well-used cat transport box.

"I think he likes me," said Cinna, gripping Quartz. He growled in response.

"I'm not so sure." Hokuren reached over to pet the cat. His growl intensified, and Hokuren jerked her hand back. "Hmm, we should invest in heavy-duty mitts for our cat wrangling. I'm worried about you getting an infection."

"I'll be fine."

"So you always say. But we'll need to repair the holes in both you and your tunic." Hokuren gripped her ever-present tan coat, which she kept spotless and intact.

"Nothing new about that."

A crowd had gathered to watch her rescue Quartz. The people tittered among themselves, some pointing at her and whispering. Cinna scowled at them. "Let's get out of here, boss. I don't fancy being entertainment for people with nothing better to do. We can take Quartz back to Lady Belladonna. As long as he's got his claws in me, he won't be running away again."

Hokuren glanced around at the crowd. "A good idea. But you should get him off you first. I imagine that hurts."

Cinna shrugged. "I'm not going to put on a show for this rabble by struggling with a cat."

"Are you so prideful that you would rather suffer in pain than risk looking foolish?"

"Definitely." Cinna had dealt with worse pain than a few cat claws in her life. She considered her ability to handle pain the upside of being mistreated in her childhood.

Hokuren's mouth opened, but no words came out. Instead, she sighed and spun on her heel to march toward Belladonna's. "Come on then, let's at least get there fast."

Cinna jogged to catch up to Hokuren, holding Quartz so he wouldn't sway any more than necessary. She whispered, "Good kitty," trying to soothe him, but he emitted a low growl all the way to the Aviary.

Home to Velles's richest citizens, the Aviary was the only section of the city with a full-time rotation of City Watch patrols. The Watch members stopped Cinna with gruff voices, accusing her of kidnapping the pampered cat stuck to her like a furry bandolier. It was only when the more respectable-looking Hokuren explained they were returning the lost cat to Lady Belladonna on commission that the Watch stood down.

"I can't believe they thought I was a thief," said Cinna. At Hokuren's wordless glance, Cinna muttered, "Well, I can't believe they'd think I'd steal *cats*."

They walked brick streets past mansions with flowers of all colors blooming in personal gardens, something not available to residents of other districts, who made do with tenements or small individual homes. Miniature statues of birds, robins and finches mostly, with a few eagles thrown in for good measure, topped streetlamps that, were it night, would be lit up with the strongest, whitest magical lights in the city. The cool sensation of the bright red brick streets under her feet, before the sun reached over the towering houses to bake them, was Cinna's favorite aspect of the wealthy district.

"Think Lady Belladonna will deduct from our pay because my blood is on her cat?" Cinna asked. The cat's white toes had turned pink from blood matted in his fur.

Hokuren clicked her tongue as she examined the blood. "Maybe she won't notice. She's old."

"Old, not blind, boss."

Hokuren hoped the trip to Lady Belladonna's didn't take long. Although the pet-finding services she provided continued to be the foundation of her investigation business, they didn't interest her. The sooner they wrapped this up and collected their badly needed payment, the sooner Hokuren could return to her office and see if a more intriguing case might arrive.

A massive iron gate stood between Hokuren and Cinna and Lady Belladonna's estate. It was the only interruption in the otherwise continuous spike-tipped stone walls that enclosed the property. It was not the most welcoming of spaces. Hokuren pressed a button that sent an entry request to Lady Belladonna. Only someone of her wealth would own magic like this from an earlier time when the wizards allowed such spells to exist.

The gate opened, revealing the mansion. The house covered more ground than the public bathhouse that Hokuren frequented. Belladonna lived here with a staff of four. In some parts of Velles, five people would find a way to live in a space smaller than Belladonna's bedroom.

Ashworth, the butler, greeted them at the front door and led them to the parlor, where Belladonna awaited. Along the way, Cinna narrowed her eyes at the gold-trimmed timepieces on display in the foyer.

"Each of these clocks is worth more than my life," she grumbled.

"Not true." Hokuren touched Cinna's arm lightly. "Remember our rule."

"Right, right," said Cinna, her voice low. "Don't complain where the client might hear."

"Let's make sure we get paid and get home."

The butler, who had pretended admirably not to hear their whispered conversation, introduced them to the lady herself when they entered the parlor.

"Lady Belladonna, Seekers Hokuren and Cinna have returned."

Belladonna's snow-white hair signified the end of her life was only a few short years away. The wizened elf wore a pink silk robe and lay upon a couch, head propped up on an arm, a caricature of absurd wealth. All she needed to complete the picture was to have Ashworth feed her grapes by hand while fanning her with a palm frond.

Cinna fought with Quartz, trying anew to coax him off her. "Got your cat," she said to Belladonna before any greeting could be exchanged. "He's part of me now. I guess we're a package deal."

"Aw, my precious kitten is back," cooed Belladonna, holding her arms out toward Cinna and Quartz.

The cat quit struggling when he spied Belladonna. He dropped from Cinna's torso and sprinted from the room, sure to be lost within the cavernous mansion.

"Don't worry, madam, I closed the front door," said Ashworth, bowing.

Belladonna inched into a sitting position with noticeable effort. She acknowledged Ashworth with the briefest of nods, then addressed Cinna and Hokuren. "I'll get him later, don't worry. I know all his hiding spots."

"We did as requested," said Hokuren, wondering if they'd done a disservice to the cat, given the way it fled this woman. "I don't wish to bother you any longer than necessary . . ." She licked her lips and held out her hand.

"Ah, yes, your payment. Of course." Belladonna waved at Ashworth, who left the room. "Ashworth will return shortly with your coin. I'm impressed with how fast you found my dear Quartz." She peered at Hokuren. "You know, you look quite familiar to me."

"I should. We met three days ago, when you asked me to find Quartz," said Hokuren, guardedly.

Belladonna frowned. "That's not what I mean. I'm not that addled yet. When we first met, I couldn't recall why I recognized you, but it came to me the day after I commissioned you. Are you from Fondence?"

Hokuren went rigid. No one in Velles had ever asked her about her hometown. She had moved to Velles ten years ago in part because its distance from Fondence meant running into someone from the town was so unlikely as to be near impossible. "I grew up there, but I'm afraid I don't remember you."

"No, I don't suppose you would," said Belladonna with a light laugh. "You are Nekane's daughter, are you not?"

"Nekane?" said Hokuren, stunned. She took a step back from Belladonna. "How do you know that name?"

"We've met, dear, you and I. You don't recall because you were but a babe in swaddling clothes last I saw you." Belladonna lurched to her feet and, with short, shuffling steps, trudged to a book tucked into the parlor's ample bookcase and began flipping through pages. "Now where is it—ah, yes."

She brought over a sketch and showed Hokuren. Cinna slid closer to peek at it as well. The image showed a younger version of Belladonna standing in a group with three women. Two were elves like Belladonna, but

Hokuren focused on the human with brown skin and black hair pulled back in braids, similar to her own hairstyle. Hokuren had only ever seen one image of the woman before, the one she carried in a locket around her neck.

It was Nekane, Hokuren's mother.

Hokuren touched this new image of her mother with her finger. "You knew her."

Belladonna nodded. "Not just knew her. We were friends. This was our bridge group that met almost every week for fifteen years in Fondence. Until, well, you know."

"You must have left Fondence shortly after she passed," said Hokuren, not afraid to mention her mother's death. She'd thought about it every day of her life that she could remember. "These other two would be Gregoire and Keshet. They never mentioned you to me. Though we didn't talk much before they both left Fondence."

"When Nekane died, our group fell apart. It wasn't the same, and Fondence became quite dreary to me." Belladonna placed the image back into the book. "I came to live here in Velles with my sister and her husband. Outlived them and got this." She waved a hand around the room.

"It's my fault," said Hokuren bitterly. "If I hadn't been born—"

"That's quite unfair." Belladonna interrupted Hokuren by touching a wrinkled hand to her cheek.

"I know, yet I can't help the feeling." Hokuren pulled back from the hand. "Could you tell me about her? What was she like to you?" All she knew of her mother was from the drawing she carried with her and stories from those who knew her. It had been over ten years since Hokuren had talked to anyone who could tell her anything new.

"Well. I like to think we were a pretty smart group of women. Bridge isn't a game for the stupid, you know." Lady Belladonna chuckled. "But Nekane was the brightest of all of us. She was so hard to play against. It felt like she'd see our moves before we even did. We took turns being her partner so we could at least win sometimes."

"I've heard similar things."

"She was always available if you needed help, too. I remember when Old Thornster's hens got loose, she organized the search party and, I believe, personally returned more of those birds than anyone else." Belladonna's eyes twinkled at the memory.

Hokuren smiled. "In stories, she always sounds perfect."

Belladonna shook her head. "She wasn't, of course, but her failings are not how I choose to remember her, or most people I have loved. And I wouldn't tell her only daughter about them, either."

"Please?" asked Hokuren. "I want to hear."

"Hmm . . ." Belladonna considered for a moment. "Well, she was a terrible cook."

"Ah." This was interesting. No one, including Hokuren's father and brothers, had ever mentioned this. "My father and brothers were too."

"Yes, when your family invited people to dinner, people suddenly found they had already made other plans." Belladonna winked. "Nekane never had the interest. Undercooked her meats, overcooked her porridge, never the right amount of seasoning, and her eggs . . . Oh, her eggs . . ." The old elf shook her head. "Every one should have been allowed to become another chicken instead."

Hokuren cast a glance at Cinna, who cocked her head to the side.

"What?" Cinna asked, her face innocent.

"I know someone else who overcooks her porridge," Hokuren said.

Cinna looked like she might deny it, but then she stopped herself and grinned. "That's why I put a lot of cinnamon in it. Hides the burnt taste."

"It really doesn't."

Belladonna cleared her throat. "There is one thing that I don't think anyone else knows about your mother."

"What is it?" asked Hokuren.

"I . . . never mind." Belladonna played with her hands. "I came upon this information in a most roguish way. Perhaps I shouldn't say."

"That doesn't bother us. We get half our information in roguish ways," said Cinna, before Hokuren could stop her. "And we'd probably get the other half faster if we went rogue."

"Please tell me." Hokuren considered getting on her hands and knees to coax the information out of the old woman.

Belladonna looked between Cinna's encouragement and Hokuren's pleading and sighed. "Nekane had secret meetings with people in the forest."

Hokuren scratched her head. "My father never even mentioned she liked going into the forest."

"Wouldn't have been a secret if he knew, girl. She told your father a number of times that she was going to a bridge game with us gals when she was really rushing off into the forest. I thought she was having an affair! I followed her once to see what secret tryst we were covering for." Belladonna's hand went to her brow, scandalized. "But though I wasn't trying to add eavesdropping to my list of transgressions, I heard enough to say I believe there was something else going on. There was talk about studying things like math and reading."

"That doesn't rule out a secret tryst!" said Cinna, earning a sharp glance from Hokuren. "Maybe she was into numbers. I'm sure someone's flirted with math before."

"That's my mother you're talking about."

"Sorry, boss."

"Fortunately for the sake of decency, I'm quite positive it was something else." Belladonna fanned herself. "She caught me watching and told me in no uncertain terms that I was to turn around, go home, and never follow her in the forest again." She shivered. "I'd never heard her so chilly."

Cinna leaned toward Belladonna on her toes. "But surely there was a second time."

"I never followed her into the forest again," said Belladonna primly. "It wasn't my business, you understand."

"Thanks for telling me." Hokuren wished Lady Belladonna had more information to provide. A story that hinted at some secret her mother was involved in would only fuel Hokuren's sleepless nights with speculation. Her first thought was some sort of clandestine study group, but hiding in the forest and telling Belladonna to stay away suggested something less than legal. The very idea her mother might be involved in unlawful activities cracked the edifice that Hokuren had built up in her mind her entire life.

Belladonna looked up to find Ashworth returning with a bag of coins in hand. "Ah, and here's your payment." She waved a hand at the butler, who counted out the agreed amount and handed it to Hokuren. "Thank you for finding my Quartz, and for allowing me to remember a dear old friend."

"If you ever remember anything else about my mother, please, let me know," said Hokuren.

Belladonna waved a hand in what could have been an assenting manner, then returned to her recline on the couch with a heavy sigh and closed her eyes. Hokuren wished they could have continued the conversation about her mother further, perhaps with a story that could counter the last one the lady told. Belladonna was spent, however, and Ashworth discreetly ushered her and Cinna away and to the exit. They didn't see any sign of Quartz on their way out.

2

Hokuren's mind was on her mother and her life that might have been on the walk back to the office. Belladonna's coins jingled in Cinna's pocket as she played with them. Usually, Hokuren would ask her assistant to stop something like that, but she was so focused on her thoughts the coins barely registered.

What if her mother had lived? It was a question that had haunted Hokuren throughout her entire life, and one that would never have an answer. She may not have come to Velles to pursue life as a seeker, investigating mysteries. From there, it was impossible to determine what things would have been like for her, but she could bet there would have been heart-to-hearts with her mother over tea. Perhaps her mother would have taught her bridge, and they could have played together. This last idea tugged at Hokuren's heart the most.

Now her imagined alternate life might need to include mother-daughter trips to the forest for secretive study groups. This one didn't quite tug at the heart the same way.

They had left the Aviary and traversed the entertainment district, quiet in the midday. Most of the businesses here, from the Grand Polemic theater to the flashy casinos to the taverns in between, stayed shuttered until the evening twilight. Promoters hawked upcoming shows with cries and fliers to the few people passing through. Hokuren ignored them, head down, while Cinna shoved aside the more aggressive ones.

Cinna jarred Hokuren from her own mind after they made it through the promoter gauntlet. "Hey, boss? All that stuff about your mother . . . are you all right?"

"Yes, thank you," said Hokuren. If she had never come to Velles, she'd never have met Cinna. The thought distressed her, so to change the subject, she said, "I'm thinking about how I'm going to clean up your wounds and mend your new tunic." She fixed Cinna with a playful stare. "Again."

"I told you to buy me a used tunic for my birthday, not a new one." Cinna held the hem out. Like her previous one, it was simple and off-white, but unlike the ratty one she used to wear, this one had yet to require any patches. "It's already become a used one. Could've saved some coin."

"I enjoyed that brief period when it was new." Hokuren had bought the tunic for Cinna's twenty-fifth "birthday," a day chosen at random because the orphaned Cinna didn't know the actual date. She'd never celebrated one before either, so Hokuren had given her a proper one with a present and everything.

"Very brief."

They remained in comfortable silence for the rest of the walk back to their office.

Thugs had destroyed the office's meager furnishings a few months previous. A new desk with chairs and shelves stacked with previous case notes replaced the old items, purchases made possible by a small windfall they'd received from a previous case. The money also allowed Hokuren to commission a new hand-painted sign out front. *Hokuren and Cinna Investigations, Seekers Hokuren and Cinna.* Sometimes she regretted the redundancy, even if she appreciated the clarity that Cinna was as much a part of the business as Hokuren. Everything else went to savings to maintain the rent payments, in case the month's revenue was too low.

Hokuren took out the first-aid kit. "Okay, lift your tunic."

Cinna obliged. Dried blood blotted the wounds on her body, courtesy of Quartz's claws. Hokuren knelt and cleaned each wound. As she worked, Cinna said, "These will heal fine on their own, boss."

"I know that," said Hokuren patiently. "You say that every time."

"But I never ask why you always do the whole clean and bandage routine. So?"

"I don't like seeing you with holes in your body." Hokuren met Cinna's eyes. "Even for a single day."

Cinna went quiet and looked away, as she often did when receiving affection.

"Done." Hokuren patted the final bandage. Her efforts were irrelevant to Cinna's physical recovery. The goddess Senara resided in Cinna's soul and would see that her body healed the wounds fast enough they'd be gone by morning.

Hokuren persisted because she wanted her assistant to feel cared for. Cinna's caregivers growing up, when she even had any, had treated her as a burden.

"Thanks, boss," said Cinna, in a voice so soft it was almost inaudible.

Three weeks passed, during which Hokuren and Cinna Investigations received two new cases. Another missing cat, found after two days and retrieved from a weaver who brought it in from the rain, and a blacksmith's hammer that the smithy swore had been stolen by a competitor. Hokuren had solved this one in under an hour by checking deep under the blacksmith's table and handing it to the abashed smithy. He had paid his fee in full, to his credit.

It was one of those days when Cinna and Hokuren had no cases to work. They lounged in the office and tossed out ideas for drumming up new business, shooting down each other's contributions. The worst involved the two of them wearing costumes and waving signs around Velles. When closing time hit with no new clients, they prepared to leave. A knock at the door halted them.

"They're late," said Cinna. "Think we should tell them we're closed?"

"I don't think you're being serious, but just in case: We are absolutely not turning them away." Hokuren opened the door, excited for a new potential case. Hopefully, it wouldn't be another missing pet case. "Hello, welcome to—"

A stitched image of a pigeon, the symbol of the Pigeon Couriers

Service, adorning a soft blue hat caught her eye immediately. The hat was atop a young elven man in matching pants and jacket. In his hand, he held an official yellow Pigeon Couriers envelope, sealed with magic only an employee of the courier could break. This was no client.

"Can I help you?" Hokuren asked. Their expensive fees meant that a delivery from Pigeon was almost always something important. They tracked down your intended recipient wherever they were, no matter what.

She couldn't help but recall the old joke her adventurer friends loved to tell. An adventurer wandered the world for years, failing to find the hidden den of a dragon that harassed her city. Then she had a stroke of genius. She sent the dragon a Pigeon Couriers package and followed the courier, who found the den in two weeks.

"Message from the estate of Mikko Tuomi for Hokuren Tuomi," said the courier briskly.

"My father's estate?" Hokuren's chest constricted as if a phantom weight had been placed on it.

"What it says. You're Hokuren." It wasn't a question.

"Yes."

"Sign here."

When Hokuren finished and handed the messenger back his documents, he held the envelope up between them. He waved a hand over the seal and muttered a short phrase in the Old Language, the words of the Primordial Ones that all magic spells used. The seal, an intricate pattern of bright purple shapes, disappeared.

With the blandness of one repeating the same line too many times to count, the courier said, "On behalf of Pigeon Couriers, we thank you and hope this item finds you well, although if it doesn't we are not liable for the contents."

"Thanks." Hokuren absentmindedly closed the door before he turned to leave.

Cinna rushed to Hokuren's side and stared at the envelope. "Boss, I can't believe this. You have a last name?"

It took Hokuren a moment to register Cinna's words as she studied the envelope. "What? Of course. Did you think I didn't?"

"Yes!" Cinna had her hands on her hips. "You've let me go along this whole time thinking you had one name like Sparklestrum."

She named the bard from Trebello, well-known for humorous songs about killing monsters long since eradicated by adventurers. Mercifully, perhaps, the monsters could only die in stories and songs now.

This broke the hold the envelope had over Hokuren, and she looked up at Cinna. "You never asked."

"Wha—" Cinna sputtered at this, but then nodded. "You're right, boss. I should make sure to ask next time."

"I'm not sure I want to open this," said Hokuren, still rooted to the spot next to the door where she'd accepted the envelope. She turned it over in her hands. "It's from my father."

"His estate," corrected Cinna.

"Yes, thank you." Hokuren closed her eyes. Dread cast a pall over her mind. She'd left Fondence a decade ago to escape his demands that she help run his import business as his heir apparent after her older brothers died. She hadn't talked to him since, as even in his letters in the intervening years he had continued to impose upon her a duty to his business. One day, she'd assumed, he would admit defeat, embrace her choice to make her own way as a seeker in Velles, and open up an opportunity for reconciliation.

With a deep breath, Hokuren slid a finger in and opened the envelope. A single piece of paper was inside, along with a set of keys and a handful of coins. She held the letter in trembling hands.

Dear Hokuren,

Looks like I'm dead. At least, I had better be dead, because I paid those seed-eaters at Pigeon Couriers a lot of coin to deliver this only after I died, not before.

Consider this my last will and testament. I leave everything to you. Mostly because I have no one else to give it all to except my competitors. And just in case there is an afterlife, I'd hate to spend it watching those fools succeed with my hard work.

I know you were never interested in Mikko's Imports, but regrettably, you must come to Fondence to settle my estate. Sorry about that. Although I love you, I am sure I left a few unpaid bills just for you. Consider it my punishment for abandoning me.

Harrison Grimes will manage my estate until you claim it. He is not very capable, so please make haste. Do not tell him I said that.

Thanks, Pumpkin. I miss you.

With love,
Your Father, Mikko Tuomi

P.S. The keys fit the safe in my basement. The coins accompanying this letter are to pay for your travel, in case you cannot afford it.

Hokuren gripped the letter so tightly it creased around her fingers. "He—he's—" Unsure of what to do, she placed the letter on the desk but kept her hand on top of it, as if it couldn't be real if she hid the words from her eyes. "He definitely wrote this. No one else would call me 'Pumpkin.'"

She took a breath. Dead. The reconciliation would never be coming.

"I'm sorry," said Cinna, in a small voice.

"I thought there'd be more time," Hokuren whispered.

Cinna wrapped her arms around her. The hug meant a lot, given how rarely her assistant gave them out.

"I don't want to go to Fondence," said Hokuren.

"Can you do that?" Cinna picked up the letter and held it up. "Ignore this?"

"Of course. My inheritance would be forfeit, but I can't be compelled to follow his wishes." Hokuren gestured at parts of the office. "I can't leave this behind, not when we're still in such a precarious state."

"What about his business?"

"That was the whole reason I left Fondence." Hokuren didn't want his business. She didn't want his estate, nor did she deserve it. Not after she left for Velles without a word.

Cinna twisted her thumbs. "But . . . don't you want to know how it happened?"

"I—" Hokuren stopped. Of course she did.

She picked through the coins her father had sent, all of them Fondencian gold in high denominations.

"Come on, let's go home." Hokuren gathered the letter, keys, and coins and stuck them back in the envelope. "We need dinner."

Hokuren glided through the motions of preparing and eating dinner. Her mind remained firmly fixed on her parents, even as Cinna tried talking to her. Hokuren gave incomplete answers and paid Cinna little attention, and eventually her assistant clammed up and excused herself to do exercises alone.

Hokuren thought about her mother, who only existed in her mind through precious few drawings and stories. She thought about her father, who had loved her but also driven her away with his single-minded obsession with his import business.

Later, Hokuren lay in bed, lantern on and eyes wide open. Sleep seemed an impossibility. She'd still shed no tears and felt guilty for that as well.

She glanced again at the letter in her hands. It was not the one from her father. Instead, it was one she'd read countless times since receiving it near three years ago. It was from Moira, the closest thing to a mother Hokuren had. She was also a witch, though she rarely invoked her magic.

Hokuren and Moira had exchanged mail after Hokuren arrived in Velles, the only person from Fondence with whom she corresponded. Moira had been encouraging as Hokuren struggled with the big city and her new life as part of the City Watch, but her letters had slowed toward the end until coming to a stop with the letter Hokuren held now. The last paragraph Moira had written all but confirmed that her long life had reached its end.

> *Even though it's been years since I've seen you, I know you've grown into the woman I knew you could be. One day, you'll be the best investigator in Velles, and then the world. I'm sorry I won't be there to see it, but even without me, you will succeed. I have never been surer of anything in my life.*

Hokuren dreaded returning to a Fondence without Moira.

She padded from her bedroom loft to make a late-night tea, holding her lantern close and tip-toeing to avoid waking Cinna. Her assistant had been sleeping on the couch for months, a "temporary" arrangement until Cinna could get her own place. They always found an excuse to avoid actually executing a search.

"Hey," said Cinna, sitting up, voice scratchy. "Can't sleep?"

"Oh, you know, just considering my regrets."

"Heavy."

"Sorry to wake you." Hokuren filled her kettle with water and activated it. The fire magic within, weak though it was, could heat the water in only a minute. It was by far the most expensive item in her possession, a splurge worth every coin. "I'll be done soon and let you get back to sleep."

"I can tell this has bothered you. You ignored me all night." Cinna was fully awake now, cross-legged on the couch facing Hokuren in the kitchen. Her shoulder-length hair, already in the throes of bedhead, was a wild mess, wavy strands sticking out every which way. "I'm really sorry about your father."

Hokuren sat on the couch next to Cinna. "Thank you. You're right, you know. I do want to find out what happened to him. Plus, I have a responsibility to deal with the estate."

"Of course you do," said Cinna. "Why wouldn't you want to go?"

"There's a part of me that's ashamed of leaving and never talking to my father again. And to go back, and he's not there . . . I don't relish facing that." Hokuren sighed. "The guilt I'll feel if I don't go back will be so much worse, though."

"Don't worry," said Cinna, as the kettle whistled. "I'll go with you, and we'll face it together."

"With you there, I'm sure it will be all right." Hokuren patted Cinna on the knee and got up from the couch to pour the water into her tea leaves. "You've never told me what you thought about me doing what I did. Leaving my father."

"You did what you thought was best." Cinna yawned. "If you hadn't, I wouldn't have met you. So I'm glad you did, although I'm also biased."

Hokuren finished preparing her tea and turned around to respond, but Cinna had already fallen back asleep. She tucked Cinna's blanket under her chin and went upstairs, where the tea relaxed her enough to allow her to finally drift off to sleep as well.

Hokuren worked over the next two days to arrange their trip. The money her father sent her was more than enough to hire old friend Captain Tulip and his ship, the *Flying Porpoise*, to take her and Cinna up the coast to Oro. From there, they would make the journey inland to Fondence.

More of her father's money bought each of them secondhand daggers, still in decent shape, for added protection on the road. Cinna, who felt her fists and feet were enough and didn't care for blades, had reluctantly agreed to carry hers when Hokuren had been adamant. While the Fondence she remembered was relatively safe, Oro was a port town with its share of thieves and smugglers. One never knew when danger might strike on a trip away from home.

Hokuren paid a visit to another old friend to see to securing her office while she was gone. Fenton ran a magic item shop on a secluded, dead-end street in Velles's business district. The ghostly pale elf greeted her the way he typically did: with jaunty sarcasm.

"Hokuren and Cinna, the demon slayers, grace my shop." He bowed deeply, head hovering just over his countertop.

"That's right," said Cinna. "No demon stands a chance against us."

Cinna and Fenton exchanged grins, then turned as one toward Hokuren, who rolled her hand in a "let's get on with it" motion. "All right, it was one demon, and we almost died ourselves. Get it out of your system."

"I've got some new items to show you, if you're interested." Fenton reached under his counter and pulled out three bottles, each half-filled with colorful liquids bubbling lazily. "Got a special deal on these potions."

"What do they do?" Cinna crouched down to gaze into each bottle.

"Don't know. That's why they're on special."

Hokuren eyed the potions with suspicion. In the center bottle, a yellow bubble floated to the cap before popping, making a sound like a dog barking.

"Okay," said Fenton, turning the bottle in his hands. "This one is for someone who wishes they had the noise of a dog with none of the companionship."

"No thanks," said Hokuren. "I actually came to ask if you would be kind enough to watch my place for a few weeks. I've got to head back to Fondence."

Fenton threw his hands up. "I should know better than to think you came here to buy something. Well, I suppose I could. It wouldn't put me out too much." He gave her a knowing look. "So did he . . .?"

"Yes."

"My condolences." Fenton, in a rare occurrence, appeared sincere.

Hokuren nodded in acceptance. "Thank you. I've got to deal with his estate. I hate to disappoint my customers by being gone so long."

"What customers?" Condolences given, Fenton returned to his teasing ways. "Neither of us has those. That's why we get along so well, I reckon. I'm sure almost no one will notice you've left. Until they've lost their cat, of course."

Cinna glanced at Hokuren. "He's got us there."

Hokuren said nothing, because it was true.

"Actually, there's something I should tell you." Fenton leaned toward them and gestured for them to lean in as well, then continued in a whisper, "This is for your ears only, and if you tell anyone, you risk not only me, but yourselves as well. There's said to be a rogue wizard in the area around

Fondence."

"Like you?" asked Hokuren, keeping her voice low. The Conclave of Wizards, self-declared keepers of magic, pronounced all wizards not part of their organization "rogue."

"Not quite. I keep my head down, don't use my magic all the time, and thus far haven't been worth hunting down. This one's active enough that the Conclave is aware of their location. I know little about them, though, not even their name or appearance. My spies have only gotten me so much."

"You have spies?" In her surprise, Cinna forgot to keep her voice down.

Fenton put a finger to his lips. "Shhh, hey, that's not something you yell out in the open." He nodded at Cinna's look of contrition. "And yes, I have spies. Any good wizard does."

"What should we do about this wizard?" asked Hokuren. She didn't relish tangling with a wizard, but if her hometown was threatened, doing nothing didn't sit right either. The Conclave had a monopoly on powerful magic, and their former members, unrestrained by the other wizards, were often dangerous. No one in Fondence could stand up to a trained wizard, should one decide to make themselves known.

"You should do nothing." Fenton shook his head emphatically. "In fact, if you somehow figure out who the wizard is, I highly recommend keeping that to yourself. Otherwise, they'll have a good reason to kill you."

"I'd like to see them try," said Cinna.

Fenton shook his head again. "You don't want to see that, I assure you. The Conclave will deal with them in due time, but it's low on the priority list since Fondence is considered an unimportant area. Avoid the wizard at all costs, especially if they've gone mad." He twirled a finger next to his head. "You'll know because they'll be wearing a velvet robe and big floppy hat. All the crazy ones do."

"My hometown isn't unimportant." Hokuren pretended to take offense.

"The official Conclave term is 'yokel backwater.'"

"I never know when I can believe you." Hokuren frowned at Fenton's grin. "Since a great wizard has deigned to go rogue in the 'backwater' of Fondence and hobnob with the 'yokels,' they must have a reason."

Palms upturned, Fenton said, "I would love to know. There were reports of a rogue wizard in the area roughly thirty years ago. I never found out who they were, and then the reports disappeared. Now the wizard is back. Could be a different one, of course."

Hokuren rubbed her chin. That would have been just before her own birth. Fondence had almost no magic, not even the simple lantern and healing potion spells Velles had. If rogue wizards had been popping up there for that many years, they'd kept themselves well hidden.

"Thanks for telling us, Fenton," she said. "We'll stay out of the way."

"I certainly hope so. You're both my favorite non-customers. I'd hate to lose the business I don't get from you." He put his colorful potions back under the counter, where the yellow potion emitted another muffled bark. "That will become irritating rather quickly," he muttered.

Hokuren didn't have money available for frivolous potion buying. Fenton knew that, so what he got from her was the ability to make jokes at her expense, even as he continued to assist her whenever she asked.

Hokuren put her hand on her heart. "One day, I'm going to make it up to you. I promise."

"Yeah, yeah. Once you're a big-time investigator, you'll buy my silly little potions." Fenton pulled over a box. "Until then, how about a penlight? You remember, it's a pen and a light? They're on deep discount."

"Maybe we should buy something, boss," said Cinna. "You keep saying we will next time."

Cinna was right. Fenton deserved a little sale, even if it wasn't much. "All right, if it's not too much." Hokuren reached for her coin purse.

Fenton yanked the box away. "Don't buy this crap, come on." He shooed them out of the store. "And don't come back until you've learned not to fall for high-pressure sales tactics."

Outside of his shop, Cinna grumbled, "He can't complain we don't buy anything and then refuse to sell us anything."

"He knows we can't afford it, Cinna."

"Oh," came the chastened reply.

Hokuren thought of the wizard roaming around Fondence. She had never met a wizard outside of Fenton, but from what she understood, he was an anomaly. Wizards were much less likely to crack a joke than they were to threaten to burn you alive for looking at them wrong.

Another thought crossed her mind, one she could not get rid of the entire walk back home, no matter how far-fetched it seemed.

Had her father run afoul of the wizard?

3

The trip to Oro took eighteen days aboard the *Flying Porpoise*. Cinna jumped off the ship and onto the pier connected to the bustling docks, where the number of crates, chests, and other containers being hauled back and forth by weary dockworkers nearly matched that of Velles. The smell of the sea mingled with the industries of wood and metal-working to create a pungent and altogether unpleasant aroma.

Cinna was grateful to stand on the dock's wooden planks, fixed in place, after the time spent on the *Porpoise*, where her footing never felt solid. The ship maintained something between gentle swaying and rocking the entire trip.

"Hard to believe you'll need six weeks in Fondence." Captain Tulip, seeing them off, had a lit cigar in hand. Cinna needed only one hand to count the number of times she saw him bereft of either alcohol or a smoke during her eighteen-day voyage with him. Given how poisonous to the body both were, according to Hokuren, it seemed a miracle Tulip wasn't already dead.

Hokuren followed Cinna off the ship using the gangplank. "I don't know how long things will take. I assumed that you might be around if we wanted to leave sooner."

"Perhaps, if we don't get some work." Tulip shrugged. "I won't turn down something good." He looked out to sea, squinting in the bright sunshine. "Though not what those men are doing." He pointed out in the distance, where a small rowboat bounced in the water like a toy as it made for the shore. "I have more self-respect these days."

"What are they doing?" asked Hokuren.

"Smuggling. You can tell because they're avoiding the docks." He blew a puff of smoke. "I probably shouldn't say this, as one shouldn't speak ill of the deceased, but there were rumblings that Mikko Tuomi got involved in a smuggling operation."

Hokuren put a hand to her mouth. "No, that can't be. My father wouldn't."

"People rumble about many things. Doesn't mean they're true. I thought you should know the rumors exist."

"Right. Thank you."

Cinna and Hokuren exchanged waves with Tulip before putting the ship at their backs. The sun blazed in the cloudless sky above them. The salty sea breeze Cinna had gotten used to on the *Porpoise* didn't exist in the protected bay where Oro had been built. Cinna perspired in the unseasonal warmth by the time they reached the end of the slip the Porpoise had tied up in.

Merchant sailors and dockhands bustled about, some grumbling curses as they dragged their enormous piles of wheeled goods around her and Hokuren.

"We're in the way, like tourists. Let's get somewhere less crowded." Hokuren scanned the waterfront, shading herself from the sun with her hand. "Come on, I know a much more peaceful place."

Cinna nodded, happy to follow Hokuren out of the overwhelming docks.

Half an hour later, they stood alone on a sandy beach. The sand was hot enough that it might have burned the soles of her feet were they not toughened from a lifetime spent barefoot. She looked out at the ocean with Hokuren, wondering why the boss had brought her here and not straight into the town.

"Do you hear that?" Hokuren asked after a time.

Cinna craned her neck, trying to hear what she was supposed to hear. "It's quiet, boss. I don't hear anything but the waves."

Hokuren wiped some sweat from her brow with the sleeve of her coat. Cinna didn't know how Hokuren could wear her favorite heavy coat in heat like this. "Exactly. No noises. No creaky boat, no sailors cursing, no Captain Tulip boasting. It's just us, and it's . . . quiet. Isn't it nice?"

"Oh." Cinna understood.

"Yeah." Hokuren closed her eyes and took a deep breath. "My father wasn't a smuggler, you know."

"Of course not."

"He was successful, so naturally his jealous rivals would spread malicious lies."

"Of course."

Hokuren sighed. "I've almost convinced myself."

"I didn't know him at all," said Cinna. "I'm just taking your word for it."

They stood for a while longer, enjoying being there together, just the two of them. Cinna gazed out into the sea, watching waves lap against a series of earthen pillars jutting up into the sky, some she estimated at twenty feet high. She dipped a foot into the lapping waves. The water was crisp and inviting.

The rowboat that Tulip had pointed out earlier caught her eye. It eased into a position behind the pillars, hidden from the Oro shore. From the beach here, she could make out two men aboard before it slid out of sight. If she brought up Hokuren's father's name to them, she wondered how they might react. Perhaps they could confirm his level of involvement with smuggling. It would bring Hokuren some peace to know the truth, either way.

Not for nothing, it was also a great day to be in the water.

"Do I have time for a swim, boss?"

Hokuren's eyes didn't open. She hadn't seen the smuggler boat, Cinna was sure. "I'm not dressed for it, but if you want to, sure. Our wagon to Fondence doesn't leave until tomorrow morning."

"Everyone is dressed for it." Cinna tossed her clothes onto the sandy beach. "You've got your skin."

Hokuren blanched. "I'm not comfortable with that the way you are."

"I see. Well, I *am* an elf. Senara told me that in the olden days, we elves used to frolic naked all the time. Elves only started wearing clothes to fit in with the humans, who were prudes." Cinna grinned. "This is natural to me."

Hokuren waved her hand toward the ocean. "Don't let this prudish human stop you from getting in touch with your inner elf."

After a bit of thought, Cinna removed her headband and placed it next to the rest of her clothes. It exposed her ears, unusually short and stubby compared to the typical elf, and if she could choose one item of clothing to wear, it would be that. She removed it because there was no one else around, and it would be far worse to lose it in the water.

When she reached for the dagger sheath strapped to her ankle, the last thing she had on, Hokuren stopped her.

"Keep the dagger, at least? You never know."

"All right." Cinna waded out, welcoming the relief as soon as the water touched so much as her ankles. "I'll be back soon." When she was far enough out that the water came up to her chest, she dove in and started swimming farther out, fighting against the momentum of the waves.

She bobbed in the water near the pillars, lying on her back and feeling the warmth of the sun's rays counteracted by the refreshing coolness of the water. If she had convinced Hokuren to join her, they could have just stayed here like this until sundown, and there would be worse things.

Shouts from the rowboat ruined her moment of peace, reminding her of the point of this whole excursion. She slithered stealthily through the water toward the boat, keeping the pillar between them.

Only now did it occur to Cinna that the two men might not respond to anyone showing up at their hiding spot and asking questions about illegal smuggling activities with enthusiastic, measured answers. Plus, they'd probably realize she was naked, which was not, as Hokuren might put it, appropriate interrogation attire.

"It's good to get away for a while," said one of the men, his deep voice not sounding nearly as relaxed as his words might suggest. "Hugo's in one of his moods."

The other man's voice was high-pitched and nasal. "Let's just hope he doesn't figure out our hiding spot. Hey, save some of that rum for me."

They continued like this for a while, obnoxious and growing more inebriated. Cinna dithered, unsure if their drinking would make it easier or harder to question them.

Then the topic switched to business, so she paid closer attention. Perhaps they would bring up something she could use to insert herself into their conversation.

"Hey, so, about those shipments," the first voice said, now hushed and tense. "Hugo says we can't sell to anyone else."

"Why not?" asked the nasally voice, making less of an attempt to whisper.

"Keep it down!" urged the first voice.

The nasally voice huffed. "Forget about managing the volume of my voice, Petros! Our buyer's dead, the silks are piling up, and we're not getting paid for them to leave. If we can't sell to anyone else, we'll be the next to die."

"Silks, he says." Petros's tone was mocking. "Don't forget the other goods. Anyway, our buyer's soon to be back."

"Back from being *dead*? Sorry, I thought that was permanent."

"Not the same person. The same *company*. Tuomi's daughter, Hokuren, is coming to take over for him and run Mikko's Imports."

Cinna clapped her sea-salty hand over her mouth to prevent her gasp from escaping. She wouldn't have to ask about Hokuren's father, because the smugglers brought it up for her.

"Oh?" Nasally voice seemed interested. "Maybe we could work something out with her."

Petros scoffed. "A contact of Hugo's in Velles said she once turned down a dragon's hoard of gold so she could put a tax cheat behind bars."

"Sounds exaggerated." Nasally voice made a dismissive spitting noise. "No one's that much of a paragon of justice."

Cinna hadn't heard that story from Hokuren, but it wouldn't have surprised her if it was closer to true than not.

"If Hokuren's even half that a paragon, it's a problem." Petros then spoke even more softly, and Cinna had to strain to hear. "Anyway, word is she and Mikko weren't talking. Best guess is she has no idea about our little arrangement and won't approve once she does."

Nasally Voice said, "That's just scuttlebutt. Maybe Hugo could go make some threats? He's good for that."

"Hokuren's ex-City Watch!" Petros sounded more scandalized than afraid for Hugo. "Bad idea. Though she's not alone. She's bringing a barefoot urchin child from the streets she took in."

Cinna narrowed her eyes. They could call her a barefoot urchin all they wanted, everyone did. Child was just flat out incorrect.

"What, she adopted an urchin?"

"Or hired her. It's unclear. She seems unimportant, anyway."

The dagger sheath caused Cinna's ankle to itch. She did her best to ignore it.

"Hmm, now there's a weak point." Nasally voice was pensive. "Kidnap the girl, scare Hokuren. She'll cough up the coin if she cares about her."

Cinna almost hoped these two nitwits attempted to kidnap her. They seemed the type that could use a good pummeling. It would be a good idea to get a look at the smugglers in case they showed up in Fondence. She paddled through the water, maneuvering herself closer to the pillars, trying to get the boat into view without attracting attention.

"Let's try bargaining before we move right to kidnapping," Petros said. "I'll discuss with Hugo. Maybe he'll—"

He stopped abruptly when, in her efforts to get closer, Cinna carelessly scraped her leg against the rough rock formation. She cried out, then swore when the men reacted.

"Someone's here?" Nasally voice turned dark and nervous.

"This is why I said to be flaming quiet. Swing the boat around," Petros said urgently.

Time to go. Cinna dove back into the water, swimming as fast as she could. When she surfaced to take a breath, she risked a look back. The rowboat had gotten through the pillars.

Both men were rowing, and she guessed they could row faster than she could swim. Her brief glance gave her only the barest of details: The bigger one had black hair, the smaller brown.

She considered stopping and leaping aboard their ship to thrash and question them. Even undressed and two-on-one, she felt confident in her odds. However, it was best they didn't get a good glimpse of her. They might figure out her identity and put Hokuren in danger.

Swim it was. She put her head down and focused on her strokes, kicking her legs as fast as she could. Her muscles burned as she pushed her pace.

Even so, when she looked back, the boat had closed enough distance that the men's grunts were audible as they rowed. When she looked back again, one of them wrangled with something big they stuffed into a tube.

It was a propulsion net.

A *poof* sound accompanied the propulsion magic firing the weighted net as Cinna dove. It settled in the water above her and fell, stretching over a vast amount of water. The weights dragged it down quickly, preventing her from swimming away. She became twisted in the threads.

Cinna pulled her legs up to her body as the net tightened around her. This put the dagger strapped to her leg within reach, even with her movement now restricted. The net rose, dragging her toward the surface and the boat like a captured fish, but she worked the dagger through enough of the net's threads to make an escape hatch.

She slipped out of the net. Her lungs tightened in her chest, demanding air, but she couldn't surface yet. She swam up to the boat and rammed her shoulder into the wood. The boat rocked back and forth, and the men shouted from above, muted by the water. She repeated this process a few more times, threatening to capsize the vessel, until the two men put oars back into the water and paddled away.

Cinna pushed up to surface and took a deep, grateful breath while checking on the boat. The two men on board headed back toward the pillars. They seemed to bicker, holding up sections of the damaged net and gesturing at each other. Satisfied and exhausted, she returned her dagger to its sheath and swam until she was close enough the waves could finish carrying her back to the shore, where Hokuren waited.

Cinna reached the beach and got to her feet, legs shaky from the exertion. She trudged further in and shook the water from her body. In the heat of the day, she would be dry in no time.

Hokuren ran to Cinna, wrapping her up in the tan coat. "Are you okay?"

"Of course I'm okay. Good idea to keep the dagger on." Cinna lay down on her clothes on the beach. She could have fallen asleep right there if her heart wasn't still thumping in her chest. "I got some good info from them before they caught me."

"Who were they?" Hokuren hovered over Cinna, blocking the sun.

Cinna met Hokuren's look of concern by sitting up to show she was fine. "Your new business partners. Congratulations, boss, you're in the illicit silk trade."

4

The coins Hokuren's father had provided paid for the two-day wagon ride from Oro to Fondence. The smugglers were right when they guessed that Hokuren would not be interested in continuing the Tuomi family association, even before taking into account their plan to extort her by kidnapping Cinna.

To take her mind off learning the rumors that her father had gotten himself involved in a smuggling operation were true, Hokuren buried herself in her novel. She saw the world through the eyes of Ms. Maplebrook, a shrewd septuagenarian who was well on her way to solving yet another perplexing crime. This also helped keep her from looking at the newly married couple that traveled in the wagon with them, who largely spent the trip cuddling and pawing at each other as young lovers sometimes did.

Cinna slapped her own book shut midway through the second day of travel. "I can't believe I'm out of *Captain Cavalier* novels. What am I going to read now?"

The words jolted Hokuren from her Maplebrook vision. Hokuren couldn't stand *Captain Cavalier*, novels in which the eponymous hero adventured in a world that relied on classical stereotypes long proved false. Goblins were always stupid and violent, witches had long hooked noses and hunched over bubbling cauldrons while cackling to themselves, pirates had ridiculous accents, and so on.

"I have some mysteries here." Hokuren held up a favorite, *Ms.*

Maplebrook and the Dapper Delinquent.

Cinna slid her eyes to the door. "Maybe I'll just walk beside the wagon for a bit."

"Did you hear about the mermaid near Oro?" asked the husband half of the couple, coming up for a short intermission from their canoodling.

Hokuren looked at Cinna, who shrugged. "I didn't know there were mermaids near Oro."

"Not just a mermaid—oh, darling, do you think we should tell them?" the wife said, wrapped up with her new husband.

He chuckled and said, "We hear it was a naked mermaid. She wasn't even wearing those usual seashells they do."

"And she was eavesdropping! The nerve," giggled the wife.

"Well, I've heard of plenty of naked mermaids, but never eavesdropping mermaids," said Hokuren, sharing a smile with Cinna. "Sounds like something a bard would come up with."

The two lovebirds tittered with restrained laughter. "Oh, Petros is no bard," said the wife. "He's just some merchant with an imagination."

"Too bad that story never reached us. We could have given Petros some information."

The couple gasped in unison. "You know about the mermaid?"

"I caught sight of it, yes." Hokuren leaned in toward them. "About this Petros. I might like to talk to him if he happens to be in Fondence."

"He's got black hair, a mustache, and dresses in fine linen," said the husband. "You'll usually catch him around with Hugo and his crew."

The couple went back to ignoring their fellow passengers, putting their hands on each other's chests after having gotten this bit of gossip off them.

The wagon arrived in Fondence and disgorged Cinna and Hokuren before continuing on. "I'm so glad to be rid of them," grumbled Hokuren as she gathered her bag.

Cinna stretched her arms to the sky. "Did you hear, boss? I'm a mermaid."

"You didn't wear your seashells, though."

"They chafe. I left them at home."

The wagon left them at the station at the eastern edge of Fondence. Hokuren stared at the town stretching out in front of her. The familiarity hit her hard, even after so long away. Already she could pick out the small smithy owned by Katerina the blacksmith, Mama Ogg's bakery, and the edge of Talainn's property where he grew his wheat and barley. She didn't know how they, or anyone from Fondence, would respond to her return after her inexplicable disappearance. Butterflies flew in her stomach like she was headed to receive a magistrate's judgment as she squelched in the soft mud created by the rains, mindful to tread with care.

"Is the whole town a mud pit?" asked Cinna, rolling her pant legs up and tromping through the muck with none of Hokuren's caution.

"The mayor wanted to pave the roads with stone, like we have in Velles, but looks like that's still on the to-do list. Don't worry. As long as it doesn't rain more, it'll dry out soon enough."

"Worry?" Cinna grinned at Hokuren. "Worry is the last thing on my mind."

"Right. How could I forget you like walking in mud?"

Cinna scanned the town in front of her, slumping her shoulders. "This place looks small. None of these buildings has a second story. Is this what being a backwater is?"

Hokuren took a deep breath and began walking toward the town center. "This isn't a big city like Velles, but it's not as bad as Fenton makes it sound." She waved her arms at the town in front of them. "It looks small, and it is, but you aren't seeing the farmland that stretches out in all directions, painstakingly cut from the forest over generations."

"Farmland, huh."

The sun crept below the horizon by the time they reached the main pavilion, which spread out from the statue of town founder Timothy Fond that marked the center of the city. His stern, patriarchal face was difficult to see in the low light, but Hokuren's memory filled in his scowl. Merchant stalls arranged in a ring around the statue, open daily for farmers and townspeople to trade and barter with each other, had closed up for the day. Stragglers finished collecting their goods in wagons to take home.

A notable absence from the town center was the play area for children. Hokuren had played games of tag and stoolball there as a small child while her father shopped for necessities. The tree from which a rope swing used to hang had been removed. Dilapidated market stalls, grimy with sludge, had been installed where the play area used to be for an expansion that seemed to have been overly ambitious. Hokuren had outgrown the childish games long ago, but it was dispiriting to see it no longer available for new generations.

A quick survey revealed that none of the lingering merchants knew where Harrison Grimes lived. Her father, in his infinite wisdom, had sent her keys to his safes but not to his house, which was now her house. She had no way to get in short of asking Cinna to pick the lock to the front door, which she'd rather not have to resort to.

"Well, well. If it isn't Hokuren." A woman called out across the desolate center, the first person to acknowledge Hokuren. She was human, like most people in Fondence, with pale skin. Her voice was hoarse and strained, as if she had something stuck in her throat. She strode toward them, dressed in plain gray clothes under a leather boiled cuirass, her gait confident. As she approached, Hokuren squinted to pick up the details of her face. She seemed familiar, but her identity lingered just out of reach.

The woman's lip twitched as she reached Hokuren. "Back in the slums of Fondence, same as me. Never thought we'd meet up again here. Town's never been worse, if you want my opinion."

Her voice was nothing like it used to be, scars crossed her once unblemished face, and her once long, luxurious blonde locks had been shorn off close to her head, yet the name came back with a rush of unrequited infatuation. Rosana.

Hokuren's cheeks flushed as she forced herself to maintain eye contact. "Ah, hello, Roz." No one called her Rosana unless she was on stage. At least, they hadn't back then.

"You remember me, Hokuren. Pretty impressive. It's been a while, and I'm a whole new gal." Roz flicked her head toward Cinna. "Got a friend, have you?"

Despite her changes, Roz still carried herself with confidence. That demeanor had made Hokuren's heart flutter all those years ago. The ruined voice did nothing to prevent that. Hokuren forced herself to remain level-headed. "Roz, this is Cinna. Cinna, Roz."

Cinna peered at Hokuren, then at Roz. "You an old friend of the boss?"

"'The boss'?" Roz laughed, the sound a breathy wheeze. "Is that your

Velles name?"

"No, no, she calls me that because I hired her as my assistant." Hokuren worried a button on her coat. "I didn't expect to see you here. Just visiting, or . . ." she trailed off.

Roz had left Fondence when Hokuren was sixteen, planning on making it big in Trebello, the city across the Sea of Expanse from Velles. Two years later, Hokuren had left, too, and she'd heard nothing of Roz since.

Roz sighed, and Hokuren could sense they could talk for hours about all that was behind it. "I'd be happier if you didn't see me here. Things didn't quite work out in Trebello. If your ears work, you can tell my voice is gone. Kind of you not to mention it."

The words struck Hokuren. Roz had created some of the most beautiful, haunting songs she'd ever heard, even at a young age. "I can't believe it. You were the best bard Fondence ever produced."

"It didn't mean a damn thing in a place where there's a hundred other towns' best bards," said Roz, her face tightening. "I never made it singing. They said my songs didn't have enough of a hook. Lost count of how many times they told me I was good but not a 'marketable voice.' Hah!" She spit near Hokuren's feet. "I didn't give up. Made ends meet as an adventurer and eventually had a bad run-in with some giant spiders. Look at this beaut of an injury." She traced her hand across a thick scar running the width of her throat. "I can't sing anymore. I can barely talk." The last few words came out as a croak, barely audible.

Hokuren put her hands to her mouth. "Oh, Roz, I'm so sorry."

Roz swallowed and cleared her throat. "Can't say too much without a break." She shifted on her feet. "It's fine, really. I've got a plan. If I stay committed, I'll get my voice back."

The conviction in her voice was discernible even in its poor state. Hokuren knew of no way to repair damaged vocal cords, even with magic-enhanced healing potions. "What sort of plan?"

Roz froze, then waved her hand. "Oh, just something I'm working on." She smiled. It looked forced. "Well, it's pretty funny your friend Cinna calls you boss. Should I be doing the same?"

"One is enough, thank you." Hokuren didn't mind Cinna calling her "boss" because it pleased Cinna, and she had learned to live with it. Potential copycats needed to be nipped in the bud.

"She's the boss, and I'm the assistant," said Cinna, hands on hips. "What's funny about that?"

"We're seekers, Cinna and I, with joint ownership of our business in Velles," said Hokuren, correcting Cinna.

"Seeker, huh? That a Velles thing? What do you seek?" asked Roz. There was an edge behind the playfulness of her tone.

"The truth," said Hokuren, unsure what Roz wanted to hear.

Roz paused for a moment at that. "How noble. Well, I'm not in the truth seeking business, but I'm your employee all the same."

It took Hokuren a moment to realize what she meant. "My father hired you."

"You got it. When I came back to Fondence, I needed work, and there's not enough for adventurers to make a living around here. I escort the goods from Oro to Fondence." Roz tapped her forehead. "That's those investigator instincts coming through. I guess I should worry about you finding all my truths."

"Only those who have done something wrong have to worry," said Hokuren, and Roz's smile faltered for a moment before returning.

Cinna interrupted the awkward moment. "If you worked for the boss's father, then do you know where the Grimes guy lives?"

"You mean Harrison Grimes. Of course I do. He's been my acting superior for a few weeks now." Roz pointed toward the west. "Down this way, last house on the road." She gave Hokuren a peculiar look. "I could describe him for you, but I'd rather you get the true experience for yourself."

"Something tells me it's not a positive one," said Hokuren. "Whatever he's like, I can't avoid him. He's the executor of my father's estate."

"Ah, right, I'm sorry about your father."

Now it was Hokuren's turn to shake off the sympathy. "We were strangers at the end."

"You were family. Don't forget that." Roz leaned in and gave Hokuren a quick, chaste hug. It still flustered Hokuren. Roz pulled back and gave both her and Cinna a little wave. "It's getting dark, and if you need to get to Harrison and back, you shouldn't waste anymore time hanging around here letting me chat you up."

"Um," said Hokuren. She wanted to ask about her father's smuggling, but her tongue failed her after the hug.

"Don't worry, we'll talk again soon, I'm sure." Roz leaned in close, and Hokuren's heart rate climbed a few beats. The smuggling left her mind completely. Roz rasped, "Perhaps next time we'll be alone."

"Perhaps," said Hokuren, her voice pitched an octave higher than she wanted.

She watched Roz go, thinking about the two of them as teenagers. She could still hear Roz's melodious voice, singing beautiful verses alongside the twang of her lute. Hokuren had been enthralled by her each and every word.

"She looks tough. I hope I get to spar with her," said Cinna.

"What?" Hokuren was shaken back to the present, reminded that the current Roz could bear little resemblance to the one in her memories, even past the appearance. "I think she could give you a proper fight."

"Those are the most fun." Cinna sidled up next to Hokuren with a grin. "Although, boss, I feel like there's something else you'd rather do with Roz. Might look similar to what those two that rode the wagon with us got up to."

Hokuren jumped and turned away. "What? No!" She peered back at Cinna. "Was I that obvious?"

"Even I could tell." Cinna tilted her head. "She might like you, too. Come on, I know there's some history there. Don't keep it secret."

Quite obvious, then. Hokuren closed her eyes in embarrassment. Roz surely must have been able to tell Hokuren's childish crush on her had life yet. "Let's talk to Grimes first." When Cinna's shoulders sagged in disappointment, Hokuren added, "I'll tell you all about Roz when we aren't standing outside in the muck of the town center, needing keys to our house."

"Gotcha, boss." Cinna started walking toward Grimes's house. "No time to waste then. Get the keys, spill the history. Let's go."

The last house on the road out of Fondence turned out to be a half-hour walk from the town center. Houses grew sparse the farther from the center one traveled, with individual plots of farmland, barns, and pastures taking up much of the space. A few of the homes were boarded up, the land gone fallow. Fondence was never prosperous, but neither did so much land go untended while Hokuren lived there.

Cinna stopped to watch goats feeding on the grass in one of the pastures. "I'm sorry, boss," she said, noticing Hokuren's impatience. "I've never seen a goat before. Only their cheese."

"We'll come back and look at all the animals once we get a good night's sleep in an actual bed," said Hokuren. "Maybe if Grimes didn't live so far from town, we'd have time to stare at animals tonight."

"Grimes must like his privacy."

The first moon, Vitreous, had risen, providing barely enough light to follow the road. Hokuren had taken the magical lights that covered Velles for granted, faded as they sometimes were outside the Aviary. Here, she worried a tree root or detritus indistinguishable to her eyes from the rest of the mud lurked.

Grimes's home was only a few years old, but seemed to have been built with the intent to make it look older. Square-shaped and painted gray, the front porch and the set of three stairs leading up to it were made of haphazard, uneven slabs of wood.

"I hope he hasn't gone to bed." Hokuren peeked over at the front window adjacent to the door, but a dark curtain blocked the inside from view.

She knocked, but the door didn't open. After a few moments, she tried again, harder. This time, shuffling inside the house grew in volume until it reached the front door.

A tall, gaunt man opened the door a crack and poked his head out, a scowl entrenched on his face. He greeted Hokuren with a grunt. "You two lost? Town's that way if you need a room for the night." He pointed a skeletal finger toward Fondence.

"We're here to see Harrison Grimes, executor of Mikko Tuomi's estate."

"Hokuren." His knowledge of her identity did nothing to improve his disposition. If anything, his frown deepened. "You showed up. It's been long enough since Mikko died, I was given to think you wouldn't."

"I live three weeks away by boat and came as soon as I was notified," said Hokuren, lowering her eyebrows. "It was all in the letter I sent to you ahead of my arrival. Did you read it?"

"No need to get snippy. I'm merely surprised to see a young person these days follow through." Grimes heaved a weary sigh. "We need to go over your father's estate, but it's late. Tomorrow, I'll come to see you. Where are you staying? The Sleepy Hollow Inn?"

"I was hoping to stay in my father's house, but I need a key. That's why I'm here tonight."

"A key." Grimes mumbled something, his eyes skyward, as if an enormous burden had fallen upon his shoulders. "I can get you a key. Wait here." He slipped back inside and closed the door. The click that followed meant he'd engaged the lock.

"He's very welcoming," said Cinna, under her breath. "Friendly, too. I can't wait to have him over for tea."

Hokuren stared at the locked door. "My father always knew how to pick them."

Grimes returned, the door cracked open to reveal his head again. "The key." He snaked an arm out to hand it to her.

"Thank you." Hokuren placed the key in her coat pocket. Before he could close the door on her again, she said, "Err, Mr. Grimes?"

"What else?" Grimes used the same tone an exhausted stall worker might towards a persnickety customer.

"I don't want to keep you long. I have one pressing question to ask." Hokuren cast her eyes down. "How did he—you know. What happened?"

Grimes glowered at Hokuren as if her asking about her father's death was some sort of faux pas. "Your father was ambushed by goblins."

"Goblins?" Hokuren looked up. "That doesn't happen here."

"Tell that to your father and the others they've killed or wounded in the past year," snapped Grimes. "The goblins have grown aggressive these days. They've sent small raiding parties into town that we've so far been able to repel, but not without the occasional casualty." He disappeared behind the door. "Tomorrow I will show you the gravesite, and you can pay your respects. Until then, good night."

The door closed, and the lock clicked forcefully.

Hokuren turned around, eyes unfocused. "Goblins. It can't be."

"I'm sorry, Hokuren." Cinna made a fist. "But goblins have those teeth and claws. It could be them."

"This isn't like your stories. Goblins! They've inhabited the woods around here for centuries, and they and the people of Fondence have left each other alone, but all of a sudden I'm supposed to believe they are rising up against Fondence and killed my father." Hokuren took a moment to calm herself. She wouldn't rest until she had the truth behind her father's death. Goblins or not, whoever had killed him would see the justice they deserved.

"Do you think Grimes is hiding something?" asked Cinna. "I mean, other than the inside of his house."

Hokuren could almost confirm he was, but what exactly she still considered an open question. "It was quite odd to hide behind his door like that. What's he hiding in there?"

Cinna shot Hokuren a sly grin. "Maybe he's got one of those—what do you call it?" She paused to think of the word. "A paramour."

Hokuren thought back to Grimes's severe appearance. He came across as detached and lethargic, quite unlike someone who had been interrupted in the throes of passion. "Somehow I doubt it."

5

Hokuren faced her childhood home with trepidation, memories washing over her.

She was six, crying over a bird that had died near the front door. Her brothers snickered while her father calmly explained that these things happened, and they could bury the bird if it would make her feel better. She was ten, grimacing as her father bandaged a skinned knee. She was thirteen, bringing home the ingredients for the first dinner she would cook on her own for the family, a dinner her father and brothers all missed because of "important business." She was seventeen, glowing from having spent the day reading a mystery novel under the shade of her favorite tree, just before learning her brothers had been killed and seeing her father's ashen face.

She was eighteen, looking back before making the journey to Velles. The last time she had seen the house, over ten years ago. It was early in the morning, and she'd just peeked in at her father's sleeping form before leaving, that being the last time she'd seen him. The last time she'd ever see him.

The steps to the front door were as she remembered, down to the squeaky plank on the porch. Many times, she had imagined returning. Not once was her father not there to greet her. With a deep sigh, Hokuren turned the key and pushed the door open.

The small entry hadn't changed, with the little bench her father and brothers had worked together to build still next to the threshold, ready to hold muddy boots. Even the smell, the wood of the home with a dash of musty odor, was familiar to her nostrils.

Cinna walked in behind her, leaving muddy footprints on the wooden floor. Hokuren held an arm up to bar her from proceeding further. "Hold on. There's a rule in this home: no tracking mud all over. I can take my boots off, but you're going to have to wipe that mud from your feet."

Making a show of checking herself, Cinna said, "With what?"

"Wait here."

Hokuren wandered past the kitchen, where despite the empty house, her father had kept the same too-small table and all four chairs. She recalled the awkward, silent dinners she shared with him following the death of her brothers. It was only now that she wished she had made more of an effort to talk.

The linen closet hadn't seen much change either, and many of the assorted blankets and towels had been there before she had left, although some were noticeably thinner. Hokuren selected the most threadbare of them, her fingers visible through the see-through cloth as she gripped it, and brought it back to Cinna. "Take care of your new mud-wiping towel."

"Thanks, boss, you spoil me." Cinna dutifully wiped the mud from her feet, then placed the soiled item on the shoe bench next to Hokuren's boots. "So, this is where you lived as a kid."

"My entire childhood."

Cinna nodded. "It's pretty nice. Cozy."

Hokuren hesitated. Cinna had spent years of her childhood sleeping in a small rooftop cubbyhole smaller than Hokuren's bedroom closet while living on Velles's streets. Hokuren didn't want to seem as if she were rubbing in how comfortable her own childhood was in comparison. "It wasn't perfect, but I have no complaints," said Hokuren.

Cinna stood over the fireplace, marveling at the size. It dominated the entry room. "You couldn't possibly complain when this thing's got a blaze going."

Hokuren's father had built it himself before she was born. He'd loved a big, warm fire, and Fondence provided many chilly nights worthy of having one.

"I couldn't."

"Did you have a big, comfy bed?" asked Cinna.

Hokuren nodded. "It seemed so at the time. Maybe it won't look so big now. Let's go see if my father left it in place." What Hokuren's father had done with her bedroom had been on her mind, off and on, the entire trip.

Cinna grabbed her arm before she could satisfy her curiosity. "Don't you think we should check the safes first thing? Grimes or someone could have messed with them." There was a gleam in Cinna's eyes.

Hokuren smiled. The bedroom would have to wait. She fingered the keys in her pocket. "All right. Come on, they'll be down in the basement."

A creaky wooden staircase, one that her father had talked about replacing as far back as Hokuren could remember, brought them down into the basement. Cinna went first, holding the home lantern. The light was from a real candle, as opposed to the magical light of most Vellesian lanterns. Even the most basic of magical items was in short supply in Fondence.

Skittering noises emanated from the stone floor as they descended. Hokuren shuddered, thinking about just how many creatures and insects probably called this basement home, their numbers only enlarged in the weeks since her father's death with the house empty. The flickering light, not even strong enough to reach every corner of the small room, did nothing to ease the tingles running down her spine.

The safes, six-foot-tall boxes with black paint and silver trim, were pressed against the back wall. Hokuren's father had told her that the typical wooden chest banded with iron wasn't good enough, so he'd commissioned the all-iron safes at considerable expense. They had been off-limits to her growing up. She'd never seen inside them, even when her father attempted to teach her his business.

"Here goes nothing." Hokuren took out the key marked with an *R* and stuck it into the right-hand safe. It clicked and swung open.

It was mostly empty.

A small bag of coins sat forlornly on one shelf. There were a few small denominations, petty cash at best. A stack of documents, which turned out to be his ledgers, was on the highest shelf. And that was all she could see.

"I rather thought there'd be more," said Hokuren, frowning.

"Seems like a waste to have this big thing hold a small stack of papers and a few coins." Cinna bent over to peer into the depths of the lower shelves. "Hang on, boss, there's something else." On her hands and knees, Cinna reached into the back of the lowest shelf and pulled out a small book. She handed it to Hokuren.

Hokuren turned it over in her hands. It was a set of loosely bound pages, held together by a cracked leather binding and several strands of rope looped through holes punched into each page. She opened to the first page and nearly dropped the book in shock.

If found, please return to Nekane Tuomi
This is her personal diary
No peeking! Not that you'll get much out of it anyway

The words were written in a light, flowery script. Hokuren traced them with her finger. Her mother's writing, here in front of her for the first time in her life. Her mother's personal thoughts, perhaps fears, hopes, dreams, anything. This was the closest she would ever get to her mother. She was almost afraid to turn the page.

Cinna peeked over Hokuren's shoulder, standing on her tiptoes. "Boss, it's—"

"I know." Hokuren blinked away tears before they could form. She turned the page and—

An incomprehensible scrawl of symbols filled the paper. Confused, she flipped through the pages, but every one was filled with the same until, about three-quarters of the way through, it ended. Her chest constricted. Her mother had died before she could finish filling up the diary.

"This is nonsense," said Cinna, gawking at the writing.

"A cipher," said Hokuren. She tried to discern a pattern in the symbols, but of course nothing jumped out at her. "And a pretty advanced one, would be my guess. I might need a key to break it."

"She must have wanted her diary to be a secret."

"This seems like overkill."

With a silent promise to study it later, Hokuren pulled out the other key, this one with an *L* on it. "Shall we check the other safe?"

This time, however, the key slid in, stuck, and didn't turn. Hokuren shook it, but the lock was unmoved. "It's not working."

"That doesn't make sense," said Cinna, holding the lantern near the lock. "You sure you're using the key correctly?"

"I won't dignify that with a response." Hokuren slid the key in and out, twisting every which way, to no effect. She growled, clutching the key so tightly it dug into her palm. "Stuff this safe in the flames."

"Sometimes locks can be finicky." An accomplished lockpicker, Cinna spoke on a subject she was an expert on. "Sometimes it's the incorrect key."

"Perhaps my father mismarked it." Hokuren shook her head. "No, he doesn't make mistakes like this. He doesn't want me to open it." She placed her hands on the front of the safe and hung her head. "This is just like him."

Cinna pulled her lockpicks from underneath her headband. "Permission to pick your father's lock, boss?"

"You can try." Hokuren stepped aside. "But these locks are pickproof."

Cinna sauntered in front of the safe, spinning the picks in her hand. "No such thing." She knelt at the lock. Despite her confidence, and several minutes of cursing and struggling, she admitted defeat.

"Pickproof," repeated Hokuren.

"I admit I've never seen one this tough before. Sorry, boss."

"It's okay. We'll figure something out and see the inside, despite my father's wishes." Hokuren waved Cinna back to the staircase. "This is enough for tonight, though."

Upstairs, Cinna fixed dinner. Hokuren used the time to explore her old bedroom. It looked exactly as the day she left. Her father had been here, though, and kept it clean. Hokuren's eyes went to the rag doll propped up against the pillow on her old bed. She picked it up, tears stinging her eyes.

Moira had made the doll and meant for it to look like Hokuren when she received it at eight years old. It was the first thing Moira had ever given her. Hokuren had written her name on the bottom of the rag doll's right shoe. Well, she had written what she could fit in her childish penmanship, which is why it forever said, "Hoku."

She replaced the doll and turned to find Cinna watching her. When Cinna saw her face, she jumped and sputtered, "Boss, were you—Sorry, I didn't mean to—I wasn't trying to—"

"It's okay." Hokuren looked away and dabbed her eyes. She'd been so good about holding back the tears. Perhaps it was this room. Many time when she was young and missed her mother she'd hidden in it to cry, trying to avoid her father or brothers seeing. "This is all a lot."

"I wish I could help." Cinna grabbed her arm nervously.

"I'll be all right."

They had a quick dinner of dried meat, bread, and cheese leftover from their travel fare, arranged into sandwiches smeared with the last of the olive spread they took with them from Velles. Hokuren set Cinna up in her brothers' old bedroom, which her father had also not touched since their deaths. Her father might have thought it sacrilege to use the beds, but Hokuren didn't believe in preserving the rooms of the dead. Spaces were for the living.

Hokuren entered her father's room before going to bed herself. It served as his bedroom and office in one, with a bed and desk on opposite ends. A portrait of Hokuren's mother adorned the desk. She picked it up and studied it. Though it was a copy of the image in the locket she wore around her neck, she liked the opportunity to see the larger version.

She placed the stack of ledgers and diary on the desk and sat. The ledgers she ignored, even though she had to admit they were more pressing. Unwinding her father's import business as she planned would require a thorough understanding of its current shape. Her mother's diary pulled too strongly, however, and she opened it back up to the first page.

Adventurers had written extensively about age-old crypts and treasure rooms, which every so often required the cracking of an encrypted text. Hokuren herself had dabbled in breaking practice ciphers, considering herself in possession of a decent grasp of the usual tricks. This cipher, though, had her stumped even as she went deep into the night. Her eyes grew heavy, and when she finally set the diary down, she didn't believe she'd made even a whisker of progress.

Hokuren returned to her old bedroom. Her bed had seemed so big when she was a child, but now she barely fit lengthwise. It didn't matter, tired as she was. She was asleep moments after her head hit the pillow, Hoku the doll curled in her arm.

6

Cinna stretched outside Hokuren's old home the following afternoon. She had been sitting inside for hours, first for breakfast with Hokuren then lounging around while the boss went through her father's records and occasionally said things like "What does this even mean?" and "My father writes less legibly than you, Cinna."

Hokuren had thrust some ledgers at Cinna at one point when she offered to help, but they were all confusing lists of numbers (Hokuren referred to this as "accounting") and she quickly bowed out. She was so far out of her depth she might as well have been in the middle of the ocean.

They needed food for the house so they could eat something fresh, so Cinna was entrusted with some of Hokuren's father's Fondencian coins and a list of items to bring back. She had been reluctant to leave Hokuren alone, as her number one job was still, in her mind, protection of the boss. Hokuren hadn't been worried, telling Cinna that Fondence wasn't like Velles. It was safe.

Cinna wasn't so sure. According to Grimes, goblins had skewered Hokuren's father, and the little green creatures had been encroaching on Fondence's territory and brazenly raiding the city. Hokuren would certainly need Cinna around if goblins showed up, but since the chances were low and they needed the food, she agreed to take the risk as long as Hokuren promised not to leave the house.

The muddy roads were drier than the previous day but still squished pleasantly underfoot. On the trip over, Cinna tried to imagine what growing up in a house like Hokuren's childhood home would have been like, with a parent and siblings, a warm, safe bed every night, plentiful food, and being taught to read and write and think about the future rather than surviving the immediate present. She could not. It was probably nice.

The sun had barely budged in the sky when she reached the central market. Fondence, at least the part that wasn't farmland, was so much smaller than Velles. Cinna wondered how people stood it. The forest and farms, never far away, that surrounded the town gave the impression of a deceptively open cage.

And the people. She'd seen few elves, and the humans lacked variety in their dress or hair. In Velles, she could walk the cobblestone streets and see all manner of outfits and styles, but here everyone wore gray and went to the same barber.

The barking of dogs rose over the light din of small-town commerce as Cinna reached the edge of the market. Three dogs with shiny, well-groomed coats bounced around and crammed their noses beneath an empty stall.

No one else seemed interested in the dogs' behavior. Cinna was about to ask a stall owner if anyone knew what had them riled up when a cat's paw swiped from beneath the stall.

The rest of the market crowd was content to let this play out, but Cinna and Hokuren Investigations left no cat unsaved. Besides, the scuffle reminded her of how the other kids had ganged up on her during her early years at the Sanctuary of the Eclipse.

The dogs turned toward her in unison on her approach, the barking intensifying.

"Shoo, shoo," she said, waving her arms at them. "Leave the cat alone." Cinna's words had no effect. The dogs danced around her, wagging their tails and continuing to bark their heads off.

A few of the market's patrons had their eyes on her, their scrutiny delivered with unkind looks. She returned a challenging stare and called out to them. "Anyone have a piece of meat?"

Blank faces met her request.

"I have coins," she added.

"Right here, then!" A stall vendor held up a small white parcel.

Cinna exchanged some coins for it, blood leaking out of the corners and smearing on her hands, and returned to the scene. As she got close, the dogs smelled the meat and went berserk, jumping and howling. One dog bumped her leg with enough force to nearly topple her, and another put its enormous paws on her stomach and staggered her.

She pivoted away from the next dog, then reared back and flung the meat as far as she could down the path leading away from the market.

The dogs tore off after the meat projectile even as it soared through the air, the cat forgotten. When they were gone and their sounds reduced to muted growling as they tore through the packaging, Cinna wiped her hands on her tunic and knelt in the mud, peering under the stall.

"Here, kitty," she said, trying out the falsetto again. "Now's a good time to leave."

The cat, barely visible as it backed away from her, had its ears pinned back. Cinna extended a hand under the stall and left it there. Before long, the cat's wet nose brushed her hand, which was soon followed by the ticklish sensation of its tongue on her fingers. Right, the blood.

She pulled her hand back from under the stall. The cat, torn between continuing to hide and tasting that blood, eventually emerged, skulking low to the ground. It was white, with a few brown spots on its nose, back, and tail. Meowing, it jumped onto Cinna's lap and purred.

"You're the first cat to appreciate my rescue." Cinna scratched the cat behind the ears.

The dogs' barking grew in volume again. They'd finished the meat and were sprinting back toward her. The cat froze at the sound, then bolted from Cinna's lap, racing away as fast as it could. By the time the dogs returned, Cinna could no longer see the cat. She stood up, giving the dogs a distasteful glance.

"Finally, a cat that likes me, and you all ruined it."

The dogs, now bereft of meat and cat, grew bored and dispersed to various areas of the market. Cinna followed them.

Before buying the food she was supposed to buy, Cinna skirted through the stalls and customers to reach Mama Ogg's bakery, hoping to purchase a slice of pie or two, which she'd been craving since the moment they boarded Captain Tulip's boat and left Velles.

They did not have pie, to Cinna's consternation. The woman behind the counter apologetically explained they only made pies once a week, but offered to sell her cinnamon rolls instead. Cinna purchased four, figuring she could afford to share one with Hokuren. She emerged from the bakery and took just two steps before someone screamed, "Goblins!"

Panic gripped the market as the word registered and self-preservation kicked in. Shouts rang out, people began shoving, and vendors abandoned their stalls, all running from the direction of the scream.

Cinna ran toward it.

She had to weave through the flow of traffic. Someone clipped her shoulder and sent her right into the path of a child, a small girl with a rabbit hairpiece. The girl tumbled to the ground. Worried that she would be trampled, Cinna tracked back, picked her up, and set her back on her feet. A woman, harried and distraught, mouthed thanks before grabbing the girl's hand and leading her away.

Once clear of the main crowd, Cinna made better time to turn the corner around a building, a temple to some god she didn't recognize, to find a battle about to begin.

Roz was there, a mace in one hand and a dagger in the other. Behind her was a taller man in uniform, his sword shaking in his grip. Together the two of them faced down a group of ten growling and slobbering goblins.

The goblins' mouths, large enough to fill half their faces, were opened to expose their sets of sharp, pointy teeth, with which it was said they could rip a person apart in mere seconds. Hairless, they wore ragged loincloths and necklaces made of teeth. Each tooth was supposed to represent someone they had killed, whether human, elf, goblin, or animal. They held branches with sharp rocks tied to one end, makeshift spears.

All of this was standard goblin appearance, at least according to the world of *Captain Cavalier*. The only thing that didn't fit was their eyes. Bright red shone from their pupils like rubies catching the light of the sun.

Hokuren was going to hate being wrong about there being no goblin attacks.

Cinna strode through the mud next to Roz, fists up. "Need some help?"

Roz peered at her, then recognition shone on her face. "You're

Hokuren's friend. Cinna?" she rasped. She shook her head. "You shouldn't be here. Do you even have a weapon?"

"Hey, we both work for Hokuren now, and I outrank you, so you can't tell me where to be." Cinna gestured at the goblins. "I don't know how long you planned on fanning them with that mace of yours, but I have some ideas of my own that involve being more direct."

"You should leave this to me, the adventurer." She nodded at the man behind her. "And the Arms of Fondence."

Cinna sneaked a glance back at the quailing Arm of Fondence. He was not acquitting either himself or his group well. "Hold this, please." She handed him her parcel of cinnamon rolls, which he took obediently. "This one shouldn't be fighting at all. He's more liability than asset. You might be of use. How many can you take?"

A goblin risked coming forward again, but Roz's mace forced him back.

"Cocky, aren't you?" Roz raised her mace to prepare for another swing. "I can handle all of them fine, but go ahead. If you die, I'm not taking responsibility."

One goblin in the rear of the small group threw his spear like a javelin. His aim was true. The missile headed straight for Roz. The adventurer flinched, but Cinna didn't. She watched the release point, calculated the trajectory, and reached out with two hands to catch it in flight.

The tip of the javelin hovered in place next to Roz's leather armor. Roz spared Cinna a stunned look.

The goblins made their move, rushing toward them.

Cinna countered the goblins' charge with the javelin repurposed as her new spear. They dove aside, hacking at her weapon with their own. The flimsy wood of the haft cracked. One more blow and the spear would break into two. Cinna tossed the worthless weapon aside.

Two of the goblins scrambled back up and rushed her, shoulder to shoulder. They thrust their spears at her simultaneously, hooting wildly. Cinna held her ground and jumped at the last possible moment. Each of her feet landed on the shaft of a different spear. She vaulted over the goblins with a somersault, landed on the ground, and kicked back, not needing to look to know where her target was. Her foot crashed into the leftmost goblin's temple before he turned around.

He crumpled to the ground. The remaining goblin wailed and stabbed at her a second time. The spear whistled as it passed her bent body, a narrow miss. One punch and a kick later, he too fell into the mud.

Four more goblins had marshaled to surround her, spitting and growling, opening their mouths wide to show their fearsome teeth in all their glory. They aimed spear points from angles all around her, likely thinking they had her trapped.

"Don't keep me in suspense," she said to them with a grin.

Speaking activated them. All four goblins roared and stabbed with their primitive weapons. A well-organized strike pattern might have had a chance to get her.

It was disorganized and their timing sloppy. She dodged all their attacks.

Though that sold her efforts a little short. She weaved and danced and spun, getting a constant view of each of them so she could anticipate their next move. The goblins grew frustrated, judging by the increased volume of frenzied spittle, as they could only nick her clothing. Each close call drove them madder and madder, but they were simply too slow.

Cinna hadn't been this focused in a long time, not since leaving the Sanctuary of the Eclipse. She tuned out everything else in the world: Roz, the Arm of Fondence, her cinnamon rolls, even the mud beneath her feet. It was just the goblins, their spears, and her body, which moved in perfect fluidity without her conscious thought.

One goblin lunged particularly lazily, a sign she was tiring. Cinna reached out, ripped the spear from her hands and, as if the spear had been in her possession from the very start, flipped it around to deflect two more spears before directing a third into one of the other goblins.

The goblins all cried out when they realized one of them had stabbed another. The red in their eyes faded, and they stood still, puzzled expressions on their faces. Their spears dropped to the ground. When they returned to their senses, they surrounded the wounded goblin, stanching the bleeding with a loincloth. None of them had any further interest in attacking her.

A goblin turned to her and spoke in a restrained, almost normal voice, but the words were garbled. Cinna couldn't understand the goblin language. She thought she heard among all the unintelligible words, "Please stop." She shook her head. Impossible. Goblins didn't speak human tongues.

Roz, who had let up as well, caught her eye and shrugged. The goblins made their escape slowly, the injured carried or supported by the others.

Cinna walked over to Roz. "Is this normal? They just . . . quit." She scratched her head. "I think one said 'please.'"

"Doubtful," said Roz, giving Cinna a funny look. "When it goes bad, they leave. We only need to hold out until it happens."

"Should we, err, stop them?" Cinna watched their retreating backs. Their bizarre behavior seemed almost to bore Roz, but Cinna had never experienced a group of people (or goblins) flipping from vicious fight to pacificity in an instant. "Won't they just come back?"

"Oh, they'll come back." Roz wiped her mace off on her pant leg. "But I'm not about to anger them into further escalation by killing them when their backs are to me."

"I'm not saying I want to kill them," said Cinna, throwing up her hands. "It's just, didn't *they* kill Hokuren's father?"

"That's what people say." Roz motioned at the young man holding Cinna's cinnamon rolls. "Hand the pastries back to Cinna and we'll report this to Commander Moira."

Cinna accepted the package of rolls. "Thanks for keeping them safe." The Arm nodded, and she turned back to Roz. "You report to a commander? I thought you worked for Hokuren."

Roz rolled her eyes and pointed to the man who'd given up the cinnamon rolls. "*He* has to report to the commander of the Arms of Fondence. I just help out with the goblin attacks."

Cinna needed to check on Hokuren. If this wasn't the only goblin attack on the town, the boss might be in trouble. "I'm leaving," she said, taking off at a trot. She called back, "See you around, Roz."

7

Hokuren set down tea for herself and Harrison Grimes. She rubbed her eyes as she sat down, simultaneously grateful for a moment's reprieve from staring at her father's figures and in despair that it required conversing with Grimes. There were plenty more pages to get through, but after her day's review, Hokuren had a good idea of the situation her father's business was in, if she believed the ledgers accurate.

He was losing money, and the losses were accelerating.

Now Grimes sat in front of her at the kitchen table, his tall, emaciated form folded into a chair too short for him. Grimes's knobby knees and elbows bent sharply to fit and his long neck craned over the table, lending him an arachnid appearance that had made Hokuren shiver more than once already.

He had brought with him additional ledgers, the most recent figures, which told a similar story to the ones she had. Many of the numbers, written in red to indicate they were losses, were larger than the office rent payment Hokuren struggled to meet each month. And they combined into a number that made Hokuren's head spin.

"The situation isn't quite as dire as it might appear," said Grimes, without preamble. "It's not good, of course."

"It could be worse?" asked Hokuren. "It looks like my father was hemorrhaging money."

"Yes, well." Grimes coughed, not bothering with the courtesy of covering his mouth. "The right person could salvage it and turn things around."

He held her gaze as he spoke. Hokuren had the distinct impression he meant someone other than her. "Let me ask you something. Were you intending to tell me about the silks skirting the customs officials' eyes, or are you going to pretend you didn't know?"

Grimes leaned back in his chair. "No, I was not intending to tell you. I don't believe it worth discussing. Per your note on your intention to come here and claim your inheritance, you don't have any desire to run Mikko's Imports." Grimes swept the ledgers up from the desk and stacked them neatly in front of him. "So discussions about the nature of the business strike me as pointless. I am happy to help you determine who to unload it onto."

"I don't see how I can sell this business. All I can tell potential buyers is that it's losing an alarming amount of money every month for some unknown reason and, oh, by the way, a large part of the business revenue seems to be from under the table deals with smugglers." Hokuren picked up a ledger and smacked it with the back of her hand. "I can't even estimate how much that revenue stream is bringing in, as it's not written down anywhere. No one with any sense will be interested."

Grimes's heavy eyebrows settled over his sunken eyes like awnings. "You know an impressive amount, seeker, in such a short time. They must be pounding on your door at all hours back in Velles." The sarcasm oozing from his mouth was almost visible.

"Do you know what else is being smuggled with the help of Mikko's Imports? Something the silks are covering for?"

He flinched, his mouth a thin line. "No, but a word of advice. Don't go digging too deeply, seeker."

There was no better way to get Hokuren to grab a shovel. "Is that a threat, Mr. Grimes?"

Grimes spread his hands, recovering his sardonic detachment. "I'm simply saying there is a buyer already knowledgeable about the, erm, unique aspects of the business, and interested. Sell it to her, and none of the rest matters."

"Who's interested in buying this falling rock of a business?"

"Someone I understand you once knew well. Moira Shadalker."

Hokuren choked on her tea. "Who?" she said, clutching at her chest.

"Moira. You were close before you left, as I hear it." Grimes seemed to enjoy her discomfit, grinning at her like she was a fly in his web.

Moira, alive. It couldn't be. The old witch had only wanted to quit communication, then. Hokuren pressed her hand into her forehead. She couldn't let Grimes see how this affected her. She cleared her throat and said, in the most neutral tone she could muster, "Moira never would have wanted my father's import business. That makes no sense."

"Ah, so I do know something you don't. At last. Hokuren, much has changed since you left. That includes Moira. Your father had already started preliminary discussions of a takeover before his untimely death."

As hard as it was to believe Moira would want to buy her father's import business, that thought paled in comparison to her father voluntarily selling it. "His letter made no mention of this."

"The man hadn't gotten around to changing it, despite frequent reminders." Grimes's mouth turned down in irritation. "He was lazy."

Her father had been many things. Lazy wasn't one of them. It was possible he simply put off a task that seemed unnecessary, as he hadn't expected to die, but perhaps there was another reason he hadn't left Hokuren any word of Moira's purported interest.

"If there's nothing else, tell me where my father's grave is," Hokuren said curtly. "I want to pay my respects."

Grimes plucked a scrap of paper from inside his jacket and placed it next to the ledgers. "This map should suffice. The graveyard is quite simple, so I hope you can find it. I can't hold your hand all the way there."

Hokuren would have sooner shoved her hand in lye than let Grimes touch it. "I'll find it." She eyed the front the door and then looked back at Grimes.

Fortunately, Grimes seemed to get the hint, and stood up. "I hope you'll consider selling to Moira quickly."

Hokuren scrutinized him. He had his eyes rolled back, an attempt to appear disaffected, but the tightness of his mouth suggested otherwise. "Why?"

"Because the longer you wait, the more difficult it will be to reverse the collapse." Grimes collected his coat and boots from the bench at the front door. "And you don't want to run it, so no one's going to give you the full story."

"Including you?"

An unfriendly smile was all she received in reply before he was gone, not even bothering to close the door behind him.

Once Hokuren had done that for him, she wandered back into her father's office-bedroom, shifting through the ledgers again. Either something in Mikko's Imports was so bad that even her father, who cared about his business more than anything, wanted to sell it, or the oily Grimes was lying.

What an awful man. A certain level of skepticism about her as the owner of Mikko's Imports, given her lack of experience with the industry, was warranted. She could accept that. However, his lack of respect went deeper. He considered himself her superior in every way possible, as if deigning to talk to her at all was a divine favor. She couldn't fathom what made her father hire and put up with him. She'd forgotten to ask what role he filled in the business.

Grimes's last words ran through her head over and over. If no one would give her the full story, then she might very well find it out herself. And when that was done, and she sold the business, she would throw in an unsolicited recommendation to the new owners to toss Harrison Grimes out like rotten food.

Hokuren considered going straight to Moira, but if she left before Cinna returned, she risked her assistant's ire. It tore at her chest that the old witch had made no attempt at contact either, as she surely would have been aware of Hokuren's impending return.

To take her mind off Moira, Hokuren dug back into the ledgers. She scanned them, finding nothing new until an entry from two months prior caught her attention. She had missed it on her first pass-through, but the initial description had been rubbed out and replaced with "miscellaneous expenses." Hokuren whistled at the red number, a vast sum for a single entry. Her father had always been rather particular about tracking his gains and losses, so dumping so much loss into miscellany was discordant with what Hokuren knew of him. She flipped through the ledgers and found several similar line items.

The initial description was no longer visible except as a black smear, but Hokuren knew a trick to reveal it. Her father had a heavy hand when he wrote, drawing his letters into grooves. Although the ink had been wiped, that depression remained.

Hokuren took the ledger outside and searched the area around her father's property. "There you are," she said to herself. She had found a stalk of hail flower, a plant native to the Fondence area. The name derived from the tiny, white pellets that formed within the plant's head. These seeds would eventually sprout feathery "wings" to ride the wind and spread. But their current state was perfect for Hokuren's purposes.

She poured the hail flower seeds onto the ledger and pressed them down into the paper around the erased section. Once finished, Hokuren brushed her hand over the paper to sweep away the loose seeds. All that remained were the seeds fitted into the impression of her father's pen, and they formed the words he had originally written: "Northern Construction Fund."

Finding the words was a victory, but it left Hokuren even more puzzled than before. Her father's house was near the northern edge of Fondence, and she didn't see any evidence of a massive construction project. This was either a hidden project or the description was a lie.

The front door banged open before Hokuren could start a cursory overview of Grimes's new ledgers. "Boss!" called Cinna. "Any goblins here?"

"Goblins?" asked Hokuren. She came out of her father's office bedroom. Cinna looked flushed, as if she'd run back to the house.

"You don't look torn apart by goblins," said Cinna, running her eyes up and down Hokuren.

"As long as we're trading compliments, you look good, too," said Hokuren. Then she inspected Cinna, covered in mud and dirt, her clothes torn. She didn't, in fact, look good. With more concern, Hokuren said, "What happened?"

Cinna placed a small package on the kitchen table, which could not possibly contain all the groceries she had been instructed to purchase. "Some goblins attacked the town right as I was at the bakery. But Roz and I took care of them. She can handle a mace pretty well."

"What? Slow down." Hokuren brushed the worst of the dried mud off Cinna's tunic. A stain in the shape of two paws, perhaps from a dog, remained on her stomach, causing Hokuren's already furrowed brow to wrinkle further.

Cinna took a breath, then launched into an explanation of her encounters with the dogs and the goblins. As usual, the parts of the story where she beat up the goblins got extra attention, but Hokuren was much less interested in the blow-by-blow account than she was relieved that Cinna escaped unscathed.

"The Arms of Fondence has a commander?" Hokuren asked. The Arms had never had one while she lived there. The organization was far too small to support such a position. She opened up Cinna's parcel to find nothing but cinnamon rolls and sighed. "I see you prioritized the sweets over actual food again."

"You know that's what I do, and yet you still sent me alone to purchase food," said Cinna, neatly putting the blame on Hokuren. "Roz said there was a commander. Her name was Moira."

Hokuren froze. Moira again. "I'm sorry. You said Moira?"

Cinna cocked her head. "You have a funny look on your face."

"You're sure she was the commander of the Arms of Fondence? And her name was Moira? And she's alive?"

"I don't think Roz would act deferential to a corpse, boss." Cinna tucked her chin into her hand. "Though I don't know her well enough to say for sure."

Hokuren released a breath. None of this sounded like the Moira who Hokuren remembered. That Moira was a witch, one who had been so kind to Hokuren that she considered her a surrogate mother figure. Under no circumstances would she have become the leader of the Arms of Fondence or interested in her father's business. Grimes must have confused this new Moira with the old one that Hokuren had known.

"So my father dying to goblins has the ring of truth to it." Hokuren paced the kitchen. "Grimes wasn't inventing the goblin attacks, at least. Yet I can't help but feel that there's more to it than that, based on what we know about the business and my conversation with Grimes today."

"I also don't want Grimes to be right," said Cinna. "Do you think your father's still alive somewhere?"

Hokuren stopped. She wanted to believe that, but the more rational part of her said, "No. My father's letter was sent upon his death. Pigeon Couriers doesn't make mistakes."

Cinna stared blankly. "What if Grimes or someone else sent a letter to them saying he's dead?"

"They'd ignore it. When you ask for a letter to be sent upon your death, they cast a spell that's tied to your soul. Your soul separates from your body when you die, ending the spell and alerting Pigeon to fulfill your order." Hokuren took a deep breath. "He's definitely dead."

"All right, I'm sorry for bringing it up," said Cinna. "If it wasn't goblins, though, we have some work ahead of us."

"My gut tells me the business with the smugglers has something to do with it." Hokuren picked up a cinnamon roll. "Is this really all we have to eat?"

"Sorry, boss. I bought them, someone yelled 'Goblins!' and then we had to fight. The goblins didn't wait for me to finish shopping."

Hokuren took a bite of the roll. The sugary sweetness strayed close to the border of overbearing, but didn't cross it. "This is good." Still, it wasn't a full meal. "I'm surprised you didn't get pie, though."

"I finally learned what being in a backwater means. They only make pie once a week."

"Thank you for putting up with my hometown's lack of ever-present dessert options." Hokuren tore off another piece of roll and put the rest away for later. "Come on. If we hurry, we might still be able to get something for dinner."

They made it back to the central market in time to purchase enough to make a solid vegetable stew. On the way back, Cinna shifted her bag of veggies. "Hey, boss, you still haven't told me what the deal with Roz is."

Hokuren's cheeks burned. She considered what she should reveal to Cinna, but decided to be honest. After all, Cinna always was with her. "I'll tell you, but please. This is one of those things where you don't tell anyone, especially Roz."

"Of course, boss, who would ask?"

"Roz, for one." Hokuren sighed softly. "There's not much to say.

She's about two years older than I am. We knew each other as kids, but we interacted little. She was outgoing and she could sing, which got her attention. I was introverted and have a singing voice like a tortured goat." She shuddered at the memory of the last time she sang, as part of a class project in school, that bubbled up unbidden. Her fellow students' shaking heads and her instructor's patronizing words (*Your talents lie elsewhere*) had never gone away.

"Your singing voice is fine," said Cinna.

"I've never sung around you." Hokuren frowned. "At least, not that I recall."

"Well, I'm sure it's fine."

"Trust me, you should be glad you've never heard it. Now, Roz took singing lessons in town, and I mostly spent my time reading, so I didn't really see her for a while. But I remember the first time I saw her perform as a bard." Hokuren smiled, recalling the memory. "I was fourteen. Her voice was lovely, but her lyrics . . . From the beginning, she was brilliant. I made sure to attend every show she had here in Fondence."

Cinna gave Hokuren a knowing look. "You were obsessed!"

Hokuren's cheeks reheated. "I was smitten, it's true. She told me after one of her shows how much she appreciated my coming to them all. I couldn't believe she noticed, but looking back, I think there were maybe ten to twenty people at the smaller ones, so how could she not?"

The feelings she had developed for Roz were new to her at the time, and had come on with such intensity she could recall them years later. It was a moment where she had missed her mother most acutely, to have someone to talk about them with. Instead, she kept them hidden, not even bringing them up to her father or Moira. She'd eventually figured them out, but perhaps not as quickly as she would have if she'd confided in anyone.

"We met a few times after that. Sometimes she would trial a new song for me, ask for my thoughts." Hokuren smiled at the memories of Roz playing her lute on stage at one of Fondence's taverns in the morning, with only Hokuren in the audience. "I was so nervous, I kept telling her they were all great."

"Good criticism includes pointing out what could be better," said Cinna.

"In my eyes, her music couldn't be better," said Hokuren. "And then she left for Trebello, where all the best bards go. The announcement was sudden, but we all knew it would happen before long. I thought for sure she'd become one of the greats. I even checked the stages in Velles, because we get Trebello bards coming through sometimes, to see if her name ever showed up." Hokuren sighed. "I can't believe she didn't make it there."

"Ah, boss, this is perfect! You can build her back up, help her start her redemption story!" Cinna's eyes shone in the twilight. "And then . . ."

"No, no." Hokuren waved her hand. "The feelings I had for her are the last vestiges of one-sided puppy love. It's been twelve years since I saw her last. We've both grown up, and our lives haven't gone exactly as planned. At most, I might ask her about getting lunch. She might be able to tell me something Grimes is hiding."

"Whatever you decide, don't forget who your best employee is, even if I can't sing."

Hokuren wrapped an arm around Cinna. "Now, don't get jealous. You're my partner, not my employee. You're far more important. And what do you mean? You have a great singing voice."

"You've never heard me—" Cinna grinned. "Oh, I see what you're doing. You got me, boss."

Hokuren told Cinna about the Northern Construction Fund over dinner, getting Cinna's agreement that hidden, large, and inexplicable expenditures often portended something shady.

"Enough about my father's foibles, though," said Hokuren as they cleaned up the remnants of their vegetable stew. "Will you come to his grave with me tonight?"

"Of course, boss." Cinna shivered. "Although I'm not sure this is a good time to pay your respects. It'll be dark and spooky."

"This is the perfect time," said Hokuren.

"If you say so."

The graveyard was southeast of the town's market center, a large clearing that required constant maintenance to stave off the forest that pressed in on three sides. The sun had set, so Vitreous's moonlight was all that lit the way. Hokuren relied on Cinna's elven ability to guide them in low light and avoid the few people who were also out.

Wood fencing surrounded the graveyard's perimeter, and the single gate was locked tight. No one had edited the sign attached to it, to Hokuren's chagrin:

GRAVYARD
CLOSED AT NITE
BECUZ OF GHOSTS

She wanted better from her hometown.

"Ghosts?" Cinna shivered again. "Is this a bad time to mention I hate graveyards?"

"Actually, yes, now that we're at one." Hokuren examined the gate's lock mechanism. Through a small gap between the wooden boards, she could see the lever that unlocked it from the inside. "Don't worry, the ghosts won't come out until later."

"The ghosts are *real*?" Cinna looked back toward the town. "Maybe we should go home."

"Real, but harmless. Just old farmers, mostly. They'll talk your ears off, but they can't hurt you beyond boring you half to death." Hokuren put her hand on Cinna's shoulder. "Are you afraid?"

"No," said Cinna, drawing out the vowel sound. At Hokuren's silence, she added, "Okay, the idea of ghosts makes me nervous."

"If we get this done in the time I think it will take, we shouldn't see any ghosts. Besides, like I said, ghosts can't hurt you."

Ghosts were a barely understood phenomenon, with the most compelling theory being that they were the souls of the dead that hadn't been recycled into their next incarnation. These souls formed translucent facsimiles of the people they previously inhabited until they were bound to a new life. They didn't wander far from their former bodies and couldn't impact or interact with the world. Ghosts talked about their accomplishments and the positive moments in their lives (many of the farmer ghosts could not stop talking, in excruciating detail, of their best year of crop yields), but had nothing to say about their deaths, rarely even acknowledging the act took place.

"Can you hop this fence and unlock the gate?" Hokuren considered the question perfunctory, but she had to ask.

"Do vampires glow in the dark?" Cinna jumped to grab the top of the fencing, swung herself over, and landed on the other side with a soft grunt. "Of course I can."

Hokuren opened the gate when Cinna unlocked it and slipped inside. "For the record, vampires don't glow in the dark."

"Huh."

Cinna took point again in the graveyard, Harrison Grimes's scrawled map in her hand, but for their first visit, Hokuren knew where to go by memory. Her mother's grave was close to the gate, and she had gone to it so many times in her childhood that the route was burned into her mind, even ten years later. She could close her eyes and find it.

Her mother's gravestone was simple and held only her name and a terse message. *You will be missed.*

Hokuren had spent an unhealthy amount of her childhood thinking of better things to put there than this plain and nondescript sentence.

"My mother," said Hokuren to Cinna.

"I'm sorry."

"I'll be all right." The hurt had faded over the years, but as always whenever Hokuren thought of her mother, she wished she could have had some time with her. Even a few years. She'd waited overnight at the grave many times, to see if her mother's soul formed a ghost, but never got her wish.

They didn't linger at the grave. Hokuren had something important to do here and couldn't let her unresolved grief hold her back.

The next visit was over to another section of plots, where her brothers Nilo and Antton were buried side-by-side. That the twins, so connected to each other throughout life, should still be together in death was poetic, at least.

Her brothers were twelve years older than her, and she hadn't been all that close with them. Their most common interaction was when the boys would team up against her to run one of their frequent pranks, especially when she was small. They would hide her favorite books and make her search for them, one would distract her at dinner while the other poured salt on her meal, or, their personal favorite, they would tell her scary stories before bed and make noises outside her room once the lights were turned off.

Still, they'd helped her father take care of her as a child, and she missed them and the opportunity to have a relationship with them as adults.

"All right," Hokuren said, looking up into the moonlit sky. "Take me to my father's grave."

"You got it, boss." Cinna held Grimes's notes up. "This guy better have given us good directions."

Hokuren followed Cinna through plot after plot. Cinna turned the notes back and forth and muttered like a translator working through some ancient culture's stone tablets. When Hokuren asked if everything was all right, she expressed confidence that it was.

"I think it's down this row." Cinna stopped in front of one of hundreds of identical rows. She peered at the gravestone at the end and made a celebratory noise ill-fitting for the venue. "Gaston Dinwitty, as expected."

"He'll be one hundred and fifty-two sites down," said Hokuren, her heart beating faster as they got closer to her father's grave.

"So much counting," grumbled Cinna, starting down the row. "All right. One . . . two . . . three . . ."

Cinna continued to announce each number as they passed. Each site had a unique gravestone, although most were simple slabs into which the gravekeeper carved names and dates of death, if known. Several families opted for custom markers, some of which were works of art in and of themselves—one farmer, for example, had a chicken carved from stone.

"One fifty-one . . . one fifty-two." Cinna sighed with relief. "This should be close enough."

Cinna's counting was spot on. They were in front of her father's grave. Grimes, or whoever had made the arrangements, had opted for the default slab. Mikko Tuomi's gravestone stared up at her, the carving fresh enough that little dirt had marred it.

"Well, here he is. My father." Hokuren's heart raced faster. What she was about to ask Cinna to help her with was wrong on many fronts, including Fondence's laws.

Cinna clasped her hands together and bowed her head. "What should we say? Any deities your family prays to?"

"No." Hokuren knelt in front of the grave with a sigh. Of the two things she came here to do, best to pay the respects first. The opposite would be awkward. "Father, I'm sorry I didn't return in time to see you again. I was afraid you'd go right back to demanding I help you run the business. I wish—" she stopped, her voice catching. "You loved me, and I loved you, even though we didn't really get along much. I thought I didn't want to take after you, yet here I am trying my hardest to run my own business. It's not the one you wanted, but I hope you'd be proud anyway."

Hokuren remained still, eyes closed, and chose to focus on happy memories of her father. His big bear hugs when she was a child, the scruffiness of his perpetually unshaven, patchy beard scratching her, that he encouraged her love of reading by using his business to bring in books Fondence otherwise might never had seen. He had ignored her for too much of her childhood, that was undeniable, but there were enough to keep her mind busy.

She shook herself out of her reverie after several minutes. Any longer, and she'd lose the motivation to do what needed to be done. "Cinna," Hokuren said, her voice wavering. "I need your help with something."

Cinna, who had treated this with such reverence she had stayed uncharacteristically still and silent the entire time, nodded. "All right, just tell me what to do."

Hokuren rummaged through her bag and removed two trowels, then handed one to Cinna. "Help me dig up my father's grave."

"Boss!" Cinna shook her head between the trowel and Hokuren, a disgusted look on her face. "Do you really need to see the body to pay your respects? It's been more than a month. I don't think it'll be, uh, open casket worthy."

"We don't do caskets here." Hokuren knelt to the dirt and scooped out as much as the trowel would allow, which was discouragingly little. "Believe me, I don't want to do this." Aside from the poor form of desecrating her father's grave, the thought of finding the body sent waves of nausea from her stomach up to her throat. "However, there might still be clues as to how he died. I need to see the evidence for myself. Maybe we can confirm our suspicion that the goblin story is a fabrication."

"All right, boss, if this is what you want."

Cinna got on her hands and knees next to Hokuren, and together they dug out the grave. Hokuren wished she'd brought a real shovel, but hadn't wanted to be caught headed to the graveyard with one. The trowels, meant for moving dirt enough to plant seedlings, made progress slow. The only positive was that the dirt, still fresh, hadn't hardened in place. At one point, Cinna tossed the trowel to the side and dug with her bare hands, displacing more dirt than with the tool by a significant margin.

They worked until Hokuren's arm was stiff with cramps and the moon had crossed from one side of the night sky to the other. For all their work, Hokuren learned only one thing from the deep hole they dug.

Her father's body was not inside.

8

Cinna stretched her legs out in front of her, ankles crossed and propped up on a smooth stone, while reclining against an old tree stump near a babbling brook. As lounging places went, it was idyllic. Close enough to Hokuren's father's house that if the boss popped her head out the back door and yelled Cinna could hear her, far enough away that until then she had only the brook breaking the peaceful silence. The sun, out for the first time since they'd left Oro, streamed through the tree canopy. Velles didn't have this within shouting distance of home.

Too bad this was about all Fondence had over Velles.

She chewed on a twig for something to do, eyes closed. She missed the rough cobblestone streets of Velles. The mud here was nice, but she'd already grown weary of it. Each step was like all the rest, because all of Fondence's mud felt the same. The variety of sensations she got from old stone and brick streets was sorely missed.

The crowds and constant action of Velles, especially during the busy market sessions, stressed her out, but Fondence swung too far in the opposite direction. There were no food stalls with their quick and tasty treats. No street shows, like juggler acts or bards telling stories. There was one tavern with music only twice a week. It felt empty, like a dinner plate with tiny portions.

Perhaps Cinna would never find a happy medium.

She thought back to the gravesite from the previous night. Hokuren's reaction to finding it empty had been to stand up, rub her hands to clear the dirt, and say blankly, "But they dug the grave."

There was now no question in either of their minds that something nefarious was afoot. Hiding his body from even his own grave was proof enough. Hokuren remained steadfast in her belief that the import business had something to do with it, and Cinna had no reason to disagree. Though this sent Hokuren back into her father's ledgers and left Cinna idle.

The crunching of boots on fallen branches and leaves interrupted her repose, growing louder as they approached. She opened one eye to see a man wearing the Arms of Fondence uniform stop roughly five paces from her.

"Err, Cinna?" he asked, trepidation in his voice. Upon closer inspection, he was more boy than man. Sporadic whiskers, untrimmed, grew on his chin. His baggy uniform hung from broad shoulders tapering into an average build that evidenced plenty of room to grow.

"Could be." Cinna wasn't thrilled that he knew her name. She removed the twig from her mouth but continued to recline. "What does the *Arms of Fondence* want with her?" She coated the words of his organization with derision.

"Nothing." The boy shuffled his feet. "I wanted to thank you for the help with the goblins yesterday." He smiled weakly. "Remember me? I'm the one you called more liability than asset."

Cinna sat up. This was the Arm of Fondence who had held her cinnamon rolls while she fought the goblins. She'd paid him so little attention she didn't recognize him. "I, um, didn't mean it," she said without conviction.

"It's all right, you were unfortunately correct."

His hangdog expression caused Cinna a small amount of regret for the statement, even if it had been true. "The goblins seem like a real problem around here."

"Commander Moira says they're testing us. Things have gone missing lately, and it started after the first goblin sighting, so they get blamed for any thefts these days. I think some people are getting away with stealing, now that the goblins take all the blame." The boy smacked his head. "Ugh, I shouldn't have said that last part. It's speculation. Could you forget I said it?"

"For some coins, sure." Cinna held out her hand. When the Arm dug into a sagging pants pocket, she snapped her hand back. "Don't actually give me any money! I didn't mean it. How about you tell me more, and I won't tell anyone else?" This was a lie. She would repeat everything to Hokuren at the first opportunity. Other than that, though, it was true.

"All right, as long as you don't tell anyone else." He looked around and seemed satisfied there was no one else listening. "Because you helped with the goblins, I'll tell you. It's mostly food the goblins take. Fruit especially. But they've also stolen household stuff. From people's kitchens."

"What, they're stealing forks and dinner plates? Even I was never that desperate." Another lie. Street urchin Cinna had once stolen a set of fancy dinner plates and pawned them off, earning enough to feed herself for three nights.

"And spoons."

"Well, what are you all doing about it?"

The Arm of Fondence shifted uncomfortably. "Well, you see, that's actually why I'm here, even though Moira wouldn't approve."

"Oh?" Cinna grinned. "Your commander? What does she have against me, anyway?"

The boy had a sour look on his face and said in a low voice, "She doesn't like you."

"Usually people meet me, *then* don't like me," said Cinna. "I'm impressed she skipped right to the second part."

"Roz told her about you and the way you fought the goblins. Moira thinks you're dangerous and unpredictable."

Cinna tasted the words on her tongue. "Dangerous and unpredictable? I'm good with that. You're saying she meant that as an insult?"

His eyes darted to her bare feet and back. "Err, Roz also mentioned that you don't wear shoes. Moira was aghast. She said everyone wears shoes."

"They do, but I'm not everyone."

The boy frowned, seemingly stumped. Cinna took in his unease for a moment. When you spent your life in shoes, it was impossible to imagine them as anything but required.

"Moira's the commander of the defense against active goblin attacks and she's worried about me? And right after I helped repel one?" Cinna played with her twig. "Well, if I'm so dangerous, why are you here?"

"I need dangerous. You beat up six goblins without a scratch. It was the way you jumped in, as if you weren't concerned at all. You *knew* you'd win. I want—" He took a breath. "I want your confidence. Please teach me."

"You want me to train you in how to be confident?" She tossed the twig aside and stood, reassessing the boy. "How old are you?"

"I turned eighteen not long ago."

He was several inches taller than Cinna and, even without filling out his frame or reaching true adulthood, might have been her equal in strength. He had the physical potential of an absolute menace. It was rather unfair. She had eaten too poorly as a child and forever stunted her growth. Though she did the most she could with the body she had, this boy wouldn't have to work half as hard to be far stronger than her.

"Hmm," said Cinna. "I'm not sure I want to help you, though. You're like the City Watch where I'm from, and we never got along."

The boy went to his knees in front of her, hands together as if in prayer and voice tremulous. "Please. We don't know what to do. Everyone capable left. Moira drove them and the adventurers away. With Roz's help, we can keep the goblins at bay for now, but not if they grow their numbers. I want to learn from you. Otherwise, we could all end up at the mercy of the goblins. Please."

"Hey, come on, this is embarrassing. Prostrate yourself like this in front of gods, not me." Cinna's cheeks heated as she grabbed his shoulder and urged him back to his feet. "Fine, fine, I'll give it a try. First, what's your name?"

"Jarmo."

"Okay, Jarmo. What's this about adventurers leaving? Roz is here, right?"

"Roz officially works for Mikko Tuomi." He blanched. "I mean, she used to work for him. Moira allows her to hang around. I think she has her do some odd jobs. But the rest of the adventurers know not to come around here looking for work anymore. Moira wants us Arms to serve as the lone defense force, but we're currently woefully undermanned."

Cinna rubbed her chin, a tic she'd developed from so much time spent with Hokuren. "All right, tomorrow at sunrise, meet me here at this spot and I'll run you through some simple exercises to see where you're at."

"Okay, yes." Jarmo put his hands together and bowed. "Thank you, Miss Cinna."

"Oh, I'm no 'miss.' You can call me Master Cinna." At Jarmo's eager nod, she added, "But before you leave today, tell me about this Moira. Why is she running the town?"

"Well, she's the commander of the Arms of Fondence, not the mayor, though she has significant sway over him. But she—" He paused, his eyes glassy and unfocused. "She's always been here and always been in charge."

"Always?" Cinna frowned. Hokuren had seemed surprised to hear about Moira the Commander, and the boss wouldn't forget something like that.

Jarmo's look was faraway. "Always."

"'Always in charge.' He said that?" Hokuren pinched the bridge of her nose. Her father's numbers had no more secrets to reveal, so she'd reattempted to decode her mother's diary. She got nothing from this besides a massive headache and lay on the couch in defeat, a small damp towel laid over her eyes.

"You know, boss. The look on his face when he said it. It was like the people who had been enthralled by the demon Julien Davenport." Cinna shivered from her perch on the arm of the couch nearest Hokuren's head. "Except it passed as soon as he said that. Then he said 'Good day, Master Cinna' and walked back into town."

Hokuren went silent for a moment before speaking again. "You know, until now I never really considered how similar 'demon enthrallment' is to what witchcraft is capable of."

"Witchcraft, boss?" Cinna shifted on the couch. "You didn't mention any witches living here."

"I didn't think there were any. There *was* one here, though. Her name was Moira."

There was a long pause from Cinna. "Do I have to say it? That's the same name as the commander of the Arms of Fondence."

The pain in Hokuren's head increased. "But the Moira I knew wasn't a commander, or a leader of any kind."

"Huh? But Jarmo said—"

"That's definitely got me confused, too." Hokuren peeled the towel off her face, opening her eyes to see Cinna looming above. "My Moira was a witch, although she kept it close to herself, and few people in town knew. More importantly, she was kind, and good to me. If I stopped by, she would give me sweets, or talk to me. She would cheer me up if I felt down. Or I left her house ready to take on any tasks I'd been putting off. For a while, I never understood that anything was being done. But she eventually told me the truth, that she'd been using witchcraft on me, just a little. She said it was to make me feel good, or push me in the right direction."

Cinna frowned. "Is that what witchcraft is? I don't want someone playing with my mind."

"My father called it 'manipulation.' An unfavorable, but not altogether untrue, way to phrase it."

"I thought witches threw bat wings and newt eyes into cauldrons and stirred them while cackling. Or ate children."

Hokuren leveled a stare into Cinna's eyes. "I keep telling you, those books of yours are full of rubbish. Witch magic is like wizard magic, except where wizards beseech the Primordial Ones for something tangible, like fire or lightning, witches ask for something more . . . subtle." She pointed at her head. "It affects the mind."

"If she could make you feel good, couldn't she also make you feel sad, or angry, or anything?"

"She wouldn't have done that to me, but, yes. And there's far worse it's capable of. That risk is why Velles banned witchcraft."

"It's a concern if Moira is a witch." Cinna grinned from above Hokuren. "She might use her powers to make me want to wear shoes."

Hokuren sat up, holding her hand to her forehead. "But I don't think my Moira is alive any longer. Though I admit, this woman having the same name is—"

"A coincidence?" Cinna looked skeptical. "There's also the matter of

Jarmo acting funny. You're saying this is a new person with the same name and she's also a witch. I don't know, boss."

Hokuren didn't want to admit the possibility, but she knew Cinna was right. This could be the same Moira. And Jarmo sounded like someone under a witch's spell, if a more complicated one than the kind Moira used to cast on Hokuren.

She refused to accept it. It couldn't be the same Moira. It just couldn't.

She closed her eyes again and leaned back on the couch. "My head is pounding like someone's banging a hammer around in there. I don't suppose I could trouble you for some tea?"

"Say no more." Cinna bounded from the couch and into the kitchen.

When the tea was hot and steeped, they drank in silence. It was made from dried lavender, one of Hokuren's favorites. Cinna had never had tea before meeting Hokuren, and she was still learning to appreciate its subtlety. ("It tastes like flowers," had been her initial, derogatory, reaction.) She would drink it, but only after mixing in honey. Hokuren could smell the sweetener from Cinna's mug.

The tea revitalized Hokuren. She set aside her empty mug. "Oh, while you were out setting up a training school for the Arms of Fondence, I received a letter from someone named Barth. He apparently works for Mikko's Imports, doing negotiations on my father's behalf with merchants in Oro."

Cinna narrowed her eyes. "Merchants, or smugglers?"

"You're thinking what I'm thinking. I don't know for sure, but he's apparently been closing deals himself since my father died, and has weeks' worth of merchandise stored in Oro. The problem is he doesn't have any money."

"So he's been buying stuff and not having to pay for it? I think he's figured this business thing out, boss."

"No, because the merchants are going to want their money." Hokuren sighed. "They'll come after me, but if my father had any money to give them, it's in the locked safe I can't open."

"Let's go to Oro, then, boss. We'll find these merchants, bang some heads, and they'll leave you alone once they realize they have to deal with me, too." Cinna swirled a finger in her tea. "And we can ask Barth if he made any deals with smugglers."

The headache pressed against Hokuren's skull with more intensity again. "We will not be 'banging heads.' We cannot solve our business problems with violence."

"Then I'm out of ideas."

"I've already sent a message to Barth to stop making deals until further notice. But it's the silk smuggling I'm most interested in. I doubt my father was killed over regular merchant deals."

A few hours passed, during which Hokuren napped on the couch. When she woke again, blurry-eyed, it was because of a pounding on the door. Cinna opened it and announced, "Roz is here. And so is a cat."

Hokuren bolted upright, wide awake. She'd forgotten she'd sent word to Roz asking her to come by to discuss the import business. With an apologetic smile, she welcomed the former bard in and guided her to the kitchen to sit at the same table she'd spoken with Grimes at. Roz even sat in the same chair as Grimes had, which she fit in much better.

"Wait, cat?" Hokuren returned to the entry to find Cinna standing over a white cat while it purred and weaved between her legs, rubbing up against them.

"It's the one I saved. She's friendly." Cinna reached down to stroke the cat. "Her name is Lumi." She fingered the tag on the cat's collar.

"It's someone's, then," said Hokuren. She bent down to pet the cat. The moment she touched the cat's fur, a sharp sensation stung her brain and she yanked her hand back. "What the—" The sensation was familiar, but she couldn't place it.

Lumi hissed and growled, swiping with razor-sharp claws, and Hokuren backed away. The feeling lingered. Her inability to recall when she'd felt it before frustrated her. Her memory rarely failed her like this.

"Wow," said Cinna, amused. "Guess you need to save her from some dogs to get pet permissions."

Hokuren stared at the cat, which now sat with her back to her. "Where did she come from?"

"I don't know. Outside."

"I—never mind." This was no ordinary cat, but Hokuren couldn't say any more until she remembered that feeling. "You're welcome to join Roz and me for a discussion. The cat cannot if she's going to be clawing at us."

"I'll let you two catch up instead. Come on, Lumi." Cinna, trailed by the strangely obedient cat, paused at the front door. "I'll be close by, just yell if Roz comes on too strong. Either to tell me to come help, or to stay away for a while."

"That will not be necessary," muttered Hokuren, as Cinna closed the door with a grin that stretched from ear to ear. For someone who had zero interest in romantic relationships, she certainly seemed entertained by the idea of Hokuren getting into one.

Roz was waiting patiently at the kitchen table, playing with a dagger that she promptly sheathed when Hokuren entered. "I've already told the commander of the Arms of Fondence that friend of yours is dangerous," she rumbled in greeting. "She took out six goblins without a weapon, and the way she moves... I've never seen anyone that fast. You aren't afraid of her?"

"I trust her completely." Hokuren sat opposite Roz, preparing a leftover cinnamon roll to share. "As for dangerous, she insinuated the same about you."

Roz made a noncommittal noise, and the air grew awkward. They ate the cinnamon rolls in silence, which continued even after they'd finished consuming the treats. Hokuren usually had no trouble striking up conversations, but now found her tongue unwilling to comply. She made tea to give her something to do.

"So, boss," said Roz finally, with a wink while the tea brewed. "Whatcha want to know?"

"Please, Hokuren is fine." Hokuren cleared her throat. "I understand your role is to escort the high value items from Oro to Fondence?"

"That's right," nodded Roz. "There's not much in the way of banditry, but there's enough." She patted her mace on her hip. "I'm usually enough of a deterrent, and if not, well, let's say that the bandits don't try twice."

Hokuren served the finished tea and sat back down at the table. "Do you escort the silk, then?"

Roz's eyes widened in surprise. "So you know already. I think I'm supposed to act surprised and say, 'What silk?'" She smiled. "I'm not much good at the innocent act anymore."

"If I'm in charge of this import business, I deserve to know. Grimes wasn't forthcoming, so I've turned to you." When Roz didn't reply, she pressed, "Where does it come from? Do you know a Petros or a Hugo?"

"Wow, you even know Hugo's name." Roz tapped her forehead. "I'd tip my cap if I were wearing one." She sipped her tea, making a grunt of approval. "This is good. Anyway, Hugo is the leader of what they call the Gregorious Consortium, but don't let the fancy name fool you. They're two-bit morons that lucked into a spectacular smuggling arrangement."

"Why is it so important that the silks aren't taxed through customs?"

Roz held up her hands. "Whoa, now you're outside my realm of expertise. The way it worked was Barth got money from your father and paid the Consortium, which smuggled them off the ship and held them in Oro. Then I arrived and oversaw their transport back to Fondence, whereupon your father and Grimes delivered them to their ultimate target, a man named Ulbricht."

Hokuren took a sip of tea to give herself time to memorize the order of operations. All this for some silk. "I have three questions for you to answer."

"Let me guess two of them. I don't know where the ship with the silks originates from, and I don't know anything about who or where Ulbricht is," answered Roz immediately.

"Hmm, that leaves me with one question you might answer." Hokuren tapped her fingers on her arm. "Are there any other goods included with the silk?"

Roz tried to keep her gaze steady, but her eyes flickered away for a split second. "No, it's just silk."

She was lying. Hokuren waited a moment to see if Roz would amend her statement, but she did not. So be it. "I assume everyone makes good money off this and all have reason to want to see it continue."

"Hugo and the rest of his Consortium boys would shit donkeys if this didn't continue."

Hokuren lifted her eyebrows at the crude phrase. "Especially if they're currently sitting on a gigantic pile of silks they've yet to receive payment for?"

"They're what you call profligate spenders of money." Roz waved her hand in a circle. "Money goes out almost as fast as it comes in. They may gamble too much, drink too much, you know how it is. This silk deal keeps them in fresh coin, but without it . . ." Her hand smacked down onto the table. "Ulbricht is a bit of a mystery. I imagine he's going to be less violent but more rich person angry if he stops getting his silks. He really wants them."

Hokuren folded her arms together. "Define 'rich-person angry.'"

"You've lived in Velles, so you know the deal, I'm sure. Happens a lot in Trebello, too. Not so much here in Fondence. A rich guy is mad, makes a stink to the people in power, suddenly you get some threats that a tax person is about to sniff around." Roz dropped her smile. "And we are currently discussing a years-long tax evasion scheme."

"So you're saying that we could either get physically pummeled by the Consortium or be dragged into tax fraud proceedings for a financial and emotional pummeling." Hokuren's headache returned with a vengeance. "Maybe I *should* sell this thing quickly."

At this, Roz leaned in over the table. "You should sell it to Moira."

Hokuren felt a pit in her stomach. "Grimes said the same thing."

"Did he?" Roz looked away, pretending she didn't know he would. All this accomplished was to convince Hokuren that the two of them were conspiring together.

Not that Hokuren could blame them. She was not the right person for this moment, with the business in peril and her own disinterest in running it.

"You know, this job with your father has been keeping me afloat. I'd really like to see it continue, and if you're unable to pay for the silks, it could be obliterated." Roz stared into her teacup. "Your father was good to me. Didn't get a lot of that ever since I left for Trebello. And the work keeps me from thinking about my lost voice, thinking about how I'll never sing again. Plus it's how I'll—" She stopped. "Never mind, it's nothing."

"I'll keep working on the silks, I promise." Hokuren saw the opportunity to move the conversation on from the business. "But Roz, your voice was never the only reason I loved your music so much. It was your lyrics. They had such a haunting quality. Did you ever consider writing for other singers?"

"Hmph. I write only for myself." Roz grimaced and traced the scar across her throat with her finger. "And I can't deal with the way I sound now. This hoarse rasp, like I've got a perpetual illness. It's some other person who is talking."

"I'm sorry." Hokuren bowed her head.

"I still do write songs," said Roz, her voice so quiet she was barely audible. "I shouldn't, because they'll never come to anything, but I can't help it. They show up in my brain and don't go away until I write them down. One day, I'll get my voice back, and I'll sing them for real. I'd do anything for that day to come."

Hokuren smiled. "If you ever needed someone to share them with, I'm an old fan who hasn't gotten any new material from you in over a decade, voice or no voice."

Red crept into Roz's cheeks. "Thanks, but I'll probably just keep them to myself." She stood up, stretching. "Oh, well, look at the time. I'd better be going."

The way Roz hustled out the door told Hokuren that the subject of music was not one the former bard was keen on. She tried to understand how Roz would feel about losing her singing voice. Hokuren didn't have a comparable skill. She could lose her investigative abilities, but in that case, she'd also suffer substantial overall cognitive damage.

Hokuren returned to the kitchen and drummed her fingers on the table. She'd been putting it off long enough. It was time to talk to whoever this Moira was and see what she was offering for her father's business.

9

Townspeople had used Moira's tower, one of the oldest buildings in Fondence, for functions like weddings or funerals in Hokuren's childhood. A minor makeover had repaired some of the worst of the crumbling stone, making it one of the very few places that looked better than before Hokuren had left the town.

A long time ago, the temple had housed followers of Sudbrisis, a god responsible for ensuring the stars in the night sky stayed lit. No one followed him anymore, and hadn't for at least three centuries, though no one knew why he lost his worshippers. Hokuren's favorite theory was that Fondence saw an unprecedented string of cloudy nights, perhaps up to a full year's worth, which convinced his followers that Sudbrisis had betrayed them and turned the stars off.

A small sign that simply said "MOIRA, APPOINTMENT ONLY" in impeccable penmanship was all that adorned the entrance as Hokuren and Cinna approached.

Hokuren wished she were visiting Moira's old house. The small but cozy mudbrick building near the southern edge of town had been torn down. Moira had praised the mudbrick, now out of fashion in Fondence, for being better insulated than the wood or stone homes most Fondencians lived in. It was incomprehensible that Moira would ditch it to commandeer the town's event venue.

The door opened before Hokuren could work up the nerve to knock.

"I saw you coming," said Moira, with a look that suggested the visit unwelcome.

Hokuren had expected to meet a stranger wearing Moira's name, but her eyes widened at the sight of the Moira who she knew and loved. Her long elven ears came to a sharp point, and her eyes had flecks of gold mixed among the green of her irises. The old witch wore a black robe that scraped the ground. Her hair, dyed a sharp white, flowed down from beneath a cowl that shadowed her face. The look was nothing like what the colorful Moira used to wear, but Hokuren knew that face, complete with a scar over her right eye, a relic of a childhood injury over two hundred years ago.

"You're Moira. You're alive," said Hokuren, taking a tentative step forward. "It's me, Hokuren."

"Of course I'm alive," said Moira, her frosty reception nothing at all like Hokuren remembered. "And I know who you are."

"Well, I had just thought, because you stopped writing—"

"I got busy here, didn't have time for someone who left the town and her father." The words gutted Hokuren as Moira glanced over at Cinna, standing behind Hokuren, and her eyes narrowed. "You must be that horrible girl Roz told me about."

"I'm that horrible *woman*, please," said Cinna.

"Moira, is it really you?" The plaintive tone in Hokuren's voice was unintentional, but she couldn't keep the hurt out. "It looks like you, but—"

"Who else would I be?" Moira opened the door wider. "You may as well come in. We've got business to discuss."

Business. If this were Moira, she'd give Hokuren a warm hug and an even warmer cup of tea, and want to discuss anything but business. She'd welcome Cinna with open arms, not call her "horrible." Looks were the only thing this Moira had in common with the old.

Inside the old temple to Sudbrisis, it looked as if Moira had taken decorating advice exclusively from Cinna's *Captain Cavalier* novels. A bubbling cauldron lurked in the corner, emitting a faint green smoke. A collection of large, pointed black hats lined a shelf along the back wall, along with three broomsticks. Another wall held a series of shelves with various animal parts, such as the obvious newt eyes and bat wings.

"Have a seat," said Moira, waving a hand at blankets on the ground.

These had images of bats sewn into them.

"There aren't any books here," said Hokuren, once she'd settled onto a blanket. Moira's favorite possession, at least when Hokuren knew her, was her bookshelf full of books along with what Moira had once considered her "witchy goods": colorful beeswax candles, glittering crystals, and small carvings of writing in defunct languages.

Moira sat opposite her and Cinna. "My place is different than you remember, I'm sure. It's been a long time, Hokuren, and I'm a new person."

Hokuren would have expected any reunion with Moira, in the event she hadn't actually passed, to be nothing like this. This all seemed so wrong.

"I'm surprised you became so . . . open about being a witch," said Hokuren, grasping for a conversation starter. "You always kept it quiet."

Moira smiled, but it lacked her old gentleness. "An old me, and a foolish, inwardly focused one. I'm really helping the town out now. I've even taken on the role of Commander of the Arms of Fondence."

"I never would have expected that."

"Some of us wanted to stay and help keep this town running." Moira's smile grew into a demented grin. "Some of us had other interests."

Hokuren bit her lip unconsciously, then stopped. She couldn't keep this up. Her insides roiling, she said, in as calm a voice as she could muster, "You were so good to me, Moira. Your letters—"

"You left, Hokuren." Moira's look of disgust would haunt Hokuren. "Without a word to anyone."

"You never told me you felt this way in any of your letters. When you stopped responding, I thought you'd . . ."

Hokuren's head hurt again. She'd been so sure this wouldn't be Moira, but now she second-guessed herself. Perhaps she'd only desperately wanted this to be someone else.

"I finally realized I shouldn't have indulged you like that. It allowed you to feel as if your betrayal of your father was justified."

"My *what*?" Hokuren put a hand to her head, which suddenly throbbed. She knew this feeling. Witch magic. But this had none of the warmth and kindness of Moira's old magic. There was something malevolent about this. "What are you doing?" she said, voice strained.

"Nothing," said Moira, innocently. She must be the same Moira, but—

"What's wrong, Hokuren?" said Cinna, coming to Hokuren's side. "You look like you're hurt."

The pressure on Hokuren's head eased. She looked back at Moira. There was nothing on her face but placid neutrality. "This isn't right, Cinna."

"And now you've returned, but too late," said Moira. "Your father's business is falling apart, and so too is the town."

Hokuren's head snapped up. "What are you talking about?"

"You know, your father and I couldn't consummate a deal before he passed, but if you want to dispose of it, I'm still willing to buy." She paused. "For a reduced price, of course, considering the losses I'm sure continue to pile up."

Hokuren took in the smug, upturned lips and steeled herself. Whoever this was might wear Moira's face, but this was not the person Hokuren once knew. "I'm not interested at this time."

Moira blinked, taken aback. "I thought you couldn't wait to get rid of it. Ah, but I have something that might seal the deal. You'll want to sell before this business goes to zero, Hokuren." She stood up and rifled through a drawer in a nearby table. "Here we are."

She handed Hokuren a piece of paper that turned out to be a letter from Casper Daily, Fondence's mayor. He'd held the post for forty-seven years, winning re-election every time unopposed. Daily worked tirelessly in the thankless role and did a decent job, which suited everyone just fine.

In the letter, Casper made a bleak case with a steady hand. With the goblin problem becoming more serious and Hokuren's father's business failing to bring in enough tax coin, the town was low on money for defenses. His suggestion was to abandon the town and disperse to neighboring towns before the goblins came in to take it. Already the population was declining.

A chart of numbers showed sinking town revenue and a rising goblin population estimate.

Hokuren put the letter down. "I just don't believe it."

Moira took the letter back and frowned. "You don't understand the goblin problem, Hokuren. They aren't content to stay in the forest any longer. They're coming, and the decades of peace have left us completely unprepared." She gave Hokuren a wicked look. "Your mother is partly to blame, did you know that?"

Stunned, Hokuren said, "For what?"

"She spent time with the goblins. Her encouragement is what now makes them think they deserve better than us!" Moira's voice rose as Hokuren shook. "Nekane betrayed the town, just as you betrayed your father. If they overrun this town, she is ultimately to blame."

The headache returned with a vengeance. A cold sweat broke out on Hokuren's neck and forehead as she fought it. Thinking became difficult, her brain sluggish. No one had ever suggested her mother having any relationship with goblins, yet she couldn't seem to argue the fact with Moira.

"It could be true," said Hokuren, without thinking. But that wasn't her speaking. She knew what was happening. The pressure in her head increased, and she held her hands against it. "Stop! You're lying to me, manipulating me."

"I'm merely asking you to acquiesce to reason. The goblins have been biding their time, and now their true colors have been revealed. It's our fault for not wiping them out when we had the chance."

"Enough!" Hokuren stood up, staggered by the pain in her temples. She leaned on Cinna for support. "You look like her, but you aren't the Moira I knew."

An explosion of pain burst between her temples, powerful witch magic hammering at her psyche. She fell back to her knees, her eyesight a kaleidoscope of blurry colors.

"Hokuren!" called Cinna, her voice sounding far away, even as Hokuren felt Cinna's hands holding her upright.

There was a voice in her head, one she didn't recognize. *Stop fighting. Accept it. This is Moira. There's only ever been the one.*

"No!" Hokuren cried out.

A wave of nausea hit her, and she collapsed to the floor. Cinna shouted and Moira responded, but they came in as garbled nonsense, as if Hokuren were listening to them talk underwater.

She was vaguely aware of Cinna picking her up and then moving, but saw nothing but blurred shapes. Something that could have been the doorway approached. When they reached it, words entered her tormented mind, clear as a bell.

How well do you really know your mother?

Hokuren's head recovered once they left Moira behind. She regained her senses along the road back to her father's house, finding herself cradled in Cinna's arms as her assistant strode as fast as her legs could take her.

"I—I can walk, Cinna."

"It's no trouble to carry you." Cinna didn't push it, however, and set Hokuren down. She wobbled on shaky legs like a newborn deer. Cinna's arm wrapped around her and steadied her, and together they continued the walk back to the house. "What happened back there, boss?"

"Moira used witch magic on me." Phantom pains remained in Hokuren's head, reminders of the real thing she had just recovered from. "Far more intense than I'm used to. She wanted to make me believe what she was saying about her, about the goblins, and about my mother. I was fighting her, but if you hadn't taken me away, I—"

"Are you okay, Hokuren?"

Hokuren considered saying she was fine. She looked at the unease on Cinna's face. "No, I'm not," she said.

Cinna seemed to struggle with something, fidgeting and stealing glances at Hokuren. After several awkward, silent steps, she tightened her hold around Hokuren for the rest of the walk back.

Hokuren breathed a sigh of relief when they entered her father's house. She planned to make some tea, curl up on the couch, and mull over what had just happened. The kitchen, however, ruined those plans.

A series of childish drawings of stick figure goblins greeted her from every wall of the kitchen, with the words "GO BACK 'HOME' BETRAYER" in block lettering scrawled opposite the doorway, all drawn in the same vibrant shade of green.

Hokuren stepped up to the drawings, heart thumping in her ears, to get a closer look. She told herself to focus on investigating them, not to consider the words themselves. The little goblins, heads portrayed with the characteristic sharp teeth and large floppy ears, were mostly engaged in a series of suggestive or vulgar activities. The paint consisted of small chunks within a sort of paste. Hokuren put her finger on the still-wet drawing of a goblin mooning her and sniffed what stuck to her.

Plant material.

"Hokuren, I have an idea for—oh." Cinna entered the kitchen and took in the room's graffiti. "Ugh, goblin bits." She pointed to a goblin drawn with a line emerging from the center of its stick figure body that reached its feet. "No one's going to believe it's actually that big."

"We weren't gone long," said Hokuren, half talking to Cinna and half to herself. "And the door was locked."

Cinna looked puzzled, wrinkling her nose when she got her own whiff of the paint. "Someone broke in and locked the door behind them after they left. That's rather polite."

"They could have had a key, but the only other person with one was Harrison Grimes, and he gave his to me. And while I don't think he likes me, it's difficult to see him doing this."

"I agree." Cinna set her gaze on a goblin drawn with its tongue sticking out while squatting for a poo. "Too much whimsy."

Hokuren snapped her fingers. "The windows."

"I'll check them." Cinna scampered off and returned after a short time. "They're all locked. Even the basement window."

"Whoever did this was at least able to lock back up. So it's fair to assume they broke in that way." Hokuren paced the kitchen, then stopped. "Wait, I'm not thinking straight. Is there anything missing?"

They searched their meager belongings and the various closets and drawers. To her relief, her mother's diary hadn't been taken, but when Hokuren went through the kitchen cabinets, she paused.

"Nothing important was stolen. But." Hokuren pointed into one of the cabinets. "There are supposed to be two red-and-white striped cups here. A matched set."

"I see one," said Cinna.

"Yes."

"Jarmo told me that people have been seeing small household items go missing lately. They all think it's the goblins."

"Hmm." Hokuren resumed her pacing. "I see no reason why the artistic capabilities of goblins would not include such simplistic doodles. Using paint made of plant material makes sense considering they live beneath a forest. Though I don't know if they can write or pick locks. Oh, and would they be responsible enough to lock the door up behind them when they leave?"

Cinna shrugged. "What if someone's watching our house and thought they'd have a little fun at our expense?"

"And steal a mug we'll barely miss?"

"It's someone who knows who you are, at least." Cinna flinched. "Sorry, I don't think you're a betrayer. But whoever did this thinks you are."

"Or they want me rattled." She held up her finger, still green from the paint. "The word 'betrayer' was the word Moira used to describe me. It's as if she wants me to know she's behind it."

Cinna scratched her head. "But unless Moira can run very fast, it couldn't be her. And doesn't she hate the goblins?"

"Unlikely she'd sully herself by drawing crude images of goblins making toilet, anyhow." Hokuren made a face at the nearest stick figure. "My Moira would never have set this up, but this one, I suppose, could. Though the timing is strange, because we showed up unannounced. How would she have known to send her goblin goons, which we are assuming she has at her disposal? As you said, she seems to consider the goblins an enemy."

"I don't know." Cinna shifted uncomfortably. "You said this was a different Moira, but she claims—"

"I know what she claims," said Hokuren, more sharply than she intended. She took a deep breath and found some rags, handing one to Cinna. "Here's my claim: She wears Moira's face in the most appalling way. Will you help me clean this up?"

They worked in silence, grateful that the paint came off easily onto damp rags. Hokuren's mind became a blur of memories of Moira as she washed the walls. Whispers from the dark corners of her brain said it was the same woman, that Moira couldn't have a clone, and no magic she knew of in all her extensive reading spoke of human shape-shifting. The scar in particular would be near impossible to replicate, and so too would the flecks of gold in her eyes. They were right where Hokuren remembered. But she refused to bow to this logic. There would be another explanation. There had to be.

Thinking about this kept Hokuren from wrestling with what the fraudulent Moira said about her mother. She couldn't deal with that until she'd gotten some rest.

Hokuren caught Cinna looking at her, concern etched on her features. "I'm all right. You don't have to worry."

"You said otherwise, boss." Cinna, standing on a chair, wiped the last of a goblin drawing near the ceiling. "You really liked Moira when you were a kid, didn't you?"

"I did." Hokuren wrung the rag in her hands. "And she was good to me. It's very difficult for me to accept that Moira seems to loathe me now. Even if it's a different person." Hokuren wiped away the word "BETRAYER" from the wall, scrubbing with a little extra force. "It is what it is, though. I have to accept it and move on. We should focus on the case in front of us."

Cinna jumped down from the chair. "Are we going to organize a defense against the goblin invasion?"

"The one that's not happening? No." Hokuren finished wiping the last of the graffiti and tossed her rag into a basin for cleaning later. "However, if Casper Daily *thinks* that is happening, I'd be interested to know what he's been doing about it."

"He hasn't been training up the Arms of Fondence, that's for sure." Cinna tossed her green-stained rag into a corner, then caught Hokuren's look and placed it in the basin. "What are we going to do the rest of tonight?"

"Tonight, I need—" Hokuren stopped, unable to finish the sentence. Cleaning the paint had given her something to do. Now she had to face this new Moira in her mind and work it out into something she could live with. "I just want to go to bed."

Cinna looked pointedly out the window. "It's barely dusk."

Hokuren rarely allowed herself to feel vulnerable in front of Cinna, but couldn't quell the tremble on her lips. "I—"

"Say no more." Cinna dashed off, returning in a few minutes in her bedclothes. "Get changed and meet me in the sitting room," she ordered.

"And what are we going to do?" Hokuren's curiosity about Cinna's intentions staved off the self-reflection for at least a little longer.

"You'll see."

A few minutes later, Cinna sat cross-legged on the floor, Hokuren's head in her lap. She'd made a nest of every blanket she could get her hands on and wrapped the two of them up in a complicated cocoon.

"This is nice, Cinna," said Hokuren, and she meant it. "But I don't think sleeping like this is going to be good for my neck."

"You aren't sleeping like this," said Cinna, more in charge than Hokuren had ever seen her outside a fight. "The blankets are because you like being held. You know how you tell me not to keep things hidden inside, and talk about them?"

"Yes, and I know you often do the opposite."

Cinna glanced down at Hokuren. "Time to set a good example for me, Hokuren."

"You want me to talk about Moira? I don't know if—" She meant to say she didn't know if she was ready to do so.

Cinna didn't give her the chance. "Whatever you want to talk about, I'll listen. I can't do a lot for you, because I don't think I can fight whatever's bothering you." She looked away, her command slipping. "This is my only idea to help you, but if you don't want to . . ."

Hokuren smiled up at Cinna's chin. "Okay."

Cinna let out a tiny sigh of relief. "Whatever you want to say, go ahead."

"I told you that Moira was kind to me. That doesn't tell the entire story. Without my mother around, she was the closest thing I had to a maternal figure. Hmm." The blankets wrapped around Hokuren were so tight she couldn't move enough to shift position. "Let's call her a positive maternal influence."

"She was like your mom, but not, okay," said Cinna, always good at distilling things to their most basic core.

"My father loved us, my brothers and me, but he was distant. His focus was always on his business."

"That sounds like you."

Hokuren started to object, then stopped herself. "That's fair, I suppose. I have put a lot of effort into the investigation business. I like to think I'd be there if I had children."

"Of course."

"Anyway, with my brothers much older than me and also engrossed in the business, I had a lot of time to myself while they and my father worked together. Moira always welcomed me in when I was feeling lonely. She helped me as I grew up by teaching me the things I needed to know that my father and brothers weren't equipped for, or she'd talk to me, or sometimes just sit in silence and read with me." Hokuren closed her eyes and drifted into some of those old memories. "I missed the times with her more than I missed anything else in Fondence when I left."

"Even though she was a witch," said Cinna.

Hokuren nodded in Cinna's lap. "For all we talked, it was mostly about me—I was a kid after all—and she kept her witchcraft close to the vest. I remember when I asked her once, when I was trying to avoid helping my father run the import business, if she would take me on as a witch apprentice."

"I assume she said no."

"You would be correct." Hokuren smiled at the memory. "She was gentle about it, but firm. Witchcraft was difficult and required a lifetime of study and work to be good at. Not like 'wizards and their little spells,' she liked to say. And by 'lifetime,' she meant an elven lifespan. As a human, she said I wouldn't live long enough to become a full-fledged witch."

Hokuren had cried that day, thinking it unfair that elves lived three to four times as long as the typical human and that, because she'd been born a human, witchcraft had been closed off for her. Moira had told her she could be so much more than a witch and had encouraged her when she first broached the idea of leaving Fondence for Velles in the hopes of one day emulating her favorite literary investigators.

"She sent me regular letters until a few years ago." Hokuren worried with her fingers at the blankets encasing her. "She was nearing the end of her life when I left, so I assumed she had passed." She sighed. "I still believe she did."

Cinna looked pensive. "Is that really not her, then?"

Hokuren struggled with the question. Everything in her wanted the answer to be no, which could not help but influence her thinking. "I can't be rational about it. I don't know how someone could look like her and not be her." Hokuren flared her nostrils. "She used powerful magic on me to influence my mind. Moira would never have done that. Never."

"Well, whether she's the Moira you knew or some look-alike, if she continues to hurt you or mess with your head, one punch is all it will take." Cinna held her fist above Hokuren's head to show she was serious. "Just one punch. I won't let her mess with your mind."

"I know you want to help, but that could make things worse."

"Then what should I do?"

"Let me lie like this for a little longer."

"I meant—all right."

Hokuren lost all track of time as she lay with her head in Cinna's lap. She mourned the loss of Moira, her Moira. Whether this Moira was the same, the person Hokuren knew was gone. Tears leaked unbidden, despite her best efforts.

Cinna's rough, calloused hands were surprisingly tender in wiping the tears away. Despite Cinna's abrasiveness and naivete, she was the only person Hokuren truly trusted. Whatever might happen, she could count on Cinna to be on her side.

Hokuren lay for a while thinking of nothing at all, just the sounds of their combined breathing. Eventually, her neck complained, and they unraveled themselves from each other and the blankets.

"Thank you," said Hokuren, wrapping Cinna in a tight hug.

"Anytime."

A scratch at the front door caused both of them to whip their heads in its direction. Cinna's expression hardened in an instant, and she motioned for Hokuren to back away. She was surely thinking the same thing as Hokuren: goblins.

"Who's there?" asked Cinna, pressed against the wall beside the door and pitching her voice down to sound more intimidating.

There was more scratching followed by a soft meow.

Hokuren silently mouthed, "A cat?"

Cinna opened the door, and in waltzed Lumi, Cinna's rescue cat. The animal purred against Cinna's legs.

"No one out there, boss," said Cinna, closing the door. "Just my cat." She picked up Lumi, who rubbed her head into Cinna's chin.

Hokuren took one step toward them to see if she might get a chance to pet Lumi, but the cat hissed and growled, so she stayed away. Lumi returned to her show of affection toward Cinna.

"I'm a bit jealous," said Hokuren.

"Oh, don't be, boss. You can nuzzle my neck later too if you want."

"Appreciated, but I meant I'm jealous of you. I don't understand why that cat hates me so much."

Cinna scratched the cat behind its ears. "This is the first cat that has ever liked me, I think. It makes sense that a cat messed up enough to like me doesn't like anyone else. Don't worry, boss. I'll have a talk with Lumi. Before you know it, she'll be purring for you, too."

"Now *you're* spoiling *me*."

10

Cinna hung from a tree branch in the chilly dawn, lifting herself until her head was even with the branch. She bent at the hips to bring her feet inches from her face, then unbent and lowered herself to the starting point.

"We'll start with twenty of those," she said, lifting herself back up to repeat the exercise.

Jarmo stood below her, mouth open. "Twenty?" he protested. "I—I don't think I could do one of those."

Cinna let herself drop to the soft forest floor and regarded him critically. "I suppose not. You have good size, but you're not taking advantage of it. You need to build both muscle and flexibility. Good conditioning is crucial to confidence."

"Yes, Master Cinna." Jarmo's head bobbed up and down.

The soft jingle of a collar tag reminded Cinna that Lumi was nearby. This morning, the cat lay on the ground and watched her and Jarmo begin their training from a distance. Lumi had remained at the house for hours the previous night, never once allowing Hokuren to come near.

Cinna turned her attention back to Jarmo and led him through a series of simple exercises, stressing the importance of doing them regularly. There were several stretches, sit-ups, push-ups, the plank, and a jog, among others. When they finished, Jarmo rubbed sore muscles while sitting on the old tree stump by the brook. Perhaps she'd overdone the workout for the first day, but she still had one assessment remaining. She wanted to see what he could do with his sword, which he'd been afraid of using against the goblins.

It rested in its sheath, leaning against a tree. Cinna drew and examined it. The sword was basic, short enough to work as a one-handed weapon. A faded red tassel tied to the end of the pommel served as the only personal flair.

Cinna thrust the sword into Jarmo's hands. "Spar with me," she ordered. "Show me how you handle yourself."

Jarmo looked alarmed. "Where's your sword? I can't just cut you to pieces."

"I seriously doubt that you could, but don't worry." Cinna retrieved a branch she'd scoured the forest floor for. It wasn't quite straight, and the balance was terrible, but it would serve as an able quarterstaff for these purposes. "I'll defend myself with this."

They squared off in the forest, Jarmo's stance earning immediate feedback. "Who taught you to stand like that?" she asked. His legs, his feet, and his hips were all wrong. He was stiff and somehow gave himself less range to attack while simultaneously providing opponents with more weak points to probe.

"No one."

Cinna nodded. "I'm familiar with having to learn on my own." She lifted the branch into a defensive position. "Let's see how it looks in action. Come at me."

He bumbled—it was the only way to put it—toward her with sloppy technique, then swung. He moved slowly and didn't put his full strength into the blow, pulling up the instant before she blocked him. She barked at him to continue, which he did in the same manner.

Frustration built up within Cinna until, after several such attacks, it boiled over. "Jarmo! I'm no delicate flower! Don't insult me by striking like I'm your ten-year-old cousin playing pretend."

"I'm not trying to insult you," said Jarmo, pausing to search for the words. "I'm afraid. I keep thinking about how I'll hurt you. Even though I know you'll block me," he added quickly. "I know you will. But it's still how I think. I can't risk it."

Cinna lowered her branch, unsure how to proceed. Any physical issues she could assess and fix, but a mental block was beyond her purview. She'd never had one because every fight, in training or not, had been another reform on either her skills or survival. She'd spent her childhood getting pushed around and beaten up, and once she learned to fight back, she never had an issue with striking first.

"Even if someone means to kill you?"

Jarmo dropped his sword to the ground. "When I was twelve, I shoved my little brother into a fence in frustration. He had been annoying me, you know how siblings are. I wasn't trying to hurt him, but I was bigger and stronger than I thought and he was easy to push." He covered his face with his hands. "The fence had a broken board, and I shoved him right into the sharpest of the splinters."

Cinna said nothing, because what could she say? It was doubtful he'd be comforted by being told it was okay.

"I didn't mean to do that, but that doesn't matter." Jarmo sniffled. "I saw firsthand what even a little violence can do to someone. He survived, but he's never been the same. Every time I raise my hand or my sword, I see him, cut up and bleeding. And I can't do it. But I need to be able to." He took a breath. "Please, can you help?"

Jarmo didn't need Cinna, he needed someone far more qualified. She had absolutely no idea how to get him to stop thinking about his brother. But no one had ever asked Cinna for help, and she didn't want to turn him down. Hokuren wouldn't. "I'll need some time to figure this out," she said. "If you come back tomorrow, maybe I'll have thought of something."

"I'll be back tomorrow," promised Jarmo.

Hokuren spent the early morning trying and failing not to drift back into her father's office to take another crack at her mother's diary. She got only halfway through the first page before finding herself scanning the symbols without thinking about them. She put the diary down in disgust. It was hopeless.

The house felt quiet and empty with Cinna out training Jarmo in the forest. This was perhaps a taste of what her father had felt once she left for Velles. His loneliness could have caused him to turn to the silk-smuggling operation, and whatever was going on with the assuredly fake Moira.

Her eyes wandered to the identical safe keys that her father had given her, taunting her from the edge of the desk. The way into the left safe required finding the other set, which meant she'd have to beat her father in a game of hide-and-seek.

Once, her father had promised a teenage Hokuren and her brothers a special cake for dessert, as a treat. However, when it came time for the reveal, he announced a twist. He had hidden the cake somewhere in the house, and only if they found his hiding spot would they get their dessert.

She never found the cake, which still made her blood boil more than a decade later. Her brothers gave up the search long before she did. She had torn the house apart, even pulling up floorboards, in her desperate need to find it. When the moon was high in the sky and she was knocking around in her father's closet to check for a false wall, he whistled. She spun around to see him munching on the cake and offering her a slice.

"I appreciate the effort, Pumpkin, but I can't let you obsess about this for the rest of your life," he had said.

In that he'd failed, because she had obsessed about it ever since. Maybe it wouldn't haunt her now if he'd told her where he'd hidden that damnable cake. Here, she could finally get closure. She could use her knowledge, honed from years of experience finding things that others wanted to stay hidden, to find what she could not in her youth: her father's secret hiding spot.

At least, that's what she told herself as she prowled outside the home, using a nearby stick to dig into the ground and poke at the foundation.

Tap tap. Tap tap. Each stone that formed the base of the house returned the same noise. It was silly, but she had to check each one now that she'd started this. If she quit after only checking half the rocks, she'd wonder ever after if the other half would have struck gold.

Tip tip. Hold on a moment. Hokuren tried the stone again. *Tip tip.* This one sounded different. Hollow. Excited, she dropped the stick and picked up the stone, giddy to find it light. Whoever had made it had done an excellent job, but what she held in her hands was no natural formation.

A small latch in the back blended in so well that it took Hokuren several minutes of running her fingers over the surface to find it. After that, it was a simple task to crack open the seam that ran around the circumference of the fake stone. She pried it open and found a small, folded note. No keys. Her heart sinking, Hokuren read the note:

Good find, thief! But this is just my fake hiding spot. -MT

Hokuren crumpled up the note and slammed it onto the ground. Even after death, he'd made a fool of her.

She stalked back to her father's office desk, fuming.

"Boss, you shouldn't look at accounting before lunch."

Hokuren jumped at Cinna's voice, having not heard her return and poke her head into the office. She checked the sun to discover she'd spent more time than she'd thought poking at rocks. Her heart rate spiking, Hokuren put her hand to her chest to calm it. "I did something even more pointless. How was training with Jarmo?"

"He's got potential," said Cinna without enthusiasm. "Except for his inability to actually use a sword. Doesn't want to hurt anyone, even goblins attacking the town. It's a mental block." Hokuren made a sympathetic noise, and Cinna continued, "Know any methods to overcome something like that?"

"Well, if someone they care about is in mortal danger, that has been known to work."

"Want to help me set up a life-or-death situation for Jarmo?"

"Absolutely not."

"Figured."

The tea kettle screamed from the fireplace. Cinna disappeared to prepare the tea, and Hokuren followed. She knew Hokuren so well she'd set up the tea without even asking. It coaxed Hokuren out of her funk.

Cinna set a cup in front of Hokuren. "So, boss, what are we doing next?"

"There are two things I want to follow up on." Hokuren put her hands around the cup to feel its warmth. "The silks are obviously important, as both Grimes and Roz mentioned them. They are going to someone named Ulbricht. We need to go to Oro and see if we can acquire some silk, and use it to find out who he is. I'm thinking of setting up a hand delivery."

"Do you think he's responsible for your father's death?" asked Cinna. She took a tentative sip of tea and made a face. She caught Hokuren watching her and said, "Tea's great."

Hokuren tried the tea and didn't know what Cinna's problem with it was. The lavender taste tickled the tongue most pleasantly. "Of course it is. And if Ulbricht thinks of these silks as very important, and if my father was seen as interfering in some way, then he may well have had the resources to have him killed."

"So, he's rich." Cinna sighed. "You know what I'm going to say."

Hokuren smiled. "And you know what *I'm* going to say. His being rich is not enough of a reason to declare him the culprit without evidence. Anyway, before we go to Oro, I want to know if Casper Daily actually thinks the goblins are that big of a threat."

"The town being in danger might not be a made-up story." Cinna frowned. "The goblins are attacking, as Moira says."

"Yes, but I believe this is all part of something bigger. I don't understand what yet. There's still too much unknown, but my father seems to have been wrapped up in it somehow."

"Ah, okay. I guess we can talk to the mayor." Cinna downed the remainder of her tea in three large gulps. "I love talking to important, fancy people."

"I think you'll find this important person less fancy than you're used to."

The mayor of Fondence, Casper Daily, lived in a small hut on the northeast road spur from the town center. Hokuren passed the walk over explaining what she knew of him to Cinna. The man was in his eighties and owned a few acres of land that he used to raise chickens, selling the meat and eggs at market.

Time had not been kind to his property. The mayor's ramshackle hut, built by himself sixty years past, looked as if it remained structurally sound through sheer willpower and inertia. Its unpainted wood rotted and the roof sagged. Dirt and grime rendered the windows opaque. A faint "YO" was written on the door. Hokuren assured Cinna that at one point, it had said "MAYOR." There were no chickens, only a forlorn and empty coop, the wood cracked and broken.

"Are you sure we don't need an appointment to see the mayor, boss?" asked Cinna, thinking of the hoops one had to jump through to meet with the prince, Velles's ruler.

"I'm sure," said Hokuren. "People have never had much need to see Casper."

Cinna stepped cautiously onto his precarious front porch, avoiding the most fractured sections where sharp pieces of wood jutted out. The wood was slimy, and she tried not to think about why that would be.

Hokuren knocked on his door with her customary three sharp raps to no response. She tried again, but when she knocked this second time, the lock mechanism failed with a click, and the door swung open.

A blast of foul odor hit Cinna in the face, causing her to gag. She turned away and held her nose. "Phew, smells like an ogre's crotch in here."

Hokuren also had her nose plugged with her hand. "Something's happened to Casper." She took a tentative step inside. "Hello?" she called out, her voice stuffy through pinched nostrils.

"It doesn't smell like death," said Cinna, poking her head into the dark room.

An old chair full of holes sat in front of a small, scratched-up table. Bookshelves lined the walls, stuffed with books, journals, and other papers haphazardly arranged with no care for their well-being. Several books were opened to a page, placed face down, and jammed into the shelves. In the rear, a desk floated in a sea of papers littering the floor.

"We should get someone," said Hokuren. "I don't like this."

"Who are we getting?" scoffed Cinna. "The Arms of Fondence? With no offense to Jarmo, I'm not sure they've got anyone up to the task here. If something bad happened, we *are* the someone."

She walked in. The floor was filthy, the grit sticking to the bottoms of her feet. Another surface of which deep consideration would be to no good end.

"Ah!" Hokuren cried out and grasped Cinna's arm. Cinna put her fists up before Hokuren released it, looking embarrassed. "Sorry, I thought I felt something skitter over my boot. I wish I'd brought a light."

Cinna's elven eyes spotted a lantern on the floor behind the chair. With the help of the accompanying tinderbox, she lit it and held it out to Hokuren. The dim flame flickered behind dirty glass, but it was better than nothing.

"Thank you." Hokuren motioned Cinna toward the desk. "See if there's anything interesting in those papers. I'll check the shelves."

Cinna didn't exactly relish the task, but not every investigation could play to her strengths. She started with the few papers still on top of the desk. There were budget meeting notes from six months ago, a request from someone in Fondence to approve new fencing (presumably they were still waiting for this), and many more incidental small farm-town things that Cinna paid little attention to the minutiae of. One was a plea from a farmer to do something about another farmer's roosters, whose crowing at sunrise was waking him too early. This was exactly what she had in mind when she thought of small-town problems.

The nest of papers on the floor seemed to be more of the same, but she dug through them anyway, tossing papers left and right to see if something was buried underneath. Her fingers scratched the floor as she swiped, and two of them caught and bent backward uncomfortably.

"Ow," she hissed, shaking her hand. It was a small latch, painted to match the dirty wood. If she hadn't caught her fingers, she would have missed it. The latch was a handle attached to a small square cut into the floor. She smiled. Secret compartments—now that was worth looking into.

Cinna pulled up on the latch, but it was locked, as expected. The lock appeared thin on inspection. She yanked on the latch, hoping brute force would be enough, and felt the bolt give. Another pull generated a snapping noise as the bolt failed, and up went the square flooring tile.

The compartment it hid was small, built only a few inches deep. A single item lay inside: a white paper envelope addressed to the Oro City Watch. Cinna reached down and plucked the envelope with her fingers. A wax seal had been melted over the envelope's flap, which complicated things only a little. She'd learned a few tricks about wax seals and how to beat them with none the wiser.

She brought the envelope over to Hokuren, who had found a folder of her own to peruse. Her mouth hung open, and she didn't appear to like what she read. Instead of bothering her, Cinna took out her dagger and held it up to the lantern's flame.

After a few minutes, she touched it. Warm, perhaps not as much as was ideal, but the weak flame had done what it could. She slipped the dagger under the wax. As she suspected, it wasn't hot enough to make the process smooth, but with patience and persistence, she separated the wax from the paper with only minimal damage to either.

Cinna eagerly removed the contents, earning a letter signed by Casper Daily as a reward for her efforts. Her excitement faded and her heart sank as she read it. The letter accused Mikko Tuomi of being a smuggler, detailing the silk scheme in its entirety while leaving out any other names.

"Boss," she said, sucking in a breath. "You should see this."

Hokuren paused her reading and took the letter from Cinna. "Where did you find this?" she asked when she finished.

"In a little hideaway," said Cinna, pointing at the still-exposed compartment in the floor.

"This is blackmail against my father." Hokuren's hand clenched around the letter. "A threat that he could send this out by post at any time. I can't believe Casper, of all people, would have this."

"Don't I keep saying that you can't trust a person in a position of power?"

"But this isn't Casper's style." Hokuren glanced at the letter and attempted to smooth out the creases she'd made to no effect. "I've ruined this." She returned it to Cinna. "Put it back. I think we've got enough to justify our little breaking and entering."

"As if we needed to justify it," said Cinna. "Door invited us in." She used the lantern flame again to reseal the wax over the envelope. It would pass a cursory glance but not a close inspection.

Hokuren showed Cinna what she had found once the letter was back in the covered compartment. "That blackmail could help explain this."

Cinna stared at a contract, signed with flourishes by Mikko, Moira, and

Harrison Grimes.

> *I, Mikko Tuomi, do pledge Mikko's Imports to Moira the druid in the event that I am unable to pay the business's debts. I am of sound mind, as witnessed by Harrison Grimes.*

"That druid Moira wasn't lying when she said there were plans for my father to turn the business over to her," said Hokuren. "Only they seem to involve bankrupting him first."

"But—but, why?" Cinna sputtered. She couldn't make any sense of it.

"My father would never have sold his business. He loved it more than anything," said Hokuren, quietly. "Unless someone made him."

"Okay, but who would want a debt-ridden import business?" asked Cinna. "I know basically nothing about how businesses work, but I think I know that debt is bad."

Hokuren tapped her chin. "It's those silk shipments. Look, Harrison Grimes signed this as a witness." She stabbed the name with a finger. "He made sure to tell me how important those silks were. Roz, too. And both of them pressured me to sell to Moira."

"Seems like everyone we meet wants Moira to be in charge of this business."

"I think my father was trying to quash the whole deal, so they got rid of him, not realizing that he'd set up the will with Pigeon Couriers." Hokuren put her hand to her mouth. "If I continue not to sell to Moira, they might get impatient and—"

"They'll have to go through me first, boss," said Cinna. "I can take care of them. I don't know who Ulbricht is, but Grimes would lose a fight to a stiff breeze."

"They won't scare me off." Hokuren set the old lantern back on Casper's table. "We need to figure out what is coming along with the silks. Moira, Casper, and even Grimes seem to have gone to great lengths to wrest control of this business from my father's unwilling grasp, and the smuggled items are the key."

They left the house, putting the door back in place as best they could. Outside, Cinna said, "We didn't figure out what happened to the mayor.

The place looks abandoned. Is he dead, or what?"

"No one's said anything about him being dead. He's just . . . absent, maybe?" said Hokuren. "Or maybe—"

She stopped, and Cinna understood what she meant. "Maybe he was against part of the plan, and they did him like they did your father."

Hokuren nodded grimly. "It's possible."

The market was visible in the distance, and it seemed empty, even by Fondence standards. Cinna was about to make a remark about it to Hokuren, but the boss beat her to the punch.

"Cinna, there's smoke." Hokuren pointed toward her father's house. Plumes of black and gray smoke rose into the air, blending in with the clouds hanging over the city. "The house," she said, swallowing.

Without another word, they ran in its direction, expecting Hokuren's father's house to be ablaze. They were wrong, however.

The Sleepy Hollow Inn, located on the same northwest spur as the house, was engulfed in flames. They licked the sky, burning so bright they illuminated the faces of horrified and awestruck onlookers. The heat broiled the air, and Cinna began to sweat despite the cool, overcast weather. They joined the growing group of gawkers that formed a semicircle around the building.

"Hokuren!" Roz, standing in the crowd, saw them coming and broke away to join them. "It's bad."

"The fire brigade?" asked Hokuren.

Roz shook her head. "By the time anyone realized, it was far too late."

"What happened?" Cinna turned from the fire with some effort to focus on Roz for a response.

"We don't know, but there are already suspicions." Roz grunted. "This fire formed fast. Too fast."

Hokuren nodded. "But why burn down the inn? Did everyone get out?"

"Lucky this was late enough in the morning that everyone was awake. One of the guests was getting a glass of water from the front desk. He saw the first flames and alerted everyone else." Roz turned back to the burning building. "And no one knows why yet, but one thing's for sure. This fire was no accident."

11

Hours later, the fire had run its course and extinguished, with the inn a complete loss. Hokuren and Cinna circled the market, mostly to listen to the conversation around the burned inn. They used the opportunity to buy more food with an eye toward breads, cheeses, and dried meats for their planned trip to Oro.

The townspeople had not welcomed Hokuren with open arms thus far in her return to her hometown. She couldn't help but notice that not a single person, other than Roz, had even so much as expressed condolences for the loss of her father. It was so unlike the Fondence that she remembered. People back then had been friendly to all, even outsiders. Now, everywhere she looked were unfriendly faces and impatience.

"A shame about the inn," said Hokuren to Caulder the cheese vendor. She had always gotten a warm smile and even sometimes a little extra bit of cheese as a snack from Caulder when she was a kid. "I'm glad no one was hurt."

Caulder wrapped up her cheese order with a grimace. "Thirty lariats," he said, holding out his hand.

"That's . . . more than I expected."

"Things are tough. Prices are high." Caulder narrowed his eyes at her. "Think I'm trying to cheat you?"

"No, no," said Hokuren, shaking her head. "I'll need change." She counted out the currency and handed it to the cheesemonger. "Thanks Caulder. Good to see you again." She put the lightest of questioning lilts into the statement.

Cinna sidled up next to her, a new batch of pastries in hand, as Hokuren received her change. Caulder grunted and turned to the next customer crowding his booth with the smile he'd denied her. Hokuren exchanged a glance with Cinna and they moved off toward the next stall.

"I guess it wasn't good to see me again," Hokuren said, with a look back at Caulder. He was nodding in rapt conversation with the next customer.

"This is the sort of friendliness you can only get in a small town. Never see the like in Velles." Cinna licked her fingers clean of the vestiges of a sticky pecan treat. "Not even a thank you for your business? Incredible."

"He's not the only one. Everyone's treating me like I'm collecting taxes at knifepoint," said Hokuren. "I really burned bridges here, Cinna."

She'd anticipated some level of animosity, but the outright contempt was as surprising as it was difficult to bear. It was as if the new Moira had poisoned the town against her.

"Stuff these people. We'll be going back to Velles soon, anyway." Cinna held out the bag of pastries and then stuck them in her pack when Hokuren refused. "Maybe they're jealous that you took the chance to leave and not be stuck here your whole life."

"Maybe."

They had nearly left the market when Hokuren spotted Harrison Grimes at a stall selling apples, peaches, and other fruits. She urged Cinna to follow, then broke off the route back home to wait for him. He filled a bag with several peaches and turned, his face darkening when he saw them. Hokuren would not have guessed the dour Grimes a peach eater.

"Mr. Grimes, how fortunate to run into you here," said Hokuren, shooting him a smile that was not reciprocated. She was getting used to that in the market.

"I'm in a hurry," Grimes huffed.

Hokuren was also used to people having other things to do when she wanted to question them. "I'll get right to it then. When were you planning to tell me you witnessed my father sign a document promising to turn his business over to Moira in case of unpayable debts?"

Grimes narrowed his eyes. "How do you know about that?"

"Irrelevant to the question, Mr. Grimes."

"The document is also irrelevant. His death rendered that agreement void."

"Please allow me to decide what is or is not relevant. My father's death remains a mystery, and every piece of information helps."

Grimes's lip curled. "There's no mystery. The goblins got him." He shifted his bag of peaches. "Surely you don't mean to tell me you're delaying the sale of his business because of that."

Hokuren restrained herself from telling Grimes she'd learned that her father's body was not in the grave. Instead of arguing further about her father, she said, "Have you seen Casper lately? He wasn't home."

"What am I, the mayor's babysitter?" Grimes shrugged. "He sleeps a lot these days. He's quite old. I'm sure you'll see him around eventually." He leaned in conspiratorially. "You ought to quit playing seeker, Hokuren. This isn't Velles. You have better things to worry about than the town's senile mascot."

"We actually have very few things to worry about, thank you very much," said Cinna, hands on her hips.

Grimes sneered at Cinna as if she were animal droppings on the bottom of his shoe. "There are stories about a certain importer's daughter and her headband-wearing friend being present at the inn right before it went up in flames."

"What?" said Cinna and Hokuren simultaneously.

"We didn't burn any inns down!" said Cinna. "We were—" Fortunately, she cut herself off before admitting to the crime they *did* commit at the mayor's house. "Er, we slept in," she finished lamely.

Grimes's smile had all the warmth of the tundra. "That's not a convincing alibi. Lots of people also think it's goblins. I'd encourage that line of thinking if I were you." He held up his bag of peaches. "If you'll excuse me."

He left Cinna and Hokuren at the stall, staring at each other.

"Cinna," said Hokuren, after allowing Grimes to get far from eavesdropping range. "Had enough trespassing for the day, or would you like to take a nap and check out the Sleepy Hollow once everyone else is asleep?"

She may as well have asked if Cinna wanted extra dessert. "I'm always good for another trespassing, boss, especially when I need to clear my name."

Cinna swiped a sign posted on the remains of the Sleepy Hollow that warned against unauthorized entry, signed by Officer Vivi of the Arms of Fondence. She crumpled it up and tossed it aside.

They had waited for the dim light of the second moon, Nebulus, to take over the night sky before investigating the inn. The late-night expedition decreased the odds of someone spotting them, but the downside was that Hokuren couldn't see in such poor light. Cinna, with her superior elven eyesight, was the only one who could see in the dark.

The goal of this foray was to find evidence of how the fire started, which might help locate the culprit or at the very least clear their names. If word was getting around that they were responsible, then it could hinder their goal of discovering the truth about Hokuren's father's murder.

"Don't you want to turn on the lantern, at least?" Cinna held Hokuren's hand and guided her into the inn. Cinna saw only in gray scale in the low light, though this would not be much of an issue. The fire had turned everything the same shade of charcoal black.

"That will attract attention. You'll need to be my eyes, Cinna." Hokuren's other hand rested on Cinna's back, cold even through her tunic. "What do you see?"

Cinna crept through the lower level of the inn. The acrid smell of burned wood lingered, and the thick layer of ash covering the floor worked its way through her toes like sand. The ceiling above them worried her. Although the second floor still stood, she didn't trust the structural integrity of the inn's husk.

"Looks like there was a fire, boss."

"An excellent deduction," said Hokuren, without skipping a beat. "Now let's find something that will explain how it started."

"What would that even look like?"

"I'm not sure, but—" Hokuren, still right behind Cinna, clipped her boot on a charred remnant of furniture. She crashed into Cinna, who kept them both upright until Hokuren regained her balance. "Sorry."

Cinna nodded at Hokuren's gray form before remembering Hokuren couldn't see her. "All right. Stay right here, and I'll go look around. You can't see, so don't move."

She released Hokuren's hand and began a circuit around the first floor, peering over the remains. Each hunk of black had been a desk, or a chair, or something else prior to the fire, but the complete devastation had rendered them all unidentifiable.

Something caught Cinna's eye. A light gray in her night vision, it stood out by the simple act of not being black like everything else.

"I found something," said Cinna. It was a striped shard of porcelain that fit comfortably in her palm, in pristine condition except for having been broken off a larger item. To identify the colors of the stripes, she'd need better light.

"That started the fire?" asked Hokuren.

"It avoided melting in the fire, which is actually more impressive."

"Bring it here, and stand close to me. I'll get us some light. Do your best to block it."

Hokuren removed a small lantern, the one she'd brought from Velles, from her coat. Old magic within produced a tiny yellow light when activated, enough to get a good look at the porcelain shard. They huddled around the lantern, and Cinna held the shard to the light. She exchanged a glance with Hokuren.

The stripes were red and white.

"Our missing cup," said Cinna.

"So this is how we get framed," said Hokuren.

A faint rustle outside sharpened Cinna's senses. It could have been a squirrel or cat, but it could have been something else. "Boss!" she whispered, reaching for the lantern to extinguish the magical light. "I think we should go."

It was too late. Another person entered the Sleepy Hollow from the front entrance, blocking their escape route. Cinna pocketed the porcelain shard and grabbed Hokuren, pulling her against a wall that might have once been in the waiting area by the front desk.

"Cinna, what's going on?" Fear caused a warble in Hokuren's voice.

"Someone's here." Cinna kept her voice low. "Don't move, get your dagger out, stab anything that comes close unless I say otherwise."

The person stalked toward them without a word. The official uniform of the Arms of Fondence covered a stout, well-built body. Their swagger and silence suggested something other than an official visit about the trespassing. A mask shrouded their face except for their eyes, over which were glasses with tinted lenses. A cap fitted over their head hid all visible hair.

Cinna drew closer to meet them before they reached Hokuren, in case things turned violent as she expected. The Arm of Fondence was human, based on the exposed ears supporting the strange lenses, but moved as if they could see in the dark like an elf.

"Sorry for trespassing, but curiosity is our curse," Cinna said, holding her hands up, ready for the Arm to make the first move.

That move came as a punch without preamble, surprising Cinna with its speed. She evaded it by a hair's breadth, then pivoted and elbowed them from behind. The attacker saw it coming and, with solid footwork, avoided taking most of the blow.

This person was much more capable than Jarmo. Another punch came as a follow-up, giving Cinna the barest of moments to bend over backward with all her flexibility. She watched the fist fly over her face.

Before she straightened up, the assailant charged and grabbed her around the waist. It was a woman who slammed her into the wall near the front door. A jolt of pain ran up Cinna's spine, but nothing was broken. The larger concern was that the building shuddered and the ceiling above creaked from the collision.

Cinna had spent ten years sparring with fellow students at the Sanctuary of the Eclipse, most of whom were bigger and stronger than her, like her current adversary. The biggest key to winning as the smaller participant was to never worry about whether or not your tactics were honorable.

The Arm pinned her against the wall, squeezing the breath from her. This left Cinna with her legs free to wrap around the attacker's knee and twist, using an understanding of leverage that existed only at her subconscious, to wrench the joint.

The woman grunted, and her grip loosened enough that Cinna slipped free, dancing out of the range of a wild swing full of fury. Despite her new limp, the woman remained dangerous. She had a knife in hand, produced from within her uniform, and with this she slashed at Cinna over and over. Cinna kept backing up to avoid the blade, left with no room for a counterattack.

They both turned in response to a noise caused by Hokuren, shifting while crouched on the other side of the inn. She had her dagger clutched in both fists, holding it in front of her.

The woman held her knife up, aiming at Hokuren.

"No!" yelled Cinna. Hokuren was a sitting duck, and the knife would easily beat Cinna to her.

The woman flicked her knife back and threw it with an expert motion at Hokuren's unaware form. Time seemed to slow for Cinna as she reached into her pocket and flung the porcelain shard. The knife and shard whistled through the air and then collided, a miracle shot that even Cinna couldn't believe she'd pulled off. The shard shattered on impact while the knife deflected off target and landed somewhere on the floor, safely away from where Hokuren knelt.

"She can see in the dark! Use the lantern and get out!" yelled Cinna, edging toward the woman, ready to pounce if she tried to produce another knife. There were no more shards in her pocket to throw.

Hokuren held up her lantern and turned it on. The woman emitted a choked cry and threw her glasses aside to cover her eyes with her hands, staggered. She picked her way out of the inn with a pronounced limp. Cinna considered going after her to get an identity, but let the woman leave to assure a safe retreat for the boss.

"We're okay," said Cinna with a sigh, working to calm herself from her combat high.

"Who was that?" asked Hokuren, breathless with fear.

"Someone in the Arms of Fondence who could take a few goblins for sure." Cinna picked up the glasses and looked them over, an idea forming in her head. "Turn off the lantern for a moment."

"What? Okay."

The lantern went out, again plunging the inn into inky darkness. Cinna put the glasses on. Her vision changed from gray to green. Hokuren and her own body glowed a lighter shade of green. "Flames alive, what are these?" She handed them to Hokuren. "Put them on, boss, but keep the lantern off."

"Oh, wow," said Hokuren, once she'd done so. "I can see."

"But I wouldn't wear them in the light."

Hokuren took the glasses off. "These feel dangerous. I wish Fenton were here, so he could tell us how they work."

"I bet he'd tell us a rogue wizard made them." Cinna glanced around the ruined inn. "Know what else a rogue wizard could have made?"

"An intense fire," said Hokuren, reaching out for Cinna to guide her back outside. "We should go home."

On the way back to the house, Cinna stretched out her back with her knuckles. "I think my spine took a direct shot on the wall." As her heart rate returned to normal, the pain asserted itself. It would be gone in the morning, of course, but that didn't help her now.

"I'll tend to you at the house," said Hokuren. "It's the least I can do to thank you for fighting off an attack on us."

"It's my job, boss. And you don't even know about the knife she threw at you."

"The *what*?"

Soon after they returned to the safety of the house, Cinna lay on her stomach as Hokuren massaged her back, prodding for tender spots and working them into submission. A fire roared from the fireplace. "Any idea why an Arm of Fondence was there to kill us, boss?"

"I don't think she was there to kill us." Hokuren worked an elbow into the proceedings. "She may have been trying to scare us off."

"If they want us gone, they could have waylaid us on the road. Why set up an elaborate arson and—ohhhh—" Hokuren kneaded a particularly sensitive spot, and the muscles tensed before relaxing. "Why wait until we've gone to the inn?"

"A good question." Hokuren went deep into thought and paused the massage, causing Cinna to regret posing it. "I suppose they want to remain as close to the law as possible. They could sell a story about finding us illegally traipsing around the inn and being uncooperative."

Cinna grinned. "That part wouldn't be a lie. I don't cooperate with the authorities."

"I'll pretend I didn't hear that." Hokuren resumed her massage near Cinna's neck. "I suspect that the false Moira is upping the pressure to get me to sell. Make being here in Fondence untenable, so I think that just selling and bailing back to Velles is the best option." Hokuren's voice turned hard. "Another way I know this is a fake. The real Moira would understand these tactics would only galvanize me further."

Cinna released another groan when Hokuren found another spot that twinged. "Is the fake Moira working with the rogue wizard then? What are they all doing here in Fondence?"

"Nothing good is my guess." Hokuren put her finger to her chin. "Moira and the others are doing this because they're afraid of what we might find if we keep looking. Maybe my father found it first, and that's why he's dead."

"Well, their plan to frame us for arson is too complex for my tastes," said Cinna. "Carrying oil in a kitchen mug to start a fire is not how I'd do it."

"How would you—no, don't answer that. The point is, they need a story. People like a story, even if it's flimsy. It doesn't have to be great, just good enough."

Hokuren finished with Cinna's back and finished with a bonus neck massage. Cinna stayed quiet, enjoying the sensations. Before she met Hokuren, being touched like this would have made her skin crawl. And if it were anyone else, it still would.

Cinna felt like putty melting into the floor when Hokuren finished. Exhaustion settled over her, and now that the danger was over and her body had gone out of fight mode, she wanted to sleep right there, face down on the floor in front of the fire.

So she did.

12

The next day saw a return to rain and gloom, fitting with Hokuren's mood. Mysteries involving both her mother and father swirled around her while answers had been in short supply. Now she shivered under the largest tree cover she could find in the light but constant drizzle, accompanying Cinna on her daily dawn training session with Jarmo.

Cinna went through her prescribed exercises with Jarmo, offering both encouragement and criticism in spades. When it came time for the sparring, Hokuren could see what Cinna had mentioned: Jarmo pulled back his attacks, even when it was clear Cinna would block him. Despite the frustration on Cinna's face, she held her tongue and dragged Jarmo over to Hokuren when they finished.

"Miss Hokuren, I hope you weren't bored," said Jarmo, who was quickly proving an overly polite young man.

"It was entertaining," lied Hokuren.

"Hey, Jarmo, we have a question for you," said Cinna, leaning in close. Jarmo seemed to find her impressive, and had already disclosed things he shouldn't have to her. Hokuren had asked her to use that advantage and lead the conversation to pump him for knowledge. "Can you tell us anything about the investigation into the fire at The Sleepy Hollow?"

Jarmo bit his lip. "Commander Moira says I'm to keep things tight under wraps."

"Oh, of course," said Cinna, waving a hand. "Let's say we ran the local rag around here, what would you tell us that's for the public to know?"

"Goblins did it," he said automatically. "They came from the north, as always. But Moira's asked us to do some searching through the ashes today." His eyes shifted away. "I'm not supposed to tell you, but she also mentioned you two as possible suspects."

"Huh? That's unbelievable," said Cinna, her mock surprise far too exaggerated. "Moira likes us so much. Especially me."

"Ah, so you already know. I don't think she's right." He spoke fast, eager to say his piece. "I even told Commander Moira, I told her, 'Why would Cinna be hanging around the fire if she set it'? That would be like a murderer returning to the scene of the crime."

Hokuren had investigated fires as part of the Velles City Watch. While Jarmo's logic made sense, she'd discovered that some arsonists enjoyed watching the show they'd created.

"Okay, so we heard we were suspects." Cinna leaned in toward him. "I'm going to need you to keep this next secret better than you keep Moira's secrets from us." Jarmo nodded, and Cinna continued, "We were attacked at The Sleepy Hollow last night when we checked it out ourselves."

"Oh, that's terrible!" Jarmo leaned down to his bag and removed a pencil and paper. "I'll take the official report."

Cinna slapped the stationery out of his hands. "Were you listening? I said we're not telling anyone!"

"But you were attacked! You should report this to the Arms of Fondence so we can take action." He said it with a straight face. He meant it, in the way Hokuren used to believe in the Velles City Watch, early in her tenure.

Cinna looked as if she'd been forced to swallow a lemon. "What if it were someone *from* the Arms of Fondence?"

Jarmo was aghast, mouth hanging open. "Surely not!"

"Well, let's see. How many women are in the Arms?"

Jarmo rolled his eyes up to the sky in thought, counting on his fingers. The answer he then provided ended up being lower than expected, given the process. "Three."

"Any of them big and strong but still dexterous enough to fling daggers around fast, like they've trained for assassinations?" Cinna flicked her wrist in emulation of the woman's dagger throwing skill.

"N—no! None of us are capable of assassinating anyone," said Jarmo, appalled. "They're good people, all. Now, Astoria's strong. She's the two-time defending hog-lifting champion, but she's no good with small weapons like daggers." He flexed his fingers. "On account of she's got big hands."

"Hog-lifting? You mean she picks up pigs?" Cinna glanced back at Hokuren, grinning. "Boss, you come from a town with *hog-lifting* competitions? Did you ever place?"

"You don't seriously think I entered," sniffed Hokuren. As if she would ever dig into pig-poop-infested mud to lift an animal for sport.

"Hmm, well, if Astoria can't handle a dagger, it couldn't be her." Cinna rubbed her chin. "But the other two, do you think they could pick me up and slam me into a wall?"

Jarmo gasped. "Did that happen?"

"I'll neither confirm nor deny someone was able to do that to me." Cinna waved off his concern. "Let's just say that if it happened, though I'm not saying it did, but if it was possible, could either of them have been the one to do that thing that I'm not saying happened, and may or may not have, but could have?"

The baffled expression on Jarmo's face suggested the tortured hypothetical stretched his mental capacity. When Cinna finished, he said, "Um, I think I get it. You're not too big . . . Still, I don't think so. Unless Vivi or Stelle learned a trick in secret, I don't think they could do what you said about the daggers, either."

Hokuren removed the night-vision lenses from her pack. "Have you ever seen something like this?"

Jarmo regarded the lenses blankly. "No, what are they?" His puzzlement appeared genuine.

"Lenses imbued with magic so us humans can see in the dark like elves can. Our attacker had them. I was curious if they were standard-issue at the Arms of Fondence these days." Hokuren stashed them away.

"Goodness, no. We get a sword," said Jarmo, holding up his short sword.

"Very nice. Thank you for answering our questions. As Cinna said, I hope you'll pretend we didn't have this conversation. We're not all that popular with Moira right now." Hokuren did her best to ignore her pang of grief, reminding herself it was not the person she once knew.

Jarmo's head bobbed. "My lips are sealed, Miss Hokuren."

He bid them farewell and trudged back to town. The rain picked up, hammering the leaves and escaping the tree cover to plop onto Hokuren's head. "Do you think he'll really say nothing to Moira?" Hokuren asked Cinna once she was sure Jarmo was too far to hear.

"Eh, fifty-fifty he squeals," said Cinna with a shrug. "That seal on his lips has leaks, as we've already seen."

"By the way, thank you for leading the questioning. You did a great job." Hokuren meant it. Like a proud mother, she had relished seeing Cinna ask questions and follow up with more. The Cinna she had met months ago would never have been able to do it.

"I was questioning him?" asked Cinna, still watching the tiny form of Jarmo walk away. "I just asked him if he could tell who attacked us by their abilities."

Hokuren grinned. "Asking questions is what questioning is."

"I see. Well, I learned from the best." Cinna looked abashed, running a hand through her unruly hair. "I'm not the only one who's been learning. It was your idea to trespass at the inn. That's some Cinna rubbing off on you."

"Don't expect it to become a habit." Hokuren turned serious. "All right, Seeker Cinna, what's your deduction? Do you believe the Arms of Fondence attacked us?"

"No, boss. Just someone wearing the uniform."

"I agree with that. Now, anything else that stood out about Jarmo's testimony?"

Cinna screwed up her face in thought. After a while, she said, "The Arms of Fondence don't get magic goggles."

Hokuren grunted. "Jarmo said the goblins came from the north, 'as always.'"

"And that's better or worse than the south because . . . ?"

"Does that not make you wonder about my father's construction fund? Which is also in—"

"The north!" said Cinna excitedly. "Wait, do you think your father was paying the goblins?"

"Not exactly." Goblins rarely had a use for coin, as they never found themselves welcome with merchants or residents of the cities. Hokuren couldn't fathom a scenario where the goblins took in the staggering amount of coin her father was flushing from his business. "I'm not even saying it's related. But if someone's manipulating the goblins behind the scenes, and our defaced kitchen last night points to that conclusion, then there might be something to the north that could tie all this together."

Cinna stopped walking, forcing Hokuren to do the same. "Boss, are you suggesting your father was funding the town's destruction?"

"He may have thought it was for some other purpose, or he may have been extorted." Hokuren turned to the northern woods beyond her father's house, woods that extended hundreds of miles over the continent. "I may never get to know the full truth of what he knew, or when he knew it, but whatever's going on here, it's not right. If my father's culpable, intentionally or unwittingly, I hold myself responsible for undoing any terrible things done with his help." She looked back at Cinna. "You with me?"

"I'm always with you, boss." She gestured to the woods ahead of them. "I'm ready to search as many acres as it takes, right now."

"Me too." Hokuren wrung out one of her sodden braids. "Once it stops raining."

The rain let up serendipitously when Hokuren and Cinna's hair and clothes dried in front of the fireplace. Dry enough for exploration in damp, murky woods, anyway. Hokuren wore a pair of old boots lying around the house and dressed in clothes her father left behind made of felted wool. These were far too big, but the wool was water repellent.

The only concession Cinna made to the soaked environs was to roll up the legs of her pants.

Hokuren bet on there being a large, obvious compound carved out of the woods that they could not miss that was still close to town. By systematically canvassing the forest, they could find it without missing any territory.

It was a good plan in theory, she kept telling herself, until the end of the first day when they'd made less progress northward than Hokuren had hoped. She suggested splitting up and covering more ground between the two of them. Cinna rejected this over concerns of Hokuren being caught alone by goblins defending their lands.

The sun was nearly set at the end of the first day, and Hokuren's legs were heavy from stalking the forest. They were about to turn back for the night when Cinna grabbed Hokuren's wool cloak and pulled her close. "There's something out here," she whispered.

Hokuren couldn't see or hear anything out of the ordinary. "Are you sure?"

"Shhh." Cinna motioned with a hand for them to crouch down into some foliage. Hokuren's thigh muscles cramped from the effort while Cinna's head whipped back and forth as she strained her neck to listen for sounds that Hokuren heard nothing of.

She was about to suggest they keep moving when she heard it for the first time. A light rustling, perhaps ten to fifteen feet away. Cinna caught her eye, and they exchanged a glance that acknowledged the noise. She pointed to a cluster of bushes in the direction the sound had emanated.

Cinna gestured at Hokuren and then down at the ground, their little nonverbal signal meaning, *You stay here, I'll go check it out.* She moved on silent feet through the underbrush. She made it halfway before there was a skittering sound that quickly faded.

She looked back at Hokuren and said, "It's gone, and it's getting dark. Let's go back home."

"Was it a goblin?" It should have frightened Hokuren, but she felt nothing but excitement. They might be close to the compound she was looking for.

"I think. Although—" Cinna looked back where the creature had been, whatever it was. "Well, I think I might have been seeing things."

"Why?"

"Because if you asked me to swear on my mother's grave, if I had a mother, that I was telling the truth, I'd say they were wearing trousers and shoes."

It took Hokuren two more days to declare that her plan to comb the forest was a failure. They found no indication of construction to represent the result of her father's money. Someone, or something, haunted them the entire time, and every so often Cinna would hear a noise and tear off in response, but she could never catch sight of the culprit again, goblin or otherwise.

None of the many adventurers Hokuren had read ever recorded goblins in fine clothing, especially shoes. Goblin toes, like their fingers, ended in wicked claws. Eagles didn't wear shoes for similar reasons. So while Cinna maintained she'd seen a well-dressed goblin, the matter was still an open question.

The notes from Barth had been arriving daily, each more stressed and pleading than the last. After three days of fruitless forest searching, Hokuren decided she could not put off the trip to Oro any longer. The only thing she felt confident about from her time spent in the forest was that there was no goblin invasion imminent. And the silks, still under the control of Hugo and the Gregorious Consortium, were now her biggest lead.

She had to tell Harrison Grimes she'd be gone to Oro, as a courtesy. Driving rain harried her and Cinna the entire walk, leaving them miserably drenched by the time they reached his door. There was no response to her knock.

"Oh, no, he's not here," deadpanned Cinna. "I so wanted to see him, especially while standing awkwardly on his porch looking like a drowned rat."

"Sometimes fortune smiles upon us." Hokuren tore a page from the little notebook she carried with her and jotted a quick message to Grimes, starting with a lie. *Sorry I missed you. Will be checking on Barth in Oro.*

Back in a few days. -H

The door opened a crack as Hokuren was halfway bent over to drop the letter, and her heart sank. It recovered when Roz, not Grimes, poked her head out. The blood vessels in the former bard's eyes were visible and red.

"Oh, it's you." Roz bit her lip. "If you're here to see Harrison, he's out. Sorry I can't invite you in."

Why Roz was in Grimes's otherwise unoccupied house was too personal a question to ask, though Hokuren yearned to anyway. She settled for raising her eyebrows inquiringly. "Are you all right?"

Roz still hadn't stepped from the door, keeping it closed as far as possible, just as Grimes had done. Hokuren's curiosity to see what was inside grew so acute she had to mop her sweaty brow with a jacket sleeve.

"Do you mean my eyes? Well, I got a little ill, but Harrison helped administer some medicine that Moira made for me, and I'm just about recovered. He's got a surprisingly nice place here, and luckily there's some good reading material to pass the time."

"What were you reading?" asked Hokuren.

"Harrison has the complete set of *Captain Cavalier* books." Roz smiled sheepishly. "Not amazing literature, but it kills time well enough."

Hokuren pursed her lips at the mention of *Captain Cavalier*, shocked that Grimes of all people would be into the insipid books. Cinna, however, grew excited.

"Even the special limited-printing story, *Captain Cavalier and the Knights of Dungeons Deep*?" Cinna looked at Hokuren. "It's the only one Maol hasn't found for me," she explained, naming their book-hunter friend from Velles.

Roz grinned. "A fan, huh? Sorry to say that he's only got the main series titles."

Hokuren handed Roz the note she had written. "I was just here to let Harrison know I'll be going to Oro to see what Barth is up to and check on a few other things there."

"That's a relief. We really need to get that silk for Ulbricht."

"I'm hoping to work out some sort of deal. Believe me, the silk has my full attention. By the way, Roz, have you seen Casper Daily lately? I knocked on his door the other day, but he wasn't home."

"Casper?" Roz flinched. "Oh, the mayor. He's not around much these days. He's closing in on ninety, you know."

"Where is he if he's not at home, then?"

"I, uh . . . don't know." Roz put a hand to her forehead, looking dazed.

Hokuren made a small noise of commiseration. "Feeling bad still? Don't worry about the mayor. Get your rest."

"Of course. Safe travels to Oro." Roz slid back into the house and the door closed.

Cinna and Hokuren walked back to Fondence's city center in silence until Cinna said, "When she was talking about the mayor, Roz looked just like Jarmo did when he talked about Moira."

"I saw that," said Hokuren. "More witch magic. I fear the worst for Casper."

"By the way, boss, do you also find the fact that Roz is at Grimes's house alone strange?"

"I struggle with anyone being friends with Grimes."

"Friends, or more?" Cinna grinned at Hokuren. "Jealous?"

Hokuren licked her lips. "Of course not. It's not like Grimes and her are . . ." She cleared her throat.

"No, they probably aren't." Cinna waited for a beat. "So if they were, though, that would bother you?"

"They're adults, they can do what they want." In reality, Hokuren hated the idea. But she wasn't going to admit that. "What bothers me is that I thought perhaps Harrison was a secretive recluse, but Roz is in on whatever's going on in there, and I'm not."

"Infuriating, boss." Cinna pulled at her headband, where she kept her lockpicks. "I can help with that. We can wait until Roz takes a nap."

"As much as I want to, we don't have a good reason to break in and enter his house. Something tells me he'd know, and that'd be the excuse Moira needs to put the Arms after us for real."

Cinna sighed. "It's bad, but I understand. We can't just break into places because we want to."

"That's not bad, Cinna. That's you becoming more responsible and reputable."

"I know. I'm becoming someone I don't recognize. Now, if he had that *Knights of Dungeons Deep* special—"

"We still wouldn't break in." Hokuren expected to look over and find Cinna grinning, but her assistant had not been joking.

The rain had degraded Fondence's paths back into muddy thoroughfares, so it was a relief when they reached the station for the trip to Oro. Their driver had seen the rains off while staying dry under cover and beamed at them a smile full of immaculate white teeth, waving at the waiting wagon.

"You've got the whole thing to yourselves!" He ushered them inside, his smile faltering when Cinna, after wiping her feet off, handed him her muddy towel. He pinched it between two fingers and extended his arm to hold it away from his body as if it were going to bite.

"Thanks." Cinna flipped him a coin. "Keep the change."

The man peeked at the coin, smile fading further as he slipped it into a pocket. "The Fondencian lariat is the smallest possible denomination of coin already, miss, but thank you."

"Will the mud be a problem?" asked Hokuren. She handed him a larger coin, bringing his wide smile back to full blast.

"No, no, not at all!" The man waved the towel at the horses' legs. "These are mudders, they are! Wide base at the hooves, strong joints, confident and comfortable in the conditions." He gave Hokuren a wink. "These horses couldn't carry wagons around here if they couldn't handle a little muck."

As before, the trip between Fondence and Oro would take two days. When they traveled to Fondence, Hokuren and Cinna had slept in close quarters, giving the lovers a wide berth. Now they had space to spread out overnight.

Once the trip started, Cinna poked her head out of one side of the wagon, vigilant for attackers, before moving to the other side and repeating the motion. Then she would start over again on the original side.

"I have two theories about the mayor," said Cinna as she continued her restless lookout. "The mayor is actually dead and no one realizes it, or the mayor is dead and everyone realizes it, but they want to pretend he's not so they don't have to decide on a new one."

"I notice you don't have an option where the mayor isn't dead," said

Hokuren. "There's definitely something strange about it." She put an arm up to bar Cinna from the nearest window. "Sit down and relax. We'll be fine. No one knew about our plans to go to Oro until I told Roz right before we left."

"Not true. Wait—" Cinna pushed past Hokuren and tensed at something outside the wagon, then relaxed. "Just a monkey, I think."

Hokuren furrowed her brow. "There aren't monkeys here."

"Oh, probably not a monkey, then. Goblin, I bet. Goblin *assassin*."

"You're seeing things and getting paranoid. Take a break."

"Boss, we know Moira has it out for us. Desolate roads are always a popular choice for ambushing and killing people you want dead." Cinna pointed at Hokuren. "And you ordered this wagon last night."

Hokuren pondered that. "Are you saying you don't trust our wagoneer?"

"His teeth are too white, and his smile too broad." Cinna, perhaps too late, lowered her voice. "No one's that happy to spend two days driving horses through a muddy forest trail."

She refused the food the wagoneer offered to share when they stopped for an afternoon rest. "Poison, sedative, or *both*," she said to Hokuren with certainty.

The wagon shuddered and jerked to a halt later in the evening, an hour before the sun would be too low to continue. The horses whinnied and pawed at the ground, and the wagoneer appeared at the door. "Sorry, folks. Just a . . . slight issue. Shouldn't be long."

"Define *slight*," said Hokuren.

Cinna stuck her head out the window. "Our back wheels are buried in mud!"

Hokuren stared at the wagoneer. "You said the horses wouldn't have any problem with the mud. They were mudders."

"The horses are fine," he said, hunched over in resignation. "The wagon's a different story."

A few moments later, the three of them were standing beside the path, arms folded over chests, viewing the predicament. The front two wheels were a few inches deep in the mud, but nearly one third of the back wheels had sunk down below the surface. The driver had already urged the horses to pull, but they got nowhere.

"Sure is stuck," said Cinna.

"This has never happened," said the morose wagoneer. "What are we going to do? The next wagon from Fondence will come through tomorrow, and we're blocking the path."

"I don't recall mud pits getting so deep," said Hokuren. "This might be a trap."

"I knew it!" Cinna waded into the mud, sinking past her knees. "Someone dug out a hole. There's soft dirt mixed in with the mud."

"It *is* a trap!" The wagoneer's teeth chattered. "Why would anyone do that?"

A trembling branch caught Hokuren's eye, from her right. She glanced at it, but there was nothing there. Unnerved, she clapped her hands together. "We need to get free, and quick. Is there any way we can lift the wagon?"

"It's far too heavy."

"We'll see about that." Cinna spat on her hands before placing them under the rear of the wagon. "Ughhhh," she said, heaving with all her might.

The wagon didn't so much as budge.

"Okay, we've seen that it's too heavy," she said, rubbing sore palms.

Hokuren thought she caught movement from the corner of her eye once again, but when she swung her head to get a good look, there was nothing but plants and trees.

"I think something's out there," she said.

"I heard it, too," said Cinna. "It's just like when we were north of Fondence."

Rustling in a nearby bush caught both of their attention. "That something's coming," said Hokuren, reaching for her dagger.

"I knew the wagoneer was up to no good. Probably got us stuck intentionally."

They stood back-to-back, daggers in hand. The wagoneer clambered back to his driver's box, where he cowered. If the fear he was demonstrating was an act, he was a fantastic actor.

Emerging from the depths of the forest were several goblins dressed in small, child-sized tunics that ended past their knees. They formed a ring around the wagon, all of them carrying branches of various lengths and widths. Hokuren counted at least twenty.

"Goblins!" shouted the wagoneer in a shrill, warbling voice.

"This is a lot of them," muttered Cinna. "Their weapons are unwieldy. That gives us an advantage."

One goblin stepped forward, halting when Cinna brandished her dagger threateningly. He coughed and cleared his throat. He pointed to himself, then at Cinna. "Me. You. Friend." The words sounded odd, a whistling sound added each time he put tongue to pointy teeth, but not nearly as strange as the fact that he said them at all.

"He can talk," said Hokuren, mouth open. "But goblins can't speak human languages."

"I guess this one forgot he's not supposed to be able to," said Cinna. She looked at the goblin. "Friend?"

The goblin nodded. "Lift. Wagon." He pointed at the other goblins. "Help."

"Why?" asked Cinna.

"Friend," repeated the goblin, growing impatient.

"They want to help get us unstuck," said Hokuren, marveling. She could scarcely believe what was happening.

The goblins converged on the wagon. Cinna and Hokuren kept their daggers in hand, but let them hang at their sides. Each goblin shoved branches into the mud at an angle beneath the wagon, then scuttled under it and pushed. Cinna, seeing what they were doing, waded back to the rear of the wagon and lifted as well.

Groans and grunts filled the twilight air, but the goblins made progress. More and more of the wagon's wheels became visible as they extracted it from the suction of the mud. Their muscles strained and veins on their foreheads pulsed, and eventually the talking goblin said tightly, "Horse! Move!"

"You heard him!" shouted Hokuren at the wagoneer, who watched the production from his perch in the driver's box. "Get the horses moving!"

"Right!" The wagoneer took the reins, and the horses pulled forward. The wheels turned and many of the branches holding the wagon up snapped, sending goblins faceplanting into the mud, but the wagon continued on, freed from the mud pit.

A cheer erupted from the mud-splattered goblins. They scampered back into the forest, melting into the foliage. The only goblin that lingered was the one that talked to them. He panted, then said, "You. Owe. Goblins." Before Hokuren could agree, he added, "Again."

"Again?" Hokuren exchanged a glance with Cinna, who shrugged. "I thank you for helping us out, but I don't believe we've ever had the pleasure."

The goblin looked as if he struggled with something. Finally, he said, "Nekane. Owe. Daughter. Owe."

Hokuren's throat went dry. "How do you know my mother's name?" she rasped. "How do you know I'm her daughter?"

"Later. Return. Fondence." The goblin bowed and ran off into the woods. He stopped several yards away and turned back. "Diary. Code. Switch, alternate." Then he was gone.

"Wait!" said Hokuren. She dropped her head. "What does that mean?"

"Should I chase him down?" asked Cinna.

Although Hokuren wanted to know more about her mother, it had been made clear that Cinna couldn't track down goblins that wanted to stay hidden. The goblin had also promised to meet again on their return trip to Fondence. "Let's focus on getting to Oro."

13

Hokuren beat her head against the brick wall of her mother's cipher once again during the following day's journey to Oro. Cinna, who had stayed up all night keeping watch, slept with her head on Hokuren's shoulder after saying she was going to watch Hokuren work with the diary "for a little bit."

This left Hokuren alone with her thoughts and a diary full of gibberish, not to mention a shoulder growing tired. She could not bring herself to wake Cinna and make her sleep elsewhere, however.

The goblin's parting words ran through her head again and again. *Diary. Code. Switch, alternate.* She couldn't come to any other conclusion than that he was giving her a hint. Though it hadn't helped much. She gripped her pen tightly. If the goblin knew how to decipher her mother's code, it would have been nice of him to tell her instead of being as cryptic as the diary itself. She muttered curses against the goblin and the cipher while turning to a different page so she could at least get stymied by different symbols, for a change of pace.

Switch, alternate. This flummoxed Hokuren for some time. She switched symbols around fruitlessly until swapping the symbols on one line with the line two below it. The biggest breakthrough came when she read only every other symbol on the page, alternating between actual diary entry and random garbage. By doing both, line-by-line, a letter-replacement system took shape—sort of. There were still oddities, as if the rules of the cipher could be broken anytime. She ended up with a page of translated text in her own hand:

> *Though we perceive our intelligence to be superior to that of the goblins, my research clearly proves this belief false and in need of reassessment. Goblins exhibit cognitive abilities on par with people. They can be taught, and they can learn. What they lack is interest, which I have determined how to provide. I must be careful, because of a massive flaw in the <unclear>. It is too simple a process to <unclear> with witch magic.*

Hokuren read it over and over and experimented with the symbols, but couldn't fill in the missing pieces. It was almost as frustrating as being unable to read any part of it, but not quite.

The god Barduk created goblins, much like Senara created elves. Scholars had long assumed he made them less intelligent because that was what the Primordial Ones demanded. If her mother had proof otherwise, that alone would be seismic, but her claim about increasing the goblins' interest, along with a reference to witch magic, placed a seed of creeping doubt into Hokuren's mind.

She had to find out what her mother had done.

Even when night fell and the wagon stopped again, Hokuren couldn't keep herself from the diary. Cinna took another full night's shift of watch while Hokuren worked through another two pages by the light of her lantern's candle with similar limited success.

> *It all works! There's no reason that my goblins could not join with human society like the elves did. What an exciting future I am on the precipice of inciting! A whole new world of interactions, of peoples coming together. And all that's required is a little motivation. If I can just fix the problem with <unclear>, I could present this to <unclear>. Until then, the*

flaw is far too serious and this work must be kept secret until I have resolved it. But I will resolve it.

Hokuren stared at both passages. Her mother was . . . experimenting with goblins. On them. Her gut twisted. Neither Hokuren's father nor Moira had ever hinted at this side of her mother. She had changed the goblins' brains, the "motivation" she referred to. Hokuren closed the diary slowly, seeing it and its original owner in a completely new and unwelcome light.

"She was a witch," Hokuren said.

"Hmm?" Cinna poked her head into the wagon through the cut-out window. "You say something, boss?"

"My mother. She was a witch." Hokuren said the words slowly, staring straight ahead at nothing. They sounded incomprehensible, like a foreign language.

"You need some sleep," said Cinna, shaking a finger. "Your nose has been so deep in that book I'm surprised it hasn't turned black from all the ink that's rubbed off on it."

But Hokuren couldn't sleep. She also couldn't focus enough to translate any more pages of the cipher, even when the sun rose the following day with them only a few short hours from Oro.

The wagon arrived in the early afternoon. Cinna rushed into the sun, complaining of muscles sore from disuse. Hokuren yawned as she exited the wagon, her sleep-deprived brain functioning so poorly she forgot they were headed to Oro, not Fondence, and gasped in surprise at the nearby ocean. She barely acknowledged the wagoneer when he asked that they not hold the debacle of being stuck in the mud against him.

"We need to get you to a bed," said Cinna, concern etched on her features.

Hokuren yawned again. Collapsing on the sandy beach nearby and falling asleep right there sounded far better than it normally would. "We're staying at the Waterview Inn."

"Sounds posh."

"It's the cheapest in Oro, actually."

"Now we're talking about my kind of place."

The Waterview Inn's name promised nothing exciting for the educated visitor. Oro required that every building have a view of the ocean, and the town bragged it would never build one that didn't. Like so many such claims, it was technically true and not worth the trouble required to fulfill it.

Cinna's first order of business upon meeting the inn's clerk was to point out that the inn was situated farther back from the ocean than any building in Oro, and she didn't believe in the veracity of either the town's claim or the inn's name. Hokuren slumped over the front desk while the clerk ignored her in order to prove both true to Cinna.

"I don't see it," said Cinna, looking out the window in the lobby's corner. The inn had elongated this corner, so the building was not a perfect rectangle, to place a window that provided the view.

"You gotta be taller, girl." The clerk, a surly woman wearing a loose gray dress and hair tied up in a tight bun, dragged a chair over. "Here, stand on this. Now, lean a little to the left—a little more. There you go."

Cinna threatened to topple over, one foot on the chair, the other hovering, while leaning precariously. "I'm as tall as I can be. And I still don't see—no, I do. The sea, it's there! You're not lying."

"Of course I'm not lying." The clerk sniffed. "Seeing the water is worth a little extra effort, don't you think?"

"I don't know." Cinna jumped off the chair. "I saw a sliver of sand and water through this window and then through two windows in that building that's in the way. Hardly worth it when I could take a three-minute walk to a completely unblocked view."

"Feh, you youth." The clerk looked to Hokuren for support. "Always need it easy, don't they? Gotta have a view with no obstructions to make it simple."

Cinna caught Hokuren's eye and elbowed her in the ribs with a wink. Hokuren grunted. Only three years older than Cinna, she wasn't considered "youth." She was too tired to pretend not to be annoyed.

"I do think seeing it through less than three panes of glass would be preferable."

The clerk slapped a room key on the desk near Hokuren. "Room six.

The promise is you can see it. Not that it's good."

"Can you see the water from our room?"

"No."

Their room turned out to be as disappointing as expected. Hokuren earned a sore tailbone by flopping onto the bed and finding it marginally more cushioned than slate. The room's single window was the size of her travel pack and had been painted shut. A lone piece of art, hung on the wall opposite the bed, depicted a scene of an old man dying alone, his expression one of regret.

"This is the most depressing drawing I've seen in my life," said Cinna, turning her head to look away from it. "The innkeeper hates us, I'm sure of it. Imagine a room in a place called the Waterview with no view of water! The only thing I'm still trying to decide is whether she hates all customers, or just us."

Hokuren tossed her bag in a corner next to Cinna's. "We can't afford to spend more at a better place." She gave the art a disdainful look. "Let's take that down. Do you mind doing that while I take a nap? I'm useless right now."

Cinna ran through her exercises while Hokuren slept. Each muscle she engaged seemed to sing with delight as she woke it from slumber brought on by the wagon trip.

Goblins weighed on her mind as she went through her routine. She could not share Hokuren's enthusiasm about meeting them again. They had helped with the wagon, yes, but the surreal nature of their appearance and ability to speak, combined with their convenient timing, hid some yet unknown motive.

The sun was setting when Hokuren stirred from her nap, her sleep schedule now thoroughly out of alignment.

"Welcome back to the land of the awake," said Cinna, finishing one of her more complicated stretching exercises that Hokuren had once said made her muscles cramp just by looking at it. "But now it's too late to do any investigating."

"Not true. We're going tavern-hopping." Hokuren got out of bed and looked momentarily puzzled when she moved to put her boots on, only to find she never took them off before falling asleep. "In a port town like this, if you want to find someone and don't know where to look, go to a tavern. Roz told me our smuggler friends like their drink, not that we should be surprised."

"Are we looking for Hugo, then?" asked Cinna.

"Or Barth. Either of them will do to start. I'm not picky."

Hokuren and Cinna emerged from the inn into the quiet of the evening. The docks were empty, the work done for the day. Ships creaked in the gently rolling waves, the sounds gradually drowned out by shouting and laughter as they approached what Oro called the "Tavern District." Four taverns pressed together atop a platform built at the edge of the waterfront comprised the district, all full of rowdy drinkers.

Hokuren stopped outside the staircase leading to the taverns. "Any preference on which one to start with?"

"Hmm," said Cinna, hand under her chin. They looked identical save for the name painted above each doorway. "People might be frigid at Rhymes with Rime. What about Three Ships and a Tugboat?"

"It's as good as any."

Cinna was not prepared for the raucous wall of sound that crashed into her when she opened the door to the tavern and flinched at its eardrum-bursting might. There was no stage, unlike what she'd find in its Vellesian counterparts. It was just as well. The noise of the boisterous patrons would annihilate any music the moment it left a bard's lute.

The floor was slick and wet underfoot. Revelers crammed into every space in the building. Dice and card games, full of shouts and slammed fists, occurred wherever a group managed to secure a small slice of table. Cinna's chest constricted and her breath grew short as she followed Hokuren into the teeming mass of people. She liked freedom, and that included freedom of movement. Here, patrons jostled her as they passed to and fro, slithering through the mass of humans and elves.

A server, armed with several flagons, bumped into another person and spilled some ale on Cinna's tunic. Without a word, the server continued on as the drink dripped onto the floor.

Cinna gave the exit a mournful glance and said into Hokuren's ear, "How should we start?" She had to scream to be heard.

Hokuren held up a finger and pointed deeper into the tavern before squeezing her way to the front bar. Cinna wrung out her tunic and followed, slipping through the crowd like water working its way through a crack in a dam. Five bartenders worked nonstop to fill requests for ever more ale from a chaotic swarm of customers.

One of the harried barkeeps took Hokuren's order for two ales. Hokuren leaned close to Cinna. "Pretend sips. It's just for show."

Drinks acquired, they continued to worm their way through the sea of humanity until they found a small pocket of free space to occupy while they stood and did whatever people do in taverns with a noise level like constant, overlapping thunderclaps.

"We can't talk because everyone's talking!" Cinna shouted at Hokuren.

"What a paradox." Hokuren lifted her ale toward the general throng. "Keep your eyes peeled."

Cinna did, looking for anyone who resembled the two men on the boat based on her limited glimpse of them, but there were too many people. She couldn't focus on any single person, and quickly gave up.

Hokuren scanned the room for the both of them, her tankard to her lips as her eyes scoured the teeming masses. Every so often, Cinna also pretended to drink. Once, she accidentally tipped her tankard too far and received a mouthful of ale. Unprepared for the bitter drink, she sputtered, and most of it ended up on the clothes of surrounding patrons. None of them minded.

Somehow, the bar got more crowded as time passed, until Cinna was sure the pressure would cause the walls to burst and the roof to collapse. Sweat developed on Cinna's forehead as the crush of humans and elves created a sauna-like atmosphere, mingling with the ale she'd already been doused with.

Finally, Hokuren tapped Cinna, pulled up Cinna's headband, and placed her mouth right up to Cinna's ear, her breath causing it to twitch. "I think we've got our man."

Cinna didn't know which man Hokuren meant, but she was happy to do anything that might lead to them leaving. She tagged behind as the boss slipped to a table near the back. Two men sat huddled beside each other, pointing at a paper on the table. They weren't gaming, and their ales sat neglected in front of them, making them stick out.

"Terrible place to do business," said Hokuren. She was nearly yelling at the top of her lungs.

The men jumped and turned around, slamming the paper upside down on the table. "We ain't interested, out-of-towner," the man on the right said. He had short-cropped black hair and a matching goatee. Muscles bulged from a shirt too small for his frame.

"I haven't told you what I want. You're Hugo, are you not?"

The men exchanged glances. "Who's asking?" said the man on the left. He had a skull tattooed on his neck.

Having this conversation while screaming was ridiculous. Cinna gestured for them all to go outside and talk like normal people, but none of the others paid her any mind.

Instead, Hokuren continued to strain her vocal cords. "I'm Hokuren. I've taken over Mikko's Imports."

The skull-tattoo man nodded. He rubbed the fingers on one hand to his thumb. "The money?"

"I'm willing to discuss options." Hokuren smiled.

The man on the right, presumably Hugo, stood up and slammed a thick fist on the table. "We want your money, not your words."

Cinna tensed and subtly placed herself in a position to intercept him if he tried to treat Hokuren like the table. She was surprised it hadn't cracked under the power with which he struck it.

"Easy, Hugo," the skull-tattoo man said, placing a hand on the other man's chest. To Hokuren, he said, "You owe us quite a bit of money. As you can see, Hugo's worried about his next rent payment."

Hugo didn't look like someone who worried about his rent payment. He looked more like someone who landlords worried about confronting when they needed to collect his rent payment.

Hokuren held up her hands. "I don't have any money with me, but I'd be happy to—"

"Where's my key, you lying—" Hugo lifted his fist, readying a punch even as the skull-tattoo man yelled at him.

Cinna threw her entire body into a clean tackle, slamming into Hugo before he could get to the follow-through. It was like tackling a bear, and she took the brunt of the hit despite delivering it, but she managed to drive him onto the table. The tankards of ale spilled and drenched them both with their contents.

This only momentarily stunned Hugo, and the next instant he was aiming one of his meaty fists at her.

She let go of him and dove off to the side, crashing into another man seated at the adjacent table before landing on the floor. The man got up and turned around, face ruddy with the effects of too much ale and newfound fury. Hugo, raging, couldn't react in time and delivered his punch meant for Cinna directly into this man's face.

The man went limp and dropped to the floor on top of Cinna, compressing her against the sticky floor. She had to roll his girth off her, a feat made difficult by the tight quarters of tables and chairs, desperate to get back up in case Hugo went for another go at Hokuren.

By the time she scrambled to her feet, the tavern had exploded into chaos.

The unconscious man recently on top of Cinna had three mates who had developed a sudden problem with a deeply unapologetic Hugo. Their scrap was only a minor part in the overall play of the tavern, where bar patrons throughout had joined in by fighting each other. They swung chairs, tankards, or their fists at anyone unlucky enough to be in their vicinity.

Cinna searched out Hokuren and found her with her head turned away, arms crossed in front of her, and backing up from the initial scuffle. She nearly shuffled blindly into another one involving two women circling each other with knives drawn before Cinna pulled her away and said, "Let's go, boss."

Hokuren needed no convincing. The bar was less crowded now, as many who weren't interested in being part of a brawl headed for the exit, but it was much more dangerous. Cinna dragged Hokuren in a zigzag around the fights. A tankard hurled through the air aimed directly at

Hokuren's head. Cinna batted it off course, earning a sharp pain in her fingers. Those things were sturdy. Wincing, she kept moving.

They burst through the door and out onto the platform outside, where several people lingered to view the commotion from relative safety, before continuing down to the docks. They were quiet, save for the ringing in Cinna's ears, a vestige of the tavern's aural assault.

"You okay, boss?" asked Cinna.

"I'm fine." Hokuren took a shaky breath. "He was going to punch me. Thank you for stopping him."

"That's what I do." Cinna plugged her ears with her fingers to reduce the ringing. It didn't help. "You know, that didn't go very well."

Hokuren made a sucking sound with her teeth. "No, it did not. We at least identified Hugo of the Gregorious Consortium, but making a deal could be more difficult than I anticipated. He negotiates like a wolverine."

"He mentioned a key." Cinna made a show of patting her pockets. "We don't have his key."

"We do not. I have no idea what he's talking about."

Cinna kept her eyes on the tavern platform as Hokuren considered how to proceed. Only a few minutes later, Hugo and his friend, the skull tattoo man, slunk from the bar. Hugo walked with a slight limp.

"Come on." Cinna grabbed Hokuren's hand and led her away from the docks as the men descended toward them. They hid behind the dock office, where the enforcers of tariffs and duty taxes operated from sunup to sundown. With the light of Vitreous now all that lit the world, the tax collectors were gone and their little office was silent. The shadowy figures of Hugo and friend passed as they headed to their next destination.

"I see. You think we should follow them." Hokuren kept her voice low. "We might find something we can use against him as leverage to enter more productive talks."

"Or we just find the flaming silks and take them," said Cinna.

"We can't—"

Cinna cut off Hokuren's protest. "You can steal from smugglers who attack you. That's the law."

"It is most definitely not."

"Well, it should be. Plus, we might even find those other goods along with the silks."

Hokuren frowned. "Let's call that plan B."

The moon hovered over the water, casting its reflection among the waves lolling into the harbor. Hugo and the skull tattoo man, walking close to the shore, stayed in constant illumination while Cinna and Hokuren lurked in the shadows of the buildings farther inland.

At the edge of Oro, the men looked behind them to ensure they weren't being followed but never glanced toward the buildings. They seemed satisfied and continued into the dense forest that began on the port town's outskirts, becoming nearly invisible once they entered. Little of Vitreous's light could penetrate the foliage.

"Following them now would be a bad call," whispered a raspy voice behind them. The hairs on Cinna's back stood on end for a second even though she recognized this voice. She turned around to find Roz kneeling.

"What are you doing here?" asked Hokuren, saving Cinna the trouble.

"Stopping you from going into a forest crawling with violent smugglers at night," said Roz. "Looks like I got here just in time."

Cinna narrowed her eyes. "We didn't ask you to tag along."

Roz shrugged. "A mistake on your part I've done my best to rectify. As someone who's worked with Hugo and his boys, I know them well, and heading into that forest after them will get you nothing. Have you talked with Hugo already?"

"For a certain definition of talking, yes," said Cinna.

"Our goal was only to discover where they went, not confront them there," said Hokuren, with a calm that Cinna wished she could maintain.

"There's a shack they've set up, nothing much," said Roz. "I've seen it myself."

Hokuren stood up and massaged her thighs. "Crouching has never been my strength. Roz, do you know anything about a key? Hugo mentioned one that he thought I had."

"A key," muttered Roz, standing up alongside Hokuren and looking down in thought. "Ah, yes. It's probably the one that opens the chest Hugo keeps Ulbricht's silks in. But the only person who ever even sees it is—" She looked back toward the town of Oro. "Oh no."

"What?"

"Barth." Roz muttered a string of curses. "If Hugo thinks you have his key, he's the likely reason."

"Why would Barth take the key?" asked Hokuren. "He sounded desperate in his letters, but never mentioned any key."

"My guess is he felt threatened," said Roz. "He'd be the only link to Mikko's Imports here in Oro, and with no payments coming in, Hugo would look for someone to take his frustration out on. He can have a short fuse."

"You don't say," said Cinna.

Roz turned toward the moonlit ocean. "Barth's probably in hiding, and I've a good idea where. It's his secret hiding spot. He thinks I don't know about it." She winked.

"Where?" asked Hokuren.

"Tomorrow. We'll need to go out on the water, and it's too dark for any reputable hired boat." Roz gave the two of them a grin. "And if I tell you now, I bet you'll figure out how to go out there without me. Cinna will talk you into it."

Cinna said nothing, because Roz had the right of it.

"Tomorrow it is," said Hokuren.

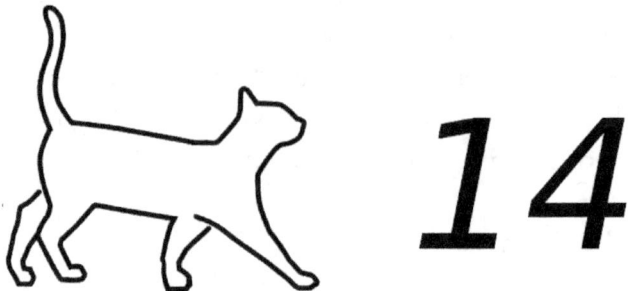

14

The Oro docks filled with workers as dawn crested, loading ships already in port and greeting ships incoming. The flow of goods never ceased to amaze Hokuren. Oro connected to several small towns in the forest, of which Fondence was one, and every item that entered or left those towns did so through their port. The docks and warehouses housed an impressive number of crates and chests, even if their count paled in comparison to the flow in and out of Velles.

Hokuren watched the scene from a seat near the beach with Cinna while the two of them ate an early breakfast of fruit, bread, and cheese. They spoke little, save for Cinna's remark that the view of the water was much better there than from inside the Waterview Inn.

"So, boss, excited for a boat trip with Roz?" said Cinna, breaking the silence.

"It's a means to an end." Hokuren glanced at the water and the crashing of the waves against the docks in the high tide of the morning. "I don't relish being on a tiny boat over these treacherous waters."

A figure on the docks caught Hokuren's attention by looking out of place among the workers. The person lurched, zombielike, toward the taverns past the far end of the docks.

"Cinna, speak of the demon. It's Roz."

Cinna stared out where Hokuren was looking. "The sun's barely cracked the horizon, and she's ready to crack back an ale. That's an adventurer for you."

Hokuren urged Cinna to join her and ran to catch Roz before she got an early start on her drinking. "Roz!" she called.

"Oh, Hokuren." Roz looked haggard. Dark circles of purple pooled under her eyes. "You're up early."

"Did you sleep at all?" said Hokuren, trying her best not to sound like a nagging parent. She wasn't sure she had fully succeeded.

"Maybe half a moon." Roz rubbed the back of her head. Grains of sand stuck to it sprinkled to the ground. "Do I have time for a drink before we go?"

"Just let me know where Barth is, and I'll go talk to him myself." Hokuren didn't want to be a party to Roz drinking after a sleepless night. "If you need a bed, we're room six at the Waterview. Please take it."

"Aw, curse you industrious early risers," moaned Roz. "Barth knows me. He doesn't know you. He might think you're with Hugo and, feeling cornered"—Roz aimed a stabbing motion at Hokuren's stomach—"he'll defend himself first and ask questions later. I have to go with you."

"Cinna and I look nothing like Hugo. We can handle—"

Roz cut her off with an exaggerated yawn. "Nope, sorry. I'll take you there, but I won't tell you where it is." She gestured toward Cinna. "Unless she wants to beat it out of me."

"Could be fun," said Cinna, dusting her hands off.

"No fighting this early in the morning," said Hokuren, stepping between the two. To Roz, she said, "Fine, lead the way."

"I'll arrange for a boat," said Roz, headed for the water.

Nezil, a tanned, shirtless, and shoeless young man with wiry arms capable of powerful rows, took them out into the bay on his chartered boat. Roz's instructions were to head for a cove to the north, outside of Oro's protected bay. He skirted the shoreline to avoid larger ships inadvertently crushing the small rowboat as they entered and exited the port in the burgeoning morning.

"Be a spot tougher go of it once we get out into the open water." Nezil licked a finger and held it up to test for wind. "Lucky we can stick with the shore." He navigated with a deft hand, keeping the little boat balanced even as every disturbance in the water jostled them.

A pit had developed in Hokuren's stomach despite how safely they had proceeded thus far, and she clung to her seat. Sailing in a ship the size of Captain Tulip's had not been an issue, but each bob and dip in Nezil's flimsy vessel reminded her how easy it would be for a wave to send her sinking to a watery grave.

Cinna had no such fears, or she hid them extremely well. She leaned over the edge of the boat and gazed into the azure water. "There are a lot of crabs," she said.

"Aye." Nezil talked and rowed, fitting his words in between each exertion. "Grab them here and you save many coins from the larcenous prices crab merchants charge."

"I'm willing to pay a little extra to avoid having to catch them myself," said Hokuren.

Nezil shrugged. "If you can afford it, I suppose."

Hokuren leaned back in her seat. She didn't eat crab legs often enough to worry about the difference in expense, but it wasn't worth arguing with the boatman. Better to let him focus on the rowing at hand.

The waters grew more treacherous once they reached the edge of the bay, as promised. They continued to hug the coast, but waves crashed into and rebounded from the rocky cliff that dominated this section of coastline. The waves hit the boat with enough height that water collected in the bottom.

"Should we be concerned with this?" asked Roz, splashing in an inch of water at their feet.

Nezil dipped his head down and made a show of considering the water, trailing his fingers in the water near his feet, his expression pensive. "No, it is no problem," he declared. "The boat has a leak anyway, so the water in and out will balance."

"That makes sense." Cinna nodded sagely.

Before Hokuren could state that it did not, in fact, make sense, Roz called out, "The cove!"

A smaller bay was carved into the cliff face, in the center of which was an open cave. Nezil guided the boat inside, able to float several paces within the cove's shelter before softly bumping into ground. The last vestiges of light barely reached their stopping point. Inky black darkness shrouded the rest of the cove.

"Is this Barth's boat?" asked Hokuren about the only other boat pulled ashore in the cove.

"It should be," said Roz. "Looks like he's still here."

"Let me see." Cinna hopped out of the boat and scampered into the darkness. A moment after she disappeared from view, she said, "The cave goes deep down from here."

Hokuren looked to Roz, who shrugged. "I've never actually been inside."

Nezil waved to Hokuren and Roz as they climbed from the boat. "I'll take care of the little water problem while you're in there."

"You'll fix the leak, too, right?" asked Hokuren. She removed her boots and tipped them upside down. Ocean water poured out. Her soaked stockings were a lost cause, but at least her feet would no longer be squelching in pools of water.

"The hole is small, so it should be no big deal." Nezil flashed a smile. "But for you, I will fix it." As if fixing his boat was only for her benefit.

Hokuren dug her lantern from her pack and turned it on. The magical spell embedded within the device lit up with yellow light, and Cinna and the rest of the cave came into view. A firepit was near the water. Hokuren stared forlornly at the pit, imagining a warm fire crackling as she shivered in drenched footwear.

"Cold, boss?"

"Just some wet stockings and boots." Hokuren put her boots back on. The lantern caught the glint of Cinna's teeth within the smile on her face. Hokuren waved her hand at her assistant. "I know, I know. That's why you never wear any."

"My feet are already dry is all I'm saying."

Hokuren grunted in response, but it was a good-natured one.

They walked into a cave made of gray rock, but veins of something that sparkled in the artificial light ran throughout the walls and ceiling, creating a wondrous glittery effect. When she pointed it out, Roz said, "Dysicite."

"This is dysicite? Should we be in here?" Stories said the gem caused the bodies of anyone who touched it to wither and lose their extremities. The old folk tales were based in reality: Dysicite was highly toxic to the touch. That combined with its tastelessness made it a popular poison. Ingestion was always fatal, the death cruel.

"Don't fondle it, and dysicite won't do anything." Roz spat. "Went spelunking with a fool back in Trebello once. He thought he would wrap it in a rag and sell it for good coin. Carried it in his hip pouch. Thin strips of cloth and leather weren't enough to prevent the dysicite from getting him."

"What happened?" asked Hokuren, stomach churning.

"Last I heard, he'll never be a father." Roz mercifully didn't go into further detail.

The cave ended in a dead end. Or it would have, were a tunnel not dug out of the ground that extended further down under the dysicite-rich rock.

Cinna crouched in front of the tunnel, peering into its depths. It descended at an angle, like a ramp, before straightening out and continuing out of Hokuren's lantern-aided vision. Cinna looked up at Hokuren. "This tunnel is unnatural."

"It's goblin work," said Roz.

Humans and elves could build tunnels, of course, but their desire to do so paled compared to goblins. They built underground warrens that could rival Velles in size and complexity.

"But why would goblins dig a tunnel here in this—" Hokuren cut herself off to examine a discoloration in the ground a few steps into the tunnel. She had a bad feeling and hoped she was wrong. The marred dirt crumbled in her hands. She sniffed and jerked back from the metallic tang, one she had firsthand experience with from her time in the City Watch.

"Blood!" Hokuren cried. "Not so old, either."

Cinna spun in place, hands in fists, ready for someone to jump out at them in the cramped confines of the tunnel. "We should leave."

"No." Hokuren let the bloody dirt slip through her fingers. "Roz, I'm hoping you're wrong about this being Barth's hideout."

Roz looked grim. "Something may have happened to Barth."

"What happened could still be down there," said Cinna. She turned to Hokuren. "You and Roz stay here. I'll go scout things out."

"I'll be going with you, Cinna," said Hokuren firmly, to stave off further argument.

Cinna, slightly stooped, descended into the tunnel built too short for people. "Stick close, then."

Hokuren bent over uncomfortably to fit in the passage. With Cinna in front and Roz behind her, she swallowed hard, claustrophobia settling in. The tunnel was growing thinner the longer they traversed it, she was sure.

"Sure is cozy," said Roz, not helping.

"I hope it's not long." The walls seemed ready to squeeze in on Hokuren. She told herself it was all in her mind.

Something in her voice caused Cinna to reach a hand back and grip one of Hokuren's. "You wanted to come, boss."

The tunnel twisted and turned a few times as they shuffled along. On the other side of an acute angle, her stomach fell. She smelled blood again, this time strong enough to permeate the stuffy air.

"On your guard," murmured Hokuren. If something had happened to Barth, the perpetrator might still be around.

Cinna retrieved her dagger from its sheath before continuing in silence in front of Hokuren. Two more twists later, the tunnel opened up into a larger room, tall enough that they could stand up straight. Against the back wall, slumped over, was the source of the smell: a corpse stained with blood from several wounds.

Hokuren grimaced. She'd never been good with dead bodies, no matter that she'd come across more than a few in the City Watch. Getting out of the Watch and into private investigation meant she was not responsible for suspected murders any longer, to her relief.

"Roz." Hokuren turned her head from the body. She continued to picture the gray skin and lifeless eyes from her glimpse of it. "Is that Barth?"

"Yeah," said Roz. She reacted to Barth's corpse with minor annoyance, similar to how she might respond to a tavern running out of her favorite ale. Adventurers such as Roz saw death all the time. Ideally, it was only the creatures they were hired to dispatch, but sometimes one of their own fell on the job. "Goblins got him, it appears."

"He has a lot of wounds, boss." Cinna knew of Hokuren's aversion to corpses, and was already checking out Barth's remains to save Hokuren the gruesome task. "Tough to say which may have done the deed, but they look like dagger cuts."

"Claws and teeth, too, perhaps?" asked Hokuren. Goblins used their deadly body parts as much as any other weapon. In the close quarters of this room, they'd be the superior option.

Cinna maneuvered the body up and down and tore off Barth's shirt to inspect a wound there. "No, these are all dagger wounds. The cuts are too clean. Claws would be more ragged."

"Regardless, don't goblins make the most sense?" said Roz, forehead knitted with tension. "They're always a danger."

Hokuren exchanged a glance with Cinna, recalling the goblins that helped their wagon out of the mud. "Cinna, help me search around. Anything of note, let me know."

Cinna saluted. "Aye, boss."

Hokuren scoured the rest of the room while Cinna prowled through the dead man's pockets. Barth's rucksack was the only other item on the ground. The bag contained a brass comb, velvet gloves, and two rings embedded with green jewels. A few more items were strewn about next to the sack, indicating someone had already rifled through it.

"Anything, Cinna?" asked Hokuren, staring again at the rings. Even if the jewels weren't true emeralds, they looked fairly valuable.

"Nothing," Cinna said, standing up and wiping her hands on her trouser legs. "I think Barth's killer got us beat. The pockets are like a cornfield full of crows. Picked clean."

"I wonder if they found what they were looking for." Hokuren pressed her finger to her chin. "Whoever killed Barth left behind plenty that would fetch a good price."

Roz snorted. "Goblins probably kill for the coin alone. You can expect they snatched those up and left everything else. It's not as if they've got anyone to sell a comb to."

"Goblins don't have much use for coin, either," said Hokuren evenly. "For the same reasons they wouldn't find an easy buyer for a comb. And we're forgetting the most obvious item Barth would have been killed for:

the key."

"It wasn't goblins," said Cinna, examining her hands and satisfied they were mostly clean. "I'm sure."

"And how can you be so sure?" said Roz, hands on her hips. It was the question Hokuren would have asked, although she wouldn't have sounded as challenging.

"There are no cuts or tears in the fabric. Goblins make terrible pickpockets." Cinna flexed her fingers at Roz. "Their claws make it impossible not to leave evidence of their hands going down your pants. They'll rip right through." She gestured to Barth's body. "But whoever went through these pockets was careful. Kept them in pristine condition, tried to hide their intentions. Not something goblins would bother with."

"An astute observation," said Hokuren, giving Cinna a nod. "Actually, I'm not sure I would have thought of it."

"Please, boss, too much praise is going to go straight to my head."

"Did you check Barth's fingers?"

"Oh, yes. Clean."

That suggested Barth hadn't fought back, either because he couldn't or he never realized he should until it was too late.

"It has to be goblins," said Roz, chewing her lip.

"It never *has* to be anyone," said Hokuren. "But the key's not here, and goblins would have no interest in it."

"Perhaps Barth never had the key," said Cinna.

"That's a possibility." Hokuren turned away from the body, having seen enough. "One we can discuss elsewhere. Let's go back."

Hokuren started toward the tunnel, giving Barth one more look. She hadn't known him, but she couldn't help the melancholy that came over her. The end of a cramped goblin tunnel was no place to die.

A slight bump on the otherwise flat dirt floor that she'd missed on first glance caught her attention. She held up a hand to ask the others to wait and brushed the dirt aside, finding it loose and easy to displace. It was fresh.

"Find something?" asked Roz, excitement in her voice.

"Maybe." Hokuren set her lantern down and used both hands to claw out a hole. She was sure Barth had hidden something here.

Her intuition was rewarded when her fingers grazed against cool metal.

Hokuren claimed a brass key the length of her hand from within the small hole she'd made. She held it up to Roz.

"That's it," said Roz, watching each movement of the key. "That opens the chest where Hugo and the Consortium hold Ulbricht's silks."

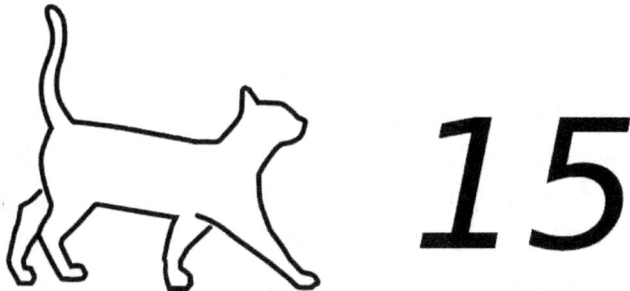

15

Cinna sat on a log near the Oro coast snacking on blueberries while Roz and Hokuren wrung out soaked stockings and set them next to wet boots to dry off in the midday sun.

They had gotten a ride back to the town from their faithful boatman Nezil, who had waited patiently for them to slog back up the tunnel. The return trip mirrored their voyage out, the boat taking on seawater like it paid its share of the fare. Both Hokuren and Roz had been silent on the ride back, morose over Barth's death. Cinna herself couldn't summon much feeling for the dead man. She knew Barth only through his shady business dealings with Hugo, whom she didn't like.

The other two women slumped on the log next to Cinna. Hokuren had the large brass key in her hand, turning it over and over, her mouth a thin line of concentration.

"What're we going to do with that key?" Cinna prodded Hokuren. "Find the chest and open it?"

Hokuren jumped at Cinna's touch, closing a tight fist over the key. To Cinna's surprise, the boss said, "Yes, I've taken your original advice. We're going to get the silks for ourselves and bring them to Ulbricht."

"You changed your mind, boss. Good." Cinna held out the bag of blueberries. "I thought for sure you'd never agree to that plan and instead suggest offering the key to Hugo in exchange for the silks. You know, keep it aboveboard."

"Hugo and the rest of the Consortium are the most likely suspects in Barth's murder. I like to do things the right way, but even I have my limits." Hokuren took a blueberry with a quick nod of thanks. "I'm no longer interested in seeing the Consortium get their cut, and besides, Hugo doesn't appear to be much for working things out like rational beings. We need that silk. With it, we might be able to get Ulbricht to reveal himself. He may ultimately be the one responsible for my father's death."

"Barth's death is my fault." Roz slammed a fist onto their log bench. "It had to be the Consortium. I said we should wait until this morning. He was probably killed last night. We could have been there to prevent it."

"You're not responsible, Roz. Only Barth's murderers are," said Hokuren. "Our best vengeance is uncovering Ulbricht's identity and putting an end to the entire smuggling operation, including the Gregorious Consortium." She tested her stockings and boots and put them back on, apparently finding them dry enough. "You said you knew where Hugo was headed last night. Could they be hiding the chest out there in the forest?"

"I'm certain their hideout includes the chest, yes," said Roz. She gritted her teeth. "I'll take you there. Anything to get back at them for what they've done."

"If we're doing this, check your dagger, boss," said Cinna. "Keep it accessible, and don't be afraid to use it. If they killed Barth, they could kill us."

"I left it in our room before we left for the bars last night," said Hokuren, with a rare sheepish look.

"You said we should always wear it, even while swimming! How could you leave it behind?" Cinna looked toward the Waterview, where they had left their belongings. "Hugo and his pals could be watching our room, though, since they didn't get the key they were looking for. Maybe it's not worth going back for."

Hokuren put her hand to her mouth, eyes widened. "Cinna, I left my mother's diary there. We have to go back."

Cinna nodded. "All right, but let's be careful." She turned to Roz. "Wait for us here."

Roz looked as if she might object, but when she glanced at Hokuren, her face changed. "You want that diary, huh? Don't dawdle."

It was a short walk to the inn. The same old woman who had been so defensive about the view of the water commanded the front desk. Cinna led Hokuren to the back entrance to avoid any interaction with the innkeeper. This poor excuse for an inn hadn't bothered to install a lock there.

Cinna slowly pushed the door open, revealing an empty hallway. She ushered Hokuren in, leaving the door open for an easier escape route if things got hairy. Their room was three units down from the rear. Cinna had Hokuren wait near where they entered, with instructions to flee if trouble started.

The rough, knotty wood floor was surprisingly quiet under Cinna's feet as she crept on her toes toward their room. A place like this usually had old, squeaky boards, but somehow the Waterview's wood defied the norm. Now that she was thinking about it, the doors made little noise when they swung on their hinges. The place was practically made for thieves.

At the door to their room, Cinna tried the knob they had locked when they left. The flimsy lock was still engaged, which meant one of two things: The room had been undisturbed, or someone had locked it back up after breaking in and now lay in wait.

Cinna prepared for the latter and stuck the key in and turned it as fast as she could. By jiggling the knob, she'd alerted anyone inside, so moving slowly and quietly no longer provided any advantage. She flung the door open to find their room precisely as they'd left it, with no sign of entry. She relaxed, feeling almost silly.

"Meow." A cat sauntered into Cinna's view, squeezing out from under the bed. Cinna rubbed her eyes, unbelieving, when she recognized the cat.

"Lumi! How'd you get in here?" Cinna looked around the room and at the tiny window, which was still closed shut. "Seriously, how *did* you get in here?"

"Merrorrrowww." Lumi became agitated and jumped against the wall to the left. Standing on her hind legs, she pawed it repeatedly.

Cinna didn't know cats well enough to understand if this meant something or if it was typical cat behavior. The boss should know about Lumi's appearance, though. Cinna poked her head out to call for Hokuren the moment the door to the left neighboring room burst open.

Hokuren cried out in surprise from the end of the hall, but Cinna called upon years of being barged in on by her rivals at the Sanctuary of the Eclipse to kick the door right back into whoever was exiting. With a grumbled curse, a man several inches taller than she and wearing a mask stumbled out and flung something silver at Cinna. She dropped to the floor to avoid what turned out to be a throwing knife that flew over her head.

Her assailant stomped at her prone form, but Cinna twisted aside and rammed a foot into his gut. The man made a hacking noise and fell back, holding his stomach. Cinna leaped to her feet and landed an uppercut to his hunched chin. He collapsed to the floor with a thud that jarred his mask loose.

Cinna took a deep breath to calm herself and quell the combat high. She had a moment of panic when she couldn't find Hokuren and dashed outside to find her on her way back with a large rock in her hands.

"What are you doing?" Cinna gently took the rock from Hokuren and tossed it aside.

"I was going to help." Hokuren's eyes were wide. She hated fighting and lacked skills beyond the basic bladework she learned in the Velles City Watch, but it was still nice to see her try to get involved.

The lanky man still lay in a crumpled heap where Cinna had left him. The unconscious face was unfamiliar.

"My bet is he's one of those Consortium guys, boss."

"I'd say there's a good chance, yes." Hokuren shivered. "Trying to end us like they did Barth."

"Thinking they could assassinate us with only one thin guy." Cinna deepened her voice to emulate Hugo. "'It's two *women*, it'll be easy, right, men?'" She snickered.

With Hokuren's help, Cinna dragged him into their room. Lumi re-emerged from under the bed again when the door reopened, meowed, and fled.

"A cat was in our room?" asked Hokuren. She looked back, but Lumi had already disappeared from view. "Hold on. Was that *Lumi*?"

Cinna nodded. "I know what you're going to ask next, and no, I don't know how the cat got into our locked room."

Hokuren made sure the door was closed and the lock set. "Honestly, the cat getting in here is less confusing than her following us all the way to Oro in the first place." She pulled a face. "I still don't like the feeling I got from her last time. I'm unsure of her motivations."

"She's a cat, boss. What motivations?"

"I admit it's ridiculous. But I stand by it."

"Is it because Lumi hisses at you?"

"There's more to it than that," said Hokuren, arms crossed over her chest.

"More to it, huh. So it *is* part of it." Cinna lifted the lanky man's hand and watched it fall back down. "I'd love to question him to see if he really is from the Gregorious Consortium, but it doesn't look like that's happening anytime soon."

Hokuren bent to check his pulse. "He's still alive, though I don't know when he'll wake. Help me tie him up in case he wakes up early and looks for revenge."

Cinna tore strips from one of the thin blankets and used them to bind the lanky man's hands and feet. The two of them hauled him onto the miserable bed and covered him with blankets.

They gathered their bags, strapped their daggers to their bodies within easy reach, and stepped back out into the mild Oro day. The innkeeper never came to check on them, so she must have smartly ignored their tussle.

Hokuren led them back at a brisk pace to the log where Roz waited. "We're ideally out of Oro before the Consortium knows we've knocked him out."

"He'll wake up with a headache, tied up. Few ways worse to do it."

Roz was waiting at the log, impatiently tapping her feet. They gave her a quick explanation of how they were waylaid at the inn and described the lanky man.

"Oh, yeah, sounds like a Consortium man," said Roz. "Not nearly the terror that Hugo is, though."

"How many are in the Consortium?" asked Hokuren.

"Four. Sounds like at least one won't be bothering us for a while." Roz nodded toward the forest. "The sooner we go, the better."

The dense brush of the forest floor provided a multitude of sensations under Cinna's bare feet, from nuts and branches to mushrooms and moss, all so much more pleasant than the tavern or the goblin tunnel. She had to disregard them and keep her attention on the task at hand.

She followed Roz, with Hokuren beside her, deep into the forest. It was uncomfortably muggy in the afternoon heat, and all of them took extra swigs from their waterskins. Cinna's tunic clung to her, sweat darkening several patches.

The path was so well-worn that they could have found their way to the end on their own. It ended at a clearing with a small shack built by inexpert hands. Moss filled the gaps between the uneven slats of wood that made up its exterior. A sagging tarp stretched over the walls, more akin to a hammock than a roof. A door leaned against a hole in the shack. To get in, they would need to physically pick up the door and move it aside.

The men of the Consortium hadn't bothered to make hinges.

"This is it," said Roz, flashing her hand at the dilapidated hovel.

It was empty, a fact confirmed by several minutes of listening outside, but they remained cautious. Cinna threw aside the door propped against the opening in the wall, fists at the ready. Beyond a firepit in the center ringed by blankets, however, the shack was indeed uninhabited.

"This should take us no time at all to look through." Hokuren entered after Cinna and gripped a floorboard, checking for a hidden trapdoor. "I'll bet they've got some type of secret underground storage for the chest."

"I'll go check around outside," said Cinna. The little shack didn't require all of them to search.

She cast her gaze across the clearing, unsure what to look for. Roz offered no help, leaning against the shack and affecting an air of boredom. She'd never make it as an investigator.

Cinna bent down and squinted for any sign of a secret passage: discolored grass or dirt, lines cut crudely into the earth, or, if they wanted to make it easy on her, a little sign that said, "Secret stash here."

No such sign was present, nor lines or discoloration. The ground was annoyingly solid. One tree remained in the clearing, the only one spared removal. It was easy to imagine why. The tree was ancient, its trunk twice as thick as the trees nearby and stretching tall into the canopy above. She paid special attention to the area surrounding the tree, crouching down to dig, but all she uncovered was earthworms.

She kept trying until Hokuren and Roz joined her, having come up empty as well.

"So, they really just have a boys' hideout in the woods?" Hokuren tapped a small stone with the toe of her boot in frustration, sending it rolling over to Cinna. "I thought for sure they'd be hiding something more."

"Smugglers need a place to feel safe, just like the rest of us," said Cinna.

"It has to be here, though," said Roz. "They come here all the time. They wouldn't keep their goods elsewhere."

"Hang on," said Hokuren. She was standing next to the enormous tree, scrutinizing it as if she were inspecting the bark for aphids. "How closely did you check out this tree?"

"I dug around it and found worms," said Cinna, worried that she'd missed something.

"Hmm." Hokuren circled the tree, then again. "Highly suspicious that it was left standing when all the others were cut down and cleared."

"Might be too much work."

Hokuren pressed her ear against the tree and knocked on the wood in several places.

"Are you all right, boss?" asked Cinna.

"Shhh," said Hokuren, pausing her bizarre work to put a finger to her lips before returning to her knocking. Finally, she stepped back from the tree. "The trunk is hollow."

"It's dead?" Cinna looked up at the massive canopy. The leaves populating the multitude of branches were still green and plentiful.

"Dying is probably a better way of putting it. No one's told the rest of the tree yet." Hokuren patted the trunk. "I can't find an opening. Could you give me a hand and bust it open?"

"Of course." Cinna strode up to the tree, doing circles with her arm to warm up.

"No, no," said Hokuren quickly. "Don't punch the tree. Just in case I'm wrong."

"Allow me." Roz strode up to the tree, mace in hand, and smashed the trunk. Her mace met no resistance, tearing through a thin layer of bark and revealing that Hokuren's guess was correct. The tree was hollowed out. A few more strikes ripped open a hole large enough to fit through.

Cinna waved Roz's mace away to look inside. Where the tree's thick trunk should have been was instead a shaft leading underground through a hole in the root system, a shaky rope ladder providing access to a tunnel below. Magical yellow lights affixed to the shaft's walls and tunnel below kept it well-lit.

Opposite the hole Roz created, there was a seam in the bark, outlined by the light from outside. "Oops, there's the door," said Cinna.

"So this is how Hokuren the seeker operates," said Roz, poking her head in to look down the tunnel.

"We need to get in and out. They'll suspect us the instant they see the hole we've made." Hokuren added a third head, and now all of them peered down inside the trunk. "Another goblin tunnel."

"I hope there's not another dead body at the end of this one," said Cinna. Though if it were Hugo's, she wouldn't shed any tears.

Roz backed up, holding her hands out. "No more tunnels for me. I'll keep watch up here for you."

"I suppose a lookout would be a good idea," said Hokuren. "If we don't come back, you can go get help."

"Or come down and save us," said Cinna. "Not that we'll need any saving."

Roz returned her mace to her hip and patted it. "If you do, I'll be here."

"Let's hope we don't," said Hokuren. "All right, let's go, Cinna. Find the chest, and get out."

They climbed down the ladder, Cinna going first because she was faster and didn't want to be stuck waiting for Hokuren to pick her way down the rope rungs. The tree's thick root system formed the walls of the shaft, sheared off and burned to black.

"How did they do this?" Cinna ran her fingers down the destroyed roots, causing charred bits to flake off.

Hokuren grunted from above her. "I only have one guess. This is the work of the rogue wizard. Explains how the rest of the tree looks so lively. It's an illusion."

"They're working with a *wizard*?" Cinna jumped the final few feet down. The tunnel ahead was empty.

"They may have happened upon a wizard's old, abandoned hideout." Hokuren eased to the tunnel floor, rubbing her hands. "The fire magic necessary to burn through the roots is consistent with the devastation at The Sleepy Hollow, however. All the more reason to get this done fast, before anyone realizes we're here."

Cinna skulked through the luminous tunnel on high alert. She was prepared to run into the Consortium boys. A rogue wizard was a different proposition altogether and gave her a rare sense of trepidation. Someone who could wield fire to create this tunnel presented a type of threat she'd never encountered.

In contrast with the previous tunnel, the construction of this one took human height into consideration. Cinna and Hokuren had plenty of headroom and could walk side by side with room to spare.

"Boss, are you thinking what I've been thinking about a wizard that can use fire magic like this?" asked Cinna, keeping her voice low.

Hokuren nodded. "It explains how devastating the fire at The Sleepy Hollow became."

The tunnel split in two directions in a *Y* shape. Hokuren bent down to peer at the dirt floor, where booted footsteps were vaguely visible. Since they went back and forth in both directions, Cinna couldn't determine the best path and was ready to flip a Fondencian coin for it.

"We go right," said Hokuren. She sounded confident. At Cinna's questioning glance, she continued, "Underneath the footprints is this wide stretch of displaced dirt, as if something heavy was dragged through."

"The chest," said Cinna.

"I'm hoping so."

Once again, the boss proved why she was the boss. Cinna led her down the right path, which quickly terminated at a dirt wall and wooden door complete with a built-in knob. They exchanged puzzled glances. Goblins didn't build doors, and they especially didn't install doorknobs. They'd done this for people.

Cinna ushered Hokuren behind her and swung the door open, ready for anything. But the small room on the other side of the door was empty save for a large chest in the center.

The box, made of lacquered wood trimmed with gold, was half as tall as Cinna and half as wide as the tunnels. Vertical straps of rope looped around the box tied it to the cart underneath. The biggest keyhole Cinna had ever seen had been built into the face of the chest. Her lockpicks, which suddenly seemed so small, may not have cracked a lock this size.

"Took a lot of effort to stuff a chest this big and heavy down in this hole," said Cinna. The stale air in the tunnel was much more tolerable than the smell of blood in the previous one, but it was still oppressive in its own way.

"Even the chest itself is worth a lot. Yet what's inside is apparently far more valuable." Hokuren removed the big brass key from her bag. "I can't imagine there's another giant lock out there."

The key fit, sliding in and clicking when Hokuren twisted it. She and Cinna exchanged grins, like they were thieves about to pull off the heist of their careers. Together they lifted the chest's heavy lid and exposed its contents.

Silks. They were neatly wrapped and came in various colors. Cinna reached in to touch them, running her hand over the expensive fabric. She'd rarely felt the soft, slippery sensation of silk in her life. It tended to be present at clothing stalls she could never afford to shop at. The original founders of the Sanctuary of the Eclipse fought in robes made of silk, though that tradition had long since died in the thousands of years before she arrived. She took a moment to close her eyes and enjoy the silk against her skin, imagining wearing one of those old Eclipse outfits, when her hand caught on something sharp, jabbing into her palm.

"Ow," she said, shaking her hand. "Something in here stabbed me."

"Let's see." Hokuren carefully removed the top layer of silk, revealing a set of six rectangular gray stones, their sides finely cut. She pulled one of the stones out and scrutinized it. "These are—"

"Looks like rocks." Cinna dug through the silks, looking for anything else of practical value, but came up empty beyond more stones further down. The precious layers of silks seemed to exist as nothing more than protective padding.

"You heard the smugglers say there was 'more to it' than silks, but these hardly seem valuable." Hokuren looked back at the tunnel. "Is this the right chest?"

"Seems unlikely there's another chest with this much silk in it." Cinna tossed a stone back and forth in her hands. In the dead quiet of the tunnel chamber, she heard the faint sound of water sloshing. "Wait." She held the stone to her ear and shook. Then she held her waterskin to the other ear for confirmation.

"What are you doing?" asked Hokuren.

"There's water inside this rock." Cinna picked up another and reproduced the sound. "Maybe all of them."

Hokuren listened to a stone as well. "We need to get them open. But how—" She turned the stone over in her hands. It looked solid.

Cinna raised a stone above her head. "We smash it open."

"Wait, wait, wait," said Hokuren, holding up her hand. "We don't know what this is. For all we know, they'll explode and hurl rock shrapnel once broken."

"Don't want that." Cinna lowered her arm and carefully cradled the stone.

Hokuren sighed with relief. "I think I know how to open them, but there's no reason to do it here. Let's take what we can and investigate further in safer confines."

They slipped their packs off and crammed in as many stones as they dared fit, using silks as buffer. It sent thrills up Cinna's spine. Theft, especially one she could justify, always did.

The unmistakable sound of footsteps, three sets of them approaching rapidly down the tunnel, interrupted her joy. Cinna closed the door. The small chamber offered little room to operate, with the enormous chest taking up half the area, but there was no escape option. They'd have to fight their way out.

Cinna waved Hokuren to a back corner, where she stood with dagger in hand. It was better than nothing, but Cinna wanted to avoid a situation where the boss had to use it.

The footsteps stopped at the door. "Hokuren Tuomi. I know you're in there." It was Hugo, his braying voice instantly recognizable. "Open up and we can talk about what happens next."

Neither woman responded.

"Hokuren!" barked Hugo, already dropping the polite act. "This door won't hold me back. If you do as I say, I might feel generous enough to let you leave."

"Did you make the same offer to Barth?" Hokuren asked. "And kill him when he refused?"

There was a moment of silence on the other side of the door. "Barth's dead?" The door rattled as Hugo tried to force his way in. "All I know is you're in there stealing our goods!"

Cinna posted herself in front of the door, waiting for it to open. She didn't wait long. Hugo crashed through, breaking the door off its hinges. Cinna got into a fighting stance, dagger in hand.

Hugo came with two associates, the skull-tattoo man from the tavern and a third man with a black mustache, aiming crossbows at her and Hokuren. Cinna hesitated.

"Move and they shoot," said Hugo.

Alone, she would have taken them. She could dodge the crossbows, maybe catch one of the bolts, pick them off one-by-one, and set herself up for an escape. But Hokuren didn't have crossbow bolt dodging or catching skills. Whatever Hugo's intentions, a fight now held too much risk of her getting hurt. So when Hugo grabbed Cinna by the arm and yanked her back the way they came, she grudgingly went along without a fight.

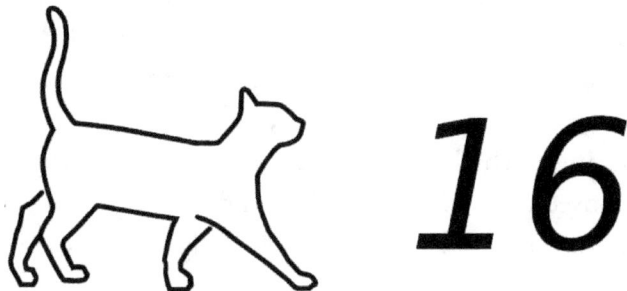

16

Cinna knelt on the ground next to Hokuren, sitting on her ankles with her hands raised at head level and visible as requested. They were otherwise treated as non-threats. Hugo and his two companions hadn't even bothered to tie Cinna up. The disrespect!

Hugo had marched them down the other path of the tunnel split, to the left, where a small room roughly twice the size of the shack awaited. A table, long and low to the floor, took up one half. Their daggers had been placed at the far end of it. Sitting at the table was the skull-tattoo man, his crossbow trained on them with unyielding consistency. He'd promised to shoot if either of them moved in any way he didn't like. Cinna didn't know how itchy his trigger finger was, and the vague instructions left her undaring to shift to a more comfortable position.

"This is your mermaid, then?" said Hugo, conferring with the other man near the room's entrance. His hushed voice was still audible in the otherwise silent atmosphere. "Hokuren's urchin?"

"She can swim like a mermaid, at least," said the other man, his mustache akin to the one described by the Fondence-bound lovers. He had to be Petros. He kept glancing at Cinna's legs as if looking for a tail. "I think we should be careful."

"I don't see any water." Hugo sneered.

Out of the corner of her eye, Cinna checked on Hokuren. The boss was holding it together well, despite being obviously petrified. Cinna swallowed her own fear. She hadn't figured out yet how to get both herself and Hokuren out of the situation safely. If only she'd tried to convince Hokuren to be the lookout with Roz and gone down alone.

Then she wondered what had happened to Roz. If the adventurer had run for help, or planned on following the Consortium in, she and Hokuren would only need to play for time. Those would be nice-to-have outcomes, but Cinna had to proceed as if no help was coming.

"Roz was working with them. I just think we should take them seriously." Petros moved up in Cinna's book a smidgen.

"Do you think I'm not?" said Hugo. The slight edge in his voice made Petros's eyes bug out.

"Of course not!" he squeaked. "You take everything seriously!"

"That I do."

Hugo pulled away from Petros and dragged a chair toward them, his lips curled up contemptuously. "So, Hokuren. Stealing from me as I suspected you would. Your father would be so disappointed in you." He held up one of their packs, still stuffed with silks and stones. In his other hand, he displayed the brass key to the chest. "Bet you thought you could steal the goods right from under my nose. You were almost right."

Fear created a quiver in Hokuren's voice, which almost certainly further emboldened Hugo. "We always intended to pay you for them. Only you refused to negotiate. You left us with no option."

"That so?" Hugo had a foot on the chair, leaning over them with his hands on his hips. With every movement, he was close to bursting out of his too-small shirt. "Well, what's the proposal?"

Hokuren swallowed. "If we can get the silks and these stones to Ulbricht, we can pay you with the money we get from him." It was what they'd discussed offering to Hugo at the tavern, had he not flown into a rage.

Hugo turned to his companions. "You hear that, boys? She thinks I offer credit to city folk and urchins." The boys chuckled, even though it wasn't very funny. Hugo returned his attention to Hokuren. "You understand that my level of trust in you at the moment is rather low."

"You don't have much choice if you'd like to get paid," said Cinna, stepping into the conversation for Hokuren. "We don't have any money."

"Liar!" Hugo thrust a finger in her face. "I know Hokuren inherited her father's business and his money. You should have plenty."

Cinna's gut tightened at his escalating anger. "Threaten all you want, but he left no money at all."

Hugo glanced at the skull-tattoo man. "What d'ya think? You believe her?"

"No," said the skull-tattoo man with a shake of his head.

Cinna assessed her increasingly urgent exit strategy. Petros blocked the path out with his stout body. He, like her interrogator, had given up his crossbow and had a dagger strapped to his person. Her move, when she made it, would ideally be made before they unsheathed their weapons.

The saving grace was that beyond the watchful eye of the skull-tattoo man, no one appeared alert for an escape attempt. Petros slouched at the door, eyes wandering, and Hugo strutted and swaggered from his perch on the chair.

The table was her best hope. Long and low to the floor, it ran almost the entire length of the shack. Hokuren could use it as shelter for her escape while Cinna distracted and battled the taller, bulkier men, somehow.

"I can tell you think I'm stupid," said Hugo, and Cinna had to catch herself from nodding in easy agreement. "I'll prove to you we ain't. Let's talk about the situation you're in." Hugo bent down to put his face directly across from Cinna's. She could smell his foul breath, a result of poor oral hygiene reinforced with the robust view of his rotten black teeth. "We know Ulbricht doesn't care about the silks. It's the stones he wants." He pointed at his head. "I gotta know my merchandise."

"The stones, yes," said Cinna, trying not to breathe his rancid breath in too deeply. "They were hidden."

Hugo laughed, causing Cinna to flinch as he showered her in disgusting spittle. "Not all that well. All I needed was to look through those silks and realize what's going on."

"But do you know what's in the stones?" said Hokuren, so tightly wound that Cinna worried she'd snap.

Hugo pulled back, to Cinna's great relief. "Something dangerous is my guess, that he doesn't want anyone knowing about." He aimed a crooked smile at Hokuren. "And so it would be bad for business if either of us did know more."

"I thought you knew your merchandise."

"I know exactly what I need to know. Tell 'em, boys." Hugo motioned to the other two men.

The skull-tattoo man didn't adjust his hold on the crossbow. "That's right."

"See." Hugo narrowed his eyes at Hokuren. "I bet Ulbricht's pissed about not getting them. He responds rather poorly to his shipments being late. I've heard stories. Something about choking the life out of you."

"First I'm hearing of that. If we delivered them, we'd get the money we could use to pay you," said Cinna, trying again to propose the best solution.

Hugo stroked his chin in a pantomime of thought. "Hmm, I'm considering it. But I still don't trust you. How about this? Hokuren takes the chest to Ulbricht, gets payment, and brings it back. To make sure she doesn't take the money and run, we hold her urchin hostage. When we have our money, we'll let her go."

Cinna flicked her vision over to the skull-tattoo man for a fresh visual on the crossbow, then back at Hugo.

"No deal," said Hokuren, through gritted teeth.

"But there's no other deal to be had." Hugo turned to the skull-tattoo man again. "We could stash the urchin in the cage while we wait for Hokuren to return. Tell 'em how nice and luxurious it is."

He never got a chance to discuss the cage's amenities, because Cinna would never consent to being "stashed" in one. She took her chance with Hugo's attention diverted.

First, she reached over and shoved Hokuren to the ground, ignoring the boss's cry of surprise.

Then Cinna lowered her shoulder into the chair Hugo preened on, tipping it backward. The unprepared smuggler pinwheeled his arms to stay upright. The skull-tattoo man shouted, followed closely by the unmistakable click of his crossbow bolt being released. Cinna dropped to the ground, the bolt whizzing past her head like an angry hornet and passing through the space Hokuren had occupied before Cinna had knocked her down.

Cinna lashed out at a chair leg with her foot, sending the off-balance

Hugo tumbling backward into Petros. The two men crashed to the ground in a squawking pile of curses.

The skull-tattoo man reloaded his crossbow. Cinna gave Hokuren, who had recovered enough to return to a seated position, a hand motion to get under the table. The boss obeyed with no argument, crawling toward it.

Cinna ran at the skull-tattoo man ahead of Hokuren and flung herself into a twisting slide that put her on her back, knees tucked to her chest and directly under the chair nearest the skull tattoo man. He brought the crossbow down as she kicked straight up with both feet at the underside of the chair's seat. The backrest slammed into his chin. He reeled, fired his reloaded bolt wildly astray, and crashed to the floor, eyes closed.

Hokuren made it under the table, so Cinna rolled out and stood up right into the face of Petros. She stepped back to avoid his dagger, tripping over the skull-tattoo man's body and crashing back to the ground in time to dodge the second swing. Petros's thrusting dagger followed as she lay draped over the skull-tattoo man. She reached out a hand, but it wouldn't be in time to stop—

A crossbow swung into view and connected with Petros's wrist with a crack. He yelped and pulled back, dropping his dagger. Cinna glanced in amazement at Hokuren, who held the skull-tattoo man's crossbow and panted. They exchanged a quick nod.

Cinna sprang to her feet again, looking for, and finding, Hugo. He yelled in rage and jumped over the table at both of them. Cinna shoved Hokuren, frozen in fear by his scream, out of the way toward the exit and spun aside from a potentially lethal punch. His back was to her now, but he loomed over a terrified Hokuren.

The daggers that had been removed from Cinna and Hokuren's possession were within reach. In a single motion, Cinna swiped one and drove it into the back of Hugo's shoulder. He howled and turned around with such shocking speed that she lost her grip. The weapon remained embedded in his body.

He threw a vicious punch that Cinna ducked, then another in rapid succession. The stab wound had merely enraged him. His swings were frenzied, but he would only need one of his enormous fists to connect to knock her out. She had to evade them all. Hugo kept coming, punch after punch, as Cinna slid back in the space between the wall and the table.

Cinna tried to catch Hokuren's attention and gesture with her eyes to leave, but Hugo's relentless assault didn't provide an opportunity. Her heel hit the rear wall of the room with her next step back. Hugo wore a manic grin. There was nowhere to go, and he had her pinned in a corner, his wide frame blocking an escape.

He aimed a punch at her torso. There was one thing he forgot to consider, however. Cinna slipped to the right, cramming herself into the corner. Hugo's fist slipped past her and followed through directly into the rough, hard-packed dirt wall with a crunch.

Hugo screamed and reared back, grabbing his broken hand. Cinna bolted from the wall and planted a kick into his stomach. He tumbled to the ground, thoughtlessly attempting to break his fall with his ruined hand. A roar of pain was followed by writhing on the ground, hugging his arm against his stomach.

Their packs full of the stolen contents of the chest were close enough that Cinna grabbed them on her way out, also taking a moment to pluck the dagger free from Hugo's shoulder as he struggled in pain. Hokuren had picked up the other dagger and harried Petros near the room's exit. The smuggler cradled his wrist and sniveled.

"Come on," said Cinna, handing Hokuren a pack.

They ran through the tunnel and climbed the rope ladder. Cinna looked back to see if any of the Consortium followed, but there was no pursuit.

Cinna breathed in deeply when she emerged into the fresh air of the forest. She helped Hokuren make the last rung of the ladder and looked around for Roz.

"Roz?" called Hokuren.

An indistinct sound came from the direction of the shack. It could have been a moan. Cinna held up a hand to Hokuren and approached slowly. She peeked into the shack.

Roz was alone, sitting on the ground, her hands tied behind her back with twine to a pin driven into the wood floor.

"Oh, so they tied *you* up. I see." Cinna cut Roz free. "Great work on being the lookout."

"They got the drop on me, all right?" grumbled Roz, rubbing red wrists. "Looks like you got out all right."

"We did. They're looking less good." Cinna nodded out the shack's door at Hokuren. "You should have seen the way she turned Petros's wrist into splinters. Saved me."

Hokuren poked her head in. "You did most of the work." Her voice shook. "Come on, let's get somewhere safe."

They hastily retreated to Oro. It was nearly dark by the time they reached the town. They'd missed the evening wagon to Fondence and would have to wait until morning. It was unlikely any of the members of the Gregorious Consortium would be in shape to hunt them down at an inn, but Roz suggested setting up a campsite to be on the safe side.

"I know a spot. It's secluded," she said.

A cozy fire crackled in the center of a small patch of dirt with room for three people to lie down. Roz called it her secret site, a half-hour walk into the forest on the other side of Oro. She shared food with Cinna and Hokuren, who'd crammed so much silk and stone into their packs no room for food remained. Cinna repaid Roz by regaling her with the tale of their capture at the hands of, and escape from, the men of the Consortium.

Hokuren stayed up for the first watch while the other women went to sleep.

She considered working more on her mother's diary, using the fire for light, but beyond the risk of setting the diary ablaze, she wouldn't be able to focus on it. The encounter with the Consortium clung to her, and she feared the nightmares she would face in the coming nights. Either she or Cinna could have been killed, or Cinna imprisoned for days or weeks while she tried to bring the goods to Ulbricht for payment. It sent shivers down her spine. Cinna was much better at compartmentalizing these sorts of things.

Roz woke up and joined her after a few hours. She was supposed to take the second watch, but Hokuren had no interest in sleeping. Roz offered to share a bottle of wine she'd hidden in her pack, and Hokuren accepted.

"They didn't hurt you, did they?" asked Hokuren. She took small sips, judiciously keeping her head straight.

"Nah. A couple of them had crossbows, I had to concede." Roz took sizable swigs of the wine and made a satisfied smack of the lips after each one. "I'm sorry. I'm glad you and Cinna got out of there in one piece."

"It was thanks to Cinna." Every time Hokuren saw Cinna in action, she marveled at how fast Cinna moved and how unforgivably brutal she could be when necessary. Fortunately, she was on Hokuren's side.

Roz finished another generous drink with a burp. She tipped the bottle toward Cinna's sleeping form before passing it again to Hokuren. "She didn't seem as shaken as you."

"Cinna believes in the invincibility of her youth."

"Aren't you two almost the same age?"

Hokuren smiled. "I've never believed myself to be invincible."

They passed the bottle around a few more times. Hokuren drank less and less until she was merely tipping the bottle back, swishing the wine around, and handing it over without so much as a drop touching her lips. If Roz noticed, she made no indication.

The bottle was nearly empty when Hokuren said, "We found stones mixed in with the silks."

"Interesting," said Roz. Her eyes were unfocused.

"Hugo suggested that they're what Ulbricht really cares about."

"I don't know." Roz shrugged. "All I've ever heard'a was the silks."

"Roz." Hokuren wanted to grab Roz by the collar and shake her. The lie was written all over her face, and it galled that she thought she could get this over on Hokuren. "If these stones are important, they played a role in my father's death. No more holding back. What are they?" She peered into Roz's eyes. "What has my father been bringing into Fondence?"

Roz snatched the wine bottle and, before Hokuren could stop her, finished it in one long guzzle. She let loose a sigh and rolled her head back, looking up at the sky.

"It's supposed to be a secret, you know, but you're the seeker of truth, ain'tcha. You'd figure it out eventually. I admit it, I knew they were the true prize of the smuggling operation. I never saw the stones myself. Barth always checked for them. I just received a locked chest to escort to Fondence and deliver to Ulbricht."

"There's something inside them," said Hokuren. "Something liquid."

"I don't want to know any more than I already do," snapped Roz, her damaged voice cracking with strain. Cinna made a noise and stirred on the ground, causing Roz to hunch in guilt. In her normal breathy whisper, she continued, "As an adventurer, I escorted goods all the time. You learn to stop caring what you're escorting, ya know? It doesn't pay to be inquisitive. Someone gives you a job to make sure no one takes their stuff, so you make sure no one takes their stuff. It can be coin, it can be rice, it can be a wagon full of filthy smut. It stops being interesting—well, okay, maybe you look at the filthy smut to pass the time. But you just want to get whatever it is where it needs to go, get paid, and move on."

Roz reached for her throat, struggling with the uninterrupted stream of words. Now so quiet that Hokuren could barely hear her, she continued, "I don't need to know what's in the stones to get what I want. They just need to make it to Ulbricht."

She had lost Hokuren the moment she said it didn't "pay to be inquisitive." Hokuren sighed. "Did my father know?"

"Maybe." Roz fumbled for the empty bottle and stared into it, as if hoping it was the type that magically refilled with endless wine. No luck, which was ultimately to her long-term benefit. "He asked a few times, that I recall, but never got an answer. He eventually stopped talking about it."

Creeping disappointment settled into Hokuren. Her father had always been proud of running a successful business while maintaining his integrity. The secrecy surrounding the items coming in should have been a red flag. If her father didn't know what he was helping to smuggle in, then he'd changed in the years since she'd seen him last. Hokuren pursed her lips, thinking of the many people she'd seen in her time in the Watch who started with the noblest of intentions before allowing their morals to degrade in the name of a little more coin. Her father may have gone down the same route.

There remained the possibility that he had been coerced from the start. Whatever happened, he'd ended up dead. It was Ulbricht, not the goblins, that emerged as the most likely candidate responsible.

To take her mind off this unhappy train of thought, she switched up her questioning. "You said you'll 'get what you want.' What is that?"

Roz didn't respond at first, creating a silence that hung in the air. Hokuren didn't fill it, and eventually Roz relented. "Guess I said too much. You already know, though." She flipped the bottle in her hands. "I want my voice back."

"You mentioned a plan when we first saw each other again, yes. I've never heard of such a thing. And how do the stones factor?"

"The stones don't, really. Look, you can't tell anyone else, but it's been promised to me." Roz twisted her mouth. "I have to take the chance that she isn't leading me along. I'd do anything to get my voice the way it used to be. To be able to sing again."

"Who is 'she'?"

Roz grabbed Hokuren's hand. "Please, I'm trusting you with this." She took a deep breath. "Moira."

Hokuren flinched at the name. "Are you sure you can trust her? She's not the same as I remember from when we were children." That was the safest way to put it, anyway.

"What do you mean?" Roz gave her a sharp look, cutting through her drunkenness. "She's the same witch she's always been, and she says she's been working on a solution. And as long as I keep Ulbricht happy, she'll provide it when it's done."

Hokuren furrowed her brow. "Why does she want to keep Ulbricht happy? Who is he anyway?"

"No one knows. Least of all me." Roz shrugged. "Does it matter? Again, I'm not asking useless questions that might only work against me."

A vague sense of dread worked its way through Hokuren's mind. "Why is he so secretive about all of this? These stones—"

"Doesn't matter," said Roz flatly. "I'm not risking my voice for curiosity. No one else is putting their neck out for no gain, either." She laughed, a hoarse snicker. "When an investigation could ruin a profit, seeker, it's the profit most of us choose. My profit is my voice. For Moira, it's whatever Ulbricht is offering her. For the smugglers and your father, it's about the coin."

Hokuren had no argument against the thesis. She picked investigation over profit and struggled to stay afloat financially. "Well, for what it's worth, I hope you do get your voice back." She kept further skepticism about the false Moira's intention to follow through to herself. Doubtful Roz would be interested in entertaining the idea.

"Me too."

The infatuation Hokuren had been fighting ever since returning to Fondence didn't die, but it had been wounded. Roz's incurious nature and single-minded obsession with her voice didn't sit well with Hokuren. If these stones were some sort of weapon, magical or otherwise, she wondered if Roz would still express nonchalance about her role in bringing them into Fondence.

Okay, if Hokuren was being *truly* honest with herself, the infatuation hadn't changed. But her desire to act upon it had been disrupted, at least.

The fire was dying. Roz got up to place more wood down. The embers turned back into crackling flames as she rejoined Hokuren on the ground with a flask.

Roz raised the flask. "To Barth." She took a swig.

"To Barth," said Hokuren, drinking from her waterskin. "Were you and Barth close?"

Roz looked away. "Not particularly, but I didn't want him to die. I'll pay the Consortium back for that one of these days."

"I'm sorry." Hokuren stared into the fire. Something about the Consortium as the murderers didn't fit right in the puzzle in her mind. Hugo had sounded sincere in his confusion over Barth's death. "The Consortium left without the key. That's a little strange."

"You almost missed the little mound as well."

"But they went out to that cove and *killed* him. They must have truly believed he had the key." Hokuren put her hand to her chin. "They should have torn that little room apart. It's not like there were many places to look."

"It's not like it was obvious." Roz threw her arms up in the air. "They're not professional investigators like yourself. Couldn't they have missed it?"

"Of course. Yet Barth had valuable items, like the comb and rings. They're professional smugglers, and doubtless a group like that could find ways to profit off those. It's surprising they would skip an opportunity to make some easy coin, given their obsession with doing so."

"They probably wanted to make it look like goblins."

"If so, they did a terrible job of it." Hokuren sighed. Barth's murder was hardly the most pressing mystery at the moment, but she hated to leave a case unsolved. She didn't even know what he'd hoped to achieve through the key's theft. If he'd worked with Hugo for some time, surely he understood that was not a man who would let him go with a warning.

"Well, who the flames knows about goblin pick-pocketing like Cinna does." Roz grunted and took another drink from her flask. "You know, the two of you've got guts, seeker, stealing from the Consortium. I worry they won't rest until they get you back."

"I'm hoping Fondence is too far away for them."

"Hey, just turn Cinna loose on them again." Roz grinned. "Sounds like she can handle them well enough." She returned to her flask, swirling the contents. "Speaking of Cinna, what's the deal with you two?"

"Cinna is family," said Hokuren, twisting to view Cinna sleeping. "We take care of each other, in our own ways."

"Family. I see." Roz faced Hokuren, eyelids heavy. "You liked me back when I was singing, didn't you?"

Hokuren's heart fluttered, like it had when she saw Roz in Fondence for the first time in years. She wouldn't act on it, she reminded herself. "I did. It was a simple childhood crush, though."

"Was it?" Roz's lip quirked upward. "Then why's it lingering a dozen years later?"

"I—" Hokuren was at a rare loss for words. She struggled to think of something, but Roz put a finger on her lips to silence her.

"It's okay." Roz stood up, wincing and flexing her right knee. "Old adventurer injury," she said to Hokuren's look of concern. "So, if you settle things and hang around Fondence a bit longer, maybe . . ." She gathered up her pack.

Hokuren wished the wine bottle weren't empty. She had the sudden urge to take an enormous pull. Her throat dry, she said, "Where are you going? It's the middle of the night."

"Take care of your family," said Roz. "I'll see you later."

"Wait—"

Roz swept into the forest brush, leaving Hokuren sitting at the fire alone, trying to make sense of the last few minutes. She'd told herself she didn't want to act on any of her feelings for Roz even as the feel of Roz's finger lingered on her lips.

Hokuren took several deep breaths, calming herself. Roz had left in such a hurry. There had to be a reason. As she replayed the conversation in her mind, puzzle pieces that weren't fitting before locked into place. She put a hand to her mouth. She knew who killed Barth, and it wasn't anyone from the Gregorious Consortium.

It was Roz.

17

Roz didn't make another appearance in Oro before Cinna and Hokuren boarded the morning wagon back to Fondence. Neither did Hugo or any other member of the Gregorious Consortium. Hokuren wasn't sure which she'd rather see less.

Their driver this time, a small elven man, had elevated suspicion in her mind by smacking his lips when he first caught sight of their packs so stuffed with the silks and stones they had taken on a spherical shape. However curious he was, he never tried to sneak a look inside.

Perhaps Cinna, once informed of Hokuren's concern, putting an arm around his shoulder, playing with her dagger, and explaining the consequences of such an action (she promised to separate him from any fingers she deemed too sticky) had put him off the idea.

In the relative security of the wagon, Hokuren told Cinna about her overnight conversation by the fire, including her ultimate conclusion of Roz's culpability.

"How can you suspect Roz?" said Cinna, shock clear on her face. "She was the one who led us to Barth's dead body in the first place!"

"It's a bad idea for a murderer to return to the scene," acknowledged Hokuren. "But she's obsessed with completing the shipment of stones to Ulbricht, because she thinks that will help her get her voice back. By putting the key in our hands, she made it possible for us to skip the drawn-out payment negotiation process. I think Roz realized from my questions that it wasn't long until I suspected her. There was a . . .

distracting conversation right before she took off."

Hokuren's cheeks heated at the memory of Roz putting that finger on her lips. This time, it was not her infatuation responsible. Roz had played with her emotions. She tugged at a button on her coat until it strained against the threads holding it in place. She should have seen through it, instead of pretending that a decade-old crush meant something.

"Hmm." Cinna pressed her fist into her chin in thought. "Why did she need to kill him?"

Hokuren cleared her throat. "Barth threw an additional wrench in getting the stones to Ulbricht by holding onto the key, thinking it gave him leverage over the Consortium. My guess is she confronted him, he refused to give up the key, tempers flared, and—" Hokuren frowned. "I don't think Barth thought she'd kill him for it."

"She still didn't take the key, even after he was dead."

"She couldn't find it. You didn't see this, but she got angry when I thought it strange the Consortium would miss the mound in the tunnel because they should have searched harder for the key. She took personal offense."

"Gotta know when to let the insults slide off. I bet I've got more experience than her in that realm," said Cinna. "Is she working with the Consortium?"

Hokuren shook her head. "I don't think so. When I accused Hugo of killing Barth, his surprise that Barth was dead seemed genuine."

"Seems that people who get in the way of these stones reaching Ulbricht get murdered. First your father, and now Barth." Cinna looked away. "If Roz killed Barth, do you think—"

"She killed my father?" Hokuren drew a sharp breath. "I hadn't even considered it, but can I really say she didn't?"

"That would be cold, boss, to have done that and act all friendly." Cinna's face hardened. "Next time we see her, I'll treat her like the threat she is."

Hokuren felt a bitter taste in her mouth. "My feelings for Roz kept me from considering her the culprit. I didn't immediately appreciate what she meant when she said she'd do anything to get her voice back." She clicked her tongue ruefully. "She's not the person I thought she was when I was young. Apparently, no one was."

"She might not have killed your father, you know."

"True. Even if she did, it would likely have been on the orders of that Ulbricht and this false Moira. They'd ultimately be responsible." She rummaged through her pack and pulled out a stone. "It's all because of these."

"Ah, the rocks." Cinna rapped on the outside of the stone with her knuckles. "I wish we knew what's inside."

"We're about to find out."

Cinna's face lit up. "We're going to smash them now?" At Hokuren's glance, she clasped her hands together and added, "If they explode and kill us, I'll apologize."

"That's the least you could do. But I have a better idea." The stones reminded Hokuren of the fake rock her father had set outside his home.

She drew the curtains over the wagon's windows and lit the candle lanterns inside the carriage. She didn't want to risk anyone looking in, no matter how remote the possibility on the forest path, hours from any town.

"What idea do—"

"Shhh." Hokuren slowly traced her finger up and down the stone, eyes closed, searching for the tiniest hint of irregularity. It would be easy to miss, so she concentrated all her focus on feeling at the tip of her finger.

There! The smallest of bumps, confirmed with another pass over. This stone was more sophisticated than the one outside her father's house. But not good enough. Hokuren smiled and used her nail to disengage the latch.

The top of the stone slid open and fell to the wagon floor, revealing the contents.

"Ugh," said Hokuren.

"A worm," said Cinna, craning her neck to get a better view.

The slender worm, faintly pink and translucent, swam in water colored brown from various suspensions and sediments. Its tiny beating hearts, five in total, were visible as it squirmed within its minuscule living area. Drops of water sloshed out with each bump of the wagon wheels over the terrain.

Hokuren fixated on the creature. She wanted to look away, but she couldn't. This thing was so valuable that silk was used as packing material for it. "What does it do?"

"A lot of wiggling, looks like," said Cinna.

"Where's the top to this?"

"Here." Cinna handed Hokuren the piece that had dropped away. "You're more than welcome to cover that back up."

The top fit smoothly back into place and locked with the tiniest of clicks. Hokuren opened two more, both worms. She and Cinna were silent for a long time, staring at the collection of stones. Hokuren's mind, in a rare experience, was stuck, like clockwork gummed up by a blocked cog.

Finally, Hokuren said, "My father made these."

Cinna's eyes widened. "He made *worms*? No wonder you left."

"No, the stone containers. I can only hope he didn't know about the worms." She buried her face in her hands. Everything she learned only seemed to make things worse. Her mother and father, implicit in a wizard's unknown scheme.

"I'm glad you talked me out of my idea of smashing it open. Imagine getting showered with disgusting water and a slimy worm."

Hokuren wished she couldn't, but of course that was all she could now picture.

The worry that Hugo, suffering from hitherto unseen levels of fury and humiliation, would chase their wagon down hounded Hokuren the entire trip back to Fondence. She didn't believe his busted hand would stop him.

Cinna and Hokuren kept the nightly watches while their blissfully ignorant driver slept. By the second night, with Fondence a three-hour morning ride away, Hokuren was more at ease. If the Consortium was going to attack them, they would have done it by then.

The whirlwind Oro adventure had left Hokuren with no time to continue her work on deciphering her mother's diary, but she managed a few more pages on the return trip. They were more mundane, describing the bridge games Lady Belladonna had spoken of or highlights of her twin brothers growing up. The last personal note tore at Hokuren's heart.

It's been twelve years since my twin boys were born, and I'd all but given up on having any more children. Though Mikko and I never stopped trying, these things are not always up to us. Yet just as I'd given up hope, here I am, with child once again. The goblin work is important. This child, moreso. I've asked for help from a trusted colleague while I care for my child during their most formulative period. I promised the goblins I would return to the work after a year with my child and finally resolve the most vexing issue of their vulnerability to witch magic because of <unclear>.

I know I shouldn't say things like this, but this is my diary and no one should be reading it anyway: I do so hope it's a girl. I could show her so many things.

Hokuren read it again in the chilly stillness of the night during her shift on watch. What had her mother planned to show her? She would never know. A tear fell and smudged symbols in the diary where it landed. Hokuren cursed and wiped her eyes dry. Crying while on watch was unacceptable.

A rustling beyond the light of the lantern hooked to the end of the wagon brought Hokuren to full alert. She froze, the coldness along the back of her neck having nothing to do with the ambient temperature.

"Don't be alarmed," said someone from the bushes. The high-pitched voice didn't pronounce the words correctly with a familiar whistle.

Hokuren wasn't alarmed, instead settling into a wary apprehension. "You're the goblin that helped our wagon. The one that could talk," she said out to the pitch-black forest.

The voice's response was strained. "I can hear your suspicions of me and understand them, but please do not call for your companion."

"Why? What if you're dangerous? You speak far more eloquently than you let on." Hokuren's hand went to the hilt of her dagger. "What else are you hiding?"

"Quite a lot," admitted the goblin. "I do wish to reveal it to you. Yet your friend is violent and protective of you. You have your hand on your dagger, but I can tell you've no desire to use it. She would. Call her, and I will have no choice except to flee, and you'll never see me again."

Hokuren had to risk it. This goblin knew her mother and could shine a light on the writings in the diary. Though Cinna would be furious, Hokuren said, "Okay. Stay at the edge of the light. Come close and I'll wake her."

The bushes rustled again. "Agreed. I'm coming out, hands up and unarmed."

The goblin that emerged was not only far better dressed than any Hokuren had ever heard of, he'd put the majority of attendees at a Vellesian dinner party to shame. He'd ditched the tunic from their last meeting for trousers held up by a leather belt and a white shirt under a black coat. His ears popped out from holes cut into his hat before flopping onto the brim. Well-made leather shoes completed the ensemble.

Hokuren opened and closed her mouth twice before coming up with something to say. "Nice outfit," she managed inanely.

"Thank you," said the goblin, pulling at his coat. "Also, a slight correction, if I may. All goblins can talk. We speak our own language. What I can do is speak a language you *understand*."

Her first conversation with a goblin, and Hokuren was immediately chastened. "I'm sorry. I meant—"

The goblin held up a hand. His claws were short and, as far as Hokuren could tell, well-manicured. "It was pedantic of me to have corrected you. Apologies, that's not what I'm here to accomplish."

"Are you here to explain what you know about my mother?"

"In part. First, an introduction is in order." The goblin removed his hat and bowed with a flourish. "I am Greeze, representative of my goblin pack. We are small, but capable of human speech, mannerisms, and dress, hidden within the forests of Fondence for over three decades."

Questions whizzed through her mind like bees running a hive, but she maintained her composure. "I'm Hokuren, a seeker from Velles."

Greeze looked ashamed. "Such introductions on your side are unnecessary, Hokuren. I know much about you and Cinna. I must apologize once again, for my pack and I have kept close surveillance on you since your arrival."

"What?" New questions entered Hokuren's mind. "Was it you who broke in and drew on my walls and stole my mug?"

"I confess."

Hokuren returned her hand to the hilt of her dagger. "You wrote that I was a betrayer. That mug was used to implicate us in an arson. I demand an explanation."

Greeze bowed his head again, this time without a flourish, and stayed bowed. "The answer is complicated. We did not do that of our own volition, please believe me. The reason we drew on your walls is why I'm here now, risking everything to speak to you."

"And that is?"

"We were, quite literally I'll add, compelled to." The goblin's clawed fingers ran over the hat. "I had hoped I'd gained some of your trust by helping you get unstuck from the mud."

Hokuren narrowed her eyes. "You dug that hole to get us stuck in the first place."

"I—well, that's—"

"It was suspicious, you showing up right when we needed you."

Greeze fell to his hands and knees on the muddy path, prostrating himself in front of her. "I admit it! But I need your help. And you do owe us. Free us from our curse!"

Hokuren lowered her gaze. Greeze slumped in front of her, and she saw for the first time the bags under his big yellow eyes, a dark purple against the dull green of his skin. "I don't understand why you keep saying I owe you. Certainly I don't if you freed us from your own trap. Plus, you've lost me with this talk of compulsion and curses."

"It's through your familial ties." The goblin looked up from the ground. "You're the daughter of Nekane, the one who first learned to dominate our minds."

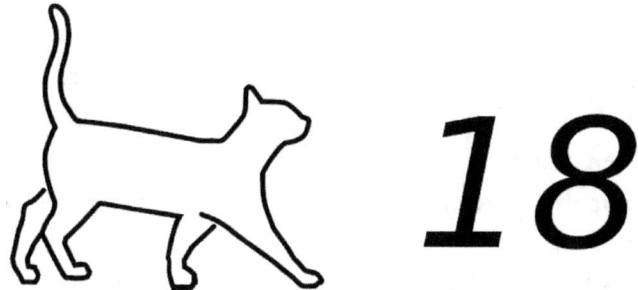

18

Hokuren said nothing for several moments, her mouth agape as she tried to process what the goblin had just told her. "My mother," she said weakly. "She never—" She stopped. She had not uncovered the full details of what her mother did from the diary.

"Nekane Tuomi, your mother, granted us the desire to learn human speech and influenced our sartorial choices," said Greeze, unfazed by Hokuren's denial. "All due to her studies into our brains that also led her to realize how susceptible we are to the influence of witch magic."

"No. My mother wouldn't do this. She believed goblins were intelligent and worth helping. She wouldn't dominate—"

"I was there for it, Hokuren," cut in Greeze sharply. "Before you were born. She knew what she was doing with her 'help.' She would not have wanted it to go in the direction it has, but Nekane provided the tools."

Hokuren tucked her arms against her stomach, bile rising. "I believe in knowing everything, but this . . . not this."

"The wizard wields significant power over us. As Nekane's daughter, I thought maybe you'd have some of the same skills to help us."

"The wizard?" repeated Hokuren. "It's witch magic that my mother used."

"You don't even know this?" Greeze stood up and wiped mud from the knees of his trousers. "Indeed, it's a wizard with access to witch magic. A great danger to us all. He calls himself Ulbricht."

Hokuren stiffened. "*Ulbricht?*" She thought of the stones in the wagon, destined for Ulbricht, now fearful of what they might contain. "There's a man with that name in Fondence. I've yet to see him, however."

"I've seen him in disguise, one of his many. None know his true face. Around here, at least."

Her father's import business and her mother's stolen witch magic research were both tied to Ulbricht, the rogue wizard. "Did Ulbricht kill my father?" Hokuren asked.

Greeze blinked at the question. "Ulbricht gave us instructions to kill him. However, we never found him."

Hokuren tucked her chin into her hand. "Then Ulbricht could have done it himself."

"I can't say." The goblin shrugged. "He stopped having us search."

Her father wasn't alive. The Pigeon Couriers spell would only end when his soul disconnected from his body, and not even the demons had figured a way to do so without death as the result. Hokuren told herself this over and over. He must have uncovered what Ulbricht was doing, or gotten cold feet about continuing the smuggling.

Whatever the reason, Ulbricht had killed her father. Or had him killed. Same difference.

"If what you are saying is true, Ulbricht is our common enemy," Hokuren said, clenching her fists. "Perhaps together we can uncover his identity and stop whatever he's doing with my mother's research."

"You know less than I hoped, but I can accept an ally." Greeze glanced around. "We should cease our discussion before it is discovered. Come find me tonight, in the woods to the north of your father's home. There is more you should know. I'd rather show you than tell you."

The goblin disappeared into the black night before Hokuren could ask anything else, including for more specific directions.

"Wait!" she cried. She jumped off the back of the wagon and ran to the edge of the lantern light's radius. "Greeze, come back!"

"Hokuren!" Cinna burst from the wagon, wide awake, and trotted to where Hokuren stood. "What's wrong?"

Hokuren stared out into the darkness. She considered asking Cinna to run after Greeze, but their previous run-ins with the goblin north of Fondence had proved they could easily evade Cinna. If the goblin didn't want to be found, he wouldn't be.

"Everything's fine. I'll explain in the wagon," said Hokuren.

Cinna had a guilty look on her face. "Actually, I know. I, um, heard the whole thing."

"You were awake?"

"I heard you start talking, and then the goblin said he didn't want me out there." Cinna waved her hands. "Sorry for eavesdropping, but if he did something, I wanted to be—"

Hokuren smiled and wrapped an arm around Cinna. "It's okay. I'm glad you heard, saves me the trouble of repeating it all to you."

Cinna relaxed. "So, are we going to head out north tomorrow night?"

"Absolutely."

Hokuren sighed and took the locket out from underneath her shirt. In the flickering light of the lantern, she viewed the image of her mother, the one she'd seen so many times it was seared into her memory.

It looked different now, though, the infallibility of her mother's person shattered by Greeze's claims that she was the reason goblins like him were subjugated by the wizard.

"Mother," she said to the picture in the locket. "Please don't let this be true."

A misty rain greeted Hokuren and Cinna upon their arrival in Fondence and persisted all day and into the night, accompanying them on their trudge through the forest in the darkness.

"I miss Oro already," said Cinna, grabbing at her increasingly wet hair to wring it out. "There's a beach, and it doesn't rain all the time like it does here. If you ignore the violent maniac smuggler who roams unrestrained with his pals, Oro's pretty perfect."

"It does rain in Oro. It just hasn't while we've been there," said Hokuren, prickly and defensive of her hometown.

Though the forest near Oro and this one were technically one, there were subtle differences this far inland. Fondence's penchant for rain encouraged trees that grew higher than the ones near Oro. The wet earth also fostered a more vibrant floor biome, the most obvious result being an explosion of mushrooms all throughout, dotting the ground like freckles.

"The goblin didn't even say how far to head north?" asked Cinna after they'd walked long enough to see the moon move behind the clouds.

"I can only assume he wanted us to get far from the city. He'll probably come find us, like he did our wagon last night." Hokuren lifted her lantern and peered into the small radius of light it provided, in case she might spot the goblin before he made himself known.

Cinna's eyes darted back and forth. "Maybe he's trying to lead us into a trap."

"I assure you, dear Cinna, I do no such thing." The voice came from the darkness behind them.

Hokuren jumped and spun around to aim her lantern light at Greeze, dressed in the same outfit he'd worn the previous night. Or it was a different goblin. If another goblin put on Greeze's clothes, she'd be unlikely to tell the difference.

"Stay back!" exclaimed Cinna. Greeze flinched and backed up a step.

Hokuren waved Cinna down. "It's okay. This is Greeze. He's into introducing himself from the shadows." To the goblin, she asked, "How long have you been following us?"

"Not long," said Greeze, recovering when Cinna lowered her fists. "We're close to the place I want to show you. Come, follow me."

The goblin scampered through the forest, deviating slightly from the path due north. His jog was their brisk walk, so they had no trouble keeping up with him. When they reached a spot in the forest that appeared no different from the surrounding acres, he stopped and declared, "We're here."

"There's nothing here," said Cinna. "Except the trap, I bet."

"There's no trap!" Greeze's words came out clipped and snarled in frustration. He calmed himself, waving a clawed hand in front of his face as if to reset it, and returned to the gentle tone Hokuren had grown accustomed to. "We must wait for what I wish to present to you."

"Can you tell us what it is, then?" asked Hokuren. "I'd rather not be caught off guard."

The goblin bowed his head. "Any explanation I make would do it a disservice, and you may not believe me, anyway."

After a few minutes of standing in silence, Cinna searched out a stump for the two of them to sit on and see out the wait. Greeze stood several feet away.

"This had better be good," Cinna muttered under her breath to Hokuren.

"Good is a matter of personal subjectivity," said Greeze. "I can only promise that Hokuren, at least, should find it worthwhile."

"He's got ears like a bat," said Cinna.

Hokuren bounced with nervous energy. She kept looking out into the forest, expecting another goblin to arrive, maybe one with more information than Greeze had.

Then a speck of bluish-white light materialized in front of them. More lights formed around it, circling the speck before swirling together into a shapeless blob sprouting the vaguest of limbs. It was a sight Hokuren had witnessed in Fondence's graveyard during her nighttime vigils at her mother's grave as a child.

They were witnessing a ghost form.

Someone had died out here, far from Fondence. Other than goblins, she and Cinna might have been the first to see this ghost. The light show continued, shaping itself into a human. As this process completed, Hokuren's hand went to her mouth. It couldn't be. The face on the ghost was one she'd viewed countless times, depicted in the locket she wore around her neck. Her breath caught, her voice almost failing her.

"Mother," she whispered.

19

Hokuren stood up and reached for the ghost. "Mother, is this really you?"

The ghost's materialization completed. The lights settled into a harsh, bright blue that bathed the forest in illumination stronger than daytime sunlight. Looking at it strained Hokuren's eyes, but she couldn't tear her gaze away. Standing in front of her was a replica of her mother as she would have been in life.

"It is her." Cinna, behind Hokuren, spoke in hushed tones. "But this isn't the graveyard."

"Who—Who's there?" the ghost gripped its collar with a blue hand. Its voice was muffled, as if it were talking from behind a wall.

Ghosts hadn't the slightest understanding of the world around them, and any interactions with them were one-sided. They would emerge into being and settle into acting out a scene of their invention, a sort of one-person play of a powerful memory the soul had stored of the person it once inhabited.

Hokuren knew all this, and yet couldn't stop herself from saying, her voice cracking, "It's me, Mother. Hokuren. Your daughter."

"Oh, it's you." The image relaxed, and a broad smile filled her face, aimed straight at Hokuren. Her heart leaped into her throat. Her mother waved to her. "I'm happy to see you. It's been a while."

"I've hoped for this my entire life," said Hokuren, ready to pretend this ghost defied all others and spoke to her, rationality be damned.

The ghost turned around and muttered, breaking the spell it had over Hokuren. She wilted. This was no special case. Her mother had died and would never return. This shade was only a collection of memories from a confused soul, stuck in limbo, awaiting another human to animate. There was no conversation to be had, only silence while the ghost waited for its invisible guest to speak.

"See!" The ghost gestured to something off to the side, whatever it thought was there. "Finally, after all these years. And you said it couldn't be done." The ghost chided its imaginary guest gently. "The combination of wizard and witch magic is complete. Oh, Moira was such a help. I couldn't have done this without her."

Hokuren's blood ran cold.

"It's the goblins, of course. They can learn everything we can, just as well as we can!" Her mother glowed with an excitement that had nothing to do with the harsh blue light she shined with. This was the person Hokuren missed out on getting to know.

The ghost's blue light blurred. Hokuren rubbed her tears away. She needed to keep her focus.

Her mother's apparition listened to someone else speaking in silence. Then, "Oh, yes, the goblins exhibit all the signs of human intelligence. They can learn our languages, and read and write with them too. Not only that, they're capable of memorization on par with us, and their ability with math can easily surpass the average person. Oh!" The ghost clasped its hands together, then listened to a quick interruption. "I'm sorry, yes, I'll get to the point. I just get so excited when I think of perfecting this process and spreading it to all goblinkind."

Hokuren's mother had been so positive. Whatever happened, she meant well.

"No, you must tell no one else about this. Look." Hokuren's mother's ghost fretted with her hands, trying to come to a decision. "Okay, I'll tell you. In order to achieve this, I've used witch magic, yes. But do you remember when the Tolliver-Evans device went missing?" She paused again. "The look on your face says you didn't know. It was I who stole it."

Hokuren thought back to the diary, playing back images of her deciphered pages in her mind. Some of the uncoded words that remained could have been references to this Tolliver-Evans device.

"Yes, I realize the Conclave would be furious with me if they knew I was the thief. But I needed its power. You see, I figured out what the others never did: It's an amplification device for our spells. I needed it in order to achieve what I have with the goblins, but it's dangerous. If other members of the Conclave were to discover its true power, and how to wield witch magic together with wizard magic, they would be far less scrupulous than I."

Hokuren's mother wasn't a witch. She was a *wizard*. A member of the Conclave of Wizards and all. Hokuren simultaneously wanted the ghostly scene to continue so she could keep seeing her mother but end before she learned even more that would upset her.

"Now, in that vein, even you, whom I trust more than anyone outside my family, will not get my full notes. Oversee this project in my stead while I am away with my child, and I will grant you associate billing. It'll be a feather in your cap, and you'll need to do little to earn it. Can you agree to these terms?" An expectant pause. The ghost smiled. "I knew I could count on you. Oh, thank you, Ulbricht!"

Ulbricht. Hokuren's fist closed tightly. Her mother had entrusted him with her work and been betrayed after her death.

The ghost faded, having exhausted the scene it wished to tell. It dissolved in reverse of the way it appeared, dispersing into individual lights that zipped around before blinking out of existence. The lantern's light, once again all that illuminated the forest, paled in comparison to the intensity of the ghost's light.

Hokuren's eyes remained fixed on the ghost's last location as her vision slowly readjusted. She felt hollowed out. She had gotten to see her mother as she had been in life, then had her snatched away again.

"Boss—Hokuren." It was Cinna, standing beside her. She hadn't even noticed Cinna approach. "Are you all right?"

"I—" Hokuren gripped Cinna's hand tightly. "Did you see how full of life she seemed? I didn't get to—Why didn't I get to—I can't—"

"Hokuren." Cinna's voice was more urgent. "The mystery. Focus on it."

The mystery. Cinna was right. Hokuren closed her eyes and tried to think of a question that Greeze might answer. She kept picturing her mother's ghost, which she'd finally gotten to see after all those lonely, futile nights in the graveyard as a child.

She stopped. Cinna had said it earlier. Her mother's ghost shouldn't be here.

"Why is she not at her grave back in Fondence?" Hokuren gritted her teeth. "Was she not buried there, either? Why was her body dragged all the way out here?"

The sound of a throat clearing brought Hokuren's attention back to Greeze. "She died here," the goblin said softly. "I'm sorry, I can understand this is difficult for you. But I will give you the truth."

"My mother died from complications from my birth," said Hokuren. It was the story she'd been told her whole life.

Greeze sighed. "That's not how it happened."

"What?" Hokuren squeezed Cinna's hand further.

"Nekane left Ulbricht in charge without giving him her full notes, including how to influence our brains to learn human speech and more, and how to use the Tolliver-Evans device." Greeze scowled. "She was serious about keeping her research and methods out of his hands. She locked her spells up with the strongest ward known to wizardry: a ward of life. Her life. Unbreakable, unless she were to perish."

Hokuren made a choked sound. "You don't mean—"

"Ulbricht learned the nature of the ward and what kept him from those notes. And"—Greeze's ears drooped—"I'll spare you the details, but Ulbricht killed her."

Hokuren collapsed to her knees. It was too much. All these memories, the image of her mother she had built up over her lifetime, the story of how her mother died: all falsehoods. "And he's been continuing what she started ever since."

"At a far different scale, and for a different purpose." Greeze pointed to where the ghost had been. "Nekane's research taught him that the access to our brains required in order to interest us in living like humans could influence us so strongly that we're essentially subjugated with witch magic. We cannot resist that influence. He used this magic on more and more goblins from my original warren, building a small army of puppets."

"Are you going to invade Fondence?" asked Cinna.

"That threat is intended to get the people to abandon the town." The goblin shrugged. "Nekane's original goal was to see us living side by side with humans, integrating goblins with humans like elves had done already. Ulbricht wishes for us to pretend to be human, but he doesn't believe we belong with humans and elves. He wants to see us use Fondence as our above ground test."

The ghostly lights returned, swirling anew. Ghosts played their scenes over and over at night, reliving that favorite memory until dawn.

"I can't—I don't want to see it again," said Hokuren. She let Cinna help her to her feet. Once was enough, and it was committed to her memory. She'd be able to view it anytime she wished.

Greeze waved her on. "Come, our warren is close by. Let me show you the incubator of the threat to Fondence."

Cinna stuck close to Hokuren as they followed Greeze to the goblin warren, doubling back toward Fondence.

She bit her lip so forcefully it nearly bled. Hokuren was listless and hanging her head, more than once tripping on a root or stone because she wasn't paying attention to where she stepped. Cinna felt powerless to help. Every time she tried to say something, her tongue wouldn't form the words, her brain afraid it would be stupid or make things worse.

So she said nothing, Hokuren said nothing, and Cinna grew increasingly uncomfortable. She needed to say something to show she cared. Finally, she gathered her courage and said, "Hokuren—"

"We're here," Greeze announced at the worst possible moment, cutting her off. He stood in front of a mound of dirt with a circular opening that resembled a yawning mouth. The goblin could fit inside by ducking down, but Hokuren and Cinna would have to crawl along the ground to squeeze through.

"You seem trepidatious," said the goblin. "Do not fear. The tunnel opens up once you're inside. Just follow me." He slipped inside and disappeared from view.

"Let's go," said Hokuren, sounding tired. She took a step toward the opening, then stopped when Cinna grabbed her arm.

"Wait, Hokuren," said Cinna. "I can't make things better, but . . . I'm here for you." She looked at the dirt mound. "If you don't want to go in there, I can report back what it looks like."

Hokuren gave Cinna a wan smile. "Thank you, Cinna. Your being here is help enough. I intend to see this through to the end. I will find out the truth, no matter how much it hurts."

"I never thought you wouldn't find out the truth." Cinna guided Hokuren to the opening. "Does it help to know your mother didn't want the goblins to be so susceptible to compulsion?"

"I . . . need time to think about it. That's why Ulbricht killed her, though. She didn't trust him enough to give him her secrets."

"Hard to argue with her instincts."

"She still trusted him too much." Hokuren paused before crawling into the warren entrance. "We will confirm Ulbricht's identity, whatever it takes."

"And then we'll do him like we did that demon!" interjected Cinna. Rogue wizard or not, she was all in on helping Hokuren get revenge for a thirty-year-old crime.

Hokuren shook her head. "And become his next victims? We took care of the demon ourselves because no one else would and it wouldn't rest until you were dead, but that's not true of Ulbricht. No, we'll return to Velles, ask Fenton to help us contact the Conclave of Wizards, and let them deal with him."

Cinna put her finger in her ear to make sure it wasn't plugged and she heard correctly. "Let the wizards—He killed both your parents! You can't let him get away with it."

"I'm not." There was an edge to Hokuren's voice that Cinna rarely heard. "Getting my personal revenge won't bring either of them back. The Conclave is much more equipped to handle him than we are."

Hokuren preferred to let the proper authorities mete out justice. She trusted groups like the Conclave to make the right decision and help.

Objections piled up in Cinna's mind. She knew almost nothing about the Conclave of Wizards. They might ignore their request. They might be on Ulbricht's side, and telling the Conclave would make them enemies.

However difficult it was to swallow, this was Hokuren's choice and Cinna would, with difficulty, accept it. "If that's what you want, boss."

"I understand what you're thinking." Hokuren's face softened, and she touched Cinna's cheek. "If we do it your way, I'm afraid I'll lose you too." With that, she lowered herself to her hands and knees and crawled into the tunnel opening.

Cinna followed, declining to argue further. Had she spoken, however, she would have said, "Your parents wouldn't come back, but at least *Ulbricht* wouldn't, either."

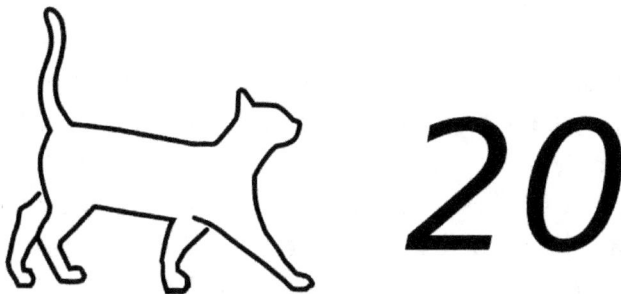

20

Cinna struggled to keep track of Greeze's path through the warren tunnels. Like the tunnel they traversed to find Barth, these were too short for standing in and formed from dirt and decaying matter. They differed through their dizzying array of intersecting branches. Doubtful she'd find the way back to the entrance on her own, should she need to.

They finally emerged into a room larger than Hokuren's father's entire house. Fully stocked bookshelves ringed the perimeter, and tables and chairs sized for goblins furnished the open interior. It could have been a room in any of the libraries Hokuren loved so much, except for the dozen goblins studying from various books.

They were all dressed as well as Greeze. With their small size, they resembled the wards of the orphanages in Velles when prospective parents visited. The goblins even wore shoes, most with slits cut in the front where their claws poked out. Even in a goblin warren, Cinna was the only one barefoot. She wouldn't have expected that.

The goblins concentrated so hard that it was several moments before one looked up at the human and elf in their midst and barked to the rest. The many pairs of yellow eyes looked up, not afraid but curious.

A goblin in a pair of glasses greeted Greeze, and they exchanged words in the goblin tongue. At least, Cinna assumed the series of grunts, whistles, and other noises was goblin language. Then Greeze introduced them. "Hokuren, Cinna, this is Viss."

"You're Nekane's daughter!" Viss said, to which Hokuren

gave a curt nod. Her pronunciation was worse than Greeze's, but still comprehensible. Viss looked at Cinna. "And"—the goblin hesitated—"Nekane's daughter's friend."

"Cinna works. Easier to say," said Cinna.

"Viss is in charge of the team that monitors the contraption," said Greeze. "She knows it better than the rest of us, and it's what I wished to show you down here."

Viss adjusted her glasses and looked away. "I can present the contraption to you," she mumbled. "But even I don't know it all that well."

"Is the 'contraption' what you call the Tolliver-Evans device?" asked Hokuren.

"So named for its human discoverers," said Greeze with distaste. "We prefer to call it the contraption. It certainly has us trapped."

Cinna had forgotten its name, and soon after Hokuren repeated it, she forgot it again. "Contraption" was certainly better in her book.

Hokuren gestured at the room full of studious goblins. "What is everyone here doing? It's the middle of the night."

"Our studies," said Greeze. "Nekane's spell grants us an almost insatiable need to study and learn. It is part of our curse."

Hokuren frowned. "Why would my mother do that to you?"

"There is a lot to learn about being human. The language, the history, the mannerisms." He tugged at his coat. "The clothes. Nekane wished for us to engage with and learn all of it, but she found our desire to do so lacking, and thus built in some—let's call it *encouragement*. Without it, we'd never bother to learn all of this."

"I see," said Hokuren, head tucked down.

"It's a very important part of the spell," said Viss, earning a scoff from Greeze. "As Nekane used to say, thousands of generations passed before the elves learned how to fit in with humans. But if we are intentional about it, we could do so much sooner."

"You know full well that's not Ulbricht's intent," said Greeze.

Viss shot him a weary smile. "He won't be around forever."

"The wizard that follows him could be even worse."

The goblins continued to bicker. Cinna ignored them, imagining goblins living in Velles among everyone else. It could be possible after a period of adjustment. The goblins talked and dressed as if they fit in. Sure, some people might need time to get over their fear of them, and Cinna included herself in this cohort, but many people were dangerous, too, so in that sense goblins would be no different.

"Anyway, I believe Nekane overcorrected," Greeze continued, bringing Cinna's attention back to him with the use of Hokuren's mother's name. "I, for example, have spent almost thirty years in near fanatical pursuit of new topics. The spell continues to compel me to learn, and I can only ever temporarily satiate that desire."

Hokuren's gloomy look deepened. "I don't know what to say. I'm sorry."

"Don't take it as me blaming you," said Greeze. "It's not all bad. A few of my colleagues and I worked on some problems we found in a book by human mathematicians they claimed were unanswerable. We have solved many of them, but alas, have no way to publish."

Now Cinna was less sure the goblins would fit in. If they arrived in town talking about high-level math and being smarter than everyone else by a large margin, that would be a tough sell. She'd seen humans rejected for less.

"I'm sure those math equations are great, but let's get to the contraption already," Cinna said. Her own study of math began and ended with basic arithmetic.

"Yes, of course. Right this way." Viss darted to another tunnel connected to the reading room, and Cinna and Hokuren followed, Greeze now bringing up the rear.

The next tunnel led to another large rectangular room that resembled a dining area. Goblins sat in front of plates and silverware arrayed as they would be for the most elegant meals in Velles. Each item was unique, not matching as was the norm, a mishmash of random forks, knives, plates, and more. Cinna picked up a fork from the closest table, earning an offended growl from the goblin at its seat.

"Where'd you get these?" Cinna asked, twisting the fork in front of her as if inspecting it. "Looks like this might have belonged to a family in Fondence not too long ago, doesn't it?"

Greeze sighed while Viss looked away. "In order to best fit into the human society, we practice," said Greeze. "Eating with a knife and fork does not come naturally to a goblin. And we cannot produce such tools."

"So Jarmo was right. You are stealing kitchen items from the town."

"We fully intend to return all property to its owner once we've sufficient practice."

Cinna snickered, placing the fork back on the table without regard for how it lined up. "Sure you do. Look, I don't care. I'm the last person you need to worry about turning you in on charges of thievery."

"All this is because of my mother," said Hokuren quietly, surely talking about more than a few stolen spoons.

"We owe Nekane so much," said Viss. "Without her—"

"Let's continue on," grunted Greeze, motioning at Viss. He readjusted the fork Cinna had placed down to its correct position before following.

More tunnels and still more intersections brought them through several rooms: a gymnasium of some sort (goblins practiced sword-fighting here, making mistakes that Cinna wanted to jump in and correct), a dormitory (they tiptoed through this one, not wanting to wake any of the dozens of goblins getting their shut-eye), and even a tavern (where goblins learned all the various intricacies of bar interaction and card games, getting experience pulling it off inebriated. Greeze called it the most popular training they did).

Finally, one last tunnel brought them to a small room, where two goblins with spears and copies of the Arms of Fondence uniform stood guard in front of the only door they'd seen in the expansive warren so far. Built oversized for goblins, the door reminded Cinna of the one under the tree near Hugo's shack.

"Greeze, sir, the contraption is ready for viewing as requested," said one of the goblin guards.

"Thank you, Poit." Greeze pulled a key from a jacket pocket and, reaching up to a doorknob level with his forehead, unlocked the door.

The party filed into this new room, brightly lit as all the others. This time the light focused on the thing raised on a platform in the center of the room. "Thing" was the only word for it. Roughly the size of a loaf of bread and made of gleaming red metal, it comprised a bewildering jumble of twisting tubes that ran into each other, like a more complicated version of the goblin warren tunnels. When these tubes connected, they sometimes seemed to disappear, or turn inside out, or halt before continuing on soon after. There were so many tubes, all the same red, that Cinna worked up a headache trying to trace their paths. No matter which she followed, she lost track of it in the central morass of metal.

"Here it is," said Greeze, with the same level of disgust he might use to point out maggot-ridden fruit. "The contraption." He snarled. "Or the Tolliver-Evans device, if you prefer."

Hokuren walked up to it, then jerked back, holding her nose. "Ow."

"There's an, um, invisible barrier," said Viss, ducking her head sheepishly.

"I found it, thanks," muttered Hokuren. She walked around the device, tilting her head back and forth for better views until she had made a complete revolution. "What does this actually do? My mother called it an amplification device, but I'm not familiar with the specifics."

"It's difficult to answer that question." Viss continued to look abashed. "We've never been provided with an explanation, and obviously none of us are wizards. Ulbricht has a connection to it through his magic. He can activate it from afar and use it to influence us with the witch magic spell no matter where we are, as long as we have the worm in our head."

"Did you say worm?" said Cinna, making a face. "And did you say *head*?"

Greeze wiggled his fingers and pointed to his ear. "One lives in all of us."

"Disgusting."

"You are correct."

"Would these worms be translucent and pinkish?" asked Hokuren.

"Yes," said Greeze, eyebrows raised. "You know about the worms?"

"Saw them myself," said Hokuren, after a while. "But I don't know where they come from."

"Neither do we. Nekane discovered their resonance with the contraption. That Ulbricht can source them too makes me think they're known to members of the Conclave."

"I fought some goblins when we first arrived in Fondence," said Cinna, to change the subject from the nightmarish worms. She rubbed the back of her neck. "Their eyes turned the same red as that thing." The more she looked at the contraption, the more sinister it appeared.

Greeze nodded. "It's the giveaway that Ulbricht is currently influencing us. We're completely at his mercy, unable to resist him. People, however, have some limited ability to fight back, even with a worm."

"Tell me what it's like when Ulbricht does that. I want to know what my mother wrought," said Hokuren, her eyes remaining fixed on the contraption.

"It's not terrible," said Viss, without conviction.

"Do not lie to me," said Hokuren sharply.

"You get a massive headache." Greeze grabbed his hairless scalp with both hands. "There's a voice in your head giving you orders. You want to obey, as if every request from the voice is the greatest idea you've ever heard. A small part of you watches, as if you're stuck in a cage, while the rest does whatever Ulbricht wants. The usual demand these days is for us to strip to a loincloth, grab a spear, and 'attack' Fondence. Or steal something, or threaten a wagon, or, well, you get the picture." He paused, taking a deep breath.

"Hold on," said Cinna. "He makes you dress like that?" Goblins though these were, it was difficult to imagine the well-dressed and erudite Greeze and Viss as snarling, nearly nude gremlins. "And the teeth necklace?"

"The teeth necklace," growled Greeze, as if describing the appearance of his mortal enemy. "Goblins don't wear those! I don't know where Ulbricht got that idea from."

"I do." Cinna waited for Greeze and Viss to give her their full attention, excited to know something the scholarly goblins didn't. "It's from *Captain Cavalier*."

The goblins exchanged glances. "Which region's military is this captain from?" asked Viss.

"A fictional one. You've never heard of it?" Everyone knew *Captain Cavalier*, or so Cinna thought.

"Perhaps their pursuit of knowledge doesn't allow for popular fiction," said Hokuren dryly. "It makes sense for Ulbricht to use a depiction from such a source, though. Surely he has access to real research and knowledge into how goblins act, but if he wants to scare people, having you emulate the goblins of the *Cavalier* series makes perfect sense."

Greeze shuddered. "He doesn't want a realistic depiction. He wants the scariest one the people already have."

"Precisely." Hokuren pursed her lips. "This is an abominable use of witch magic."

"There have been some benefits," muttered Viss.

"Ah, Viss does like to look on the bright side," said Greeze, waving his hand dismissively. "Ulbricht seems to have taken to witch magic. Wizards can create images, but Ulbricht can do more. He can twist your view into what you need to see to make his illusion work." He tapped his head. "Your own memories are used against you."

"What does that even mean?" asked Cinna.

Hokuren stiffened, then snapped her fingers. "Cinna, describe Moira to me. What did her face look like?"

Cinna called up a mental image of Moira. "Umm, it's hard to say, boss. No real standout features."

"Did she have a scar above her eye?" Hokuren traced a finger above her own right eye. "It would be light, half hidden beneath her eyebrow, but there all the same."

"No, I don't think so." Cinna hadn't paid close attention to Moira's face, but she would have noticed a scar.

"So that's how it's done." Hokuren tucked her chin down into her hand and muttered to herself. "That's why this Moira looks exactly like the original."

Cinna sidled closer to Hokuren. "Want to fill me in, boss?"

"It's witch magic. To me, this Moira looks exactly like my memory of her because it *is* my memory of her. The magic tells my brain to see her as I remember. Ulbricht hasn't created a perfect replication of Moira! He's merely told me to believe he has. She has a scar, but you don't see it because you didn't know about it." Hokuren snapped her head toward Greeze. "Could the false Moira be Ulbricht in disguise?"

The goblin nodded. "I've long thought it possible. She knows witch magic, which only Ulbricht should know. My orders include a direction not to approach Moira, which I suspect is because he's worried I could confirm that she is Ulbricht."

Cinna shivered. "I really don't think I like witch magic, boss."

"Like any power, in the wrong hands . . ." Hokuren shook her head. She gestured to the contraption. "How can we get in there and destroy this?"

"You can't!" shouted Viss. At everyone's glance, she cleared her throat. "What I mean is, there's no way to get past the barrier. If there were, we'd have already destroyed the contraption. Please don't try. You'll hurt yourself."

Cinna put her hand out and approached the contraption until she met the resistance of the invisible barrier. Her whole body tensed. Some wizard could place an indestructible fence around what amounted to a goblin mind-control device and no one could do anything about it.

The Conclave of Wizards had lied and told the world that powerful magic was gone so they would be the only ones who held it. Their reasoning, that magic shouldn't be allowed in the hands of those who would abuse it, was sound, but they forgot to include themselves in the list of abusers. The contraption and the indestructible fence around it served as an example of their hypocrisy.

Her fingers curled into a fist and willed her righteous anger into her arm. She wondered if these super-intelligent goblins had tried something as simple as smashing the barrier.

"What are you doing?" asked Hokuren.

"Destroying the barrier."

"Are you—Wait, don't—" yelled Viss.

Cinna ignored the goblin. Her first punch would be light, a test of the barrier's strength. If it was like punching a brick wall, she'd rather not pulverize her hand the way Hugo had in the tunnel.

The instant her fist hit the barrier, she froze as if she'd been seized in midair. Then, with a popping sound, she took an invisible blow to her chest that sent her flying backward, tumbling head over heels before skidding to a stop on the dirt floor.

"Flames," she said, taking stock of her body. Her rib cage was as sore as if she'd taken a Hugo-sized punch. Her elbows and knees were skinned raw from the crash. She picked herself up from the ground, groaning at aches and pains all over her body. Hokuren arrived next to her and held her arm to steady her.

"The barrier has a special property," said Viss, once again embarrassed. "Any force dealt to it is paid back threefold."

"Another thing that would have been good to know beforehand!" said Hokuren.

"I did say not to try anything," said Viss, reproachfully.

"I'm fine, boss." Cinna stood with Hokuren's help. Either the room was wobbling, or she needed to clear her head. She'd barely put anything into her strike. Threefold wasn't a high enough multiplier.

"Come now, I know when you're lying," said Hokuren. She continued to hold Cinna's arm. "One more question, Greeze. This warren. How did all these rooms get built? Was it my father?"

It was Viss who responded. "Your father's generous donations were a considerable help. We will miss him."

"The Northern Construction Fund," Hokuren said to Cinna. "This must be it. He's been subsidizing these goblins for—wait, how long has he been doing this?"

"Since Nekane's death." Viss lowered her head solemnly.

"My whole life? He never said a word!"

"For a while, the amounts were small. However, they increased substantially in the past few years," added Greeze.

"And why is that?" asked Hokuren.

"Because Moira asked him to."

Hokuren grunted. "I suspect it was more of a demand."

They remained near the contraption for a few more minutes, a never-before-thought-of way to defeat the barrier failing to materialize. Greeze led them to an exit he said would let them out much closer to home, extracting promises from Cinna and Hokuren that they wouldn't reveal this secret entrance to anyone. They passed more goblins along the way, getting more of those curious looks. No doubt they figured their overwhelming numbers versus the two above-grounders gave them no reason for alarm.

They left the winding tunnels and turned into a flat straightaway. Neither Hokuren nor Greeze seemed to have anything left to say, so Cinna stayed quiet as well, occasionally rubbing her sore chest. Finally, an end appeared in sight: a tall, thin metal door.

"You might find this exit amusing," said Greeze. One look at Hokuren's face told Cinna that the boss would find little amusing on this night.

When they reached the door, Greeze put on his best butler imitation and waved them through. The walls and the staircase at the far end of the room looked familiar, but it wasn't until they walked in that Cinna recognized where they were.

They had stepped out into Hokuren's father's basement, through the left safe.

"Flaming bones and gristle," said Hokuren.

Cinna shut the safe door behind the quickly retreating Greeze, who had declined to stay for Hokuren's reaction. "At least we solved the mystery of how the goblins broke in."

As anticipated, Hokuren was not amused.

21

The second moon, Nebulus, had already traveled a quarter of the way across the sky by the time Hokuren settled into her childhood bed. She lay wide awake, wasting the precious little time available before sunrise. She clutched Hoku the doll against her chest, the way she used to as a child when she was afraid of monsters under the bed. Only now the monster was real, and her own mother had fed it.

Digging up secrets and exposing truths intentionally hidden could be painful. In her City Watch days, she investigated the theft of a painting from the parlor of a noble married couple. While recovering the painting she had also proved both husband and wife were committing adultery—with the same person, the painting's thief. The couple's marriage ended, as did the thief's.

This time, it was Hokuren damaged by her own discoveries. In a single night, her perception of the two women she admired most, her mother and Moira, had been upended. Moira's kindness toward her could never be undone, but now Hokuren would always wonder how much the witch had hidden from her.

As for her mother, Hokuren didn't know where to start. It was clear her mother hadn't given the goblins a choice in whether they would experience her *encouragement*. She'd also foolishly entrusted her still vulnerable work to a fellow wizard. Hokuren had always known, deep down, that the image of perfection she had built up in her mind was not a realistic version of her mother, but she hadn't prepared herself for it to be irreversibly shattered this way.

Though it wasn't all bad. Hokuren had held herself partially responsible for her mother's death her entire life, an unfair guilt that reason could never completely shake. That guilt, built over her lifetime, had already eased by learning it had nothing to do with her. She hoped she would finally be free of it entirely one day.

It was Ulbricht who had taken a life with her mother away from her. Hokuren squeezed her doll harder at the thought of him. When Cinna had suggested they go and get revenge, a part of her yearned to agree. It had been difficult to say no. But that was not who she wished to be.

She would not rest until she knew the Conclave had dealt with him. Once she confirmed he was disguising himself as Moira, or someone else, she and Cinna would get back to Velles and beg Fenton's help. She was prepared to travel to the Conclave itself, wherever it was, if that was what it took.

With all that settled, and her mind wrung out to a point beyond exhaustion, Hokuren finally collapsed into sleep.

"I want to see you hold that plank longer this time," said Cinna, performing the exercise alongside Jarmo.

"I . . . can't . . ." Jarmo, his face red with effort, collapsed onto the forest floor.

Cinna held the position for a few more seconds, having barely broken a sweat, then let up and joined him on the ground. "You do have more to hold up than me," she admitted.

When Jarmo asked her if they would continue the morning routine when she returned from Oro, she hadn't been sure if it was worthwhile. After all, she'd gotten no closer to resolving his mental block against hurting people. But now that they were out here, she enjoyed taking him through the exercises.

Cinna had always been proud that she'd become a success within the Sanctuary of the Eclipse. No one taught her these exercises she showed Jarmo. She'd learned them on her own, by watching the others and experimenting, because the alternative was remaining weak and at everyone else's mercy.

It was the same before that, when her caretaker died and forced her onto the streets at the age of ten. She had to figure how to steal food without getting caught and keep it out of the grasp of her fellow urchins, because there was no alternative. She'd succeed or die. That was how it'd always been.

It was Hokuren who showed her a different way. Cinna learned to read not by being threatened if she didn't, but by Hokuren painstakingly running through letters and words and sounds, over and over, until Cinna could read simple texts, then gradually increasing the difficulty. She'd actually taught Cinna, the first person ever to do so.

That was how it was supposed to be. How it should have been. And now Jarmo was getting lessons from her. She liked that.

"I just need . . . more practice," Jarmo wheezed.

"Practice helps." Cinna waved him up. They sat cross-legged across from each other. "Break time."

They drank water, basking in the crisp dawn sunlight. Jarmo stared at her with a funny look on his face, so Cinna raised her eyebrows at him in question.

"Master Cinna," said Jarmo, fidgeting. "Is this how you learned to fight? How you learned to let go and hurt people? By doing exercises?"

"No," said Cinna. "Exercises are how I got strong enough to do so."

"Teach me the way you learned. Maybe that's the way."

There was a time when Cinna would have agreed that would be the only way anyone could learn. Sink or swim. In order to break Jarmo, she could punch him until he got tired of it and fought back. Eventually, he would. Everyone had a breaking point.

But she couldn't punch Jarmo for the same reason she wouldn't kick a puppy.

"Jarmo, have you ever worried about where your next meal was coming from?" Cinna asked. "Or where you would sleep that night?"

"Can't say I have," he said. "My parents always had food for us, and my bed was the same every night."

"Did you ever have something, like . . . a toy that you had to hide because if someone else found it, they'd hit you and steal it from you?"

"Well," said Jarmo, thinking with a hand massaging his chin. "My older brother would sometimes take my favorite ball. But my mother would make him give it back."

Cinna shook her head. "You can't learn the way I learned. You *shouldn't*. I don't want to do that to you."

"But—"

"We'll have to find another way. And that's final." She stood up. "We have more exercises to go through, and then more practice with your sword. Best not to waste any more time."

"Yes, Master Cinna." He bobbed his head. He was so agreeable, so eager.

Cinna couldn't punch that.

Hokuren was making breakfast, eyes heavy from a lack of proper sleep, when Cinna returned from her resumed dawn workout with Jarmo, a sheen of sweat present on her forehead beneath her headband.

"Jarmo still hasn't figured out his mental block," Cinna announced the moment she walked in the door. "I learned I won't punch him."

Hokuren frowned. "Why would you punch him?"

"I said I won't."

Cinna leaned over the cooking breakfast and, before Hokuren could react, snatched a sausage from the hot pan and gulped it down.

"That's not even fully cooked," said Hokuren, swatting Cinna away from the rest of the food.

Cinna grinned as she skipped out of range of Hokuren's arms. "Close enough."

Hokuren almost smiled. Cinna was doing her best to lighten the mood, but it would take some heroic work for Hokuren to recover her bonhomie.

"Hey, boss," said Cinna, dropping her voice into a more serious tone. "I'll accept not going after Ulbricht right now. That being said, I think we should figure out if we can get past that barrier and bash up that contraption."

"The Tolliver-Evans device?" said Hokuren.

"That, sure. I don't like knowing it exists." Cinna twisted the hem of her tunic. "I know it was a prized possession of your mother—"

"There's no question it should be destroyed. I'm not sure how we can do that, though."

"We'll figure it out," said Cinna, with more confidence than Hokuren felt.

"In the meantime, we're going to continue with our plan to confirm Ulbricht's identity." She waved her hand to cut off a response from Cinna. "Before you say anything, we're not confronting him. We follow the stones to him, get an identity, and get away without being spotted. We'll go see Grimes after breakfast."

"Ugh, worm stones and Grimes. Which is worse, honestly?" Cinna looked longingly at the sausage and eggs cooking over the fire. "Why don't we go back to Velles now and tell the Conclave of Wizards to go after that fake Moira? You and Greeze seemed pretty convinced that's Ulbricht in disguise."

"Because we have no confirmation," said Hokuren. "Without proof, it's mere conjecture."

"What if we shoved a stone in Moira's face? Couldn't her reaction to seeing the stones be our confirmation?" asked Cinna, not ready to let up.

Hokuren nodded. "It would be perfect if not for the fact that doing so would suggest we suspect both Ulbricht and Moira. We must do this in the right way. If he knows we're onto him, then—"

"Yeah, yeah, he'll try to kill us," said Cinna, resigned. "So instead, we follow the stones to Ulbricht."

"All we need is the identity, then we can return to Velles."

"Wait." Cinna looked up at Hokuren. "If we leave, I'll have failed my training with Jarmo."

"That's really important to you, isn't it?" Hokuren scratched her head. "I'm not sure we have a way around it. You know we have to get word to the Conclave as soon as possible."

"Yeah." Cinna sighed. "I'm not saying we shouldn't leave. I *am* saying that it'll be disappointing to Jarmo."

"Perhaps you could keep up a written training correspondence." Hokuren judged the food cooked through and served it on two plates, giving Cinna the larger portion. "Now let's eat and get moving."

"Don't have to tell me twice," said Cinna, digging in.

They made the long trek to Harrison Grimes's house on the outer edge of Fondence once again. Hokuren wanted to avoid Roz, even if she were back in Fondence, so Hokuren's father's most mysterious employee (in the sense that it remained a mystery why her father hired him) represented their best lead on delivering the stones to Ulbricht.

Cinna carried a single stone in her pouch in case Grimes worried they were lying. She complained about carrying around a worm with a penchant for living in brains. Hokuren assured her the odds of the stone breaking open and releasing the worm were exceptionally low, to which Cinna responded that "low" was not zero.

Grimes answered the door at Hokuren's knock as before, sticking his thin head out and glaring imperiously down on them like they were plague-ridden solicitors. "You're back. How wonderful. Were you able to deal with young Barth's, ah, problems?"

"We can safely say Barth will not have any more problems," said Cinna, earning a light elbow from Hokuren.

"Barth was murdered." Hokuren paused, but Grimes merely raised his eyebrows. She could have told him rain was in the forecast and elicited a stronger reaction. "The prime suspect is goblins."

Cinna turned to look at Hokuren, but thankfully kept her mouth shut. Grimes closed his eyes and muttered something that could have been a prayer. "I see. I told you they're more dangerous these days."

"As with my father, the evidence is sorely lacking."

"Have you come to argue this again with me?" Grimes fingered the door, as if threatening to retreat inside and slam it on her. "Because I'm quite busy."

Hokuren doubted that. For all his griping, he didn't seem to do anything at all. "I came here to ask if you could tell me how Mikko's Imports delivers Ulbricht's shipments to him."

Grimes licked his lips, his interest in Hokuren higher than ever. There was an urgent note in his voice. "You retrieved the chest from Hugo? You have the silks?"

"Not all of it." Hokuren snapped her fingers and, as instructed, Cinna flashed the stone from her bag. "I also got a fair number of these."

"Rocks," said Cinna, holding the stone in her hands up to him.

"Wh—what's this?" Grimes's play at surprise didn't fool Hokuren. Unlike when he was genuinely caught off guard, he didn't try to hide it. He exaggerated his shock by reaching around his door with a slender arm to take the stone from Cinna as if he'd never seen a rock in his life. "Where are the silks?"

Cinna removed a wad of silk from the bag. "Oh, here. But Hugo told us the stones are more important."

"I see," said Grimes, eyes narrowed. He moved the stone around in his trembling hands to look the entire thing over. "Have you opened them?"

"They open?" It was Hokuren's turn to feign ignorance. She grabbed the stone to take it back, meeting initial resistance. He gripped it for a moment before relinquishing it with obvious reluctance. "How would you know that if you've never seen them before?" she asked.

Grimes's hooded eyes regarded her with distaste. "Perhaps Ulbricht has entrusted me with more information than I wish to share." His eyes went to the stone again before he tore his view back to her. "Normally Roz handles the delivery. Where is she?"

Hokuren shrugged, carefully placing the stone back in Cinna's bag. "Haven't seen her in a while. I know how important these are to Ulbricht, so I don't think we should wait for her to decide to show up. Can you help me arrange a meeting for the handoff?"

"You don't, under any circumstances, *meet* Ulbricht." Grimes emerged from behind his door and shut it immediately, before Cinna could finish leaning over to look inside. With a sharp glare at her, he said, "You meet his gofer, Garrett Hawthorne. Come, I will take you."

They set off behind Harrison Grimes's long, gangly stride. Along the way, Grimes was effusive in his praise of Garrett, calling him "incorruptible." When Hokuren asked what made him say that, Grimes responded that one could just tell these things.

Hokuren, fresh off learning of both her parents' and Roz's various corruptions, didn't reply.

The rest of the walk to Fondence was full of awkward silence. Grimes was not a chatty man. When they stopped in front of a house on the northwest spur road, near the town center, Grimes said the first words spoken in quite some time.

"We're here."

The house was small and well-kept, a single story painted a drab gray. Hokuren remembered the family that lived there when she left. The Kolusians. Given Garrett's last name, it seemed they had moved on.

Grimes waited far from the door, gesturing to Hokuren. A tall young human opened the instant after her first knock, as if he'd been standing next to the door waiting for her. Startled, she said, "Oh, hello. Is Garrett in?"

"You're looking at him. How can I be of service?" Garrett bowed and rose back up with practiced ease. He had a voice of such depth and delicacy a bard would envy him. He made eye contact with Hokuren and held it. His stare was intimidating. She had trouble identifying what made it so eerie at first, but eventually she realized there were several seconds between his blinks.

"I have some silks for Ulbricht from Mikko's Imports," Hokuren said, struggling to maintain eye contact. "I'm told you can help me get them to him."

His face fell. "Ah, business. It's always business when I'm summoned. Perhaps another time I might get a personal call." He bowed again, his form identical to the first. "I'll come by tomorrow, so have everything ready. My uncle tells me you're staying in your father's old house, correct?"

"Your uncle?" said Hokuren, wondering what uncle was keeping tabs on her for Garrett's benefit. "Do I know him?"

"Well, I don't want to make a big deal about it, but I'm sure you do. Casper Daily."

"Really?" Casper was famous for speaking so little of his family that when she was growing up, most townspeople assumed he didn't have any. "I missed him at his home. Does he stay with you here?"

"Oh, no, nothing of the sort. Honestly, I barely know him." Garrett blinked again, slowly, as if still learning how. "Tomorrow morning, look to the west, and I shall be there, cart in hand." Garrett performed another bow, this one with an extra hand flourish, then stepped back into his house and closed the door on Hokuren.

"He talks like one of those nobles in Velles," said Cinna, once they'd stepped away from the threshold. "You know, all stiff and formal. Also, what was that about being 'summoned'?"

Hokuren looked back at the front door. "He's . . . odd."

"Garrett is a fine young man," said Grimes, who had never come close to the house. "Self-taught, I believe." In what, he didn't say. "He's in high demand, and often feels as if he does nothing but work."

"Is his family from Fondence?" asked Hokuren. "Other than Casper, of course."

"Yes, but both his parents have moved on to find work elsewhere." Grimes shook his head. "Poor Garrett had to take care of himself at an early age. He has handled it better than most would, I should say."

"Not all of us who had to take care of ourselves get a free house to do it in," grumbled Cinna.

"Well, I've taken you to Garrett. He'll pick up the stones, and that will be the end of your involvement. Then, perhaps, you can resume plans to sell." Grimes turned to leave, then thought better of it and remained to say, "Take care not to follow young Garrett. Ulbricht wishes to remain anonymous for a reason."

"I don't intend to follow Garrett," said Hokuren, who absolutely intended to follow Garrett.

Grimes wore his fake smile again. None of his were ever genuine, but the shadows cast over his face by his hat made this one seem especially unfriendly. "Good. Because the last curious person who did was never seen again."

"What do you mean by that?"

"Enjoy the rest of your day."

Before Hokuren could say anything else, Grimes's loping steps were already taking him down the path back to his house.

22

Cinna returned from her training session with Jarmo before Garrett arrived the following morning. Butterflies fluttered in Hokuren's stomach as she and Cinna set up the improvised delivery method they'd come up with the previous night: a spare linen sheet converted into a handy sack full of precious worms.

Seeing the stones leave the house would be a relief. Hokuren hated the worms from the moment she saw them, and knowing their purpose made them so much worse. Cinna had argued in favor of killing the worms before handing them over, but Hokuren refused. Doing so would alert Ulbricht that they knew too much.

Garrett arrived on the path to their house after they'd finished preparing the linen sack.

"Good morrow to you, fine ladies," said Garrett.

Cinna scowled in response to his overly formal speech.

"Good morning, Garrett." Hokuren toed the linen sack on the ground. "Your goods are right here."

Garrett took one look at the package and recoiled as if it were an animal carcass. "What is this shabby display? Usually there is a fine chest of wood, a delivery vessel worthy of one such as Ulbricht." He undid the knot holding the line together and pawed through the silk, counting the stones. "Just ten? Is this why you have worked extra hard to remove these from the chest, to hide the true number? There should be more."

"I assure you, these are all the stones I have. I couldn't bring the entire chest back. Does Ulbricht not want the silks as well?" Hokuren kept her voice steady.

After a long pause, where Garrett stared out into the distance, never blinking, he said, "You didn't open the stones, did you?"

"Everyone knows stones don't open." She flashed her most innocent look, channeling an expression Cinna wore when claiming not to understand that dessert shouldn't be eaten before dinner proper.

"I shall report this to Ulbricht." It sounded like a threat.

Garrett transferred the stones into his wagon, turning down an offer of help, covering them with the silks. "You will return to Oro and retrieve the rest."

Cinna positioned herself in front of the wagon, arms out. "Hey, don't we get paid for what we brought?"

"I shouldn't have to explain how this operates. Step aside, servant."

That was not the right way to address her. Cinna stood her ground with a face like thunder. "You won't leave without paying us for our work."

Garrett looked to Hokuren for support, but received none. She also wanted to know why they weren't receiving payment. With an exasperated sigh, he said, "Once Ulbricht takes control of the stones and ensures they are as expected, he will remit a prorated payment based on the delivery of ten stones."

"Sounds like a raw deal, boss," said Cinna.

"Let him take the stones and trust we'll receive the payment as promised." Hokuren nodded at Cinna, who shot Garrett one last glare before reluctantly moving out of his path. "If we don't, I assure you both they'll be the last stones he ever receives."

"Thank you." Garrett huffed and swung the wagon back the way he'd come.

Hokuren and Cinna watched his retreat. "Nice acting," said Hokuren. "I think he really believed that we were focused on the money."

"That was no act. We could really use that coin. We're low on money for food." Cinna jerked her thumb in Garrett's direction. "I don't know where he thinks he's going. There's nothing but forest that way."

"That's what you'll find out." Hokuren put her hand on Cinna's shoulder. "Remember, follow, don't engage, get an identity and get out.

And watch out for Garrett. There's something off about him. He's fishy."

"Fishy?"

"Fish don't blink, and neither does he."

"Fishy eyes. Got it, boss. Stay here. I'll come back once I know where he's taken these."

"I won't leave. He's almost out of sight. Good luck, Cinna."

With that, Cinna trotted into the forest after Garrett.

Hokuren wrung her hands the moment both of them were out of sight. If this worked, she could make plans to return to Velles and get in contact with the Conclave of Wizards. If it didn't . . .

There was nothing to do but gather up the linen sheet, which Garrett had damaged through his careless handling as he relieved it of the stones.

A voice from around the corner, near the front door of her father's house, called, "Oh, where is she?"

Hokuren dropped the sheet. The voice was that of her mother's ghost.

But it couldn't be. The literature specified that ghosts lingered in specific spots and didn't roam.

It could not be ignored. Hokuren rushed to the front of the house to once again see the shimmering blue form of her mother. Her knees buckled, and her hand went over her mouth.

The ghost spotted her. "My daughter," it said, continuing to defy everything Hokuren thought she knew about ghosts. This time it addressed her. "There you are."

"Mother?" Hokuren's voice shook. "How—"

"Please hurry. He's coming, and—" Her mother's figure looked wildly off to its right, toward the center of Fondence. "Oh, no."

"Who's coming?"

"Daughter, I won't let anything happen to you. Please, you must follow me. Hurry!" The ghost ran—no, that wasn't the right word. It *floated*, its legs losing definition as it moved. It was several feet down the road back to Fondence before turning back to a frozen Hokuren. "Come on, we don't have much time before he arrives!"

This was too much. It was clearly interacting with her. Hokuren's head spun, a headache developing as something grasped at her mind. Witch magic, just as when she visited the false Moira. She sucked in a breath.

"Who arrives, mother?"

The ghost's eyes narrowed. "You know."

Hokuren winced at a sharp pain deep within her head. Ulbricht. Her mother's ghost was acting out the last moments before Ulbricht came to kill her. Hokuren swallowed a lump in her throat. Her mother had known what he was about to do and had tried to get away.

She took a couple of steps toward the figure, then stopped again. No, this was wrong. There were too many unexpected things happening at once. She held her hand against her splitting headache, which continued to worsen. Like last time, she was losing the fight, and Cinna wasn't here to carry her away. She said through gritted teeth, "I know what you're doing."

"What do you mean, dear daughter? I'm your mother, and I'm trying to get you to safety."

Another jolt of pain coursed through Hokuren's brain. Then another. They kept coming, hammering away at her mind. "No," she said, struggling to remain standing. "Even if you were the ghost of my mother—argh—I would have been a newborn. You wouldn't have talked to me like—ugh—like this."

"You think far too much, dear daughter." The ghost waved Hokuren toward it. "Ulbricht is on his way, and you need to flee."

More pain, harsher than any previous, washed over Hokuren, and she collapsed to her hands and knees. A change came over her. She could see now that while this was her mother's ghost, it wasn't acting out her mother's death. It was telling her that Ulbricht was coming *now*. It was trying to save her life, and she needed to listen.

"Okay." Hokuren stood up. The pain in her mind eased as she told herself this was the right idea.

Some part of Hokuren's mind, barely audible, as if calling from the back row of an auditorium, cried out. *No! This isn't right. You know it's not right! Don't fall for the witch magic!*

But of course it was right. Hokuren knew that now, and the fading pain in her mind confirmed it. This wasn't witch magic. It was her common sense saving her.

"Follow me." Her mother flitted down the path away from Hokuren's father's house, and Hokuren dutifully trailed behind without another word. The voice in the back of her mind continued to object, but she easily dismissed it.

What about Cinna?

This made Hokuren stop. If she wasn't at the house to tell Cinna to stay away, her assistant could indeed run afoul of the wizard. The pain in her head returned long enough for Hokuren to realize Cinna could take care of herself, and anyway, remaining at the house wasn't an option. Cinna was elsewhere, and Hokuren needed to focus on her own safety.

Hokuren's mother led her directly to Moira's converted temple home. Of course Moira was the safest person to seek shelter with. She had always been there for Hokuren as she grew up.

This isn't Moira! You know that!

Hokuren shook her head to dislodge the voice in the back of her mind. Wherever it came from, it was clearly trying to lead her astray. She lifted her chin and continued to follow the ghostly form. It passed straight through the wall to get inside. Hokuren had to go around to the front door.

Moira stood behind a lectern on the great dais in the back of the old temple, as if ready to give a speech. She wore a velvet black and red robe and a matching large, floppy hat. Her long white hair spilled out from under the hat.

"Hokuren," Moira said, smiling with her teeth. "I need your help to defeat Ulbricht and save Fondence."

"Yes, Moira." Hokuren had been such a fool. This was Moira, the old Moira, the only Moira, the one Hokuren knew and loved. A different wardrobe and a more commanding presence didn't change that. She wanted to protect Fondence from the threat of the goblins, and Hokuren wanted to assist with this noble goal. She had wasted so much time believing their objectives were at odds.

This. Isn't. Moira. This is Ulbricht, you idiot!

Hokuren shoved the irritating voice in her mind aside. Her mother would never lead her into a trap like this, and anyway, Moira and Ulbricht couldn't be the same person. That didn't make any sense.

"My dear Hokuren." Moira stepped down, robe trailing along the ground. She touched Hokuren's chin with icy fingertips. "A powerful mind, but everyone has their limits. You're safe now in my influence."

"Please help Cinna," mumbled Hokuren. "I want her to be safe as well."

Leave Cinna out of this!

Moira smiled the way Hokuren remembered . . . didn't she? "Don't worry. She'll be much easier to bring over to our side than you were. Your mind is strong, with one specific weakness. Cinna won't require as much effort."

She released Hokuren and bade her kneel. Hokuren didn't see any issues with obeying.

"Good," said Moira. "The first step in defeating Ulbricht and helping both you and your dear Cinna is to find out how much you already know about his plans."

Don't tell her anything! What is wrong with you? With me?

Hokuren nodded. "I'll tell you everything I know." Moira deserved no less.

Cinna stalked through the forest on quiet feet, the only sound the creaking of Garrett's wagon. It made following easy, as she could hang farther back and lower the risk of being spotted.

Not that he appeared particularly interested. His gait had an eerie perfection to it that grew clearer the longer Cinna watched him. There was no wasted movement, each step efficient and sharp to the point that only his arms and legs seemed animated. His torso and head stayed unnaturally straight, even as he pushed a brisk pace over the bumpy forest floor and dragged the cart behind him.

Garrett pushed east, deeper into the forest, for half an hour, until he stopped at what seemed to be a random tree. Neither the house nor any other building in Fondence was visible. He stood stock-still in front of the tree, staring at it as if transfixed by the patterns in the bark. This lasted long enough that Cinna seriously considered blowing her cover to get him to do something.

He solved that problem by finally turning around with military precision, facing Cinna and locking eyes with her from her hiding spot within some brush. "Cinna, was it? I know you're out there, because of course you followed me. We knew you would. If you're looking for Ulbricht, why don't you go see Moira?"

Then Garrett was gone.

He didn't walk away. He simply . . . vanished, like a snuffed candle flame. Cinna first thought Garrett had cast an invisibility spell, which she'd seen once before. The wagon lead he had been holding had fallen to the ground with a thump the moment he'd disappeared, ending that speculation.

This was, to say the least, the last thing Cinna had expected. When she and Hokuren had run through the plan to follow Garrett and tried to conceive of potential hurdles, "Garrett blinks out of existence" never came up. That flaw in their planning merited further discussion with Hokuren later.

Magic was difficult to account for, however. The wizards claimed spells were requests made to the Primordial Ones, the world's creators, in the Old Tongue. In theory, if one knew the language well enough, they could ask for anything, though the Primordial Ones didn't answer every request.

For now, Cinna wasn't sure what to do. Ulbricht or a lackey would eventually claim the wagon and stones if he truly desired his worms, but flames knew how long that would take. She played with Garrett's final words in her mind. He had all but confirmed that Moira and Ulbricht were one and the same.

Her stomach twisted when she realized what that meant. Ulbricht wasn't concerned that she knew.

She ran through the forest back to the house. Garrett had expected she would follow him. Now worried this had been planned to separate her from Hokuren, Cinna sped up, ignoring the sharp branches and hard seeds underfoot.

The front door was open when Cinna arrived, a terrible sign. She did a quick run through the house, calling out Hokuren's name, but this only confirmed what she already suspected: Hokuren was not here.

She stood in the empty house, panting. If Hokuren had been taken,

Moira was the only answer. Surely, she would be waiting and ready for Cinna to arrive. Cinna clenched her hands into fists. Whether Moira was the witch from Hokuren's past or Ulbricht the wizard himself, or even both, it didn't matter. Cinna would go and rescue Hokuren.

She made it only to the front door when Roz appeared in the doorway, blocking her exit. "Sorry, but I can't let you leave," the traitorous adventurer said in her scratchy whisper.

A reunion with Roz wouldn't be a moment for celebration in normal circumstances, but Cinna had no patience for her now. "Move."

"No. It's for your own good. If you'll listen—"

Cinna threw the first punch. Roz reacted quickly enough to duck under it, following up with one of her own that Cinna spun away from.

They fought like old sparring partners. Neither landed a good blow on the other, with Cinna able to avoid Roz's slower attacks and Roz, for her part, raising an arm to shield herself from Cinna's that she couldn't avoid. She was a formidable opponent and held a decent size advantage.

Cinna would have to fight smart or dirty. Or both.

The fight shuffled onto, and back off of, the couch, then into the kitchen. They circled each other, backed off, feinted, made for openings—they did everything but talk. The table and chairs ended up scattered about. Cinna tried for the exit twice, but Roz was quick to react and keep her from leaving the house.

Roz jumped over a trip attack and efficiently flowed into a takedown attempt. She slammed into Cinna and threw her to the ground, pinning Cinna under her larger frame. One of her hands smashed into Cinna's nose, which started bleeding, while the other grabbed for Cinna's arms to wrestle her into submission.

Cinna twisted, bucked, and most effectively, poked Roz in the eye to enable an escape. Roz grunted in frustration as Cinna wormed away and grabbed her ankle, lifting it up and sending Cinna toppling heels over head. In an act of desperation, Cinna planted her hands on the floor and shifted her weight to put as much as she could behind a kick with her free foot, which connected with Roz's chin with a satisfying crack.

Roz freed the captured ankle and lurched back a step, wincing when her right knee took too much weight. "I can't tell if you're good or just flaming lucky," said Roz, rubbing her chin.

Cinna wiped her bloody nose with the back of her hand. The cartilage was miraculously unbroken. "That grab you did. And your knee." She looked up at Roz in horror. "The inn. It was you."

"No, it—it—"

"You got an Arms of Fondence uniform from Moira. You were going to kill Hokuren with that knife!"

"I missed on purpose. I was only—" Roz grimaced in pain, struggling with something. She shook her head and faced down Cinna again. There was a reddish tint to her eyes now. Not as strong as in the eyes of the goblins they'd fought, but enough.

"A worm," said Cinna in disbelief. "You've got a worm in your mind." Had Roz allowed it in or had it been against her will? Either way, Cinna had to get to Hokuren. They could sort out Roz once the boss was safe.

"Stay here, and no one gets hurt," said Roz, more confident.

"I don't take orders from worms." Cinna juked toward Roz, eliciting a left jab in response. A second false step got the same result. The path to winning the fight had shown itself. "Moira's going to hurt Hokuren, and you're on her side."

"No, that's not true." Roz looked momentarily stricken, but it was only a moment. Her face hardened again. "Moira's going to help Hokuren see the truth."

"You talking about the truth is rich. You even pretended to like Hokuren."

Roz set her chin. "It wasn't pretend, but it's like I said. I'll do anything to get my voice back."

"Have it your way."

Cinna stepped forward again, and for the third straight time the left jab was the counter. She expected it was there to set up Roz's right hook, so this time she dodged the jab to place her head in prime position to give Roz a target for a direct hit.

Right on cue, Roz obliged. Cinna was ready, ducking under the punch and delivering one, then two punches to Roz's undefended face. She swayed back and forth, unable to gather her wits before Cinna barreled into her, sending both of them through the front doorway and out into the mud. Roz toppled to the ground, bleeding from a wound on her forehead.

"Wait," she wheezed, rolling to face Cinna. The red in her eyes had faded. "You don't know what you're getting into. Moira's like . . . like a god. If she got Hokuren, she'll get you too."

Cinna ran toward the converted shrine without another look back. Not even a god could stop her from going after Hokuren.

23

Cinna flung open the iron-reinforced door to Moira's converted shrine. Rare Fondencian sunshine shone into the otherwise dark room. "Moira!" said Cinna, stepping into the tower, dagger in hand.

"I didn't expect Roz to stop you, but it was worth a try." Moira stood near the back next to her cauldron. It bubbled over with water that disappeared on contact with the floor. She wore a new hat, but her face had the same smarm as before.

"Where's Hokuren?" Cinna stayed alert for traps, keeping her eyes moving.

"Right here." Moira swept her hand to the right, where Hokuren was slumped against the wall. Her eyes were open, but she hadn't responded to Cinna's entrance. Thankfully, her eyes weren't red. "We've had a long talk, and it's clear you know far too much. Once I pick up the worms you brought me, I'll be able to ensure you don't go around telling anyone else what they shouldn't know."

There'd be no reaching the worm stage if Cinna had anything to say about it. "What have you done to her?"

She took another step forward. Moira waved her hand and spoke in a different language. Cinna had heard similar speech only once before, when Fenton used it to create a potion. It was the Old Language. But this seemed different, the sounds heavier and more guttural.

A massive pressure built within Cinna's skull, so painful she collapsed, dropping the dagger and grabbing her head. An urge to obey Moira permeated her thoughts like tendrils from the edges of her mind.

There was a voice in the back of her mind. It sounded like her own, but deeper. *No.*

Moira hacked out more unintelligible words, speaking louder. The pressure continued to build. Cinna writhed on the floor, the pain almost intolerable. A change came over her. Maybe Moira was right, and they did need the worms in their heads. They should be doing what Moira wanted, but without the worms, they'd be unpredictable. Cinna couldn't be trusted to obey and would fight the witch at every opportunity. Of course she should accept the worms so that didn't happen.

Do not be foolish, Cinna.

The pain stopped as the voice in the back of her mind spoke. What had she been thinking? Moira wasn't right. Cinna shook her head and rose to unsteady feet.

"What—" Moira's shock was temporary, morphing into a chilly smile. "So you can resist witch magic. Rather unusual."

Senara. It had to be the goddess in Cinna's soul, canceling the witch magic. Cinna had never been more thankful for her presence. She felt wrung out, like she hadn't slept in days, a result of the goddess using her body as a conduit for the counter magic. Last time Senara had done something like this, Cinna had needed to sleep immediately after. She didn't have that luxury at this moment.

"Your tricks won't work on me," said Cinna, as if she hadn't just learned Senara could block witch magic. "Release your hold on Hokuren, or I'll make you."

"You don't command me, even if I can't command you, either." Moira set about chanting. The Old Language contained sounds that no other language did, and grated against Cinna's ears, but Moira brought the noises together almost in song. The words echoed off the walls of the old temple, amplified by the magic they summoned.

Cinna ran toward Moira, hoping to beat whatever the witch had planned. But she didn't make it. Moira finished, flourishing her hands. Fire shaped like an arrow formed in the air and lanced across the room. Cinna dodged to the right as the fire hit the floor where she had stood an instant before. A searing heat hit the soles of her feet and ran up her legs before it dispersed. Small flames erupted from the floor, the wood burning.

Now this was wizard magic. They had been right: This *was* Ulbricht in disguise.

"You'll need to do better, Ulbricht," Cinna said, pushing against the floor to pop to her feet.

The false Moira made a tsk-ing sound with her tongue. "You know so much less than you think."

There was no time to consider what this meant. Moira chanted and waved her hands, casting new spells Cinna had never seen before. Chunks of ice fell from a cloud inside the temple. A black sphere formed behind Cinna and dragged her toward it, and she had to get down on hands and feet, digging fingers and toes into the cracks between wooden floorboards, to pull away. A puddle of green liquid appeared and ate through the floor, requiring her to jump over it.

The gap between Cinna and Moira had closed. A few more steps and Cinna would be in punching range. The wizard's chanting continued, her voice louder and echoing throughout the old temple. She pointed at Cinna. The area around Moira seemed to darken, as if the very world itself was involved in the spell.

Cinna prepared to dodge whatever was coming this time, but an unseen force swept her into the air before she could react. She dangled three feet off the floor as if pulled up by a harness. Invisible bonds restricted her as she struggled, holding her in place in midair. The bonds tightened, and soon her body was rigid as a statue, blinking the only movement available to her.

"It appears one trick works on you," said Moira, sweeping her robe behind her, restored to her position of power. "The air is frozen in place around you until I say otherwise."

Not even a finger would budge. This was bad enough, but Cinna had a larger problem. She couldn't breathe.

Moira's grin grew as if she could sense Cinna's fear. "Yes, no airflow means you'll soon suffocate. You're immune to my influence and too troublesome. Don't worry about Hokuren, though. She'll be a useful pawn for her old friend Moira."

The panic settled in. The wizard had barely needed to say a few words to end Cinna's life. She struggled to break whatever invisible force held her, unable to make any muscle so much as twitch. Her lungs screamed for air and her heart pounded with desperation. Out of the corner of her eyes she saw Hokuren, sitting against the wall with her head dropped, unresponsive. Cinna made one last ditch effort against the futility of her invisible prison. She could not fail here. She could not!

Her hand moved. It was like pushing through the thickest cold Fondencian mud, but it moved. Spirits restored, Cinna redoubled her effort, straining to push further before time ran out.

A white blur shot past her and leaped at Moira with a screech. It was Lumi, claws extended. Moira had enough wherewithal to tilt her head to one side despite her surprise. Lumi landed on her shoulder and, howling, sliced deeply into Moira's cheek.

Moira screeched and swatted at the cat, the big floppy hat sliding from her head to the floor. Lumi deftly jumped over the attack and onto her now exposed head, digging her claws in. Moira grabbed for the cat, getting nothing but a tuft of fur in her fist.

The spell restraining Cinna weakened. Her whole body now moved as if wrapped in heavy chains underwater. She swam through the frozen air, every action stressing her to breaking, searching for breath. Her hand punched through, and fresh air rushed to fill the gap she created with a popping sound. She gulped in precious air with a gasp as the last vestiges of the spell dissipated.

Cinna crashed to the floor, limbs heavy and chest heaving.

"Where are you hiding?" Moira said to Lumi, her focus entirely off Cinna. She had the cat in her grasp by the scruff of her neck. "Now that I know you're still around, I'll find whatever hole you've been hiding in."

This was Cinna's chance. Exhausted, lightheaded, and sore, she willed the energy for one final push. She rushed at the distracted Moira, rearing back and putting as much force as she could into a single punch aimed straight for the wizard's nose.

Moira didn't see her coming until it was too late. Cinna's fist slammed into Moira's face.

CRASH.

Cinna's fist continued through as if shattering a pane of glass, throwing off her balance. Moira only had time to say, "You—!" before her body cracked and exploded into thousands of pieces. Rainbow-colored shards, reflecting the sunlight, clouded the air and floated down, disintegrating into nothing before they reached the floor. Cinna fell to her knees, following her unexpected momentum, and rolled to a stop.

She looked over at Hokuren while lying on the rough wooden floor. The boss grimaced as if in pain, but ran over and pulled Cinna into a hug. "I'm so sorry. I let her spell influence me. I tried to fight it, but she came in the guise of my mother's ghost and I—"

"It's all right, boss," said Cinna, slumping in Hokuren's grasp. The threat was over, and Cinna was spent. "Remember when I said one punch was all I needed? Heh. Not quite how I saw it happening."

Hokuren squeezed Cinna harder. "If the cat hadn't broken Moira's focus—" She stopped. "Cinna, what's wrong?"

"Nothing," mumbled Cinna, lowering her head. "A little tired is all." She closed her eyes, unable to keep them open despite her best efforts.

"Can you stand?" asked Hokuren, her voice tense. "This place is on fire."

The smell of smoke registered in Cinna's brain, and she opened her eyes enough to view the fire originally started by the bolt of flame. It had spread and now threatened to engulf the entire interior. "I guess I'd better."

But her body wouldn't budge. With how much energy Senara had used to push out Moira's witch magic, she'd apparently left enough to escape the frozen air and throw a single punch, no more. Cinna summoned what remained of her willpower and, with Hokuren's assistance, made it to her knees before her head drooped. Walking suddenly seemed the most difficult endeavor in the world.

"I'll carry you," said Hokuren.

"Let me help." It was Roz's whispered voice. Cinna tried to tell Hokuren that she couldn't be trusted, but all that came out was a murmured gurgle, and then powerful arms took her from Hokuren and dragged her out of the burning temple.

She passed in and out of consciousness, catching glimpses of Hokuren and Roz in awkward conversation followed by Hokuren sitting alone. She emerged from this state lying on the forest floor, Hokuren's coat wrapped around her. The boss sat next to her, giving her a relieved smile as she stirred.

"You're awake," said Hokuren, rubbing her own arms. She reached over and touched Cinna's forehead. "Good, the fever's gone."

Cinna sat up and tried to get her bearings. "I had a fever?"

"You rejected Moira's witch magic." Hokuren accepted her coat when Cinna offered it back. "I suspect Senara had a hand in that."

"She puts me to sleep when she does that," said Cinna. "Better than if she hadn't, though."

The sun had moved across the sky, which meant she'd been out for hours. A candle lit in a lantern provided some extra light in the shadows of the trees. Cinna's stomach rumbled. Flames, she was hungry. The memories of the encounter with Moira flooded back, and she gasped.

"Where's Roz?" Cinna asked, whipping her head around.

"Gone," said Hokuren, lips pursed.

"You can't trust her." Cinna explained her fight with Roz, how she'd delayed Cinna's appearance at Moira's tower, and that she had a worm in her head like the goblins.

Hokuren nodded. She produced a parcel of bread and cheese from her pack and handed it to Cinna. "I know. Here, eat."

The bread was dry and the cheese firm. It was delicious nonetheless in Cinna's current state, and she chomped her way through it with a muffled thanks. She would have eaten unprocessed wheat and milk fat.

"Roz told me everything," continued Hokuren, "and it matches what you said, so she was telling the truth. She helped get you out of the temple and out here in the forest, where we might be safe for now." She thumped the ground with her fist. "But the false Moira wasn't Ulbricht, or even a person at all. I'm not sure what she was—some kind of image, but stronger. We have to assume that Ulbricht knows what she knew."

"Ah, yeah," said Cinna. "Garrett was an image or something also, and told me that Moira was Ulbricht."

"So he suspected we knew too much." Hokuren blew out a breath. "He won't let us go back to Velles. We're stuck."

Something furry rubbed against Cinna's back once she finished eating. It was Lumi, purring while sauntering in a circle around her.

"Our hero," said Cinna, feeling guilty she hadn't remembered to check on Lumi's condition. She reached to pet the cat, but Lumi extracted herself and moved over to rub against Hokuren.

"She likes me now." The cat settled onto Hokuren's lap. "Lumi followed us here and watched you sleep along with me. When I pet her, there's still that familiar feeling that I can't quite place, but I get this strange sense that . . . I trust her."

"You didn't back in Oro."

"Things have changed."

Lumi bounded out of Hokuren's lap, meowed and spun in a tight circle, and then scampered several feet away before another spin. "I think she wants us to follow her," said Cinna.

"Yes, she's been suggesting we do so for a while. I keep telling her I won't leave you behind." Hokuren had her hand on her chin. "We have nowhere we can go, Cinna. Fondence won't be safe, and I'm sure Ulbricht will be watching the wagons leaving for Oro. This sounds crazy, but I say we do it. We follow the cat."

"It does sound a little crazy." Cinna got up from the forest floor and stretched aching, tired muscles. "I like a little crazy."

24

Cinna and Hokuren picked their way through the forest as Lumi led them northeast out of Fondence, Hokuren relying on her candle lantern to augment the weak sunlight trickling in under the increasingly thick foliage. She didn't know where the cat was leading her, but it was her best chance of figuring out the source of that familiar feeling she had when she touched it.

"Hey, Lumi," called Cinna. The cat, which moved unbothered through the tangled mess of roots, vines, and mushrooms that made up the forest floor, kept scurrying far out in front of them, then circled in agitation waiting for them to catch up. "Slow down, you know Hokuren doesn't move fast."

"You're moving slower than usual, too," Hokuren pointed out. Cinna said her sleep had fully revitalized her, but her yawns told another story. Her usual surefootedness was missing as well. Hokuren caught her tripping over forest obstacles. "Are you sure you're okay?"

"I'm good enough, boss," said Cinna truculently. She'd never admit weakness in front of anyone other than Hokuren, including cats. "You know, I've been thinking about my fight with Roz."

"Oh?" Hokuren shuddered, thinking of the worm in Roz's head. It had come too close to happening to her, as well.

"She telegraphed her last punch. Adventurers often fight like that, because they normally deal with monsters. You don't exactly need advanced tactics against a giant rat. But she still should have known better against me."

"You're saying she could have telegraphed it on purpose." At Cinna's nod, Hokuren continued, "It's a thought. The compulsion might have forced her to fight, but it didn't say she had to win. Greeze also told us that people had some limited resistance, even with the worms, that the goblins don't have."

When Hokuren learned of Ulbricht's ability to coerce the goblins' minds with the worms, she hadn't considered he would actually take the concept to people. Perhaps he had done to Roz what he intended to do to Hokuren and placed a worm in her head against her will. The thought sickened Hokuren.

"Hssss." Lumi had backtracked during this discussion and now stood imperiously upon a small tree stump, hissing.

"Okay, okay, we'll keep moving." Cinna reached down to pet the cat, but Lumi bounded off.

A half hour later, Hokuren's calves burned and her feet had grown sore. She took a long swig from her waterskin and prepared to explain to Lumi all the reasons she would take a break and the many ways the little furball could stuff herself into a fire if she objected, lifesaver or not.

She didn't get the opportunity because the forest ended in a green wall in front of them.

"This isn't natural." Hokuren walked up to the wall, which extended out both to her left and right at least as far as she could see with her lantern.

"Oh, really?" Cinna plopped down onto the ground and stared at the wall. "If this is a trap, I'm not sure I have it in me to fight back."

The wall shimmered where the candlelight hit, wisps of green snaking throughout its opaque surface. It rose into the air higher than the light reached.

Cinna scooted closer and extended a finger out. "What's it made of?"

"Don't touch it," said Hokuren, leaning down to grab Cinna's hand. "I don't know, but it could be the same as what surrounds the contraption in the goblin warren. Or worse."

"More magic." Cinna threw her head back and sighed.

"Hey, where's Lumi?" Hokuren swept her lantern around her. No sign of the cat was visible in the limited light. "She's gone."

Cinna made a cursory glance around to confirm. "If she led us for all this time to see a magical wall we're stuck behind, I'll—"

Lumi's head appeared by their feet, poking out from the other side of the green wall, the remainder of her body obscured behind it. "Meow." She tilted her head in a very human fashion toward the wall.

Hokuren and Cinna exchanged glances. "Magic," said Cinna, extending her hand out again.

Her finger went first, smoothly entering the wall. Little ripples formed around her finger. Hokuren cringed as Cinna shrugged and pushed her hand in. "It feels like I'm pushing through the surface of a lake."

"Meow!" Lumi bared her teeth.

"Clearly we're moving too slowly," said Hokuren.

"This cat has no patience at all. Let's go through together." Cinna got to her feet and held Hokuren's hand with the one not yet penetrating the liquid wall.

They walked through. Hokuren couldn't help but squeeze her eyes closed as she did so. It was a strange sensation, like walking through a veil of water that didn't dampen her hair or clothes. The other side of the wall looked much like the side they had crossed from. Trees, brush, mushrooms, the whole lot. The only difference was a small mudbrick house, spewing smoke from a chimney.

"Someone lives here," said Hokuren.

They approached the house with caution. Bunting on the windows and a cheeky hand-drawn broomstick on the pearl-white front door greeted them. Next to that was a carved woodpecker door knocker. Hokuren could almost smell peppermint tea, triggered by the sight. "Cinna," she said, her voice catching. "These things on the outside of the house. They're Moira's."

"The real one?" Cinna touched the string emerging from the woodpecker's bottom.

Hokuren knew she shouldn't, but she allowed herself a small hope that Lumi had led them to Moira. Her Moira, hidden away deep in the Fondencian forest.

Cinna stood in front of Hokuren at the front door. "Let me go first, boss."

"Right." Hokuren had been so focused on the idea of Moira being here, she'd forgotten the potential dangers of this unknown house.

Cinna pulled the woodpecker's string to trigger its beak to knock on the door frame, then backed off, pushing Hokuren behind her.

The door creaked open, the entry matching Hokuren's memories. At first, it appeared empty, but once the door opened wide, it revealed a wizened old elf with white hair and a bright green dress, a small smile on her face.

Hokuren hesitated. It looked like Moira, but so had the false one thanks to memory manipulation. "Moira," whispered Hokuren. "Is it you?"

Moira waved her hand. A gentle sensation settled over Hokuren and her mind received the equivalent of a warm embrace. This was Moira's magic, *that* couldn't be faked. She ducked past a protesting Cinna and ran up to the witch, wrapping her in a real hug. "It's you."

"I'm glad to see you, dear girl," said Moira, squeezing Hokuren tight. "You've done me proud, becoming the investigator you were always meant to be."

"You're alive." Hokuren pulled back from the hug. "Why have you not said anything to me until now?"

Moira dropped her gaze. "Please come in. We have much to discuss, but little time to do it. I'll put on tea." She gestured past Hokuren at Cinna, who lingered behind and shuffled her feet awkwardly at the reunion. "Your friend is welcome as well, of course."

Lumi waltzed past them, head held high.

Hokuren sat in Moira's oversized chair, her favorite when she was a child, tea in hand. Cinna perched on the chair's ample armrest, forehead knotted as she peered into the tea, trying to determine what was in it.

"Drink it, please, Cinna," said Moira. "I can tell you're still drained from fighting off the witch magic. This should help."

Cinna gazed into the tea, then at Hokuren.

Hokuren patted her arm. "It's okay. This is the real Moira."

She took in Moira's sitting room, basking in the familiarity. A shelf full of books composed one entire wall. Hokuren guessed they were the same books she remembered from her childhood. The outside looked different, and the interior was bigger, but this was Moira's house. Of that there was no question.

The house provided Hokuren with a greater sense of belonging than even her old childhood home had. Though perhaps that had more to do with Moira, alive and well, in front of her.

Her old mentor sat on her small couch opposite them, settling in with her own tea. "I made your favorite, peppermint, for you."

"You remembered." Hokuren watched Lumi excitedly bat a small ball of yarn around the room. This playfulness was much more cat-like behavior, unlike what she'd expressed ever since their encounter with the fake Moira. Watching the cat, she could almost pretend she and Cinna weren't in danger.

Almost. "We're not safe," Hokuren said. "And my mother is partially responsible."

"I know," said Moira, hands clenched tightly around her mug. "I owe you an explanation."

Hokuren went immediately to the biggest question in a mind full of them. "My mother said you helped her learn witch magic and how to compel the goblins." At Moira's furrowed brow, she added, "I saw my mother's ghost."

"I didn't know at the time that I was helping her." Moira leaned back on the couch, sighing. "I didn't see any harm in performing a few spells when she asked, but she memorized my words and actions and could repeat them all on her own."

"She stole your magic."

"Stole is a word for it, I suppose." Moira stared into her tea. "Though it's more that she derived it. I didn't think it possible, but she hid her abilities well. I learned only after her death that she was a rogue wizard who'd once been a part of the Conclave. Had I known, I would never have let her watch."

"Did you know all this while I was coming over to your house, talking about how perfect my mother was?" Hokuren bit off the words.

"I can hear the accusation, Hokuren. You were a child, and you loved your mother. I—I didn't want to take that from you."

Hokuren fingered the necklace containing her mother's portrait. "I loved an idea of her. Perhaps I wouldn't feel so foolish now had I been told the truth. She meant well, but at the same time . . ." Hokuren made a helpless gesture with her hands. "She never consulted with the goblins to ask if they wanted what she offered, and she has some responsibility for what's become of her work."

Moira shifted on the couch cushions. "I meant to tell you one day, but I never could work up the nerve. And then you went to Velles, and putting it in a letter felt wrong."

"Fine." Hokuren dropped it. There were too many more important subjects to get to. "What was the false Moira we fought? And why an image of you?"

"A simulacrum," said Moira, spitting out the word. "As I pieced together what he was doing, Ulbricht wanted me dead. I retreated here, where he can't track me behind my magic. He thought I died, and he replaced me."

"What's a simulacrum?" asked Cinna, from the armrest.

"A being that isn't quite real, but isn't a simple image, either," said Moira, quietly. "An illusory yet autonomous creature only possible by combining wizard and witch magic. And by punching it, Cinna, and seeing it react like it wasn't supposed to, you literally shattered the illusion." She paused. "Magic like that is a feat in and of itself. Few simulacra have been created in anyone's living memory."

"People aren't supposed to be able to manage both wizard and witch magic," said Hokuren for Cinna's benefit.

"The cadence, the tones, the words, just ever so different." Moira held her fingers close together and peered at Cinna through them. "Of course we know it's possible, but people stopped bothering because of the difficulty. Few could master either if they attempted. Best to specialize."

Hokuren's mother had done it, at least to some extent. Then Ulbricht rode her coattails.

"What I don't get is what Ulbricht hopes to achieve. The goblins seem to think they're in some long-term experiment." Hokuren shook her head. "It doesn't make sense to me."

"I'm almost afraid to tell you what his ultimate plan is. I don't want to scare you children." Moira looked her age, over two hundred and fifty years old, ancient even for an elf.

"We're not children," said Cinna, arms crossed. "I'd have thought you learned your lesson about withholding things from Hokuren."

Hokuren laid her hand on Cinna's arm with affection. "What Cinna means is, tell us, please."

Moira looked between the two of them, a sad smile on her face. "You are both still children to me. But if you insist. His goblins are to take over Fondence."

"Yes," said Hokuren. "He doesn't have a plan for where the people living there should go."

"He does." Moira twirled her finger in her tea. "They'll remain in Fondence as the goblins' servants."

Hokuren and Cinna did nothing but gape at Moira for a long while. The very idea was so absurd that Hokuren would have thought it a joke if not for the grim look on Moira's face. If his goal actually was to turn the town into a collection of mindless drudges, then Ulbricht had taken her mother's research to terrible new levels.

Finally, Hokuren said, "Can he really do that?"

"*Why* would he do that?" asked Cinna. "I'm sure he's not interested in the ethics questions, but it seems like a lot of work."

"To answer the first question, he believes he can. As for the second, *because* he can. He's a wizard. This is what they do. They test the bounds of their power and take it farther and farther. He's been saving up those worms, and he's got close to enough. It'll be the newest ultimate test of his abilities."

"All the more reason to get the Conclave here as soon as possible to stop him," said Hokuren. "He's rogue."

Moira's laugh was mirthless. "I see you haven't lost all your childhood naivete, Hokuren." She leaned toward them. "Why do you so easily believe he isn't doing this with the Conclave's blessings?"

"Because—" Hokuren froze, realization dawning on her. "Of course they'd be interested in combining wizard and witch magic."

"Oh, outwardly they'll call him rogue and say they'll deal with him when they have the chance. But the inner circle of the Conclave, at least, absolutely knows what he's up to, and has approved it." Moira sipped more of her tea. "If this goes well, and Fondence ends up in service to the goblins, who's to say the wizards couldn't take it further and find a town that could be in service to *themselves*."

Cinna jumped off the chair. "Enough with this. If the Conclave supports him, it can't be allowed to go further. We have to stop him!"

"How? We barely survived his simulacrum." Hokuren pointed at Lumi. "And only because the cat assisted."

"It will take him some time to create a new one, so he'll be at his most vulnerable," said Moira thoughtfully. "Even still. He can marshal a sizeable goblin force to his aid and of course, knows plenty of magical spells, like the air-freezing spell used on you, Cinna."

"Maybe we just need Lumi's help again." Cinna hunched down to pet the cat. "We beat the simacrulum or whatever, we can beat him."

"Hold on," said Hokuren. "Moira, how did you know what the simulacrum used against Cinna?" She thought back to earlier in the conversation, when Moira said something she should have picked up on. "Or that Cinna shook off the witch influence?"

"I'd still like to know how Cinna did that." Moira peered at Cinna. "The influence of witch magic can be resisted with varying degrees of success, though it's harder when Ulbricht can use the worm. I've never heard of someone outright rejecting it, however."

"Trade secret," said Cinna.

Hokuren held her tongue. Though she trusted Moira, Senara's existence in Cinna's soul was her assistant's story to tell, and if she didn't want to tell Moira, Hokuren wouldn't either.

"We're all allowed some of those." Moira raised her palm and placed it perpendicular against her nose, saying a few words in the ancient language of the Primordial Ones. Lumi jumped up into Hokuren's lap. The cat kneaded her trouser legs before curling up, purring.

"This feeling . . ." Hokuren's eyes widened as she recognized the magic. It had eluded her when she first felt it from Lumi. Now she couldn't believe she didn't know what it was from the start. "It was you."

"I have a special connection with Lumi. I can be Lumi and see through her eyes, if I wish."

"You saved us."

"Wait," said Cinna, catching up on the conversation. "It was you in Lumi?" When Moira nodded, she frowned. "Thanks, then. But were you—with the dogs?"

"I was," said Moira.

"She was testing me, boss."

Moira laughed softly. "No, I wanted to follow you and see who you were. When Hokuren arrived in Fondence with a friend, I was curious. You two seemed close, and I wanted to know more about the person who'd cracked Hokuren's exterior. She usually keeps people an arm's length away."

"Come on," said Hokuren, cheeks heated. "I don't." Her denial had little strength behind it.

"If you say so."

"I couldn't recall that was your magic I felt when I touched Lumi before now. Why?" The answer hit Hokuren as soon as she finished the question. "You made me forget."

Moira's smile fell. "I had to. If you had recognized my magic, you might have asked about me, or been more open to calling the simulacrum an impostor early on. You could have alerted Ulbricht to resume his search for me."

Hokuren opened her mouth to say that she wouldn't have jeopardized Moira like that, but shut it without saying anything. She wouldn't have known the dangers, and very well could have blown Moira's cover.

"Okay," she said. "You're right. I just—"

"I wanted to see you, Hokuren. I wanted to tell you that I was here." Moira's head was down. "Most of all, though, I wanted you to be safe. When you were notified of your father's death, you were supposed to come, sell the business, and leave. You weren't supposed to get involved and make yourself an enemy of Ulbricht. Now you'll have to stay here."

"What, forever?" said Cinna. "In this little house and pocket of forest?"

"You can't go back to Velles. Ulbricht knows you know too much. He won't let you."

Cinna stalked back and forth in the little room. "I'd rather risk the wizard than this cozy prison. You and Hokuren stay here, and I'll go deal with him."

Hokuren made a calming gesture at Cinna. She agreed that staying with Moira indefinitely was no option. Neither she nor Cinna would be able to live in the sterile safety for long. But they needed time to think. "We should not do anything rash, Cinna."

"Why didn't you sell Mikko's Imports and go back to Velles?" said Moira, face drawn. "You'd have been safe, unaware of what was happening here."

Hokuren shook her head. "I couldn't let my father's death go. The goblin explanation was lacking. I needed to know. It's why I came to Fondence."

"About that." Moira wrung her hands. "I know something about what happened."

"What?" Hokuren shot to attention. Even Cinna stretched toward Moira in anticipation. "Tell me," ordered Hokuren.

"You're going to hate me."

"I doubt that."

Shuffling feet approached from the back rooms of the house. The source entering from the kitchen left Hokuren utterly speechless.

"Hello, Pumpkin," said her father.

25

Mikko Tuomi stood in front of Hokuren, looking far more than a decade older than last she'd seen him. His beard, always so neatly trimmed in her childhood, had grown scruffy, and the gray that had peppered his chin when she left had completed its takeover. What were once wrinkles on his forehead were now creases. His deep brown skin was weathered, almost leathery. His smile was awkward, as if he'd forgotten how.

"My daughter," he said, a catch in his voice. "I've been wanting to see you for so long."

"Father," Hokuren sputtered, closing her mouth when she realized it hung open. She got up from the chair and gave him a tentative hug. He wrapped her up and lifted her from the ground like he had when she was a child. This at least was as she remembered. "You're alive," she added, idiotically.

"That explains the empty grave," said Cinna.

Moira cleared her throat. "I've been protecting him here."

Her father's smile turned guilty as he released Hokuren. "I waited to give you a little time with Moira. You weren't supposed to find out I 'died,' Hokuren. Things didn't go as planned. I'm sorry, Pumpkin."

Hokuren buried her face in her hands, unsure how to respond. First Moira, now her father, back from the dead in rapid succession. Of course he faked it without telling her, and of course he wanted instant forgiveness. He never much considered how she might feel.

Cinna's hand touched her shoulder. "Hokuren, are you all right?"

"Who's this?" Hokuren's father waved his hands to usher Cinna aside. "This is a family reunion. I haven't seen my daughter in ten years. Please don't interrupt."

Cinna shrank back, but Hokuren grabbed her hand. "This is Cinna. She's family now, too. Don't treat her like she doesn't belong."

"I—" Her father's eyes slid between Hokuren and Cinna and back again. He pressed his hand to his chest. "I see. I'm sorry. What can I do to make it up to you?"

He often did this, asking Hokuren to tell him how to fix things when they argued, rather than making a genuine effort to right things himself. Exasperated, she ignored his request and said, "You let me think you were dead. How did you break the Pigeon Couriers spell?"

"Ah, yeah," said her father, scratching his head. "Moira didn't know I'd done that. She offered me sanctuary here after I overheard the false Moira discussing the worms in the stones." He shivered. "And she caught me and threatened to kill me if I spoke a word about it. I agreed out of fear, but that wasn't enough, apparently. Goblins broke into the house, armed and frenzied. Those red eyes are frightening. I barely escaped."

Moira cut in. "My magic cuts us off so completely from the world that it severed the Couriers's spell. *If* he had told me about it, I might have been able to work out a way to maintain it and keep you from getting the letter announcing his death."

"Then I'd never know what happened to either of you." Hokuren turned back to her father. "I can't believe you've been working with Ulbricht. Do you even know what those worms of his you've helped to bring in are used for?"

"I do now, but not until Moira, *this* Moira, told me. Before, I didn't know, I didn't, I swear." Mikko held up his hands. "Things were getting tight a few years ago. He approached me about a deal to import silks. Said his previous contact quit the business. It seemed easy and lucrative, so I agreed." He tapped his forehead. "Wasn't thinking. In my younger years, I'd have seen it for what it was and said no, but . . . I'm worn down and not as careful as I used to be. Before I knew it, I was waist-deep in the smuggling muck, with no easy way to extract myself. And the money wasn't even good! I was sending so much to help pay for the goblins' warren."

"And you didn't wonder about that, either?"

"I had no idea it was"—he waved his hands around—"witch magic or wizard magic or what have you. I thought they were just unusually smart little critters."

"You used to care about what you were bringing in, beyond the money," said Hokuren.

Her father didn't meet her eyes. "I used to have a lot of things."

Hokuren pursed her lips. "Not now. We can't do that now. We're all in trouble. You said Ulbricht approached you. So you know who he is, then." At long last, they might finally get an identity.

Her father shook his head, however. "He came to me in a guise, and I've never seen him since." He put his hand on Hokuren's shoulder. "If I could have stopped the Pigeon Couriers package from being delivered, I would have. I never wanted to bring you into this mess."

"Well, I'm here now, in the thick of the mess." Hokuren gripped the edge of her jacket. "And if we don't figure out who Ulbricht is, and stop him, we're all stuck here until he finds us, which he can probably do eventually, right?"

"That seems to be about the extent of it," agreed her father. "Or perhaps he never finds this place, and we're here in safety forever. Know any good games to pass the time?"

The past few hours had been overwhelming, and the tendrils of exhaustion pulled at Hokuren's mind. Moira and her father stood alive in front of her, and all she could do was try to puzzle out Ulbricht's identity. Focusing on that kept her from breaking down in front of them.

"I need to think," Hokuren announced to the room. "Alone." Cinna's hand, still in her grip, tightened. "And by alone, I mean with Cinna."

Cinna breathed a sigh of relief. "I suppose I could come with you, boss," she said, a pretense of insouciance.

"But we just reunited," said her father quietly.

Hokuren pushed her rising guilt aside. Their reunion meant little if they were to soon become Ulbricht's minions through inaction.

"We're safe behind the wall," said Moira. "For now. If Ulbricht knew we were here, he'd have already breached it. But if you go beyond, you risk all of us."

Hokuren nodded and left the house, Cinna in tow. When they were outside, Hokuren's composure collapsed. She slumped over, remaining upright only because of Cinna's quick reflexes to support her.

"Hokuren, what's wrong?" said Cinna, steadying Hokuren.

"It's too much, Cinna."

There was bright sunshine in Moira's little domain, the sun's static position unmoored from the world outside. A gentle breeze played with the plants and flowers in the gardens surrounding a rockery. Cinna led Hokuren to this rockery, taking care not to step on the flowers.

They sat on the rocks, feet dangling a few inches off the ground, for a few moments without a word until Cinna said, "I'm sorry both your parental figures led you to believe they were dead and didn't tell you. If this is what having parents is like, maybe I'm better off without them."

Hokuren laughed, choking back tears. "There are good moments, too."

"We should rest," said Cinna, her haggard face full of concern. "I got plenty of sleep, but I bet you didn't. You always say not to think when you're tired and distracted."

"I do say that. Sometimes there's no other option. We've got to figure out who Ulbricht is."

"All right." Cinna thought for a moment. "The problem is that it could be anyone."

"I have a hunch."

"I like your hunches, boss. Tell me."

Hokuren returned a grin from Cinna. With little fuss, Cinna had agreed to a brainstorm session and put Moira and her father to the side. She swallowed, ready to start with her least favorite option. "Let's talk about Roz."

"What?" Cinna boggled at Hokuren. "You think he disguised himself as Roz and followed us around this entire time?"

"What better way to keep tabs on us? Roz presented as a friend, but that throat injury. Convenient, no? Ulbricht's spell could make us see what we wanted to see, but maybe he couldn't get the voice right, or he didn't know her songs, so instead he gave her a croaky, ruined one. The real Roz could still be in Trebello, singing away, with no idea there's a doppelgänger of hers that's been working for my father for years."

"We fought though," said Cinna. "Me and Roz. He could fake his appearance to look like her, but he couldn't have those fighting skills without actual work. Work he can't possibly have had time for, what with all the wizarding and witching."

Hokuren nodded. "And if he was going to look like her, I'd imagine he'd pick something closer to what she looked like before she left. Why cut the hair off and bulk up? I never really thought it was her, but I had to mention it." She adjusted her coat lapel, thinking of her next guess. "Okay, what do we know about both Fenton and my mother?"

"They keep secrets?"

"Granted, but there's one more thing they both keep: low profiles. They work on their magic in secret while presenting a very normal townsperson persona."

"I see." Cinna frowned. "I don't know many of the townspeople."

"I've got one in mind. Casper Daily."

"The mayor?" asked Cinna. Hokuren could almost imagine the gears turning in Cinna's brain. Cinna snapped her fingers. "I get it! He keeps a low profile by being a useless mayor in a town that runs itself. And the other person who's not real, Garrett, was supposed to be his nephew."

"Yes," said Hokuren. "He also had the blackmail letter in that secret compartment in his house. The reason we didn't see him at all is that he's Ulbricht, and talking to us would threaten his cover. Remember, we aren't under any of the spells he cast on the townspeople."

"So he's a coward."

"I'd call it more carefulness than cowardice. He was helping the fake Moira drum up concerns about the goblin threat and pressuring my father to sell the business."

"Perfect." Cinna jumped from the rockery. "It's him!"

Hokuren held up a hand. "There are some issues with the theory."

"Like what? I'm already convinced."

"You're forcing me to be the one to destroy my own theory?" Hokuren waved Cinna back to her seat on the rockery. "For one, even though his mayoral role is mostly ceremonial, he's still one of the best-known people in town. Hardly the most inconspicuous persona for a wizard in hiding." Hokuren held up two fingers. "But the second, and most damning, is the testimony from my mother's ghost."

Cinna side-eyed Hokuren. "Not to be disrespectful to the memory of your mother, boss, but I'm not sure a ghost's testimony will hold up in a trial."

Hokuren smiled. "This isn't a trial. Casper's been mayor so long that his time in the position predates my mother's first conversation with Ulbricht. She wouldn't have needed to call him in from the Conclave, like my mother's ghost insinuated she did."

"Ah, but boss," said Cinna, waving a finger at Hokuren in the manner in which Hokuren liked to do when she disagreed. "Ulbricht's able to change how he looks, right? Couldn't he easily have just killed the real Casper and replaced him after arriving in town?"

The thought shook Hokuren, not least because she hadn't even considered it. "For no one to notice, he'd need to change more than his appearance. That would require a thorough understanding of Casper's mannerisms, his way of speaking, his—" Hokuren stopped herself, discombobulated. "Wait, how can I say he couldn't do it? He did it with Moira. He could use our memories as a guide for how he looked, and a witch spell to handle the rest."

Hokuren held her hand to her forehead. *Had* Ulbricht replaced Casper so long ago that she was still living in Fondence at the time? She could have been under the influence of a spell of his for years and never have known. It was difficult to feel confident in her thoughts when she couldn't trust her own memory hadn't been magically altered.

Cinna pressed her fists to her hips in pride at coming up with a point that made Hokuren reevaluate. "Right, he cheated with magic."

"We never even saw Casper. Maybe for a while they worked together, but then Casper found out what was going on and Ulbricht got rid of him? Maybe he's an image now, like Garrett. But it all feels so . . . unnecessary."

"Everything about the whole goblin experiment thing feels that way."

Hokuren frowned. "You know, the goblins have been bothering me since we met them."

"Is it because they're better at math than we are?"

"No." Hokuren gave Cinna a strange look. "It's about what happens when Ulbricht compels them. The loincloths, the tooth necklaces, the lousy spears. They snarl and snap. They're made to masquerade as farcical versions of themselves."

"Well, it's just like Moira pretending to be a witch, right?" Cinna waved a hand at the house. "Not that one, but the fake one. She had a bubbling cauldron, broomsticks, and bat-themed blankets."

Hokuren nodded. "And the pointy hats. Unlike the true Moira, she was a caricature of a witch. If you want people to buy an act, it's easier if you present what they already expected. Like characters from a book."

"A specific book. Or books, if you will."

"That's right. *Captain Cavalier*." Hokuren slapped her forehead. "I didn't put it together until now. I believed Moira was Ulbricht and never gave any other possibilities a thought."

"Put what together, boss?"

"Who's been involved in all these machinations between Ulbricht, the fake Moira, and Casper?" Hokuren barreled on before Cinna could interrupt with an answer. "Never the leading actor, always in the cast. He witnessed the pledge my father made to sell the business in case of overwhelming debt. He pressured me to sell it to her. He led us straight to Garrett and warned us about following. No one likes him, and he keeps to himself as far on the outskirts of town as you can get. He knew the stones opened. Has a house he keeps hidden from people who don't have a worm in their head so he can't easily manipulate their memories." She pointed at Cinna. "What books did Roz tell us Harrison Grimes has a complete collection of?"

Cinna's mouth made an *O* shape. "I think you've figured it out."

Hokuren pounded her fist to her palm. "Grimes is Ulbricht."

At first, neither Moira nor Hokuren's father accepted the idea that Grimes was the wizard.

"He's creepy, I'll admit, but he's also quite lazy," said her father. "Just because he reads some popular books, you think he's a wizard?"

"It's not only the books, and he's not lazy. That's the show he puts on to deflect attention." Hokuren paced the sitting-room floor. "If you thought he was creepy and lazy, why did you keep him employed?"

"Well, the fake Moira told me to—oh."

Hokuren stared at him. "I wish I had known that sooner."

"All right, let's say Harrison Grimes is Ulbricht. How does that help?" asked Moira. "He'll still kill us."

"Obviously, we've got to get to him first," said Cinna. "We're not going to sit and wait for him to find us and get the upper hand."

"He'll no longer be able to sneak up on us in the guise of Grimes," said Hokuren. "We need help. If we can destroy the Tolliver-Evans device"—Hokuren caught Cinna's confused expression—"*the contraption* my mother brought to Fondence, I think the goblins would become our allies."

"Ah, yes." Moira seemed to shrink in her chair. "Nekane used a special bit of witch magic in the barrier that surrounds that thing. You'll never get past it on your own."

Cinna rubbed her hand. "So we discovered."

"Moira, my mother got her knowledge of witchcraft from you," said Hokuren. Their only hope rested with the old witch. "You must know how she did it. And, more importantly, how we can bypass it."

Moira averted her eyes. "I think so. Witch magic can only be cast on others. The power required means I can only cast a counter to Nekane's spell on one of you."

"Me," said Cinna instantly, stepping forward. "I'll go into the goblin warren and bash that thing up before you can brew another pot of tea."

"It's not that simple." Moira shook her head. "I need to get into your head, and there's only one of you I know well enough to trust doing that."

They all turned to Hokuren, who blanched. "Me, then." It was right that she be the one to undo the mistake her mother made. "I can do it."

"I'll be right there with you, boss," said Cinna.

"Now wait a minute," said Hokuren's father, holding his hands up. "Are we sure this is safe?"

"It's not safe, but we have to do it." Hokuren channeled bravado she didn't feel. It helped to think of what Cinna would say.

"There's another problem," said Moira, tentatively. "The moment Hokuren leaves here with my magic, I expect Ulbricht to feel it immediately. A powerful spell like that is going to attract his attention. He'll send every goblin he's got, and if they don't get you, they'll at least slow you down before he can arrive to finish you off."

"Hah," said Cinna. "His too-smart goblins fight like mathematicians, and if he's still in Fondence, we have a big head start. We can make it."

"He will beat you to the contraption, I guarantee it."

"Well, then, what? It's hopeless?" Cinna glared at Moira. "You can cower in fear behind your magic all you want, but don't keep us from dealing with this."

Moira rose from her chair, showing more energy than she had since Hokuren's reunion. "You have no idea—"

"We can distract him," said Hokuren, interrupting whatever Moira was going to say to Cinna. "If someone were to engage with him, perhaps he wouldn't notice us long enough for us to get to the contraption."

Moira cut off her stare at Cinna. "But who can we get to do that?"

"It has to be me," said Hokuren's father, rising from his seat. "My return from the dead should prove a shocking enough distraction."

"Father, he wanted to kill you, and I don't think that's changed." Hokuren gripped her coat buttons. She couldn't handle the whiplash of him going from dead to not dead to dead again.

Her father's eyes twinkled. She remembered that look, from those too rare moments where he paid attention to something other than the import business. "I might stave him off long enough if I come in with an offer to sell the business. Listen, Pumpkin, I've been complicit in all that's been going on. Perhaps it's what I deserve." He held up a finger to Hokuren's protest. "If it'll keep the only child I have left safe, what sort of father would I be if I turned this down?"

"Father—"

Knock knock. Everyone in the house turned to face the door in sudden silence.

Moira had her hand over her mouth. Her spell should have made it so that no one else could see the house or the bubble, but someone had. Hokuren's hand went to the hilt of her dagger.

It was Cinna who motioned the others back and tip-toed to the door with her dagger in hand. She threw open the door and pointed the weapon at the interloper.

"Roz?" she said. She didn't lower the dagger.

"The very same." Roz's mace was at her hip, her hands up and open. Dried blood flaked from the wound she'd received from Cinna on her forehead. "I came to offer my help again. You're doing this all wrong."

"How did you find this place?" said Moira, hand to her throat and eyes wide. "Is Ulbricht right behind you?"

"Doubt it," said Roz. If Moira being here and alive was a surprise to her, she didn't show it in the least. "I followed these two." She pointed at Cinna and Hokuren. "I caught them following that cat, and I couldn't figure out why. Lucky for me, none of them realized."

"I would have. I'm just tired," said Cinna.

Hokuren spoke up from behind Cinna. "How long have you been listening?"

"Since the beginning." Roz grinned. "Heard you talk about me as Ulbricht. Thanks for discarding the idea so easily." She gestured at Cinna. "Can I get a nicer welcome than a blade in my face?"

"We all know about your worm now," said Cinna. "You're not trustworthy."

"Let her in." Hokuren waved her hand. "Keep your dagger at the ready."

Cinna stepped back, and Roz joined the rest of them in the sitting room. Moira fretted about Ulbricht finding the hidden cottage, while Hokuren's father wore a look of puzzlement at both Roz and Cinna's mention of the worm.

"Nice place." Roz nodded with approval. "So this is the real Moira."

"Why have you followed us here, Roz?" Hokuren crossed her arms over her chest. "I thank you for helping to get Cinna out of the temple, but you tried to kill me, toyed with my emotions, and delayed Cinna from coming to my rescue. You'll do anything to get your voice back, right? Has Ulbricht made you promises now that his simulacrum is gone?"

"You tried to kill my daughter?" asked Hokuren's father. He marched up to Roz and leaned over her. "After I gave you a lifeline when you came back from Trebello with your injury? That's how you repay my generosity?"

"No!" said Roz, straining her voice. "Hokuren, I meant to scare you. Cinna put up more of a fight than I anticipated, so I threw the knife as part of an attempt to flee. It was never going to hit you. I did it so you'd want to sell the business and get out of Fondence." She lowered her voice. "You have to believe me."

"Do we now," said Cinna.

Hokuren regarded Roz warily. The fluttering heart and nervous stutter she'd previously had around Roz was gone, the childhood crush laid to rest. At best, Roz was unreliable. At worst, she was an adversary.

"I'd like to believe you," said Hokuren, quietly. "But you killed Barth, didn't you?"

Roz sighed. She ran her tongue along her lips, apparently thinking through what to say. She settled with a simple, "Yeah."

"You—You killed Barth?" said Hokuren's father, stunned. "Barth's *dead*? Why, Roz?"

"He figured out how to open one of those stones! The worms are in there, and he didn't like the look of them. He stole the key to the chest so the goods would be stuck. His plan was to confess to the Oro Watch and make a deal with them by ratting out the rest of us. Said that with you dead"—she pointed at Hokuren's father—"it was a good time to end the smuggling." Roz looked down at her boots. "I told him he could leave, and it'd be like he was never involved, but he wouldn't relent. And I was overcome by this, this . . ." She looked up at Hokuren, stricken. "It was Moira. The simulacrum. Her voice was in my head, telling me to kill him, and it seemed like the most logical thing to do. The only logical thing to do. And then, it was over."

Hokuren recalled the way she'd felt when the simulacrum had used witch magic on her. When the false Moira's influence was strongest, she wondered if she'd be able to resist an order to kill.

"I see," said Moira. "You received a worm, Cinna said?"

The poise Roz had entered with was gone. "Moira said she could get me my voice back if I made sure the shipments continued. If I let her put the worm in me, and did what she asked, she'd make it happen. She *promised*."

"You *let* her put the worm in you?" said Cinna, horrified.

"I didn't know what it could do."

"That doesn't make it better!"

"I keep telling you, I'll do anything to get my voice back. But even then, I didn't want to kill Barth. I—I lost control of myself." Roz pulled her arms close to her body to hug herself. "It was the same when I was trying to stop you from reaching the inn. When I received orders like that, it's like I couldn't disobey. I didn't think I would be asked to do any of . . . that."

"And what are your current orders?" asked Cinna, still in a fighting stance.

"I . . . I don't have any," said Roz, as if the very idea was alien. "The fake Moira is gone. No instructions in my head, no constant presence. And since she's gone, I can't get my voice back from her anyway. I think—I think I'm free."

"Could it be?" asked Hokuren. "If the simulacrum was the one who influenced Roz . . ."

"It's possible that the spell to influence Roz doesn't work for Ulbricht," conceded Moira. "He'd have to cast it himself. Though if he sees you, it would be rather easy, what with you already having a worm in your head."

"I'll accept punishment for Barth's murder," said Roz. "But first, let me help you. I've been listening to your plan, and I think you need me."

"We've got it all figured out, thanks," said Cinna. "Someone who may still be little more than a wizard puppet only hampers us."

"I know I don't deserve your trust, but if I had wanted to betray you, I could be halfway to Ulbricht already." Roz clasped her hands together. "Please, at least hear me out."

"Tell us," said Hokuren. Cinna scowled, but said nothing further.

"Ulbricht doesn't believe that Mikko died," said Roz, jerking a thumb at Hokuren's father. "He also knows everything that Hokuren knows, because she told him through the fake Moira when she was under the influence. He'll guess, or at least worry, that Hokuren will eventually figure out Grimes's identity, and activate his defenses. Surround himself with compelled goblins. Hokuren, your father will never get close to him. Ulbricht means to kill you all."

Hokuren nodded. If he was spooked, that rang true. "All right, sounds bad. What do you propose?"

"You still need to destroy the contraption in the goblin warren, and you still need to distract him. There's only one of us who could truly hope to distract Ulbricht for any appreciable length of time." She pointed at Cinna. "Her."

"Oh, no," said Cinna. "I'm going with Hokuren to the contraption. She can't go alone, and neither Moira nor her father could fight off even a single goblin to protect her." She turned to Moira and Hokuren's father. "No offense."

Roz shook her head. "I heard Moira say that witch magic can't affect you. That's why it has to be you. He can lock any of the rest of us up too easily." She pointed at Hokuren. "She'll be coming with me."

"Absolutely not." Cinna waved Roz off. "Do you think I'd trust you with Hokuren alone?"

"You're right, Roz, that Cinna is the only one who could fight off Ulbricht's witch magic to have a chance at distracting him." Hokuren fussed with the buttons on her coat. "But wizard magic can still affect her."

"That's true," said Roz. "She'll just have to survive until we destroy the contraption."

"You going with Hokuren isn't happening." Cinna crossed her arms over her chest. "Right, boss?" When Hokuren said nothing, Cinna looked at her, betrayed. "Hokuren?"

Cinna's reticence was easy to understand. They'd have to split up, and Roz had been guilty of heinous actions hoping to recover her voice. However, Hokuren couldn't see how the plan would work otherwise. "Cinna, please. I think Roz is right. This is the only way."

"Do you really trust her?"

Hokuren forced herself to sound confident. "Enough."

Cinna put her hands on Hokuren's shoulders, her eyes full of fear. "You can't die, Hokuren. I need you."

Hokuren pulled Cinna into a hug. "Same, Cinna."

"Ahem." Roz cleared her throat. "You know, Cinna, I've never wanted to hurt Hokuren."

"Listen, you." Cinna turned to thrust a finger in Roz's face. "If anything happens to Hokuren, I will have nothing better to do than spend all my days hunting you down, do you understand?"

Roz blinked at the tenacity in Cinna's words. "I don't doubt it for a moment. I'll keep her alive. I owe both of you that much."

"When should we leave?" asked Moira.

"Now." Hokuren made sure her tone brokered no argument. "The longer we wait, the more time Ulbricht has to plan."

26

Hokuren bid Cinna farewell and watched her run into the forest back to Fondence to distract Ulbricht until she was no longer visible through the trees, wondering if she would ever see Cinna again.

"I know you're worried, but I'd be surprised if she could actually die," said Roz.

Hokuren didn't reply, listening to the breeze rustle nearby leaves. She closed her eyes and said a silent prayer to Senara to keep Cinna safe and to not let her sacrifice herself on Hokuren's behalf. Even though the goddess couldn't hear her and had no control over Cinna and her reckless nature, the prayer made her feel a little better.

Neither Hokuren nor Roz knew the way to the goblin warrens from the bubble Moira hid them in. Hokuren's father, however, knew the forest as if he lived in it as a ranger. "I've been to the warren and back so many times, the goblins should consider me an honorary citizen," he had joked. No one had laughed.

He walked beside Hokuren to the warrens, Moira and Roz following at a short distance to let them talk. They spent a long while in awkward silence until he said, "Anything on your mind, Pumpkin?"

Hokuren swallowed. "Were you aware of what Mother had been doing with the goblins?"

"No," her father grimaced. "I knew nothing until Moira told me a few weeks ago. She told me she was playing bridge!"

"She did sometimes."

"Not always." Her father glanced into the treetops. "Once I learned of it, I tried to see her side of it. I believe she meant well, I truly do. We discussed goblins from time to time, and she always told me that she hated the way they were treated. Are treated. She believed they could be a part of society, that we could trade with them and live among each other. We didn't have to be such enemies."

"Do you think she considered the potential consequences of what she was doing? It seems easy to see how influencing their minds opened up the potential for something like what Ulbricht has been doing." Hokuren's voice cracked. It was like she was a little kid again, talking to her father and asking for an answer that would make her feel better.

"Your mother was an idealist," said her father. "She thought that if your intentions were pure, things would work out in the end."

Hokuren grasped the locket with her mother's picture and held it in her hand. "Mother's intentions were not completely pure."

"That's true, but don't be too harsh with her."

"I'd like to think that if she were alive now, and saw what Ulbricht was doing, she'd join us in stopping it, even if it meant destroying the contraption." Hokuren released the locket from her hand. "You knew her better than I."

Her father grabbed Hokuren's hand and squeezed. "She would. You're doing the right thing, and wizard or not, she believed in that." He smiled at her. "There's a lot of her in you, you know. You're smart, you believe in justice, and you will do what's necessary."

Even if he only said all that to make her feel better, it worked.

"What about you, Father?" His role in all of this still bothered Hokuren. "When you started smuggling the silks for Ulbricht, something had to seem off, didn't it?"

"You're not wrong. It took very little time for the whole thing to become unsettling." Her father looked off into the woods for a while. "Well before I knew about the worms, I asked if I could back out. Ulbricht made it known that wasn't an option, and if I tried going to the authorities, he'd come after the one thing I cared about more than anything."

"Ah." Hokuren nodded knowingly. "He'd destroy your business."

"No. You."

Hokuren startled. "Me?"

"Of course it's you. I know I was terrible to you after your brothers died. Losing them, after losing your mother—I didn't handle it well. They were supposed to take over the business, and you were supposed to do whatever your heart pleased. And then they died, and I wanted to make you a part of the business, and didn't understand why you pushed back so hard." Her father gave her a wan smile. "My biggest regret is how I pushed you away and lost the only family I had remaining. Even though you were far away and never spoke to me, you were always the most important thing left for me, far more than the business. And Ulbricht knew it. He knew you were in Velles, and explained in no uncertain terms that the distance was no matter should I ruin his operation."

"I—" Hokuren stopped. She didn't know how to reply. All this time, she had thought her father cared about the business above all else. Certainly above her.

Her father waved his hand at her. "Ah, but this is too heavy a topic when you've got an important job up ahead. Tell me about this friend of yours, Cinna."

Hokuren gripped a braid tightly, thinking of Cinna facing Ulbricht alone. "I hired her as my assistant originally, but we quickly bonded in a way I've never done before with anyone. She's family to me now, Father. I can count on her in a way I can't anyone else, and if I were to lose her, I—I don't know what I'd do." Even the thought of it scared her like nothing else could.

"I see." Her father put an arm around her and pulled her against him, as he had when she was a child. Back then, it felt like he could protect her from the monsters. That feeling was no longer present, but it was a comfort nonetheless. "Do you think she can handle her role as a distraction?"

"Of course," said Hokuren automatically, keeping her worries to herself. "I believe in her."

"Then I do, too." He pointed to a gap between two trees ahead. "We're almost there, Pumpkin. We'd best get you ready to go. I want to see you survive as well, understand? Focus, get in, get out."

Moira interrupted the conversation, catching up to them. "We're close, aren't we? I should cast my spell on Hokuren before we're right up against the warren entrance."

"This is probably close enough." Hokuren's father brought them all to a halt. "This won't hurt my baby girl, will it?"

"Father, I'm nearly thirty," said Hokuren, covering her face with her hand.

Her father took Hokuren's chin in his hand. "You'll always be my baby girl."

"*It* won't hurt her," said Moira. "The goblins, on the other hand—"

"Leave them to me," said Roz. She'd already taken the mace from its loop at her hip and now held it up against her shoulder. "Cinna was right that when Ulbricht compels them, they are poor fighters, worse than goblins acting on their own. If we run straight to the contraption, we should be fine. You remember how to get there, right?"

Hokuren nodded. She would once she reached a room she recognized from her last visit. Her father had provided instructions to get to that point.

Moira put her hands on Hokuren's head, covering her ears. "This might feel strange, but that's normal." She began chanting in the language of the Primordial Ones to cast her spell.

At first, Hokuren felt nothing, but slowly the spell insinuated itself into her mind. Unlike the simulacrum Moira's invasion, this was warm and inviting, evoking the same feelings as when she'd received a warm cup of peppermint tea from Moira when she was a child. A vague euphoria settled over her, and she smiled unconsciously.

"Done," said Moira, with a deep sigh. She wiped sweat from her brow.

"Are you all right?" asked Hokuren.

Moira found a patch of bare ground to sit on. The euphoria dissipated as Hokuren checked on her old mentor.

"I'm fine." Moira waved away Hokuren's concern. "Or I will be in a moment. I put as much as I dared into that spell, to give you the best chance of getting through the barrier. I only hope it's enough."

"All right. I'd better not waste your effort." Hokuren looked to her father. "Make sure Moira's all right. Roz, with me. Let's go. Cinna's waiting for us."

Hokuren's father saluted as Roz fell in line behind Hokuren.

"I hope Cinna pulls off her distraction," said Roz. "Or we'll be walking into a hornet's nest of goblins."

Hokuren smiled. "I trust Cinna. If there's one thing she can do better than anyone, it's needle someone she doesn't like into frustration."

Cinna kept a steady pace through the woods back to Fondence, gritting her teeth and pounding her feet into the ground with each step. Roz had secretly opposed them the entire time, and they had entrusted her with the most valuable job of all: keeping Hokuren safe.

In a way, of course, Cinna's job was the same. And, as much as she loathed to admit it, Roz was right. No one else could confront Ulbricht and keep him occupied. That didn't mean she had to like the arrangement.

The edge of the Fondencian farmland came into view. Cinna increased her speed and was soon in the town proper. Mud splashed up her trousers as she ran through the town center, unusually empty in the early evening. The only person among the abandoned stalls, the last resident of a ghost town, was Jarmo. He ducked behind the statue of Fondence's founder, unaware that the statue didn't completely conceal his tall, broad frame.

"Jarmo!" Cinna called. "What's going on?"

"Master Cinna!" Jarmo popped out from his hiding spot. "I thought you were more goblins."

"More goblins? Where did the others go?"

"T—to Mister Grimes's house." He put his hands over his face and wailed. "All of them ran right into his house. There were too many!" A sniffle emerged from behind his hands. "Mister Grimes is in trouble, and I—I ran away."

There wasn't time for Jarmo's tears, but Cinna patted his back anyway. It's what Hokuren would do. "Grimes isn't in trouble yet, but he will be soon." She motioned for him to crouch behind a stall. "Stay here. I'll take care of it."

"Alone?" he said, eyes wide. "Can I help you?"

She averted her eyes while swallowing a protest against any "help" from someone with his lack of killer instinct. "I'll be fine. Watch for any additional goblins running through here."

Cinna continued on toward Grimes's house, looking back to see Jarmo staring after her. A clock in her head told her she was behind, that Hokuren was already in the warren and subject to Ulbricht's undivided attention. She picked up speed, churning through the slippery mud, reaching Grimes's house in record time.

The house looked the same as it had on all their previous visits, except the door was wide open. Cinna burst through the threshold without slowing, skidding to a stop once she was inside, stunned by the sight.

The inside of the house was far larger than its exterior, extending two stories up to a vaulted ceiling and three times as far from front to back as it appeared on the outside. Cinna stood on a marble floor in the ballroom-sized entry. Ivory pillars placed on either side held up a second-floor balcony that wrapped around the enormous space's perimeter. Doors to other rooms ringed both floors, all of them closed, and a grand staircase at the far end provided access to the balcony. Shelving units along the walls held items from books to intricate clocks to precious vases and candelabras. Red stained glass windows covered the entire front and back walls above the balcony. The place rivaled Lady Belladonna's for its size, all while looking like a typical modest Fondence house on the outside.

Grimes stood on the balcony at the opposite end, framed by the blood-red stained-glass window. He looked much as he had the last time she'd seen him, except for the black cape that waved behind him as if he were standing amid an extremely localized and steady wind. A group of ten goblins surrounded him, standing with the butts of their spears on the floor. A dozen more stood on the first floor, guarding the staircase. Their eyes glowed bright red.

All of this was distracting her when the goal was to distract *him*. Cinna pushed aside the opulence and impossibility of the space and grinned up at Grimes while catching her breath. "Getting to see the inside of this house was worth the wait. Nice illusion you have out here."

"Cinna, what a surprise," purred Grimes from above. "Where's

Hokuren? I thought you never left her side. And you did so just for me. I'm honored." He frowned slightly. "Though I wish you wouldn't be so uncouth as to track mud on my freshly shined floor."

Cinna shook the mud off her feet and wiped caked mud from her trousers, flinging as much as she could onto the marble. "I'm sorry about the floor, but I left my towel at home."

"It's no problem," said Grimes, waving a hand at the goblins. "My friends and I will see you receive the punishment you deserve."

Cinna was almost relieved at the rapid escalation. She hated having to pretend. "Good luck. Better than you have tried. We figured out your secret identity. *Ulbricht*," she said, pleased to earn a slight downturn of his thin lips.

"I expected nothing less from Velles's top investigator and her plucky understudy," said Grimes, or Ulbricht. He clapped slowly. "Though I am curious, why are you making the grand accusation and not Hokuren? I daresay you're playing the role she should be in right now." He held up a finger. "Ah, but she must have more pressing business in the goblin warrens, doesn't she?"

Cinna's stomach dropped out from under her.

"Oh, yes," said Ulbricht, leering. "Hokuren's wearing a spell from Moira like a beacon down there. I know exactly where she is. What is her goal, do you think?"

The distraction would have to be good if he had such a close bead on Hokuren. Cinna couldn't trust Roz to fight off a whole warren's worth of goblins, minus the collection she now faced herself.

Cinna narrowed her eyes at Ulbricht. "Your creature tried to make Hokuren and me her pets. Hokuren isn't here because I know she wouldn't approve of what I'm about to do as payback."

Ulbricht raised his eyebrows in anticipation. "Are you not planning on arresting me and bringing me to justice? That's Hokuren's thing, isn't it?"

"It is her thing, but not mine today." Cinna smiled without humor. "I'm here to kill you."

The warren was even quieter than the first time Hokuren had been inside. The first two rooms she and Roz walked through, neither of which she recognized, were empty. They had yet to encounter a single goblin.

"I wonder where they all are," said Hokuren, under her breath.

They exited a tunnel into a mail room. A pile of letters and envelopes awaited sorting into the slots and shelves surrounding it. The scope of the goblin operation seemed to grow with every new room.

Roz pushed Hokuren forward, mace in hand. "Come on, the only thing we should care about is the location of that contraption."

Two goblins jumped out at them from behind a huge mail basket in the center of the room. They were well-dressed, and one even wore a wig with a slicked-back ponytail, but their eyes burned red, and they shrieked and slobbered as they attacked with their spears.

Hokuren froze at their reveal, but Roz didn't. She caught one with her mace and the other with her foot. Both goblins collapsed with a thud at Hokuren's feet, unconscious. Hokuren bent down to check if they were still alive, relieved to find they both had pulses.

"Looks like the wizard knows we're here," said Roz. "The welcoming party was light. That's a good sign. Let's pick up the pace."

Each room had multiple tunnels, but Hokuren had the path her father provided memorized. He knew where the goblin library was, and from there her own memory of the path to the contraption could take over.

They traveled a few more rooms into a kitchen, a savory aroma wafting from a pot that made Hokuren's stomach rumble, reminding her it had been hours since she'd had more than tea. From behind the pot, goblins appeared, speaking their own language to each other.

Roz readied her mace, but Hokuren held her back. "Wait."

The goblins were calmly discussing something in the pot, with none of the red that indicated Ulbricht's influence visible in their eyes. One of them, wearing a chef's white apron and hat, said to Hokuren, "Are you Nekane? It's been a while."

"Not quite," said Hokuren tightly. "Do you know where Greeze or Viss are?"

He and the other goblins shook their heads. "Many of us were made to join Ulbricht for protection."

Hokuren thought of Cinna, worried anew. "How many?"

"At least a couple dozen to start with."

"Let's hurry," said Hokuren to Roz, headed for the next tunnel. As they passed through, she said, "Cinna can handle herself, but I'm not sure even she can take that many goblins at once plus a wizard."

"Cinna's definitely started distracting Ulbricht," said Roz as they entered the next room. It was a bakery. Several goblins bowed to the two of them as they moved through. "This is easy now."

"Don't say that," said Hokuren. "That's when things go wrong."

Things hadn't gone wrong for Cinna, at least not yet.

They weren't *great*. Ulbricht had not taken her declaration of intent to murder lightly. He had sent the dozen goblins on the first floor after her while taking shots at her with bolts of magical fire similar to the ones his simulacrum had wielded. She certainly had his attention.

Cinna ran toward one of the pillars, jumped to plant a foot on it, then pushed off into a backflip. Three goblins that had been chasing her crashed into the pillar and fell to the side, spears clattering on the marble floor. She sidestepped a spear thrust at her the moment she landed, then another bolt of fire flung from the balcony.

"Come on!" she goaded. "You'll need to do better than that!"

Compelling this many goblins at once seemed to limit Ulbricht to rudimentary tactics, so she was in effect dodging spears wielded by toddlers in both size and strategy. She'd already pulled off the pillar trick twice.

The one thing she couldn't do was fight back, as all of her time needed to be spent avoiding the attacks. Poor as they were, the goblins had far superior numbers, and they kept coming.

The floor swirled underneath, a black and gray vortex. Cinna flung herself forward right before a spike trap, opaque like jelly, jutted up from where she'd been. The spikes faded into a fine mist before disappearing completely, and another vortex formed where she lay.

"Flames," she growled. She pushed herself up and dove to the right to avoid this new set of spikes.

She did so successfully, but slammed into an invisible barrier that may as well have been made of brick. Crumpled on the ground, she needed a moment to gather herself. This was enough time for a goblin to grab her around the ankle. He opened his mouth and set his needle teeth on her calf.

"No!" Cinna kicked his head with her other foot. His chomp missed her leg, and he fell off her with a squeal of pain. She instinctively rolled aside as another bolt of fire whizzed toward her, singeing her hair.

"Luck is with you, but for how long?" Ulbricht shouted, throwing another fire bolt that Cinna deftly skirted. It scorched the marble floor before sizzling out.

Cinna evaded two more goblin spears. "Nothing lucky about it," she muttered. Hokuren and Roz needed to get to that contraption pronto.

Ulbricht chanted more magic spells from his balcony. A mirror image of herself appeared, popping into existence like a reversal of the way Garrett had disappeared. Ulbricht didn't have much imagination if he thought having her destroy copies of herself would faze her.

She punched herself, the image shattering like the false Moira had.

Another one appeared, but on this one her face was twisted into a mask of fury, snarling the same way the goblins were. Cinna had to get out of the way of more goblin spears while the image advanced on her, fingers like claws. Another punch shattered this one as well before it did any damage.

Cinna was about to boast when a third image appeared. This one, however, resembled Hokuren. It wasn't real, it wasn't Hokuren, but Cinna still hesitated for an instant. That was enough. The image-Hokuren dove at her and tackled her, dragging Cinna to the marble floor.

Goblin spears harried Cinna as she tussled with the image. It was stronger than the real Hokuren, with significantly better grip. She heaved the image back and forth to roll them away from spears that clinked against the floor with each narrow miss.

"Oh dear, Cinna, are you not going to listen to the boss?" said the image-Hokuren, in a voice that sounded close enough to Hokuren's to feel uncanny. The image was on top of her, and used this advantage to punch at Cinna's head. She tilted her neck to avoid it. "This is insubordination!"

Another goblin spear headed toward Cinna. She grabbed the Hokuren image by her faithfully modeled coat and yanked. The spear hit the image in the neck, and Hokuren shattered right in front of her.

Cinna let out a low moan at the horrifying sight. Goblin claws scratching marble brought her back to the immediate present danger. She rolled away from the goblins and their spears and pushed herself back to her feet. Her mind replayed the Hokuren image's "death."

"She doesn't talk like that!" Cinna yelled up at Ulbricht, as much to remind herself as to inform him.

A goblin grabbed her from behind. She was getting sloppy. Ulbricht threw another bolt of fire at her, which she spun away from, taking the goblin with her. With an elbow to the snarling creature's face, she wiggled free and narrowly avoided more spears.

Ulbricht's face had turned red, and stress lined his face as he labored with his fire bolts, spike traps, and images while maintaining his direct influence over the goblins. She'd seen first-hand that the mental energy needed for each spell was not an inexhaustible resource. Even a powerful wizard, such as she assumed Ulbricht to be, had a limit.

Her fatigue grew with each momentum-shifting dip, dodge, and jump. Already her steps were slower. Soon they wouldn't be good enough. Although she could hold out for a little while still, she needed Hokuren to smash the contraption soon.

Then things went wrong.

Ulbricht muttered under his breath, and the goblins all stopped chasing Cinna. They grabbed their spears and walked (or limped if necessary) to the back of the giant hall.

Cinna looked up at Ulbricht and the smug smile he aimed at her. "I know the goblins weren't doing their job, but what's going to stop me from getting up to where you are now?" she asked, grateful for the break.

"Our guests are finally here, and I suspect you'll be too busy with them." Ulbricht lifted his arms, palms out, and gestured to the front door behind her. "I trust you're familiar."

Cinna turned around to the unwelcome view of the Gregorious Consortium filing in, with an incensed Hugo at their head. The skull-tattoo man, Petros, and the lanky man from the inn followed. Her heart sank.

"We found you, urchin," growled Hugo, waving his damaged hand. It resembled a club thanks to the bandages wrapped all around it. "We have a score to settle."

"Better to say that I alerted them to come here the moment you entered, Cinna," said Ulbricht. "Caught them wandering around town asking about you or Hokuren and offered a chance at a happy reunion if I saw you and, well, here you are."

None of the Consortium members' eyes were red. They were here of their own free will and would cost Ulbricht's magic reserves nothing. Worse, even if Hokuren destroyed the contraption, it wouldn't impact the men now arrayed in front of her.

"You shouldn't have," said Cinna through gritted teeth.

Hokuren and Roz had nearly reached the library via her father's instructions when a familiar face intercepted them and briefly halted their progress.

"Heard you were back. Greeze wanted me to check in on you and see what you need," said Viss, the contraption's expert. She moved her head to look at Roz from several angles. "I'm always bad at telling humans apart, but you smell different from Hokuren's previous companion."

"Better, I hope," said Roz.

The goblin smiled politely but said nothing.

Roz pointed the head of her mace at Viss. "And don't think I'm not watching to see if Ulbricht jumps into the driver's box in your head."

"That won't happen!" said Viss, shrinking from the weapon. "Greeze and I are considered too valuable for that these days."

"We're here to destroy the contraption," said Hokuren, pushing Roz's mace aside. "And we're in a hurry."

"You—you are?" Viss's ears flattened against her head as she moved to block Hokuren. "The barrier—"

"The barrier will not be a problem anymore." Hokuren trusted in Moira, but if the witch's magic didn't work, Cinna would be in deep trouble. Her restless stomach continued to do flips. The goblin stayed in her way, so she added curtly, "Either come with us or move. This isn't a social call."

"Right, of course. My apologies." Viss scampered toward the library. "I'll take you there."

Though Viss's guidance was unnecessary, Hokuren allowed the goblin to lead them. When they reached the library, they were not greeted by studious goblins with heads down in their books as last time. Six goblins snarled at their entry, their movement jerky and their eyes bright red.

"Ulbricht knows you're here!" cried Viss, diving behind a table in the corner.

Roz stepped between the goblins and Hokuren. "You know the rest of the way, right? If we get an opening, run for it."

"Okay," said Hokuren. She fingered the only weapon she had, her dagger. She wasn't keen on slashing the goblins, but if left with no other choice...

The tables proved to be to the goblins' advantage at first. They hopped over them to charge at Roz.

"Come on!" said Roz. She motioned for Hokuren to run to the right, away from the goblins. The two of them had no hope of outrunning the goblins, but Roz's plan became clear soon enough.

The goblins gave chase, stretching their line out instead of maintaining group cohesion. It was as Roz said. They didn't use their numerical supremacy to its fullest. Instead of six goblins at once, Roz could deal with one at a time.

She did so with terrifying efficiency. The first three goblins leaped at her with claws out, only to take one crunching mace blow each. The last three, showing some semblance of lucidity, regrouped in the center of the room.

There was a thudding march approaching from the library's other side. Pinpoints of red light streamed from deep within the dark tunnel, illuminating dozens of goblins in haunting crimson outlines. There were far more than she and Roz could possibly handle. She backed up a step, the dagger in her hand shaking.

"Go!" said Roz.

Hokuren broke into a run for the exit tunnel, Roz right behind her. The goblins poured into the room as Roz displayed her strength by grabbing a table, tipping it on its side, and hauling it to the tunnel entrance. She jammed it there, blocking the tunnel.

Goblins threw themselves at the blockage, slamming into the table. It shook, but held firm. The frustrated snarls of the goblins on the other side faded as Hokuren and Roz sprinted down the tunnel toward the contraption.

Four more goblins met them in the next room, the dining area. Roz dove into a melee with three of them, leaving one focused on Hokuren.

She backed away, holding her dagger. "Stay away. Don't make me use this," she begged, but of course in his Ulbricht-compelled state, he didn't listen. Only now did Hokuren realize the problem with her dagger. She couldn't use it without letting the goblin close enough to sink its sharp teeth and claws into her.

The goblin charged Hokuren, mouth wide to show off all its teeth. Hokuren backed into a table and, without further thought, grabbed a dinner plate from behind her and swung. The plate crashed onto his head and shattered. The goblin fell to the ground, stunned but not unconscious.

Someone pulled Hokuren by her elbow. She nearly reached for another plate before she realized it was Roz. Blood flowed from a wound in her arm. "There'll be more if we wait here," she said, grimacing.

"Roz, your arm."

They were already in the tunnel to the next room. "It'll be fine." She sounded like Cinna.

The two guards who stood in front of the door in their custom-made Arms of Fondence armor met them from within Ulbricht's control. Roz sighed and lifted her mace. Their armor and swords didn't help them fare any better than the rest she'd already dispatched. All that stood between Hokuren and the contraption was the door.

It was locked.

"No!" said Hokuren, banging her fist on the door. "Cinna's in trouble! We can't wait any longer!"

Roz bashed the door with her mace to no effect. She turned around at the sound of approaching goblin footsteps. It was Viss, panting as she ran to catch up with them.

"Wait!" she cried as Roz held her mace up again. "It's me. Viss! It wasn't easy to sneak by all those goblins."

There was no red in her eyes. "Can you get this door open?" Hokuren glanced up the tunnel, straining to listen for other goblins. "And fast?"

"I think so," said Viss, digging into her trousers for tools that resembled Cinna's lockpicks. "The other goblins are all under Ulbricht's control, but with so many he can't give them good instructions. They'll be stuck for a while."

"So, then," said Roz. She turned to Hokuren. "Hey, about everything that's happened—"

Hokuren bounced on the balls of her feet, every moment that passed torture as her mind strayed to Cinna. "It can wait," said Hokuren. She didn't relish this conversation, particularly at this moment.

"It can't," said Roz, putting her foot down. "Not like we've got shit else to do until this door is open." At Hokuren's silent nod, she continued, "Once this is done, you won't see me again."

Hokuren shook her head. "I doubt that."

"Just listen to me. I'm not asking for anything. I want you to know something about what I've done."

"Look, Roz, I know you wanted your voice back—"

"Wanted my voice back?" Roz spat on the floor. "That's not even close to strong enough. I *need* to get it back. You're hoping for a chance to forgive me as long as I've learned my lesson and, well, I'm here to disappoint you. Ulbricht cheated me, but there are other wizards out there. Other witches, too. I aim to find them. One of them can help me."

Hokuren blinked, taken aback. She hadn't expected full remorse from Roz, but she had expected *some*. "Your singing can't be the only thing that defines you."

Roz's lips curled. "You don't get it. You never will. That's okay. I can't stand listening to myself with this thick, curdled, frog-sounding voice, and I'm the only one whose opinion matters." She jabbed a finger at the scar across her throat. "I wake up every day and try to sing, just in case it's miraculously healed. It never is. I gave a wizard the opportunity to compel me for a chance to go back to the way I used to be, and I'll do it again if that's what it takes. One way or another, I'll get my voice back, or I'll die in the attempt."

"I suppose talking you out of it is pointless."

"By the way, what I said at the campsite . . ." Roz turned back to Hokuren, a half smile on her face. "That was real. I meant that. Though it's a good thing we never did anything, all things considered."

Hokuren's breath caught. "There was never a chance between us, Roz. Anyone you end up with will always be second place at best to your voice."

"That's—" Roz's nostrils flared, then relaxed. "Completely correct."

Hokuren turned to Viss, still fiddling with the lock. The goblin's effort had waned. Hokuren didn't have Cinna's lockpicking skills, but she knew slacking when she saw it. "Hurry it up," she snapped. "Are you even trying? This door should have already been open."

"Of course I'm trying! I—I don't know if I can get it," Viss said, shrinking from Hokuren's glare.

"The key! I have the key!" Another goblin was running down the tunnel toward them. Greeze, holding a key in his hand. "If I had known you were here to destroy the contraption, I'd have come sooner, even with all the chaos in here."

"Who told him that Hokuren was here?" Viss muttered under her breath.

Hokuren ignored Viss. She could have kissed Greeze as he stuck the key into the door the contraption room and swung it open.

The four of them entered. Greeze shut the door, engaging the lock again. "The rest won't be bothering us in here now."

"The barrier still stands," said Viss, rubbing her hands together with nervous energy. "I'm not sure if there's any point in all this."

"We'll find out soon enough whether there was or not. I've got a spell to get me past that barrier, I hope." Hokuren held out her hand. "Roz, your mace, please."

Moira hadn't been sure if the spell in Hokuren would dispel the barrier entirely or merely allow Hokuren to pass through. If the latter, she would need to destroy the contraption herself, so the safest play would be to take Roz's mace with her.

The handle brushed Hokuren's palm. She closed her fist over it.

"Happy bashing," said Roz.

Hokuren looked down at the mace. "It's about time we ended this. Not much longer now, Cinna."

Greeze's eyes were wide. "Will I actually see it destroyed in my lifetime?"

The mace was heavy enough that Hokuren required both hands to hold it up against her thudding chest. She approached the center of the room, the barrier invisible but all too present in her mind. She took a deep breath as she neared where she remembered it being.

"Hey—argh." Roz grunted behind her, and over the quiet hum of the barrier magic and contraption came the unmistakable squelch of a knife entering a body. When Hokuren turned around, Roz fell to her knees, a blade hilt sticking out of her gut. Blood bloomed from the wound on her shirt.

"Viss—what are you doing?" said Greeze, frozen in shock.

Viss's eyes narrowed, and she held a small crossbow aimed at Hokuren. "Not another step, human."

The Gregorious Consortium, fresh and energized by revenge, had the upper hand on Cinna from the beginning. Despite carrying various injuries she'd inflicted upon them, they worked together in the open space in a way that the compelled goblins didn't.

Every time she avoided one attack, another man would be lying in wait, trying to predict where she'd dodge and get in a blow before she could react again. It didn't always work for them, but it worked often enough. She had already taken an elbow to the back and a kick to her thigh, hobbling her. It was only a matter of time before they caught her with a strike she couldn't get back up from.

Ulbricht tittered with laughter from his perch on the balcony and urged on the Consortium like a punter at one of Velles's underground boxing matches. When she took her second blow to the thigh, he said, "This isn't even fair. Well, I'm sure you and the Consortium boys can work this out. I should see what Hokuren is up to—wait, I know where she's headed! And Roz! What are they—" He went quiet, standing still.

Cinna spent too much time focused on Ulbricht, a mistake the Consortium men didn't make. It was the skull-tattoo man who caught her square in the chest with his punch, knocking the wind out of her. She crashed to the marble and slid on her back, gasping for air.

She groaned, trying to recover her breath. Hokuren must be close to the room with the contraption to get Ulbricht so alarmed. She hoped she had done enough, even if Ulbricht had now turned his mental gaze back to the warrens and she had no way to stop him.

Hugo loomed over Cinna, massaging the club at the end of one arm with his good hand.

"You could have been our hostage," Hugo said, satisfied smile on his face. He lowered his disgusting, blackened teeth closer again. "But our best client wants you dead, and we are big into customer service, you see."

The pressure in Cinna's chest was easing. If she could buy a little more time, she could get up and continue to fight. No matter how dire the situation, she would never give up until it was over.

Jarmo appeared in the doorway behind Hugo, his disorientation at the enormity of the house's interior replaced by a grim determination when his eyes caught Cinna's. Hugo had thick muscles, but Jarmo was taller with wider shoulders and possessed an intensity Cinna hadn't believed the timid boy capable of. None of the other men saw him approach in time to react before he grabbed Hugo under his arms and tore him away from Cinna. The stunned Hugo squawked as Jarmo hurled him aside and stepped between the rest of the men and Cinna.

"I'm with the Arms of Fondence," he said, making an attempt at authority undermined by the warble in his voice. From her position on the floor, Cinna had a good view of his quaking knees. "You're all under arrest."

"That's a funny one," said Hugo, with a chuckle. He picked himself off the floor, the only thing hurt his pride. "You're big, but that ain't going to be enough."

Cinna got up, stiffening her muscles to hide shaky legs. "Jarmo, I told you to stay away."

"An order I could not obey, Master Cinna," he replied, continuing to act like someone who replaced the real Jarmo. "Who are these guys?"

"Lousy smugglers with bad teeth." Each breath hurt, but Cinna could push past it. "Since you're here, I could use your help, I admit."

He dropped his voice to a low whisper, so faint Cinna almost couldn't hear it. "I still can't punch them." Now this was the Jarmo she knew.

"That's fine, because I want to do that myself." She watched the Consortium men, waiting to see when they made their move. "You remember the exercises, right?" she said under her breath. "Do them when I call them out."

"What?" whispered Jarmo. "Is this really the time for—"

"Trust me. Please."

There was no further time to explain. It was Petros who moved first, with the lanky man right behind. Cinna recognized what they were doing, a move they had used already that had earned them the shot to her chest. They were both decoys, setting up the skull-tattoo man for a punch he was already rearing back to throw. She saw it coming this time.

"Toe touches!" shouted Cinna.

Jarmo obeyed, despite the confusion on his face, bending at the waist to reach his hands to his feet. He couldn't actually stretch all the way to touch any toes, but she didn't need him to. She needed him to be about half as tall.

She put her hands on Jarmo's rear to lift herself up, spin clear of Petros and the lanky man, and swing her legs. Her momentum drove both of her heels into the skull-tattoo man's neck before he understood what was happening. He crashed to the floor.

One down. "Plank!" she yelled.

Jarmo dutifully dropped to the floor, supporting his body weight with his forearms. Petros reached for his dagger, so Cinna picked him as the next target. She jumped onto Jarmo's back, poised like one of Velles's champion surfers.

"Up!"

He lifted himself upright with his core strength. With Cinna on top, he didn't rise as much as he normally would, but it was enough for Cinna to use him like a spring, propelling herself into a backflip and extending a foot to catch an unsuspecting Petros in the chin. He fell next to the skull-tattoo man.

Two down.

"Get the Arm of Fondence!" roared Hugo, raising his club hand into the air, while the lanky man brandished his dagger with the tentative nature of one who'd witnessed two of his associates knocked out in the past few seconds.

Jarmo stood petrified, eyes wide, as Hugo brought his club hand down to crush his head. Cinna shoved him out of the way with an encouraging "Move!" and sent them both tumbling as Hugo's club whiffed, slamming into the floor and cracking the marble.

"What the flames is under those bandages?" moaned Jarmo, lying next to Cinna on the floor.

"Stay with me," said Cinna. The lanky man advanced on them to take advantage of their weak position. "Sit-up!"

She was worried he wouldn't do this one, but he rushed to take the exercise position while a man with a knife bore down on him. She couldn't buy trust like this.

This time, Cinna didn't need his help, calling out the first exercise that entered her mind. She stayed down behind him and grabbed her arm, pantomiming injury. The lanky man approached cautiously, no doubt expecting some exercise related trick. Cinna popped up from around Jarmo's sit-up. The lanky man, caught by surprise, slashed awkwardly with the dagger. Cinna easily ducked under it to elbow him in the ribs. A kick to his knee followed by rapid punches to his head brought him down and out with the others.

Only Hugo remained, snorting and standing over the mud Cinna had wiped off when she entered. Cinna risked a look up at Ulbricht. He was catatonic, his eyes shining red, his goblin charges inert. She hoped Hokuren was all right.

She turned her attention back to Hugo, who was between her and the wizard. The smuggler was apoplectic with fury. "There are no walls here for you to trick me into punching this time, urchin. Come at me if you dare."

Once Cinna finished him, she could deal with Ulbricht. No time to waste. She pulled her dagger from its ankle sheath. Keeping her eyes on Hugo, she said, "Jarmo. Spin me and throw me at him. I need the speed."

"Um—" said Jarmo, beginning to object.

"Do it!"

"All right, Master Cinna."

She put her hand out and he grabbed it, his larger hand engulfing her own. She ran in three circles around him as he twirled in place on his heels. He let go to slingshot her at Hugo, who had crouched down like he was waiting for the ball in a game of catch. Cinna used the momentum to sprint at him at top speed. Hugo was ready, and she could already predict what he was going to do. Let her stab him with her little dagger, figuring it wouldn't penetrate far enough past his muscles to do meaningful damage, and slam his club hand into her. Cinna held her dagger in front of her as if planning to do just that.

He fell for the deception.

When she reached him, Cinna dove onto the freshly mud-slick marble floor, sliding on it between his legs as if on ice, the club arm swinging harmlessly by. As she slid under him, she slashed with her dagger in a wide arc. His muscular body lacked the dexterity to react in time. Her blade sliced deep into his heel, through the boot and down through the tendon.

Hugo screamed and fell to the ground, clutching his ankle.

Cinna groaned and picked herself back up. She hurt all over, but no rest for the weary. The goblins watched her run for the staircase, but made no move to stop her. As she reached the stairs to the second-story balcony, a goblin prodded Ulbricht and brought him back. "Hmm, already?" he said, his eyes losing their red tint. "I suppose I'll have to leave it up to Viss to finish. She's doing well on her own."

"What'd you do to Hokuren?" said Cinna, pointing her dagger at him.

"Me? Though I tried, I've done nothing. Not every goblin wishes for the hold I have over them to be broken, if you can believe it." Ulbricht sneered. "You have the bigger problem." He glanced down at the fallen smugglers. "I am far more dangerous."

He raised his hands to the ceiling, chanting in the language of the Primordials, the discordant set of sounds that made Cinna uncomfortable. He was shouting, the spell taking some time to recite. She bolted toward him, two steps at a time, and reached the landing.

Only a few feet separated them when, with one last guttural recitation, the spell finished. He lowered his arms to point at her. Cinna, anticipating the frozen-air spell, slid to the left, but Ulbricht had a fresh trick. A blast of gale-force winds slammed into her, lifting her into the air and carrying her backward. The howling winds whipped her hair into her face and twisted her into a wild spin. She clenched her eyes closed and covered her neck and head with her arms as best she could as she hurtled on a collision course with the stained-glass window on the other side of the house.

She smashed through it. The sound of the window shattering into hundreds of tiny red glass shards gave way to tinkles as the shards fell with her to the ground from the second story. Cinna's stomach lurched as she entered a brief free fall, arms flailing. The ground rushed toward her, and she hit the path leading to Ulbricht's illusory house on her back with a squelchy thud.

Everything hurt, but she was alive. The mud, thick from the frequent rains, had cushioned her fall.

She wouldn't get a chance to celebrate. The goblins surged from the house and surrounded her, jumping on her arms and legs to pin her down. Weak and weary, she couldn't free any of her limbs.

"You really are tough to kill," said Ulbricht, eyes bright red, emerging from the house. "Vermin often are." He swept toward her, cape still flowing, flanked by more goblins. Jarmo followed close behind, giving Cinna the vain hope that he would simply pound the wizard into the ground with those huge hands of his. This could be his moment where, in a life-or-death situation, he finally got over his mental block and hit someone.

Then she saw the red tint in Jarmo's eyes. "No," she said. "Not you."

"I could, of course, have the goblins eviscerate you right now. Though it strikes me that goblins killing you wouldn't be as fun as using this Arm of Fondence. You two seem fond of each other, and I cannot pass up the irony." Ulbricht waved his hand at Jarmo. "I put a worm into the head of every member of the Arms of Fondence, just in case. Though"—he lowered his voice to a whisper—"don't tell them. They don't know."

"Jarmo, don't do this," said Cinna, ignoring the wizard.

Jarmo, expressionless and silent, pulled his standard-issue Arms of Fondence sword halfway from its sheath, then hesitated.

"Don't stop," barked Ulbricht. The red in his eyes flashed with greater intensity.

Jarmo winced, then pulled his sword out all the way.

"Come on, Jarmo, fight it," said Cinna. He was standing over her now. "You hate this! You don't want to do this!"

He raised the sword up, his mouth a straight line, as if he couldn't even hear her. The tip of the sword hung above her. The first person he'd hurt again, breaking that mental block, would be her. She closed her eyes and hoped Hokuren at least figured out a way to survive.

"Viss, what are you doing?" gasped Hokuren, unable to stop looking at the point of the crossbow bolt trained on her.

The goblin waved her away from the contraption with her weapon. "Throw your mace down and move."

Hokuren's mind raced, trying to determine how to proceed. Cinna was still out there, perhaps still struggling against Ulbricht's magic. Viss's eyes weren't red, so this wasn't him. It was a goblin double-cross. "I don't understand. This device allows Ulbricht to dominate your mind, compel you to do things you don't want to do, and puts you and all your fellow goblins in danger."

"Do as I say, or I'll shoot!" Viss shook the crossbow menacingly.

"This makes no sense, Viss. Stop this instant!" said Greeze, reaching out with a hand.

"Stay out of this, Greeze," said Viss, venom in her tone.

Hokuren moved a step closer to the contraption, almost daring Viss to shoot. "I could easily slip behind the barrier, and you couldn't touch me from there."

Viss grunted. "And then what? Do you plan to live behind the barrier forever? Look at my eyes. This isn't Ulbricht. You destroy that contraption and I'll shoot you when you eventually re-emerge."

"You'll have no reason to shoot me once the contraption is gone," said Hokuren, hoping it was true. The goblin could still shoot if she felt petty, even if it wouldn't bring the contraption back. "I have to destroy this, not only for current and future victims of Ulbricht's, but for Cinna's sake as well."

Viss looked over at Roz and turned the crossbow on her. The former bard knelt heavily on one knee, pale, both hands pressed against the wound in her stomach, trying to stanch the blood. She breathed in gasps, head down.

"Okay, then, I'll shoot her."

"Coward," rasped Roz between heaving breaths.

Hokuren tossed the mace to the ground. She'd have to talk her way out of this one, but fast. "Fine. Tell me, though, why are you doing this?"

"Without the contraption, Ulbricht can't turn any more of us. We'd be free, yes, but the few that we are will live alone with only each other until, one by one, we die out." She snarled, her goblin accent more pronounced in her anger. "You would doom us to that outcome? Just like your mother made the decision to do this to us without asking, you shouldn't get to make the decision to take it away."

"Surely that's not true, though," said Hokuren. "My mother believed you were all always capable of this."

"She's right, Viss," said Greeze, calm and collected. He inched closer to Viss every time he thought she wasn't looking.

"Lies!" The crossbow shook in Viss's hands. "No goblins have spoken human languages without either Nekane's or Ulbricht's encouragement. It's not what Barduk made us to do!"

"There's no reason we couldn't teach other goblins."

"Stay out of this, Greeze, or I'll get rid of you and say the humans did it." She swung her crossbow and pointed it at the other goblin.

Greeze held his hands up, but didn't back down. "We've been over this. We don't need the contraption. It doesn't make us *more intelligent*, it makes us more *willing to learn*. We can serve as an example and convince others to join us once we rid ourselves of the contraption's significant downsides."

"None of them will want to," said Viss, her focus entirely on Greeze. "Even you would rather go back to the way it was."

"I would," admitted Greeze with a sigh. "I'm much smarter now, and I have all sorts of esoteric knowledge of things human. Yet I'm not the same Greeze I was before Nekane began her experiment. And I never will be."

"You're better."

Greeze sputtered a laugh. "Am I? I would give anything to undo all of this, all thirty years of learning, to be the goblin I used to be."

Hokuren crawled to the mace to pick it back up while Viss argued with Greeze, careful not to disturb even a single grain of the dirt floor lest she draw the goblin's attention. She crept toward the barrier with short, careful steps, checking over her shoulder to see if anyone noticed. No one did.

"But what about the plan to integrate with the humans, like the elves?" cried Viss. "I thought you wanted that!"

"I've been pretending!" roared Greeze, causing Viss to flinch. "For the sake of the man who can and would end any of us with a snap of his finger, because of that . . . that thing!"

He gestured at the contraption, drawing every eye in the room to Hokuren. She froze like a child caught with her hand in the cookie jar.

"No!" said Viss, bringing her crossbow to bear on Hokuren.

"Rrrgghh," said Roz, springing to life and tackling Viss as she released the bolt. She hit the goblin in time to alter the bolt's trajectory. It missed Hokuren and hit the barrier, from where it deflected somewhere else in the room.

Viss hit Roz with a vicious kick near her stab wound, sending her sprawling to the ground, and produced another bolt to reload.

"Go!" yelled Greeze.

The yell brought Hokuren to her senses. She turned and ran for the contraption, squeezing her eyes shut when she reached the invisible barrier. A slight tingle played across her body as she passed. It was all she felt as she made it to the other side as if the barrier didn't exist. Viss's next crossbow bolt proved it did as it bounced off the barrier behind her.

"Don't! Please!" cried Viss.

Hokuren gripped the mace, heaving it over her head. "Sorry, Mother, but you never should have used this," she said, too quiet for anyone else in the room to hear.

Hokuren brought the head of the mace down on the center of the contraption.

Cinna kept her eyes closed as she heard Jarmo grunt and sensed the sword falling. If she had to die, she didn't want to have to see it happen, at least.

The sword made a squish sound, and Cinna's entire body tensed in response. She waited for the pain to tell her where she had been stabbed, and for the darkness she'd heard awaited when it was all over.

A few moments later, she was still waiting for either, confused and wondering if Jarmo had executed such a surgical strike that she'd been killed instantly, and everyone was wrong about there being no afterlife.

She opened her eyes.

The blade of the sword was in her peripheral vision, sticking out of the mud beside her face. Jarmo had a puzzled look in his red eyes, staring at the sword as if trying to figure out how it got there.

"How did—how did you miss?" said Ulbricht, as surprised as Cinna.

"I don't know," said Jarmo, his voice hollow.

Cinna almost laughed, despite the still-present danger. Jarmo's aversion to violence was so strong that not even Ulbricht's worm-enhanced influence could overcome it. He resisted the compulsion. He didn't have it in him.

The red in Jarmo's eyes disappeared, replaced by his normal blue, as if Ulbricht was so disappointed he didn't even want to compel him anymore.

It wasn't only him, however. The red in the eyes of the goblins holding her down faded as well, leaving them questioningly looking around at each other.

"Just in time, boss," said Cinna.

Hands fell off Cinna as the goblins gathered in a group. Ulbricht backed away. "No, no, she couldn't have gotten past the barrier. How is this happening?" he said in a panic-stricken tone of voice more musical to Cinna's ears than the greatest bard's melody.

Her former captors had shoved her so far down into the mud that she needed time to wiggle out of it. She hadn't quite wiggled free when Jarmo offered a hand to yank her up. The mud made a sucking sound as she popped upright with his help.

His eyes were enormous and his mouth agape with horror. "Master Cinna, I almost—I mean, I don't know why I almost—"

"It's all right, Jarmo. Let's talk later." Cinna staggered in place. "I've got to get back—"

The goblins yelled out a war cry, drowning her out. All of them faced Ulbricht, who put his hands up to ward them off.

"Stay away." His tone remained commanding, even in the face of retribution. The lines on his face looked deeper. That he wasn't already attempting to cast a spell suggested he'd spent the last of his capacity summoning the hurricane in his house.

The goblins marched toward him, no longer his to command. He turned tail to flee, but the goblins easily overtook and encircled him. They drew closer, tightening the circle.

"What are you doing? Don't you understand? I—I did this for you," Ulbricht stammered. The goblins didn't stop, snarling and gnashing their razor-sharp teeth.

Ulbricht had killed Hokuren's mother, had tried to kill Cinna, and magically dominated the minds of goblins for three decades simply because he'd been able to do so. Cinna couldn't muster much sympathy for what was about to happen.

"I'll give you anything." Ulbricht's voice pitched up as he tried desperately to stop the inevitable, his facade crumbling. "I'll even teach you wizard magic. You'd like that, right?"

Jarmo stood next to Cinna, a troubled look on his face. "I think I know what's going to happen. Should we do something?"

"This isn't our decision to make," said Cinna. "Even if the goblins killing him won't be very much fun."

She lifted her hand high and covered Jarmo's eyes. He was too innocent to watch the goblins throw their spears down and enact their justice, three decades in the making, with their claws and teeth. Jarmo heard Ulbricht's screams ring out until they faded into nothing, though, wincing the whole way through.

Cinna felt light-headed. She was only standing now due to force of will, but even that had its limits. "Jarmo, I know this is awkward, what with that gruesome death and all, but I'm going to need to ask you to carry me to Hokuren."

27

The contraption lay on the floor, no longer glowing red or emitting the ever-present hum. Hokuren, wanting to be sure, had smashed it several times with the mace. The silent silver hunk of metal barely resembled the delicate piece it had been.

Viss didn't follow through on her threats to shoot anyone, Hokuren included. She was on her knees and hanging her head, muttering, "It's gone, it's gone," repeatedly.

All that remained of Roz was a small pool of blood. More blood dotted a trail that led out of the room. Hokuren tossed aside the mace.

"Your friend left," said Greeze. "We could chase her down for you."

"Don't bother," said Hokuren. There was little chance of ending Roz's obsession with reclaiming her voice, and the goblins had more important things to worry about. As did she. Her only concern was Cinna's status.

"He's gone," said Greeze, full of wonder as he examined the ruined contraption. "He's out of my head."

"He was in your head?" asked Hokuren.

"At all times, yes. A small part of him, even when he didn't directly interfere in our minds. It was sort of like when you're trying to remember something, and it feels like it's right there but you can't recall it. That's what his presence in our minds felt like."

Hokuren shuddered. "I'm sorry, my mother—"

"Your mother gave him the ability to do this. She did not sanction it." Greeze shook his head. "We cannot undo what happened in the past, but

I can look forward to the future."

"What will that look like, Greeze?"

"I'm not sure. We never really planned for this part." Greeze laughed, a hissing sound. "We'll discuss it. All I know for sure is that we'll party." His needle-like teeth didn't quite undermine the joy in his smile. "And we'll grant you whatever you wish."

"All I want is to make sure Cinna came out of this safely."

"I will send scouts to find her."

Several goblins entered the room, confused and holding their heads. Once they received an explanation from Greeze and marveled at the ruined contraption, they split up into groups to arrange for tracking down Cinna and leading Viss away, her hands bound.

"What will you do with her?" asked Hokuren. She was careful not to make any suggestions.

"She'll either embrace our new reality or she won't." Greeze shrugged. "I hope she does."

The goblins brought Hokuren to a mess hall and fed her soup, which she ate with Cinna-like gusto. When she finished, she lay down on one of the goblin dormitory beds. Telling herself she was only going to rest her eyes a moment while waiting for the goblins to find Cinna, she fell asleep instantly.

Hokuren woke with a jolt, her mind immediately on Cinna, only to have her concerns resolved just as quickly. Cinna lay on her back in the bed adjacent, sleeping soundly. One of her hands hung over the edge of the bed. Hokuren reached over to take it, holding it softly to avoid waking her. The hand was gritty, covered in dried mud, as was much of the rest of her, but Cinna seemed otherwise fine in her peaceful slumber.

Hokuren gazed around the room before spotting her father, standing awkwardly in a corner. He met her eyes and gave her a small wave. She gently placed Cinna's hand on the bed and joined her father.

He wrapped her in a hug. "I'm so glad you made it out in one piece, Pumpkin."

"When did Cinna get here?" she asked.

"A bit ago. The goblins found Jarmo carrying her, lost in the forest. She was unconscious."

Hokuren looked back at Cinna's sleeping form, alarmed. "Is she all right?"

"According to Jarmo, she said, and I quote, 'Tell the boss I'll be fine.'"

Hokuren pursed her lips. It sounded like something Cinna would say, but coming from her, it could mean anything from "I'll be fine" to "I've suffered several potentially mortal injuries but am not, technically, dead yet." She waved her father over and checked Cinna for injuries while they talked.

"Where's Moira?" she asked, brushing aside flaking mud to look for tears in Cinna's tunic.

"Moira returned to her house when she learned what had happened to Ulbricht."

"Hmm," muttered Hokuren. She wanted to see the old witch again, as their reunion a few hours ago had been tense with danger, but she'd have to wait for now. "And what happened to Ulbricht?"

Her father frowned. "Sounds like the goblins got their revenge. Jarmo seemed rather traumatized."

"I see," said Hokuren, shivering at the thought. She didn't need further details. "What do you think of the fruits of your profits?" She waved her hand at the dormitory and the warrens.

"This place has far more amenities than Fondence." Her father furrowed his brow. "Though they all sleep in an open dorm. Not sure I'd want to trade, to be honest. I like my privacy at night."

There weren't any obvious injuries on Cinna's body. It seemed she *was* fine, but exhausted. Hokuren let her rest.

"So." Hokuren looked away from her father. "Now what?"

"Now what? Oh, I see." Her father patted her head, like he'd done when she was young. "Can you forgive me for bringing you back to Fondence with my fake death?"

She turned her eyes up toward the hand on her head. There was a comforting nostalgia to it, even though the touch also felt like that of a stranger. "Perhaps, but that's not what I'm talking about. I'll be going back to Velles in a few weeks."

Her father sighed. "I suppose I hoped you might have found the import business so enthralling a decade later that you'd want to stay this time." Before Hokuren could retort, he added, "A joke, Pumpkin. I hope that maybe you'll stay in touch with your dear old father from now on?"

"I was wrong to ignore you when you contacted me, but even then you kept asking if I would return and help you with the business." Hokuren took a moment to tamp down renewed frustration. "You've never acknowledged I don't want to do that. It's got to be different going forward."

"You're right." Hokuren's father ran a hand through his thinning hair. "You're right," he repeated. "I'm sorry. I can't undo that. But maybe I can . . . do that now? Support what you're actually doing? You are a seeker in Velles, aren't you? You're better suited for that, anyway."

"You had better mean that." Hokuren wanted to believe him.

"I do. I've spent far too long pushing you away. There's a lot of missed time to make up for, but we have to start somewhere, and I . . . maybe I don't deserve it, but can I have a second chance at a relationship? A real one?"

"I'd like that, Father."

If he followed through, she'd have her father back.

Hokuren sat by Cinna's bedside so that when her assistant woke up, she could be right there to squeeze her into a tight hug.

"Happy to see you too, boss, but let me breathe," Cinna said blearily.

"I heard you needed to be carried here," said Hokuren.

"There were minor complications," said Cinna evasively. "And Jarmo wasn't supposed to tell you I had to be carried."

"I know how to speak Cinna, so I know that means you don't want to tell me the full truth," said Hokuren with a smile. "But I want to hear it anyway. I'll tell you about my own *complications*."

They traded stories of bringing about the end of Ulbricht's reign. Cinna loved hearing about Hokuren smashing up the contraption, less so about Viss firing a crossbow at her. Roz's departure didn't bother her. Hokuren fretted about how close Cinna had come to being impaled on the end of Jarmo's sword.

"I never managed to teach Jarmo how to overcome his mental block and hurt people," said Cinna. "It's a good thing I'm a lousy teacher, because otherwise I'd be dead by his sword."

"I'm just glad you survived," said Hokuren.

"Oh, no doubt. You'll need the company on the three-week trip back to Velles so Captain Tulip doesn't bore you. All of his stories are about being on a boat," said Cinna, back to her usual flippant self now that the danger had passed. Then her eyes dropped. "I'm glad you survived, too. If you hadn't—I meant what I said at Moira's. I need you."

Hokuren put her hand on Cinna's shoulder. "We need each other. Especially if we're going to get our investigation business restarted."

"I wonder how many customers we'll have missed." Cinna counted on her fingers. "I guess five."

"We'll have been gone three months!" said Hokuren, playing along. "I know we don't get many customers, but there are more lost cats than that."

Cinna grinned. "Forgot about all the cats, boss. Okay, eight."

They left the warren soon after with Hokuren's father, ready to let the goblins determine their next steps. Greeze led them to the long corridor that ended at Hokuren's father's house.

"Good luck, Greeze," said Hokuren.

Greeze acknowledged her with a tip of his cap. "Come and visit anytime, see what we accomplish. I warn you, though. We may act more goblin than human next time, if I have my druthers."

The goblin tottered off, and the three began their long walk home. Cinna said to Hokuren, "We should give the luck to Fondence, not the goblins. Can you imagine these goblins organized? They could take the town."

"I'm not worried about that," said Hokuren, looking back at the warrens. Greeze was gone. "I don't think they *want* the town."

"Well, I guess they won't if Greeze has his druthers." Cinna frowned. "Whatever those are."

"Greeze has already informed me they won't be accepting any more coin from me," said Hokuren's father. "Which is fine. There'll be a lot less of it to go around now that they've torn my best customer to shreds."

"Don't forget he was also one of your three employees," said Cinna helpfully. "Oh, and your only remaining living employee killed the third and has now, I assume, quit."

Hokuren's father sighed. "I wish you hadn't reminded me of Roz. I'm rather disappointed in her."

"Granted, Roz killed someone, but I still think Grimes was your worst hire," continued Cinna. "I don't know much about Barth, though he'd have to be some kind of monster to beat Grimes for that title."

"Hokuren, Pumpkin, do you plan to install some of the Tuomi tact into her?" Hokuren's father said, arching his eyebrows.

Hokuren put her arm around Cinna's shoulder. "One of us needs to be willing to speak our mind all the time. Do you disagree with her?"

"Well, no," admitted her father. "But no one needs to say it, do they?"

Hokuren smiled, walking with Cinna on one side and her father on the other. Her family, such as it was.

They arrived back at the house, emerging from the safe. "You didn't give us the key to this safe door," said Hokuren, irritated all over again.

"Obviously," said her father. "I didn't want you to open it."

"You said you hid it somewhere. I need to know where."

"I'd have thought you'd have figured it out by now." At Hokuren's silence, because that comment increased her irritation by a sliver, he continued, "What is the one place I would think is safest, that no one would think to look?"

"If I knew that, I'd—" Hokuren caught his hand slip into his trouser pocket, and she couldn't believe she'd never figured it out. "Your own person."

"Bingo." Her father pulled a set of safe keys from the pocket and jingled them.

"That's where you hid the cake!" Hokuren said, raising her voice too loudly in the small basement. "You had the flaming thing the entire time!"

Both Cinna and her father wore puzzled expressions. "What cake?" asked her father.

But Hokuren, having solved a mystery she'd been thinking about for half her life, wasn't listening. She pranced up the stairs to the main floor of the house, the sense of relief palpable. "His pocket!" she said to herself.

The townspeople of Fondence struggled through the next week, their shared hallucination courtesy of Ulbricht's spell coming to an abrupt end. Hokuren helped where she could, clarifying the situation to town elders who could disseminate her words to the rest of the town. No one would miss Grimes all that much. The water tank full of translucent pink worms found inside his illusory mansion spooked its discoverers, and Hokuren met little resistance when she insisted they kill the worms.

With Ulbricht's influence gone, the town now remembered that Casper Daily had passed away three years ago. As far as Hokuren could tell, Ulbricht hadn't even bothered with a Casper image. He'd simply made everyone believe the mayor was still alive.

Once the town had come to terms with Ulbricht, the goblins, and the magic, Hokuren finally had time to have a proper conversation with Moira. She and Cinna ventured out to the witch's home behind the green bubble, which remained in place. Cinna waited outside the house, exploring the garden with Lumi, to allow Hokuren to speak with Moira alone.

Of course, once they were together, tea in hand, neither said anything. Hokuren couldn't think of a way to start that didn't sound too petulant to her ears, so she waited to see how Moira would take the lead.

"You and Cinna actually did it," said Moira, finally breaking the silence. "I must admit, I would never have had the guts to do what you did."

"I would have come sooner if I had known how bad the situation was." Hokuren almost believed herself. She would more likely have come later, and not alone. "I could have brought help had I known the full scope."

Moira let a fresh silence hang over them. When she spoke again, she said, "I didn't want you to come at all."

"Didn't you want to see me again?" The hurt in Hokuren's voice raised it higher in pitch.

"Of course I did." Moira's eyes flashed with anger. "How could you think otherwise?"

"You stopped writing. I—I thought you were dead." Hokuren dug her fingers into the armrests.

Moira's anger disappeared. She sagged in her seat. "I stopped writing once the fake Moira was in place," she breathed. "It hurt me to do so, but I thought if you believed me dead, you'd have less reason to return. I knew things were getting dangerous here. Plus, Ulbricht might have intercepted a letter I sent out. I didn't want to give him even more reason to think about targeting you."

"I know you did it to protect me, but still—"

"I understand you feel hurt, and that's fair." Moira folded her hands around her teacup. "I sent letters to the Conclave of Wizards, hoping they'd come stop their rogue wizard from enacting his plans. I never received a response. That's how I determined this must be happening with their consent."

"What about my mother?" Hokuren's throat went dry. "My mother started this. Was she also doing it as part of the Conclave?"

Moira spoke slowly, as if searching for the right words. "Your mother was part of the Conclave at one point. She was too skilled a wizard not to have been. But I believed she went rogue and started this on her own. She trusted Ulbricht, and he betrayed that trust to bring her work within the organization."

"You knew her. I didn't. What did my mother really want?" Hokuren braced herself for the coming answer. She could handle her father's immorality, but the same from her mother pained Hokuren deeply, given how she'd built her up.

"I really don't know," said Moira. At least it was honest. "I believe she wanted to see the goblins better off, but I also believe it was presumptuous for her to decide for them." She cleared her throat, clearly uncomfortable. "And Nekane may have wanted to see if she could do it. Many wizards are that way."

"I see," muttered Hokuren. It was not the answer she hoped to hear, but one she'd expected. Her mother would forever be complicated in her mind now. It hurt, yet she felt a sense of satisfaction as well. She knew more about her mother and who she really was—never the perfection that had existed in Hokuren's mind, but a person with strengths and flaws and goals. Few might agree with her, but Hokuren preferred it this way.

"Witches are like that, too. It's the power." Moira sighed. "You once asked me why I wouldn't train you to be a witch like me."

"You told me it was because, as a human, I wouldn't live long enough to truly master it."

Moira laughed and waved a hand. "A lie, but you know that now, I'm sure. The truth is that once I discovered how these powers can be used, I vowed to train no one else. Ulbricht is a prime example of what I feared. Experimenting with people's minds is something our world can do without, and I refused to play a part in perpetuating it."

"For what it's worth, I'm glad you turned me down." Hokuren shuddered. "I like to think I wouldn't abuse the power, but I'm glad not to have to worry."

"Where I erred was in believing that as long as I didn't teach, no one would learn. Nekane proved me otherwise." Moira stood up and collected the empty teacups. "To prevent that from happening again, I'll be seeing out my days here in seclusion."

"Won't you be lonely?"

"It's been years already. I've grown used to the solitude."

Moira left to put the cups away while Hokuren chewed on that. Before she met Cinna, she too had become used to being alone, and thought that she was prepared to live like that for the rest of her life. Cinna's friendship had taught her how wrong she was.

When Moira returned, Hokuren said, "I had hoped that if I ever saw you again, it would have been in happier circumstances."

"I want you to keep building your life in Velles."

"The only part of my life in Velles I truly could never leave behind is Cinna." Hokuren looked out Moira's window and glimpsed Cinna sitting on the rockery, her back to the house. A small breeze played with her wild mane of hair while she rubbed Lumi's belly. "She thinks she needs me more than I need her, but she's wrong."

"Ah." Moira smiled. "While I was in the guise of Lumi, I tried to learn more about Cinna. After all, I wondered what made her so important to you. I figured it out when you first came to my place here. Do you know what I determined?"

Hokuren shook her head. "Guessing would be pointless. Please tell me."

"Such a Hokuren answer," Moira said with a laugh. "You're very different people, of course. Yet I noticed that neither of you backed down when the situation with Ulbricht went sideways. You did what needed to be done, at great personal risk. You both have the same heart."

"I don't disagree." Hokuren smiled at Cinna's back. "I'm confident that as long as the two of us are working together, we'll be successful."

"I think you're right." Moira stood up, signaling the end of the conversation. They shared a hug. "I'll miss you, Hokuren," said Moira.

"I'll write," said Hokuren. "Please don't let me think you're dead again. Unless, you know, you are."

"I promise."

The next few weeks before Hokuren and Cinna returned to Velles passed quietly. News filtered in that the Gregorious Consortium was broken up and its members sentenced to imprisonment in Oro for smuggling. The Oro City Watch wanted Roz for Barth's murder, but a person matching her description had already been spotted on a ship bound for Trebello.

Hokuren hoped Roz at least found some peace, if not her voice.

Cinna still spent mornings training with Jarmo, but she no longer included martial skills in the lessons. To Hokuren, she reported encouraging increases in Jarmo's strength and flexibility, and the pride in her voice was clear. Jarmo might not ever punch anyone, but he remained a willing student.

"I just hope he turns out all right," said Cinna one evening. "I've never been so invested in someone else."

"You've helped him quite a bit," said Hokuren. "I think you've done a lot to make sure that happens."

Hokuren spent the time helping her father reshape Mikko's Imports. They paid for and retrieved the non-smuggled goods trapped in Oro during his lengthy absence, made new deals, and interviewed for replacement employees. Her father thanked Hokuren for her help, repeatedly acknowledging she was not obligated to do so, perhaps to make up for the way he took her involvement in the business for granted prior to her leaving for Velles. For the first time in her life, she enjoyed working with him.

However, by the time Captain Tulip was due back in port, she wished to return to Velles, and Cinna felt the same way. Cinna wanted the action and bustle of the city, but for Hokuren it was the opportunity to plug away and build her investigation business. Mikko's Imports dulled her mind. She needed mysteries and challenges, and Fondence had none to offer with Ulbricht defeated.

Her father saw her off at the wagon stop, giving her a long hug with tears in his eyes. "I got my daughter back, and now I have to see her leave again," he said, sniffling. "I can only bear it because I know you will be happier back in Velles."

"This time I'm not leaving forever," said Hokuren. She touched his shoulder. "There will be letters. And if you find the time, you can come visit."

Her father dabbed at his eyes. "It's just dusty, that's all."

Hokuren's eyes rolled. "No lies on my last day here, Father."

"Worth a shot." He turned to Cinna. "Take care of my daughter."

Cinna gave him a salute. "That's my job, so you got it, Hokuren's father."

"I trust she's not too . . . overzealous?" asked her father, leaning in toward Hokuren.

"What Cinna means is that we will take care of each other, right?" said Hokuren.

"Of course, boss."

The wagon arrived at the station a few minutes later. Cinna and Hokuren tossed their belongings inside and had one foot on the step leading into the coach when Jarmo, huffing and puffing, ran up to them.

"I just . . . made it," he said, sucking in breaths.

"Jarmo, we said goodbye this morning," said Cinna.

"I wanted to give you something, Master Cinna. It just got finished. I'm glad I won't have to mail it." Jarmo removed a small package wrapped in linen and handed it to Cinna. "My way of saying thanks for all your help."

Cinna looked stunned into silence, staring alternately at the gift and Jarmo. "Uh," she said. "I owe you more thanks. If you hadn't shown up when you did—"

"Nonsense, Master Cinna. I know how to keep myself in shape now, and thanks to you I've figured out what I want to do. I'm going to study to be a medic." He smiled sheepishly. "If you beat up anyone, send them to me and soon I'll be able to patch them up."

"A medic?" mumbled Cinna. "Good idea." She was still looking at the package as if in disbelief.

"Why don't you open it?" said Hokuren, elbowing Cinna.

Cinna unwrapped the cloth to find a small blue tassel, looped with some string. It matched the red one Jarmo had attached to his Arms of Fondence short sword.

"I had it made for you. It's the same color as your headband. I assumed you might like that. Hopefully, it helps you remember me," said Jarmo.

"I—thanks," said Cinna, uncharacteristically dumbstruck. She tied it to her headband so that it dangled in front of her ear. "How's it look?"

"It looks great, Master Cinna."

"I have nothing for you," said Cinna, embarrassed. "It's unfair. I didn't know I was supposed to exchange gifts." She brightened. "Oh, wait, hold on." She rummaged through the wagon, emerging with one of the pastries Mama Ogg's bakery had prepared for her to take on the trip. "It's almond," she said, handing it to Jarmo.

He took it gracefully. "A pastry," he said, bemused.

Hokuren leaned in and whispered to him, "Perhaps you don't realize how unusual it is for Cinna to give up a treat like that."

"Oh, I see." He bowed to Cinna. "Thank you, Master Cinna."

Cinna grew flustered. "It's not much, you know, I—" she stuttered and stopped herself. "For someone who can't throw a punch, you were a fine partner in a fight."

"From you, I believe that is a great compliment," said Jarmo. "Goodbye, Master Cinna. I'll be rooting for you and Miss Hokuren down in Velles."

"Knock them dead as a medic," said Cinna, then she blanched. "Not literally."

Soon after, Cinna and Hokuren were bundled into the wagon's coach, Hokuren exchanging one last hug with her father. Cinna sat quietly, a finger toying with the tassel.

The wagon moved, starting the two-day trip back to Oro. Hokuren leaned out of the wagon's open window, waving to her father. She watched until he disappeared behind the trees of the forest and turned to find Cinna unmoved.

"I don't get gifts from people who aren't you," said Cinna, looking straight ahead at nothing in particular. "I didn't know how to respond."

"You did fine. I told you that you made an impression on Jarmo." Hokuren put her arm around Cinna and squeezed.

"It feels good." Cinna turned to Hokuren. "How do you feel, boss?"

"Well, you made a friend and set him on his path in life, my father didn't die and I reconciled with him, and together we saved our friends and family, an entire town, and a group of intelligent goblins from a wizard with far too much influence." Hokuren took a breath. "I even learned a lot about my mother. I have a much greater sense of who she was, and the parts of her I want to emulate along with the ones I don't. I feel pretty good as well."

"All in a month's work for Hokuren and Cinna Investigations," said Cinna, grinning. "Though we forgot not to work free of charge."

Hokuren returned her grin. "My father promised a small payment to be sent to us on behalf of the town, but yes, we did it with no hope of recompense." She put her finger on her chin. "You know, someone told me that I'm foolish for pursuing the truth instead of financial security."

"Hmm," said Cinna, cocking her head at Hokuren. "If you didn't, you wouldn't be the Hokuren I like so much."

"Don't worry, I didn't take her criticism to heart."

The wagon hit a bump in the path, a tree root growing over the muddy trail that they'd hit on all their back-and-forth trips between Fondence and Oro. It reminded Hokuren that she missed the comfort of her home in Velles, where there was no mud or tree roots.

"When we get back home, what's the first thing you want to do?" she asked Cinna. "I'm going to sleep in my big, soft bed."

Cinna had an answer immediately. "Before you go to sleep, we're going to get blueberry pie. A whole one, not just a slice."

Hokuren laughed. "You know what? We deserve some pie."

Acknowledgements

Huge thank you to my beta readers: Natalie, Jesse and Trevor. Your insight and highlights pointed out the pain points and helped make this the best novel it could be. Thank you!

Thanks to my editor, Kyra Rogers, who caught and helped me correct a great many of my worst mistakes. Any remaining errors are the fault of the author.

Thank you to the Regional Authority: Ethan, Daniel, Jeff and Sheila. The first version of Cinna existed because of our game together, without which the Cinna and Hokuren series never gets started.

Thank you to the Exeggcutors: Malia, Stars, Milton, Pat and Kaido. You all helped mold Cinna and Hokuren into the duo they are today.

Thanks Mom and Dad for your love and support.

About the author

Quinn lives in the Pacific Northwest and spends time each day either writing or thinking about writing. Other activities include playing Dungeons & Dragons, walking around the neighborhood, and reading as many other books as possible.

Along with Columbo, who takes on a dual role as lead writing assistant and very affectionate cat, Quinn is excited to present novels starring Cinna and Hokuren with the world.

Visit quinnlawrencebooks.com to sign up for Quinn's newsletter and get a free short story starring Cinna and Hokuren delivered right to your email inbox.

Email: quinnlawrencebooks@gmail.com

www.ingramcontent.com/pod-product-compliance
Lightning Source LLC
LaVergne TN
LVHW010310070526
838199LV00065B/5515